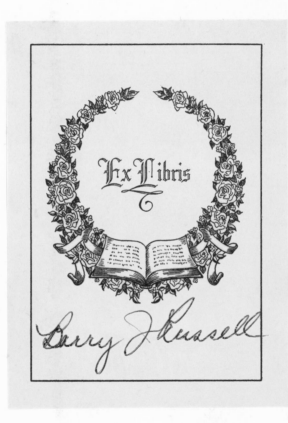

Crosswind

ROBERT HENRY

Crosswind

A NOVEL

Published by

THE VIKING PRESS

New York

1961

First published in 1961 by The Viking
Press, Inc., 625 Madison Avenue, New
York 22, New York

Published simultaneously in Canada
by The Macmillan Company of
Canada Limited

Library of Congress catalog card
number: 61-15701

Printed in the U.S.A. by Vail-Ballou
Press, Binghamton, N.Y.

For Ollie

CONTENTS

PART I   3

PART II   105

PART III   147

PART IV   215

Crosswind

PART ONE

Chapter 1

FLIGHT 0900 was numbered for its departure time from Santa María. They said it seldom departed on time.

At a little after ten a.m. I walked into the *cantina* at the airport to tell Johnny Michaels I was going to replace him on this trip. There was a piece of paper in my pocket from Coronel Romirez that made me Chief Pilot now.

Michaels was sitting at the bar with an olive-skinned, almond-eyed stewardess. There were *café puros* in front of them. According to the local character assassins, the coffee Michaels sipped would be his fourth or fifth cup, and the passengers scattered around at tables in the place wouldn't know that his demitasse had been steadily laced with dark rum. That was why he was out and I was in. I felt a little sorry for the old lush, but I wanted his job.

Like other airlines operating in Central America in '47, Líneas Aéreas Ruedo Central had picked up a couple of war surplus C-47s—DC-3s, if you'd rather call them that—and tried to look like the big lines. LARC was kind of a laugh, but not the money it paid me.

I had three reasons for taking the job.

First, I was no kid. Coming out of the war a pappy guy of thirty-four, compared to the twenty-two-year-old Air Force lieutenant colonels, I hadn't been as happy as they were with a co-pilot job on American for $380 a month. Romirez was starting me at a thousand.

Second, to be behind in alimony is not an extraditable offense in the little country of Ruedo.

Third, I hated cold weather.

I put one of the last of my Luckies in my mouth, forgot to light it, and walked over to the bar. I stood close to Michaels with what I hoped was a TS expression on my face. He ignored me, but the stewardess slid off her stool and went out of the *cantina*. I took the seat she had warmed.

Johnny must have known what was coming. He ducked in a comic way, showing me the top of his grizzled gray head. Without looking up, he said, "Things are getting Christ-awful up-to-date in the tropics when they tie the can to a flyer for drinking in the morning."

He pushed the demitasse away and made a quick switch from happy drunk to mean drunk. His seamed, weather-beaten fifty-year-old face had a surly expression, and a broken nose helped him to look tough.

"So you're Romirez' new fly-boy," he said.

"Yes," I said. "Name is Luke Hadley."

"Do I ride co-pilot? Show you the route?" He flicked his questions sarcastically.

I didn't say anything for a few seconds, thinking, did I want the rummy around—even as co-pilot? Well, I could give him a check ride. LARC was short-handed, and I hadn't flown with the native co-pilots yet. I shook my Luckies at him. He refused them and lit the dark tobacco of one of his own Mex cigarettes. Then he held a little wax match to my unlit Lucky. His hand was steady enough. We blew smoke at each other.

"All right. Come along," I finally said.

"Thanks. Ship ready?"

"You ought to know."

He vented a dirty laugh. "We may never get off the ground!"

Michaels pushed off from the bar stool and walked ahead of me out of the *cantina* with deliberate steadiness, shoulders squared in his sky-blue Ruedan Air Corps uniform. Quite a hell of a guy. Maybe he could shape up—stay off the sauce at least in the mornings. I hoped so. The passengers looked at him with undisguised admiration and, by contrast, I was some bum in a floral-print sport shirt, unpressed slacks, and a baseball cap. I carried everything I owned in my old Air Force B-4 bag.

Santa María, Ruedo's capital, was our home base and had a PA system for calling the passengers to board the flight. The station agent's voice was loud and pompous as he made the announcement in Spanish. He sounded less certain and hurried calling the flight in a memorized English version.

Outside, the sun was glaringly bright. When it hit old Johnny, it made him waver the slightest bit. It was well over eighty degrees already, and felt like July at home, but it was only January.

The architecture of the terminal building was such a modern abstraction of concrete and tinted glass it looked like it might fly better than the old tin crate parked beside it. But I had a warm feeling for that DC-3 because it was mine. And I liked the way the soft, warm air made my bones feel in the middle of winter. I liked the sound and the smell of the lazily hissing water sprinkler on the piece of manicured green lawn in front of the terminal. I almost smiled at the peacock preening himself there and at the big red blossoms on the hibiscus hedge nodding in the little breeze.

Then the breeze stopped abruptly, and I could feel the heat reflecting from the asphalt. That would make our take-off run longer. I looked up at the limp Ruedan flag on the terminal roof. It was yellow and green stripes, which, according to ancient Indian lore, stood for the sun and the earth. The same colors were striped on the sides of the LARC plane, but were faded and flaking off here and there.

"It's your green and yaller basket," Johnny said, and then he introduced me to our stewardess, who was waiting at the foot of the steps below the plane's open door. Teddy was her *Yanqui* name, short for Theodora something, Indian and unpronounceable. She was a short girl, which is helpful for working a DC-3, and she was kind of hippy and chesty.

"Capitán," was all she said, looking at me frankly, her Oriental eyes as dark as black olives. She politely stepped aside to let me board first.

Through the windshield on the left side of the cockpit I could see a lot more of the *aeropuerto.* There was the TACA Loadstar I'd come down from the States in three days before, now back from Peru and heading north again. There were also nine lethal-looking P-51 Mustangs parked along the edge of the field and a couple of AT-6s as well—the Ruedan Air Corps. They seemed unnecessary and expensive toys, those peashooters, but they were apparently amusing to my boss, the Minister of Aviation, Romirez, whose toys they were. I hoped he could afford them.

And there were lots of soldiers around the airport. They leaned on their rifles, standing a sullen guard duty. I had seen them in the city, too. Santa María was calm but, with *Federales* everywhere, the capital seemed to be in a brooding state of siege. Other people looked right through the soldiers; maybe I'd get used to them too.

I watched my passengers coming toward the ramp. To me they were a straggle of eight natives, because I hadn't yet learned to distinguish better than that. There was also what I had learned to call a *North American* couple—*turistas.*

With our DC-3s capacity of twenty-one, we had a fifty-per-cent load factor, which is airline talk meaning we wouldn't break even on the trip with fares based on six cents a mile. Because I wanted to buck for chief of operations, maybe take over sales too, I would have to study the traffic and do something about it. Why not? But wait a damn minute, I told myself. I had come down to the tropics for a sweet flying job at good dough and to get away from the rat race. I was a cinch to have a fine time with a minimum of effort. What the hell did I want to run the whole airline for?

Johnny gave me a mumbled reading of the check list, and I flipped most of the dozens of switches, levers, and knobs myself. We fired up, and I taxied us out on the field. Then Johnny handed me a crude mimeographed chart and flight plan.

The map of Ruedo looked like an inverted triangle, blunted at the bottom. I was going to see a lot of the country on this meandering all-day trip. From Santa María in the north, near the Atlantic coast, we would fly west to Puerto del Sol, the Pacific port city, then southeast to the central city of Matanzas in the highlands, finally south across the jungle to Las Piraguas, on a river that emptied into the Caribbean. Our two aircraft crisscrossed this run south and north four to five times a week. On other days we had to haul small-town local freight and passengers, and one DC-3 made a weekly round-trip to Mexico. If there was a printed timetable, I hadn't seen one, but down here, who reads? Johnny's chart also contained penciled drift corrections, headings, and bearings.

"Up to date?" I asked.

"Same as yesterday," Johnny mumbled sleepily.

Swell, I thought, and took off. Once we were off the ground and on cruising rpm for the hour-and-fifty-minute run to Puerto del Sol, Johnny didn't show me a damn thing. He slept off his rum.

I made out okay, though. I'd been flying four-engines during the war and since then had had co-pilot time in 3s. No sweat.

When I turned off the No Smoking and Seat Belt sign, our stewardess came up front, very sure-footed in the little turbulence we had. She sniffed at the sleeping Johnny Michaels, rolled her Chinese eyes at the rum fumes, and gave me a smile that was dazzlingly white-toothed in her pretty dark-skinned face. She also gave me a paper cup of strong black native coffee, thick with coarse native sugar, then ducked out quick, but left a tingling impression of hard, honest curves where she had brushed against my shoulder when leaning over to put the coffee in my hand. I made a mental note to find out if south of the border pilots rated the way they did up north when a trip was over. I hoped so. It's funny the way a hot sunny day in the tropics works on the endocrines; and it's hot and sunny most every day.

The airport at Puerto del Sol was just a packed dirt strip at the top of a cliff above the craggy Pacific shoreline. I sat us down nice as you please. Johnny didn't wake up until I parked and cut the switches. Sudden silence in an airplane will wake up a dead pilot.

"Everything okay?" he asked, sitting bolt upright.

"Sure," I said.

"Next leg is tougher. All uphill," Johnny said, slouching back down in his seat. He closed his eyes and was gone again.

I wiped my sunglasses and watched from the side window as four of our dark-skinned *pasajeros* and the tourist couple deplaned. We took on two sunburned guys from the resort town. They came toward the plane, laughing and kidding with Teddy in their lousy Spanish, prosperous businessmen types whose belts squeezed well-fed bellies. Their luggage, dragged under the plane for loading, contained tackle boxes and aluminum rod cases. So Puerto must be good for sport fishing, I thought, and I wondered if they'd had luck with the sailfish.

I daydreamed over the chart on my lap. I was supposed to be studying it for landmarks and elevations, but I couldn't help thinking of the tourist attractions along the route and how maybe I could help the airline with some advertising ideas and how, if they worked, Romirez would promote me to sales manager on my way to becoming the line's president. Some daydream!

I didn't use yesterday's figures to plot our course on the next leg to Matanzas. The winds were different in both direction and velocity and would probably change some more en route, so I measured out all the check points I could find on the chart—roads, mountains, valleys, rivers, and streams. There were no towns along the way. This dead reckoning would let me know where I was if weather closed in on us, and in the mountains I would have to know—quick. We'd move nearly half a mile in the ten seconds it would take to look at a chart.

We took off at 1240 hours with a satisfying roar from the two Wasp engines. The DC-3 always has a way of sweeping off the ground that makes me believe in her as a flying machine. People like me were already getting sentimental about 3s back in 1947. Mine was a pretty venerable aircraft. According to her log, which I looked at while checking out George, the automatic pilot, she had started life ten years before for United and then, when war came, had been painted olive-drab for the ATC. LARC had bought her a year ago for only three thousand bucks on the surplus market, but had spent several times that on reconditioning. She flew as good as new with more than four million miles behind her tail. There must be ten thousand DC-3s scattered around the world, I thought, and with an engine change and spare part every so often, they just might go on flying forever. Still, I wanted to give mine a thorough preflight inspection before heading back in the morning.

It was a long climb, heading southeast toward the town of Matanzas in central Ruedo. We crossed brown hills, wrinkled with erosion, then above steeper rust-colored, burned-looking hogback mountains that were grooved by dry arroyos that would be spilling over with flash floods when the rainy season came.

I tooled us through a pass at seven thousand where the mountains grew into the long chain of Sierra Madre. Occasionally I could see the turning, twisting mountain road from Puerto to Matanzas. Then I saw the damnedest thing. The southbound road crossed the deep canyon carved into the mountains by the Río Barranco on a great arched bridge, but on the opposite side of the gorge, the bridge didn't meet the northbound ribbon of asphalt. Somebody had goofed and they had to build a connecting road between.

I woke Johnny up from his second nap and pointed out the highway snafu to him.

Johnny yawned and said, "Some relative built the lower road."

"Must have been a hell of a scandal," I said.

"Nah," Johnny said, "Everybody laughed. They have a funny sense of humor down here. When there was a change in government, a couple of years ago, that road engineer ran for his life—to Miami, I think. They laughed even harder then."

I watched cumulus clouds make dark moving blots on the desolate terrain and thought about how that land was milked by the *políticos*.

At ten thousand feet we were in the clouds, and I went upstairs on instruments. Johnny stayed awake and scanned the gauges. He wasn't satisfied with the altimeter and made sign language that said go higher. When he reached for the wheel on his side, I was glad for the chance to get up and stretch my legs, which were always three inches longer than the space allotted to them in every aircraft I'd ever flown.

I stood up in the slot behind the pilot and co-pilot seats and hung on during the turbulence in the clouds. I watched the altimeter go over twelve thousand before we broke out on top of most of it. Some of the mountain peaks reached up as high as we were. Most were unnamed on the chart, but the tallest on our route had a name penciled in by Johnny. He called it Bust-Your-Ass Mountain. I checked my wrist chronometer as well as the clock on the panel and, estimating our position, found the chart we flew by to be anything but accurate about elevations. There could be clouds with hard centers at twelve thousand. Johnny looked over his shoulder at me and at the chart. He shrugged the way the Latins do. This flying was real bush.

"Radio at Matanzas?" I asked.

"Yes."

"Any in between?"

"Negative."

With nothing more for me to do but let the miles roll under us, I went down the narrow aisle to the rear of the plane. Most of the passengers dozed. We were too high to make smoking much fun, but I wanted my last Lucky anyway, only I couldn't find my matches. I chewed on the cigarette and looked around for someone to practice my Spanish on. I'd had three years of it in high school, and I learned more about speaking the language in thirty hours with Berlitz in New York. Anyway, I knew how to ask for a light.

I guess the natives weren't too impressed with their sloppy-looking captain. They ignored me. The fishermen from the States said hello and bragged a little about hundred-and-twenty-pound sailfish. One of them gave me a light after I'd patted myself all over. He told me matches were scarce in Ruedo. There was some kind of monopoly on the little wax *fósforos*.

The gabbier of the fishermen introduced himself and started telling me his life story. "I'm Sam Warren," he said, "I sell US machinery, farm machinery, all kinds. Got a big deal in Matanzas. I live in Santa María. Look me up. You're new with LARC, aren't you?"

I allowed as how I was new and went on back and had some more coffee with Teddy at the buffet. She said I'd better get fitted for a uniform.

"People down here go for uniforms, Capitán Hadley," she said, implying that she could go for a uniform herself.

I ducked into the single washroom, which was a stinking mess, and when I felt better I looked into the little mirror over the basin. I forced a crooked grin on the somewhat sad, gaunt face of Lucas Hadley and tried to imagine how I'd look in the sky-blue uniform my coincidental commission in the Ruedan Air Corps entitled me to wear. It wouldn't have a jacket—just a short-sleeved tunic-blouse open at the neck, and gold boards on the shoulders. I would get an officer's cap and put a fifty-mission crush in it. Well, I'd flown my fifty missions over Germany; the memory of them wiped the grin off my face.

Up front again, I watched Johnny Michaels fly. He worked with a bored sort of competence I admired. What I had heard about him, besides his drinking habits, was that he'd learned to fly too late for the First World War and was too old or, more accurately, too beat up for the Second. Between wars he logged a lot of airline mileage in the United States. The way the story went, pieced together from things Romirez said and what I heard at my hotel, Johnny's eyes could put a DC-3 into tough airports like Salt Lake City's for Western, but all of a sudden in 1940 his eyes couldn't pass the Army physical. That was when he started to drink. After he missed a few flights, the airline retired him. He went to Miami for a while and tried to drink the town dry. They say he stayed drunk for six months and then one half-sober day he bought himself a pair of prescription sunglasses and a ticket to Venezuela, where pilots were scarce, and even half-blind ones, for whatever reason, could make the desperately needed runs.

There aren't many roads or trains through the mountains and jungles of Latin America. The people down here had made it in one jump from ox carts to planes flown by men like Johnny who worked for the highest bidders in Venezuela, Bolivia, and Costa Rica, where he bent his beak when he nosed over an old Fairchild. Finally he wound up here in Ruedo as Chief Pilot for LARC. But now there were plenty of ex-GI pilots and lots of competition for flying jobs. It was my turn.

I took over the controls again as the central highlands of República de Ruedo appeared beneath us, the sparsely timbered slopes and monotonous scorched mesas with only an occasional lonely *finca* where galvanized iron roofs reflected the sun like mirrors. Then, in the middle of this worthless-looking country, I got my first look at the Copa Verde, a great green valley, shaped like a cup. Matanzas lay in its irrigated bottomland. On the other side of the valley floor was Mount Diablo, a cone-shaped volcano rising nearly five thousand feet. A small grayish cloud hovered motionless over the crater.

Johnny called the tower during the letdown into the cup. He told me to line up my downwind leg in the traffic pattern with the volcano behind us and the cathedral spires ahead. The church loomed up over the squat white and pink stucco buildings of the farm-rich four-hundred-year-old town in the middle of the valley.

As we turned base, Johnny switched on the *No Fumar* and Seat Belt signs and got the gear down. The tower cleared me to land. I wanted to make it a good one because the northbound flight was already on the field, and my boss, Coronel Romirez, was its pilot. He liked to keep his hand in.

In the strong wind on the runway I popped the wheel forward quick enough for a wheel landing as soft as a dropping pair of nylon panties. Now the big boss of the Air Ministry could point with pride at his new Chief Pilot.

Matanzas had a nice airport. It had been developed by TACA, but they no longer made the interior stops now that Ruedo had its own airline. I taxied up to the terminal building that looked like a Spanish palace with its walls of latticed brick, shiny mosaic tiles, and iron grillework gates. When I came down the steps after our passengers, Romirez greeted me fondly. He was a hell of a sight to see even for the second time.

Coronel Juan Miguel Romirez was a pumped-up blimp of a man who bulged his sky-blue uniform and jiggled its loops of gold ornamental braiding. He was about my age, maybe younger, because a lot of him still looked like baby fat. His cap had a *Wehrmacht* peak and visor, and underneath it was a soft, lardy face with a black mustache he let grow to look fierce and the biggest cigar I had ever seen. I was pinned down by a couple of small and utterly pitiless black eyes that dominated all the easily dominated and most of those with a little guts. I wondered how much guts I'd have to have for the Coronel to keep on being nice to me.

His flight north had been on time, but he'd waited for us so we could have lunch together. The fat Coronel was very hungry, and he ordered both flights to have delays for mechanical reasons, so I guessed we would have a leisurely lunch, complete with siesta. The temperate highland country in Ruedo was a good place to have an appetite for five-dollar steaks that cost only forty cents.

Teddy and the stewardess from the other flight ate by themselves. Caste system. Romirez and his pilots were served by the manager. We talked shop, and it looked as if Johnny Michaels was worming his way back into the Coronel's good graces, which was okay with me if the old guy would take his demotion in the airline and stay reasonably sober. Otherwise out. I guess he knew it was his last chance because he shamelessly brown-nosed Romirez and that made me feel uncomfortable.

The co-pilot of the other plane was Lieutenant Ramón Fuentes. He was a sharp-looking guy with lots of carefully combed hair. His face was the face of old Spain—thin-nosed, thin-lipped, white-skinned. He was built like a welterweight boxer, which is as big as most Latinos get, but he packed a lot of insolence in his small package.

Fuentes kept looking past me toward the stewardesses' table and permitted himself a smile when the Coronel decided that he should join my flight as co-pilot to the end of the run at Las Piraguas. The Coronel and Johnny, who had sobered up nicely, were going to fly the rest of the northbound trip. Then the Coronel briefed me on LARC's other two pilots, whom I would meet in Matanzas tomorrow. I was glad one was a Yank, a pro.

When we left the terminal restaurant a crowd outside cheered Romirez, and he loved it. Johnny came with me to my plane to get his overnight bag and he looked over his shoulder a couple of times, making a point of not speaking to me until we were out of earshot of the others.

"Fuentes is a good flyer. You'll like that," he said. "I've been here two years and taught him all I know."

He stopped talking to laugh with a false gusto. I had a feeling he had more to say. He did.

"Remember, Hadley, these guys down here, like Fuentes, are on the inside. They're the real Air Corps officers. You, me, and Reynolds, we're just hired hands. If Ruedanos could handle operations at night and in bad weather, we would be out of work."

Johnny was entitled to his opinion after two years in Ruedo, but I felt, somehow, I had more to sell than my instrument rating. "What else do you think they want besides my green card?" I asked.

"There's something big cooking," Johnny said, looking over his shoulder again. "It's politics. Romirez is getting hot for the top job. And down here they don't have elections. They have overthrows. You have your loyalty for sale."

Then Johnny left me in the cockpit before I could ask another question. He went down the ladder from the forward hatch because the aisle was full of cargo now. I watched him stop under the wing. He turned his leathery face my way and said, "Take care." He grinned at me.

I didn't know what the hell to grin at, but I waved good-by.

Chapter 2

THE TRIP down the south side of the tableland and across a high pile carpet of green jungle called for some pinpoint navigation. It was more than six hundred miles to Las Piraguas, and the only changes in the landscape providing check points were three rivers that, according to Lieutenant Fuentes, zigged when they should zag on the chart. Our compass, wobbling in its liquid, had to be right.

With a heavy payload, foodstuffs mostly, our speed wasn't much over 180 mph. I let Fuentes fly and worked him hard to see what he had. He had plenty all right. Really had it. He was a born flyer and obviously enjoyed it. To this I tried to add something that was missing, something that Johnny hadn't emphasized in his teaching, an understanding and appreciation for the book, for flying by the numbers and not just the seat of his pants. I made him work out our ETA. It was the distance times sixty divided by the speed we were making, our arrival time a mathematical certainty if only Fuentes would take his eyes away from the windshield and put them on the gauges once in a while. He had faith in his well-coordinated hands on the wheel and feet on the rudder-pedals. He seemed to think that was enough. When he had faith in the gauges, and when they once saved his life, then he would have it all. Then he would be a pilot.

After three hours and ten minutes—we had picked up a little tailwind

—there was the Río Culebra, winding its way toward the Caribbean coast, and then, in the deep tropical darkness that comes suddenly without twilight, we had a corrected heading for Las Piraguas. Or we thought we had. A river bend we depended on for our heading was inaccurately mapped. This led us off course enough to have missed the city altogether if we had been running out of gas, or if visibility hadn't been good enough to see the lights of the town. I didn't get very far trying to impress the gravity of this situation on Lieutenant Fuentes' mind. He was much more interested in shooting a practice night landing.

My radio call got the runway marker lights turned on, all four of them. On final, I switched on our landing lights, and ten million bugs destroyed themselves in head-on collisions with us. Fuentes made a good landing and then he strutted all the way to the administration shack as if he had just flown the Atlantic upside down.

I was introduced to Alvarez, the station agent, and he had held a rickety old taxi, vintage '34 Chevy, to haul Teddy, Fuentes, and me into town. That was one way to ingratiate himself with the new Chief. The passengers had to take a lopsided old bus with room on the roof for more.

LARC crews always stayed at the Gran Hotel. It was on the main drag and had two squat palms out front that looked like pineapples with overdeveloped thyroids. In the lobby slowly revolving four-blade ceiling fans barely moved the thick humid air.

After checking in and changing clothes, we met again at the bar that featured a pet toucan. It squawked as if it had sat on a tack and then walked up and down the mahogany bar surface pecking at crumbs of *tostadas* with its banana-like beak.

Fuentes was dressed for a night on the town in the kind of white suit that's always seen in the tropics. The best I could do was a clean sport shirt. Teddy had on a red dress, really less a dress than a two-piece outfit great for suntanning. The halter top tied in a bow at the neck and had its work cut out for it.

The problem of two men and one girl could be rectified almost at once, according to Teddy. There were supposed to be dance hostesses at all the joints in town.

I tried calling Teddy and Ramón by their first names with the informality we have back home, but even under easy-going circumstances I remained Capitán to Ramón. Teddy just talked to me without a handle. The hell with it, I thought. Latinos are a funny people, full of contradictions.

My crew steered me to at least five different clubs along the Río Culebra waterfront of Las Piraguas. They were bamboo or mud and plaster huts with thatched roofs. They had either tile or waxed stone floors and the occasional lizard skittering up pink stucco walls. They were noisy joints, and some of the acrid smoke clouds were from marijuana. We ate in one of the spots, which took some courage on my part.

At midnight we wound up in a dive called the Club Zerape. By then we were as rumpled and wet as we would have been if caught in the rain. Sipping maybe our tenth frozen daiquiri, we sat in rattan chairs, grateful for their open weave that gave us the benefit of whatever breeze came in the open door.

The Club Zerape was crowded with Caribbean Negroes, because it had the best music *conjunto* of them all. The musicians were also black, and their music was Afro-Cuban, every instrument played for percussion. Their piano had a crisp drum sound and the actual drums, in addition to the *timbal,* which was played with conventional drumsticks, were a half-dozen shapes and sizes, being finger-slapped, heeled and kneaded. The deep *tumbadora* was slung in a harness from naked ebony shoulders. Several medium-sized *tambores,* each with a different depth of sound, were held between the drummers' knees, as were the *bongós.* Sometimes, because of the humidity, the drums had to have their skins tightened and tuned with a lighted candle held inside the wood frames. Dented cow bells were smacked with sticks for their special junky sounds. More rhythm was coaxed from *maracás,* and a dry, clacking bop tone came from *claves,* which were nothing more than two round, polished hardwood sticks tapped together while one is held over a cupped hand to make a sounding board. Then there was the *güiros,* arm-long serrated gourds, scraped with a stick to sound like syncopated crickets. You would have to be very square not to feel the beat of that primitive band. I know it worked into my bloodstream like an injection and pulsed hardest in the pelvic area.

Up north I had danced what I thought was a rumba, but my shuffled hula was a joke to Teddy and Ramón, who demonstrated how it should be done.

Teddy was fun. I tried to have fun with her. Maybe I tried too hard. That can happen. Or maybe it was the threesome, which doesn't usually work out. I don't know. I do know that I just didn't get *with* the party the way I wanted to. Instead I caught a kind of sadness. I thought about how it had been a tough war and an even tougher homecoming to a wife who didn't remember me too clearly after one of those hurry-up marriages on leave. It had turned out that Cynthia and I wanted different things, and the things she wanted were probably correct but to me they were mostly just *things,* and to get them I would have had to go back to Madison Avenue and give up flying. Maybe it was immature of me, but I just couldn't do that for her.

I didn't want to think about the past. It didn't make me look especially good to myself, and I sure didn't want to think about the alimony that Cynthia and a smart lawyer clobbered me with.

When Teddy and Ramón were dancing again, I began to wish all the dance hostesses weren't busy and then I began to wish there was a crap game in one of the back rooms and not what was obviously there. My gambling had been another reason for fights with my wife, and if I had a crazy urge to go for broke, she certainly accommodated it.

I went to the bar to get away from myself and shook six dice in a leather cup for a drink. I lost. The guy who was tending bar owned the joint. We introduced ourselves. He was Fidel Salas, at my service, which service included corralling one of the dance hostesses for me.

Carmen was a *mulata* with skin the color of *café con leche.* She also wore a bare-midriff thing with a tight skirt starting so low at the waist her deep navel showed. But her face was so surprisingly beautiful I hardly looked at the rest.

We danced. Only it was more like melting together, and I let myself go enough to learn the movement. If you don't know what the Cuban movement is, I can show you, but I can't tell you for sure. It is better to learn it as I did, in a hot tropic night, and it is better still to be born with it, to inherit the movement the way Carmen and Teddy did from African or Indian forebears who walked over uneven jungle trails in their bare feet with bundles on their heads. The upper part of your body shouldn't move at all. What the lower part does would be asked to leave the floor at the country club dance.

I got good enough at it to accent the beat, and I even began to hear the music as well as the rhythm, especially the flute that sounded like a jungle bird in heat. When the vocalists were quiet, Carmen sang unpublishable lyrics into my ear in a husky, half-whispered voice that talked more than sang the Spanish and *ñañigo* words. Sometimes she was quiet, too, and her tongue teased my ear, and other times she told me what the music was. She told me that the slow, languid pieces were not rumbas at all, but boleros. The music called *guajiras* featured the guitar and a ten-line verse —no more, no less—as formalized in its way as a sonnet. Then the band played something new she called a *mambo*.

Carmen didn't teach me to dance the *mambo*. A little open break-step we did became an abandoned solo dance for her. The syncopated, dissonant, horn-blaring *mambo* put her into a state close to ecstasy.

Carmen became the floor show; she was that good. Everybody sat down to watch her. Me too. She kicked off her high-heeled shoes, and her bare toes had a way of sliding forward as if feeling for the floor and grabbing it, finding the beat there and letting it come up her long legs in a wanton motion.

The musicians shouted some lyrics that let us know the *mambo* was called "Mi Culebra," meaning "my snake," and she gave lots of sensuous meaning to the title with nautch gestures that had everyone in the place making pecking motions with his neck to the off-beat rhythm she set. I guess I was flattered that Carmen danced mostly for me, close to my chair, and finished by sitting in my lap.

Carmen was an entertainer. I was being entertained. I liked it without feeling especially involved. The fact is I had kind of wanted Teddy and wasn't accepting a substitute.

Some of Carmen's lipstick had rubbed off on my shirt, and she had found a red hibiscus blossom somewhere and put it behind my ear. I must have looked like a guy having a hell of a night on the town. Both girls started calling me Luke—with two syllables. I was "Loo-kay." And maybe I was feeling the rum, because then I spilled a drink and had to go to the men's room to mop up my pants.

Ramón came with me, smiling sardonically because he hadn't lost *his* dignity. "You know, Capitán"—he sneered—"you will have to give this Carmen some money for the dancing. She is a paid hostess like the others."

"So what?" I said, a little belligerently. He was irritating me.

"She will sleep with you, too. For a price."

"What are you, her pimp?" I shouted at him as I washed my face with cold water.

When I looked up, Ramón handed me a towel, but his face was set hard, tight-lipped. He said, "If you wish to be killed, it is easy in my country with insults such as that."

"Oh, hell," I said, holding my hand out to him and smiling, "I'm sorry."

He took my hand but didn't smile back, "It is my fault," he said. "I provoked you."

"I have a short fuse," I said. "Let's go back to the girls."

"Un momentito," he said. He was combing his hair meticulously. My own short haircut I comb with one swipe of my hand. I left him there.

"Loo-kay!" Teddy crooned at me when I sat down between the girls. "Did Ramón try to make trouble?"

"Why should he?" I asked and signaled the waiter for another round. Carmen rubbed my knee with hers.

"Ramón is very jealous," Teddy said. "He thinks I am his girl. He thinks he owns me."

"I got that impression myself," I said.

She laughed at me. "You don't know anything about Ruedo," she said, as if it were the funniest thing in the world.

Ramón came back. He sat down next to Teddy and whispered something to her.

"Do you know what he said?" she asked, turning back to me. "He paid me a compliment, a flowery Latin compliment. He tells me how beautiful I am, how desirable; that life without me is like death. I like to hear it, but I do not believe it. I have heard it too many times from too many men. What do *you* say, Looo-kay?"

I didn't know what to say. I looked at Ramón, who was scowling darkly. I looked at Carmen, who was drumming her long pearl-tinted fingernails on her empty glass to the tempo of the music. I looked at Teddy again and just grunted with my nose in my drink, and Teddy patted my hand. I hated that.

I pulled out my wallet and signaled the waiter for the check. I'd had it. The party was over. It had reached a stage where it's a bore to keep a party going.

The waiter came. Fuentes fumbled for his wallet, but I had to make a big show of paying the whole check and ordering another round. They sure as hell didn't mind that, and when the drinks came they drank to their host. Maybe I was a fool. I felt like one. It was true, as Teddy had said, that I didn't know Ruedo yet. Perhaps I didn't like the place either. So far I hadn't found it very hospitable. Well, there were other places, other jobs.

Ramón put his arm around Teddy possessively and I saw her squirm out of his grasp. She said, "It is my belief that you cannot own a person. You can only enjoy him."

I nodded. That made sense, I thought, the way all sorts of ideas make sense when you are full of drinks. Teddy smiled and squeezed my hand. That was better. When you're lonely in a strange country, a touch of honest affection, and whatever might or might not come next, can create a sense of belonging. That's what I wanted.

I got my wallet out again and pulled three fifty-duro bills from it. This brought the waiter to my side, and I gave him one of the pink bills to give to the musicians. The other two I folded and slipped under Carmen's glass. She was wetting her lower lip with her tongue.

"Be nice to Lieutenant Fuentes," I said.

She pouted. "I want to be nice to *you,*" she said, but she picked up the money and tucked it inside her brassière.

I stood up and lifted Teddy out of her chair. The musicians began to play a rumba just for us. We danced well together now. Everything was going to be all right, and the dancing let me know it. There was no sentiment involved, but Teddy said, *"Yo te quiero."* Literally that means "I want you," even though the same words also mean "I love you" to Spanish-speaking people, who closely associate love with desire.

I didn't say the words back to her, but I held her tightly as we danced near our table. Over the top of her straight, jet-black Indian hair that rubbed coarsely under my chin I saw there were still two empty chairs between Ramón and Carmen. Teddy scooped up her purse as we passed by, and we all said *"Buenas noches"* to each other, and there wasn't too much strain. Anyway, Ramón didn't shoot me.

Then Teddy and I danced to the open door and went out.

It was only a short walk to the Gran Hotel. She went to my room with me, without any coaxing or coyness. It was the most natural thing in the world.

Chapter 3

IT WAS the first light of the morning, or it was the strangeness of having someone in bed with me, that awakened me at five-thirty. When I stood up on the cool tile floor, I rocked a little and my head ached. My naked body felt clammy in the humid air coming in from the rain forest.

Tepid water from the one working faucet in the corner sink put some of the hangover fires out. I washed and shaved as quietly as I could. When I waked Teddy, I did it by touching her lips with a finger. They were slightly puffy, with the lipstick eaten off them. I said, *"Buenos días, niña."*

Her slanty, wide-set eyes opened, and her arms reached up for me. Then she saw I was dressed, packed, and ready to go.

"Looo-kay." She sighed reproachfully. Pronouncing my name made her cheeks sink in and accentuated her high Indian cheekbones.

"Don't go now." She pouted. "Johnny wouldn't go now."

So *that,* I realized, had been part of Johnny's trouble. Then I knew I had been right in the way I planned the morning.

"I have to go to work," I said gently. "And you better go to your own room." I sounded priggish to myself, but I had to prove something out at the airport.

When she saw I was all business, she stamped around the room, snatching at her clothes. Her top-heavy nakedness almost changed my mind, so I said quickly, "See you at the airport at eight o'clock, and don't be late." Then I left.

The lobby of the hotel had a damp, moldy smell, and there was nobody around. I had to get a *café puro* in the kitchen from a sleepwalking old Indian woman. I had one, just one, dash of dark rum in it. It was easy to see what had happened to old Johnny. It wasn't easy to run this airline on time.

Out at the airport, nothing stirred. The air was thick with a finely atomized mist. Our airplane was half shrouded in ground fog.

The station agent, Alvarez, who doubled as night watchman, slept in a hammock slung under the wing. He awoke at the sound of my footsteps and lowered a shotgun at me in slow motion, but he recognized me quickly enough and rolled out of his hammock to open the plane's doors for me.

I climbed in and went up to the cockpit to open the side windows and air out the cabin. Then I pulled the log book, the dog-eared manual, and the check lists from the pocket where they were supposed to be and looked them over. The instructions were all in English. A hell of a lot of help, I thought, to Ruedano pilots. I knew right away how I was going to spend the next couple of hours before I'd trust that aircraft again.

I went to work on the preflight inspection. I was thorough. I checked everything.

Alvarez brought me a broom so I could brush the fungi loose from the fabric control surfaces. The climate bred mildew on everything. I also opened the drain holes in the trailing edges; they were plugged with dead bugs. The elevators would get us home, but I was going to see that they were re-covered before another trip. Methodically, I went all around the airplane. I gave the landing gear a complete inspection, looking up into the wheel well for leaks or slipped or slack cables. I wiped the main hydraulic strut clean of gritty dirt and checked the safety pinning and made sure the down lock was properly engaged. I checked the radio antennas and went over the visible parts of the engines too.

Another Indian arrived to help Alvarez refuel the ship from a row of fifty-four-gallon gasoline drums. The gas had to be wobble-pumped by hand through a hose up to the wing tanks, where it was strained through an old felt hat. The wages for this work were the couple of unused gallons that remained in the bottom of each siphoned gas drum. I went out on the wing myself to see that each of the tanks was topped off.

I was so busy, time went by fast. At 0820 hours, just a Latin twenty minutes late, Ramón and Teddy showed up. They were scrapping. It was a loud, yelling fight in Spanish too rapid for me, but I could tell it was about me.

"Spaniard!" Teddy shouted at Ramón, using the word like an epithet. "Long-nose! Stop bothering me. I do as I please. No one owns me, especially you. You should go get some Indian girl in trouble. Go make a baby with eyes farther apart than yours, with a mind not so narrow. Go improve the breed!"

I interrupted her with a bawling out. "We will report for all flights exactly one hour before flight time. The co-pilot, not the pilot, will do the pre-flight inspection." I handed Ramón the check list.

"The stewardess," I said, giving Teddy the hard eye, "will get the flight manifest for the captain and help check the cargo weights and passenger list. She will also be responsible for a clean cabin, a clean toilet, and the stuff in the galley."

They were visibly surprised. Teddy sort of flounced off to the wooden bungalow that served as a terminal.

"*Puta!*" Ramón spat at her back.

"None of that," I said.

"That mestiza is my girl," he said ruefully, "but she always wants to get in good with the *capitán*. You better be careful, Capitán, or this will be her plane."

"Want to bet?" I said. Then I took him inside the cabin and showed him what I wanted done before every trip. I made him use a flashlight to inspect the tail cone through an opening back of the lavatory, to make sure all the cables, pulleys, and brackets were the way they were supposed to be. We also checked off equipment that had to be aboard in case we were forced down in the jungle, stuff like the first-aid kit, a machete, a folding shovel, a flare pistol.

Just before our 0845 flight time, Alvarez opened the radio shack and called Matanzas for a weather check. From the door of the shack he signaled okay to me with circled thumb and forefinger.

Then we took on our passengers. Everybody's clothes were rumpled and wet through the back with sweat.

I let Fuentes fly. It did him good.

Teddy served the Continental breakfast of rolls and coffee. She had a smile that was both warm enough and remote enough to make the men want her and still keep hands off during working hours. She slept around, but she was still a nice girl to me. If you believe the fallacious theory that there are two kinds of women, you are a sucker or you are nuts or you are a Latin American.

We churned through the air with a tailwind on the way north to Matanzas, and it was a beautiful morning. I had the feeling that everything was going to be just fine. I would learn something new everyday and I sure as hell wasn't going to be homesick for Westchester.

Maybe because I was feeling too good, we ran into a lot of turbulence over the mountains. What had been a ceiling ten miles high of cirrus clouds was now slamming down in front of us, all cheesy cirro-cumulus and the curdled milk of cirro-stratus. I could barely see the cone top of Mount Diablo ahead where its crater was mixing dirty smoke with the cloud deck of a warm front that closed the valley of Copa Verde. We were bouncing around good, so I put the Seat Belt sign on and I cursed the idiot at Matanzas who had radioed CVU to Alvarez.

I called Matanzas tower. They told me the ceiling at the airport was less than two hundred feet and might get worse. I took over from Fuentes and held on top. Circling around, I thought about the instrument landing systems in the States, and wished they had ILS or GCA here, but knew my wish for radar was fanciful as hell. LARC didn't even have radio at all its fields. I leaned out the gas mixture and circled some more while we burned it at the rate of a gallon and a half a minute.

There was only emergency refueling at Matanzas Airport, and if I couldn't get in and out soon, I'd have to overfly this station and head for Puerto del Sol, where gasoline came in by ship.

My hands got a little damp on the wheel as I watched clouds settling into the valley below us. Fuentes didn't look worried. In fact he looked a little glad, which is something about men of Spanish blood I was going to have to remember. It makes them, and hardly any other people, good bullfighters. They get a personal, prideful kick out of working close to mortal danger.

Then a hole opened in the cloud deck and gave me a brief look at the terrain before it closed again. I took us down fast, sort of by Braille, and the steep descent must have given the passengers who didn't know how to blow their noses some painful earaches. My own sinuses felt it. The air was rough, too. We bounced plenty, but I had a bearing for the airport. I sneaked into the valley, around Mount Diablo, and dodged the church steeple. The wind was strong and quartering across the runway. I crabbed in with only half flaps, getting the glide path right because I didn't want to overshoot and have to go around again so damn low. I picked my touchdown spot on the runway. Then I looked ahead of the spot and back to it, ahead and back, over and over, and watched the far end of the runway flatten out as the terminus spot rushed at me, getting bigger and bigger, and, just beyond it, the runway seemed to break and rush away, a change of perspective that always let me know it was time to flare-out and hold off. Then it was wing down into the crosswind and a goose of the throttle to touch down wheels first and pretty hot. I popped the wheel forward soon enough and hard enough to grease her on the runway and hold the tail high for steerage.

As much as Ramón may have hated my guts, he gave me a spoken *"Olé!"*

Before we could leg it to the terminal building we were caught in a sudden heavy shower, a tropical downpour that was rare at this season, and it soaked us like a high-pressure hose.

The southbound flight from Santa María and Puerto had got in before the weather. Fuentes introduced me to the crew at lunch. The American captain, Ken Reynolds, had been flying in Ruedo for several months. He was an ex-GI pilot like myself and seemed a nice quiet guy. His co-pilot was a high-strung Ruedano named Pepe Lopez, who Teddy said was a cousin of Coronel Romirez.

I hadn't paid any attention to the other stewardess the day before. Now

I did. She was a Panamanian imitation of Rita Hayworth who answered languidly to the name of Carlota. I dropped the separate-table caste system and looked the new girl over in the way men south of the border always did. The Latinos have a way of giving everything a girl has the long stare, starting at the feet, with their eyes pausing at interesting sights along the way. It is intended as a compliment. Teddy caught me doing it and said something to Carlota that I didn't catch, but I guessed it was all right because the girls laughed together in a good-natured way. Pepe Lopez, however, seemed as jealously watchful of Carlota as Ramón was of Teddy.

Lunch over, I checked the weather again with such scientific devices as my twenty-twenty eyesight, a sniff with my nose, and a phone call to Puerto del Sol. Puerto, they reported, was only catching the edge of the front. The sun was trying hard to come out in Matanzas, with some reluctant scud still hanging around.

I was almost dry again when I walked over to the plane. I saw and regretfully smelled the paper puke bags that littered the asphalt outside the plane doors, where the stewardesses had dropped them after collecting them from the airsick passengers. I decided to make an official stink about that because there was a rubbish bin at the gate. On the radio I called the tower and asked them to tell the ramp agent to call the flight. Then LARC, the Airline of the Slobs, took off again.

It was all routine to Puerto and then home before dark in Santa María. While the passengers went out the door and Teddy said *adiós* to them sweetly, I made out the squawk sheet, mostly about recovering the fungus-rotted elevators. Then I took Teddy by the arm and started for the terminal with some hope that this might become a steady shack job, provided nobody got too involved. That smugness got blasted when a long blue Cadillac sedan came out on the field apron and two blue uniforms got out of it. One was the unmistakable fat Coronel, and the other was Johnny Michaels, still wearing his captain's shoulder boards and now sporting the golden wings of the Ruedan Air Corps. Bang!—like that Teddy ran to Johnny and threw her arms around his neck and pressed hard against his brass buttons. I didn't mind too much, but poor Ramón, his face was a study. I thought about how it was said that old Johnny was bitter about missing two wars and never getting his wings. Well, he had them at last. Not eagle wings; they were condor wings—but official. He had a pretty girl, too, the way a military pilot should; and, despite a demotion in the airline, he had something cooking with Coronel Romirez, who beamed at him. I decided to wonder about that later, not on my own time.

Chapter 4

WHEN the birds go south for the winter they come down here to Ruedo and make a lot of pleasant noise in the morning to wake you up.

The bright warm sun streamed in through the two jalousied windows of my hotel room. I could have started my tan right there in bed, but I had a better idea for my Sunday off.

I shaved and put on my swim trunks and went down to the turquoise mosaic tile pool. After a dip, I ordered breakfast at a table beside the pool.

The Hotel Mirado was new and of extreme modern design. Frank Lloyd Wright would have admired it. Ruedanos were proud of it. It made me feel successful to live in it.

A white-jacketed *camarero* with long black sideburns and a constant expression of amusement on his face brought me a big stack of tropical fruits, some of which he identified for me as mangos. He also identified himself as Paco, a Cuban.

The pineapple, the little red bananas, and the tangerines were good eating, and so was the papaya. When I asked for more papaya, Paco thought it was very funny. He called it *fruta bomba,* and told me that in Cuba papaya is something else again, the sweetest part of a woman, and didn't I think it was a little early in the morning for that? Paco was a card. He brought me a fine Upmann Monte Cristo cigar and said it was the kind Romirez smoked. It lasted until it was time to go swimming again.

Time went by with a nice pattern of lazy moves into the pool and back to my blue sailcloth pad, which I dragged around to follow the brassy sun. But when the sun has finally ironed out the kinks, just lying there can get monotonous. I wished I had a book. I explained this need to Paco, but all he could find for me was a book of plays by a Spaniard named Lorca, and it was in Spanish, as had to be expected. After a frustrating few minutes with the poet, I sent Paco after a Spanish-English dictionary.

Looking up some words made a hell of a difference. This Lorca's verses were strong medicine, especially a play called *Blood Wedding*.

By afternoon, when I was sipping an ice-cold rum and Coke in the shade, some of the scenery improved. I knew I would want company soon, and a hotel swimming pool is a good place to pick it up when you like to be sure the company has nice legs.

I had a choice that disturbed me. There was one girl who was a knock-out in a Bikini swimsuit, and redheaded too. But she was obviously an American, and I was drinking the wine of the country; at least that's what I let myself believe was the reason the other girl attracted me. Actually, the other girl wasn't a beauty. Her legs were a trifle skinny. And yet there was something special about her. She had a way of touching her close-cropped black hair, of moving her hands, her whole cinnamon-tanned body, that wasn't just dancer-graceful; it was enthralling. Even from across the pool I thought I saw a flashing in her dark eyes.

There was an older woman with her who looked like a relative, a non-dieting, non-swimming relative. The young one swam like a playful otter, but mostly they sat at a table and talked in a very animated way. The girl was never left alone and she never looked my way. After a while she got up, gathered their robes, sunglasses, tanning lotion, bathing caps, and cigarettes (I watched every move she made), and they left. I felt deserted and alone. From thirty feet away across a pool, it was a ridiculous way to feel about a stranger.

I looked back to where the gorgeous redhead had been teasing the boys with her legs up on a wheeled chaise longue that had been moved under an umbrella to protect the sensitive complexion redheads have. Now she had a guy who had bought her a drink. There was nothing to do but get up and go in to dress. My one summer suit and bright tie made me feel a little gayer.

But at dinner alone in the hotel I still must have looked like I'd lost my last friend, so Paco tried hard. He brought me some *Carlos Tercero* Spanish brandy and heated the snifter glass over an alcohol fire. He held a match to another fine Cuban cigar and by then was calling me Don Lucas. He made his final pitch for a big tip by telling me about a whorehouse, but my plan for the evening was a lonely prowl of Santa María, the town I wanted to call home.

The capital was trying hard to outgrow its Spanish colonial architectural heritage with tall, starkly modern office buildings and apartments of glass and shiny metal. Their builders had achieved some fine effects that blended with the old part of town by using different colors in cement and textures of stone, tile, and brick. Of course Ruedo had that essential symbol of progress, neon signs. The capital was a big city now, all right, but a barnyard too. I could hear roosters crowing. The new and the old, the sophisticated and the earthy, were both here, and the more I saw of Ruedo, the better I liked it.

I turned off the Calle República, which was the main drag, because I was getting thirsty from my walk in the warm evening and because I was ready to be with people again. On one of the narrower, crookeder side streets I found a congenial-looking bar, and then, as Papa Hemingway wrote it somewhere, the town came to me. In walked Sam Warren, the sunburned, loud-talking fisherman and machinery salesman I had met on the plane. He had friends with him and introduced me to Harry Donahue, a crewcut attaché with the American Embassy staff, and to some fellow called Jim, who was also new in Ruedo and who had the tourist trots.

They sat down, and Sam Warren picked up a conversation where he had left off, telling Jim what to get at the drugstore for his trouble. I listened, too, and we both wrote it down. The Mayan Revenge could strike anybody.

"Get Sulfaguanidina and Entero-Vioforma—that'll fix you up," Sam said heartily, "but if it's amoebic dysentery, you'll need Milibus and Arelin."

Harry Donahue changed the subject and said I should check in at the embassy and get acquainted with the Ambassador. I bet him I wouldn't.

He said, "Seriously, Luke, there's trouble brewing. You're on the hottest spot in Ruedo, the airline. Romirez can control the whole country with his planes. How many roads did you see when you flew over the mountains and the jungle?"

"Damn few," I admitted. "None south of Matanzas."

"That's right," the earnest young Yale type said. "And when the rains come next month, nothing will move except by air. See the situation?"

"Hell!" Sam Warren rasped, "We ain't had a good revolution here in years. Might stir things up. Be good for business. Too many goddamned Commies in this new government anyway!"

Jim, the one with the trots, had just come back from the toilet and heard what Sam said, so he asked, "Do you think it's safe to stay on here? I hoped to go to Puerto for the fishing."

"Sure, kid. Don't worry none," Sam told him, and then he began a private conversation with Jim about his recent fishing trip. I would rather have been in on that kind of talk than the serious crap I had to listen to from Harry Donahue.

I got an earful about Ruedan politics. It was a monologue, and I didn't pay close attention. After a while Harry smiled ingratiatingly and said, "I talk too damn much. I don't listen enough. That's why I'll never make it in the diplomacy racket."

I nodded agreement. He frowned, but he bought me a drink.

"I think you're just looking under the bed, expecting to find Romirez there with a Tommy gun," I said. "He seems like a fairly harmless fat clown to me."

That started Harry off again, and it also made him argumentative. I finished a brandy I didn't need and got up to leave. He got up too and nudged me toward the bar, still talking.

"Of all the pleasures of man," Harry said, "the Irish like to lean on a bar and talk all night. With a drink, of course," he amended and signaled the barman for another round.

He rubbed the small beginning of a pot belly and held forth. "We Irish are full of blather. We will speak on any subject if only somebody will listen, and it doesn't matter whether or not we know what we are talking about. As a general rule, we won't say much that matters. That's because the Irish are really a stupid race of people."

"You said it; I didn't. Why brag you've got a corner on stupidity?" I said, and I thought I was pretty stupid myself to listen to him.

"I can prove we Irish are stupid by listing our chief pleasures—after talking, that is. Next comes drinking, or rather, getting drunk. We really don't like to drink. We like to get drunk.

"The next pleasure to an Irishman, after talking and getting drunk, is fighting. I almost said arguing, because I love to argue. Most Irishers do, and most of us will spoil for a poke in the eye, too. Haven't you felt like poking me in the eye yet? I've felt like belting you a couple of times for not taking me seriously." He went into a boxer's stance.

"This is pretty silly," I said, towering over him and looking down on his crewcut and button nose that women probably called cute.

He looked up at me belligerently and read my mind. "Don't let my size bother you, fly-boy. I played half at the Cross."

So it wasn't Yale, but Holy Cross, and a football player. He'd probably rush me swinging, the way all football players fought, and I'd stop him cold with a couple of straight punches the way another Irishman, Arthur Donovan, had taught me back in the Depression when I had the mistaken notion that the ring was an easy place to make a buck.

As it turned out, Donahue and I didn't exchange punches, maybe because he was sure he had gained my attention for what he called his primary pleasure. Anyway, he leaned back on the bar, looked into his glass of brandy, and said, "So there you have it. Talk, drink, fight—that's the Irish. With the dagos, it's sex that's first among the things they enjoy. All the Latins go for the sheer joy of screwing, but not the Irish. Latins make it glorious; the Irish make it dirty. We punish ourselves about it. We get our church mixed up in our sex life and screw to make kids, or occasionally otherwise if greatly moved, but our sex is lust, which is a sin, and we hate ourselves in the morning."

So, I thought, a long night's talk finally got around to the big topic. Maybe this mixed-up Mick would rather talk about it than do it, and I was beginning to wish I could remember where the house was that Paco had told me about. I was fed up with the embassy's big mouth. But there was no polite escape.

Then he was holding on to my lapels, which I didn't like, and saying, "Maybe Irish proclivities have something to do with the climate that spawned the race. It's about the same as Scotland, you know, cold and damp; and the dour Presbyterians also rate sin very high."

I removed his hands and backed away from his brandy breath as more talk spewed out of him, about how the Irish were hyphenated Americans, always professionally Irish and Catholic, and often crude, too, and insensitive enough to become caricatures of themselves as bartenders, cops, politicians, and hard-nosed priests. He went on with some historical stuff that sounded like nonsense to me, about how the Irish had got mixed up good when Drake chased the Spanish Armada into a storm off the Irish coast and the Spanish sailors went into the beds of Eire's women and made a lot of black Irishmen. He said his own family name, Donahue, was probably once Don Ajo, allowing for the Spanish "h" sound for "j."

"But the Latin strain is weak in me," he said, on the verge of a crying jag. "I have a surface sentiment and not the real passion of the Latins. To prove it, I'm not sure I want what's good for the people of this stinking little country. Could be I just want an uneventful tour of duty in Ruedo and a transfer to a better post in Europe. A revolution here would be an inconvenience to me, but I'm politician enough to read the signs. It's coming, fly-boy. Sure as shooting, it's coming."

Harry stopped talking. He had finally run down, and damned if I was going to wind him up again. Sám and the poor guy with the trots had already left. I said good night and left him ordering another drink.

I felt depressed. Maybe it was because I shared Harry's lack of enthusiasm for trouble coming in this country. I wanted to keep my life nice and simple. I was trying to take it from day to day and play it as it was dealt, without having to think too much about the future—or about the past, either.

I walked back to the Mirado and went to bed and dreamed about a girl with a cinnamon-colored tan, a girl who was altogether adorable and separated from me by a castle moat that looked like a tile swimming pool and had guards posted on the other side. They were all as fat as Romirez and wore sky-blue uniforms. They shot at me with toy pop guns.

Chapter 5

IT WAS Monday morning, and I didn't have to fly because my plane was still on its way back from the weekly Mexico City run with Reynolds and Pepe Lopez.

I visited the recommended tailor, a Spaniard from Madrid who, before the Civil War, did work that rivaled that of Bond Street, according to the testimonials he showed me. He took the measurements of my lanky frame, clucking over my shoulders and the length of my legs, and he said not to worry. I wasn't worried. I ordered two uniforms and a suit of tropical whites.

He insisted on payment in advance, shaking his head sadly. "It is a pity," he said, "but sometimes I have finished uniforms here in Ruedo just in time for the military funeral."

Then I worked on my tan again beside the hotel pool and almost felt as if I were in Ruedo on vacation. The hardest job I had to do all day was watch the entrances to the pool patio for the girl of my dreams. She didn't show up again, and neither did the redhead. I didn't know how to get in touch with the well-stacked Teddy either, but I didn't fret about it.

During dinner I got the address I needed from Paco, who didn't even raise an eyebrow, and, since it wasn't far from the hotel, I began walking in that direction. Actually, I didn't need an address, because there were a couple of slowly cruising taxis that edged up to the sidewalk alongside of me with pandering drivers. But I stayed on course and kept walking and puffing on a strong-smelling Ruedan cigarette.

Maybe I did feel a certain reluctance about a roll in the hay with a pro, because when I saw a sign that promised entertainment to fill a bachelor's evening, with bulbs spelling out the word *Frontón* and *Jai Alai* in neon script underneath, I went in. I had never seen the game played, but I'd heard you could gamble on it.

I bought my entrance ticket and tipped the usher for a scarce center-court seat in the steep grandstand that was built on one side of the Jai Alai court. Spectators were separated from the game by a heavy wire screen, a necessary protection.

I tried to puzzle out the game. The players used the green concrete walls on the other side and both ends to slam a hard ball around in a kind of handball gone crazy. There were four players on the court, two pairs of partners. One team wore blue shirts, the other white. On their right forearms they had scoop-shaped wicker baskets called *cestas*. In one motion, because a pause disqualifies the action, a player would catch the ball from either in front or behind, and with a roundhouse arm sweep and some tricky wrist action hurl it at the end wall at any angle or speed that would make a return difficult or impossible for his opponents.

My eyes were just getting used to the back-and-forth motion of the game when the usher came to the section where I was sitting and tried to clear a row of ten seats. The stands were jammed, but the usher wasn't kidding. He wanted a whole row vacated, and *now*.

At first nobody budged, and hot Spanish oaths were spat at the usher, who puffed his thin chest out against his oversized purple uniform coat and made a little pronouncement: *"Señoras y señores,* if you please, the seats are respectfully requested for the party of Coronel Romirez, Minister of Aviation for our beloved nation of Ruedo. Ten of you will now volunteer to find other seats. I thank you."

A hushed quiet came over the people within sound of the usher's words. Several directly in front of me rose and looked at one another with blank faces that still managed to reveal the quiet, patient hatred of the Central American Indian that goes back to their conquest by Hernán Cortés. But they did move to seats in the end zone; that is, all but two.

Left in the row were a young man and his girl friend. They didn't get up. Hundreds of eyes were on the immobile young couple.

Slowly the young fellow stood up and pulled his girl to her feet, but he didn't move out. He began a harangue that was nothing more or less than a political speech. He got a lot of whistles, which in Spanish countries are boos, but from a few he got halfhearted cheers.

The game stopped on the court, and the players watched the fuss. The usher waited resignedly, knowing the young man would sooner or later have to stop talking and leave. The young man knew it too, if the nervous sweat on his forehead was any indication. His date also knew it, and her eyes had already begun to visit with people in nearby seats.

The young speechmaker shouted, "Listen to me! I will go now, but not to give that fat pig Romirez my seat. No, I leave because I will not share this *frontón* with him!"

I thought the guy got out of his predicament fairly neatly, and so did some others, who clapped for him as he left, holding his head high and steering his girl out by her arm. The usher went away then, leaving a row of ten empty seats in front of me, and the game began again.

A blue-shirted player dove to the floor, trying to pick up a low rebound off the back wall, caught it, but couldn't get his shot away. When he got to his feet, there was blood on his elbow. The crowd cheered much louder than for the speech.

That retired the blue shirts, who were replaced by another two-man team in orange shirts. As long as the whites remained unbeaten, they would hold the court and be challenged in succession by other teams. They called this system of play a *quiniela;* the first team to score five points would win. The score flashed in lights on a tote board along with changing odds in the betting. The odds on the *Blancos* were lousy. They already had three of the five points needed to win and were favorites all the way.

Next up were the *Rojos,* long shots that would win me a thousand duros if I bet a couple of hundred. The red-shirted players looked eager coming onto the court. They had previously scored a point, too. Why not? I figured. It's only duros.

I caught the eye of one of the official bookies who walked the narrow aisles. He was identifiable by his panama straw hat with a sign in the hatband. He tossed me a tennis ball with a slit cut in it holding a betting form and an indelible pencil. I wrote down my bet and my seat number, stuffed the money with the paper into the slit, and threw the ball back just as Coronel Romirez and his entourage paraded in. Polite applause greeted the fat man.

Johnny Michaels was with him, and so was Teddy. There were two other Air Corps officers and four very attractive party girls.

Romirez hoisted his hams onto two benchlike seats, and I knew why he'd had ten cleared.

Then the Coronel spotted me and, wheezing with exertion as he twisted around, said, "Capitán Hadley, it is good to see you!"

He was very cordial. He bought beers for everybody in the party and included me. He tipped the vender big. He called the skinny usher and tipped him big too.

Romirez elbowed me in the knees. "So you like the Jai Alai—*bueno!*" He said it as though I was now a member of his club.

I drank my free *cerveza* and didn't say anything.

"How did you like the performance of that student?" the Coronel asked me. I took it as a rhetorical question, delivered with a twitching of his gross mustache and the blowing of blue clouds of cigar smoke. I guessed somebody had filled him in on the disturbance. I hadn't known the young man was a student.

The *Blancos* team finally lost, which was due, and left my red-shirt team on the court as winners. Odds dropped on them, but I let my winnings ride against the *Amarillas,* in bright yellow shirts.

The Coronel didn't bet but watched my tennis ball wager with amused interest. "I do not like to bet on sports," he said. "Athletes are too unreliable, not like politicians. I asked you what you thought of that student's big act."

So he did want an answer, after all. I answered him with another question, "Was it just an act?"

"*Sí! Sí!*" Romirez said and laughed explosively. "It is expected of the university students to display certain revolutionary tendencies. It is their tradition to make a riot now and then or else they will be thought to be *maricones!*" He stabbed his cigar and another question at me. "What are *your* politics?"

His question came just as my *Rojos* were defeated. I said, "I like to back a winner."

The fat Coronel laughed and wheezed until he could scarcely breathe. I had to pound his back for him until his asthmatic breath came again. Johnny turned to look at me and grinned because I was playing his game.

Romirez said, "Jai Alai amuses me, but I do not bet on it because the game cannot be fixed. So this honest game is my relaxation. The players belong to a guild, and a portion of their winning purse is always put into a retirement fund. If they are only suspected of throwing a game, they forfeit their retirement money. It is a good way to keep them out of gamblers' clutches, no?"

"Yes," I said.

The Coronel knew his Jai Alai, and he explained some of the finer points to me, such as how a player's right arm is larger than his left. But I only half listened as I wondered about Ruedan politics and if I too wasn't a bought and paid-for by Romirez.

"The ball bounces at two hundred sixty kilometers per hour and can kill a man if he doesn't catch it correctly or duck out of the way," Romirez said with satisfaction.

I believed it. I also believed the fat man with glittering eyes knew a lot about killing.

The ball was rebounding with the cracking sound a rifle makes. It blurred past my eyes. A Basque on a team in green shirts had a way of taking the ball out of the air and getting rid of it fast that reminded me of Joe Gordon making the double play at second base for the Yankees. I got a sizable bet down on the *Verdes* just in time to lose it when the Basque's teammate goofed one that had too much spin on it off the side wall.

"You like to gamble?" Romirez asked.

"I fly your airplanes, don't I?" I said.

That gave him another belly-laugh, and he got up and said, "*Vámonos!*" to all of us, adding, "We will now go to the Casino Palace."

I never knew if the *Blancos* finally won the match, because the Coronel led us all out of the *frontón,* his brass-buttoned stomach working like a snowplow through crowds of deferential humanity.

We piled into two blue Cadillacs. I rode with Romirez, and on the way he told me that casinos had been legal in the previous regime, under Sagasta, but since the election of *El Presidente* Ortega and the exile of Sagasta, gambling had been outlawed. This thought tickled Romirez' funnybone, too, and through guffaws he said that the regrettable reform tendencies of *El Presidente* merely presented further opportunities for graft on the part of the *federales.*

The Casino Palace had once indeed been the baroque palace of a Ruedan dictator. It had Roman columns in front and was built into the side of the foothills that mark the inland suburbs of Santa María. A uniformed attendant parked the Coronel's Cadillac next to a number of others.

In my sweat to get to the tables I was only half aware of the lavish decor of the casino. I did sort of feel the quietly rich, velvet hush of the place, laid over with ankle-deep carpet and the opulent light of crystal chandeliers hanging from a very high and ornate ceiling.

I picked a roulette table that wasn't getting a big play. I bought a stack of chips, thinning my wallet down to all but my last two pink duro bills. I didn't have enough money left from my salary advance for my big game, so I decided to go to work with my system first.

Don't believe all you hear about system players dying broke. That's propaganda the gamblers spread to keep you playing hunches. I say that to cheer myself up. It takes confidence to gamble, even with a system.

I've got a system for playing any kind of even-money chance that can make expenses for me just as though the roulette wheel were a lathe in a factory that I worked for wages. That is all I make at it, however— modest wages. If you're impatient to make a quick killing or to lose it all fast, don't play my system. Don't get the idea, either, that my system is a sure thing. The only guys who have a sure thing in a casino are the owners.

Based on a kind of doubling, as all systems are, mine has the advantage of increasing the size of the bets at a relatively slow pace, and you can make your score by actually winning less than half the times you bet.

I placed my bets on red or black, or on odd or even, or on high or low. I didn't have to bet consistently any one way. For instance, I could switch from black to red if red seemed due to come up, and that gave me an extra edge. Well, of course that's not really true, but it is nice to believe in, like Santa Claus. There isn't any such thing as a law of averages. Professional gamblers repealed it long ago. What they know is that the odds remain exactly even on every spin of the wheel—on red or black, odd or even, high or low. It is always possible to lose. All you've got going for you is the law of probability, and a merciless roulette wheel could keep you there for a week or a month to see it work *for* you. Hardly any bankroll is big enough for any doubling system in a run of bad luck, and just in case there is a Farouk in the game, there is a house limit on the size of bets. And besides, because an even break for gamblers is too much to ask of casino stockholders, they have green zeros on wheels to take a percentage away from even-money chances.

Yet eventually I had about ten thousand duros of the casino's money added to mine in a mountain of chips. I was ready to quit working and start gambling. It was quite late, maybe two in the morning, but I didn't notice it then. I was living high on the excitement that comes with the whirring of the wheel and the kikaida sound of the little white ball rattling across the grooves. I hadn't even taken a drink in over two hours, but now I wanted one, which a waiter brought me. It was a Fundador brandy and soda. It was on the house. They would have been happy to bring me more, but just one was fine. I sipped it and didn't play right away. I fingered my chips, stacking them different ways on the smooth green felt. I could count them by touch almost as well as the croupier could.

I drank slowly and watched the wheel. It was different from those I'd first learned to play in the South of France when I took my leave there right after the war. This one had both zero and double zero on the green, and they came up regularly enough to interest me. I decided to sort of feel for them as I began to play.

The right way to gamble in roulette is to do it as masterfully as possible, with no sense of insecurity. My plays had a calculated, don't-give-a-damn speed. Maybe it looked as if I just scattered chips around, a lot of them, but I knew what I was doing and what the odds were on the lines and on the corners.

I hit right away at eight to one. Then I hit at seventeen to one; at eight to one again; at five to one; and had a couple of big hits at thirty-five to one. I let my winnings ride, not dragging back a single chip. My identifying chip color was a wine red, and the chips spread out so that damn little green felt showed through.

The croupier's thin brown fingers spun the wheel with a flicking motion, and he let the little ivory ball go in the opposite direction. As it rode high on the polished slope of the light-grained mahogany bowl, I moved a couple of big stacks to the line between zero and double zero just before the croupier said, "No more bets, por favor."

I watched the ball hard and let the excitement build. You can feel what I felt then by walking across Park Avenue at Forty-Sixth Street against the lights. I chewed an unlit cigarette as the ball dropped and bounced crazily along the chrome slots and, when the wheel slowed, it made just a little trickle of noise. Then there was silence. The ball rested in the green slot on double zero. I was rich.

Well, I was rich in Ruedo anyway, with over a hundred thousand duros. I could buy my own Cadillac now if I wanted to and even pay the hundred per cent duty. If I wanted to.

Perhaps you wonder why I didn't quit then. They always do, those who haven't got the gambling fever. The truth is I wanted to win a whole hell of a lot more. I was gambling for untold riches, for the pot of gold at the end of the rainbow.

I scattered some more stacks of chips, and there was a little crowd around me now. I lost a little. I knew that black and even hadn't come up for a long time and I honestly felt right about moving all of my chips onto those even-money positions to double my winnings. I was betting four times the limit, and the croupier had to call the manager to okay exceeding it.

The manager nodded approval and spun the wheel himself for the simple chance. It's sheer superstition to resent a change of touch on the wheel but I did, and I didn't watch the ball. I just listened to its dry clicking sound and watched the croupier's and the manager's expressionless faces. When the wheel was silent, I got my news from the groan of the people around me.

I backed up from the table about six inches and right into Coronel Romirez' fat stomach.

"Muy mala suerte," he commented on my luck.

I took out my wallet and opened it with my fingers shaking only the slightest bit. I took out my last two pink bills and calmly tossed them to the croupier.

"Para su propina," I said, matching his faraway expression with my own.

"Muchas gracias," he replied politely while his hand, like a claw, closed over the tip and then proceeded to make the table clean for the next play.

I went to the bar. The Coronel followed me, and it was a good thing he bought the drinks, because I was flat broke.

I hardly tasted the brandy, the gall in my throat was so strong. I hated to lose. I think it is so much Freudian crap about how compulsive gamblers unconsciously play to lose, to hurt themselves, or to slowly, excruciatingly give in to their death wish with a kind of money suicide.

Gambling is an addiction, all right. I accepted that. But it started with how I felt about money—what money or, more likely, the lack of it did to me. I wondered when gambling had got to me, and not just the cards, the wheel, or the dice, but the gambling of myself, of sticking my neck out. I got to thinking about the time during the Depression when I couldn't afford to go to college, the time when a second five-cent cup of coffee downtown meant a long walk home instead of a bus ride, the time when things were tough enough and I was hungry enough to box in preliminaries in little fight clubs after all day at the paint factory where I worked in the sales-promotion department. Poker was just a penny-ante way to kill some time in those days. Was it because life then was enough of a gamble?

I remembered how I got better at my writing job than I did in the ring and landed with an ad agency on Madison Avenue as a copy cub. I didn't shoot craps or play the horses or any of that then either, because I had rediscovered airplanes and went for them the way some guys get a yen for cars or boats or the theater or anything outside of what they're doing for a living. I saved my money for weekend flying lessons. Was that another way to gamble?

When the war started and the government taught people to fly for free, I became an instructor, and along about then I got some expensive instruction myself in poker and crap shooting. It was in England, with a B-17 squadron, that I began to play poker like there was no tomorrow. For some of them, the ones who always kept an ace as a kicker, there was no luck on the ground or in the air. But the endless poker game we kept going was a way of saying money is a funny joke right now and life is serious as hell.

I was married by then, if having been on a ten-day honeymoon and separated for nearly three years in the service is being married. What a hell of a gamble that was! And before long I wanted to lose. A "dear John" would have been better than her V-mail about FHA loans and the lay-away plan for buying furniture at Bloomingdale's. I wanted to come home to a bride, not a bookkeeper, so I often raised bets with nothing but my openers. It was a waste, but there is another kind of waste that's worse.

I saw myself in the big mirror behind the bar, a tall, lazily slouched-over loser with a faraway unhappiness in his face and an unlit cigarette in his mouth. Gambling! It never made any sense!

Romirez broke in on my reminiscence. "Permit me to buy you another drink," he said.

"If you don't buy one, I won't be able to have one until payday," I said and didn't succeed in getting a chuckle into my voice. I was beginning to feel crummy.

"You want another advance?" he asked me.

"I guess so," I said.

"It is all right," he said, and he pulled an enormous roll of bills from his pocket. "I do not have dollars with me, but here is twelve-fifty in duros. Now you have been paid for three weeks," the Coronel said as if he owned me, and he counted out a sheaf of pink bills.

Johnny came over then with Teddy. They were winners at Black Jack and happy about it. I thought: For Christ's sake, I wasn't even lucky in love!

For taxi fare I broke one of the bills Romirez had given me, and at the entrance of my hotel I bought a Ruedo National Lottery ticket from a blind man.

Chapter 6

A TELEPHONE call early in the morning reported a low ceiling at Puerto del Sol, so I delayed the Tuesday flight until they called back and said the fog was burning off.

The delay gave me time to look over the travel agency counter at the Hotel Mirado. It provided LARC's only city ticket office. The posters were all Pan American's. A chrome DC-3 model had TACA markings. LARC had a burned-out neon sign. I made some mental notes for improvement of our point-of-sale effort. That wasn't my job, but whoever the sales manager was, he wasn't working at it.

Getting away late also gave Teddy a chance to nap and recapture some of the glamour a hard night had cost her, and she was almost cheerful when we finally took off. Ramón Fuentes' mood stayed sour because he knew where Teddy had been all night, and even the bright sunshine we found at Puerto did nothing for his humor.

I guess I was a little glum myself and would have been in a door-slamming mood if it hadn't been for the flying. If there was something missing in my life—and God knows I felt a big lack, like a hole inside me, at times—I had hoped to find something in Ruedo to fill the gap. But that's expecting a lot of just a place. Flying, which was my work, the concentration it required to do it competently, helped a lot.

I always got to know my aircraft the way a sailor gets to know his ship, a farmer his north forty, a musician his piano, or a lover his woman. Headed for Matanzas, my DC-3 was responsive to my touch. I made her do everything she was designed to do and just a little bit more as I planed her down to the cruising altitude I wanted and made her ride right on the step with the absolute minimum of drag for maximum speed at the horsepower setting I chose. I had her trimmed so clean and nice she'd fly hands off better than you could drive her.

Then, on the Las Piraguas leg, the feeling of emptiness got too big for ordinary flying to alleviate. With no difficult flying problems to solve, I began to think of filling the dull void with more work than skippering a flight in on time. How much added responsibility for the airline's operation I might take on would depend on how much of a vacuum Coronel Romirez left in my path; or, in other words, how much attention he really paid to the LARC business end as well as to the Air Corps.

I thought of putting into effect some stateside operations procedures, some proven methods for safety and on-time performance. This would demand a lot of improvement all along the line. My mind was so busy with the problems, the hollow feeling disappeared, and so did the last of the daylight as Las Piraguas, the river town, came into sight.

I gave Alvarez, our jack of all trades, a workout on radio procedure. It tested my Spanish at the same time.

"*Aeropuerto Piraguas,*" I called, and read the numbers on the wing: "LARC *cinco, cero, nueve, sobre Río Culebra . . .*" And I requested landing instructions. I got quite a surprise and was proud of Alvarez when he responded correctly and told me a Pan American Constellation was turning final and that I'd be number two to land.

"Roger and *gracias,*" I said, grinning into the mike I held beside my mouth.

I watched the Pan Am Connie drop her high-efficiency Fowler flaps and flare off to touch down beautifully short on our jungle strip. It was smart to use all the runway. If you overshot, going around again at Las Piraguas meant clearing the hills and high jungle trees at the far end. Why did they always pick such lousy spots for airports?

The big four-engine ship taxied out of my way, and I came in. Two airline landings in two minutes; the air age was coming to Ruedo!

Alvarez introduced us to the Pan Am crew in our bungalow terminal building. He had already gone all out with LARC hospitality and given them some native coffee.

"Greetings, Yank," the blue-jacketed captain said to me and then added condescendingly, "Nice little bush outfit you've got down here."

Right then I wished I had my own uniform, but I'm not the type to embarrassedly scuffle dirt with a shoe. I said, "Welcome to Las Piraguas. You slumming or lost?"

"Got some pressurization trouble," the captain said seriously.

"If you didn't bring your own mechanic you're bad off, because pressurization is one luxury we don't know how to fix here. But you picked a fun town."

"So I've heard," the captain said, staring at Teddy as she walked up with a rumba motion in her hips. The clean-cut faces of the American stewardesses sort of came apart with helpless jealousy. They got busy herding their fifty passengers toward the bus, which would have to make two trips. I told the captain, who shared a taxi with me, that I'd see what I could do about straining the facilities of the Gran Hotel. I begged off joining their tour of Río Culebra night spots.

"Believe it or not," I said, shaking my head with enormous world-weariness, "I have a report to work on tonight, entitled: 'How To Take Líneas Aéreas Ruedo Central Out of the Bush League.' "

I didn't stir out of the hotel lobby all evening. I ate a turtle steak there at a little cocktail table made from a cross section of mahogany tree trunk and I compiled a list on a pile of hotel stationery. I wrote under the heading of "Things to Do":

1. Complete an accurate aerial survey of routes.
2. Translate all check lists and maintenance bulletins into Spanish.
3. Oil the dirt strip at Puerto del Sol.
4. Move emergency supply of gasoline in drums to Matanzas by truck from Puerto or fly it from Las Piraguas when payloads are light.
5. Before rainy season, pave strips from loading docks to ramp areas so cargo trucks will move easily, or use rails and carts on train wheels.
6. Obtain 300-pound CO_2 fire extinguishers on two-wheel carts for use at all fields when starting engines.
7. Provide uniforms for ground personnel; also repaint Ruedan colors on planes (good for Latin morale).
8. Build a tower at Las Piraguas for radio. Also construct a wind T. (Good for my morale, because crosswinds bad there.) Need more runway lights, too.

The list was just a start, I knew, but it *was* a start. I slapped at some mosquitoes and called for a *mojito*. After drinking it down, I nibbled the frosted mint leaves, and then added another item to my list:

9. Purchase three additional USAF surplus C-47s, one of which we will cannibalize for spare parts; also spare engines (being offered by War Assets Administration).

I thought it would be a good idea to try for really high-density seating in the DC-3s. I could order small, lightweight, buslike seats, a non-reclining type, and carry up to forty passengers. Ruedanos weren't very big people anyhow, and that way we could lower fares while furnishing the only available transportation to more of the population. But of course I had to remember that this was a government-owned line, and that Romirez probably wanted first-class accommodations for the brass. And one thing I liked about the present seats was the way they folded up against the side of the cabin to make room for cargo when it had priority. I chewed on my pencil and then wrote down one more ambitious idea before turning in:

10. Purchase a C-54 for long-haul non-stop flights such as the Mexico run.

The next morning I showboated an on-time departure for our Pan Am guests to watch. Alvarez was great, making the hand signals like a big airport lineman to guide our taxiing, just as if we always had a lot of traffic. The Connie got out right after us, their engineer-mechanic having done what was necessary to make their high-altitude pressurization system work again.

It was a routine trip back to Santa María, but I kept Fuentes after school. I made him show me the whole maintenance set-up, while he sulked because Teddy had rushed off somewhere in a taxi.

In a corner of the hangar I found a dusty, yellowing sheaf of bulletins from the Douglas factory, stuck on a spike behind a pile of worn-out tires. I looked them over. There were no notations of compliance by LARC, no way to find out if the airplanes we operated had been de-bugged according to what the factory advised.

There was one flight safety bulletin that made my blood run cold. It read: "Inspections have revealed that there exists an improper load distribution in the wiring of the AN/ALT-6A equipment. Modified wiring within the equipment will be necessary prior to using, to eliminate possible fire." Unquote. It was dated 17 December, 1946. It was now

29 January, 1947. Nothing had been done about it. *Fire!* Fire in an air-plane! Oh, brother!

There was another beaut: "Information has been received concerning fuel-selector valve malfunction. If a faulty fuel selector is positioned to a particular tank, fuel may be drawn from or transferred to one or more other tanks. This can result in sucking air from a tank which is inadvertently run dry. Such a condition has in some cases resulted in simultaneous stoppage of both engines. . . ."

Fuentes shrugged. He said, "On the other plane we noticed a change in fuel level on the tanks we were not using."

"What did you do?" I asked, incredulous.

"We switched from tank to tank, so none got too low, but sometimes we got an overflow," Ramón said.

"With gasoline overflows and faulty wiring, do you realize what could happen?" I almost screamed at him.

"*Sí,*" he said ."We go *boom!*"

"Okay," I said. "We will put the mechanics to work on our ship right now; the other one as soon as it comes north."

"The mechanics have all gone home," Fuentes said.

"Then send for them. Send soldiers in jeeps after them!"

"Yes, sir," Ramón said, saluting. The soldier part seemed to satisfy a craving he had for authority.

While he pulled rank on some noncoms and sent them for the mechanics, I mentally underlined the item on my list about translations of bulletins.

When Fuentes came back, I asked him, "How do you keep discipline among the ground crews? How are you sure of their work?"

"Coronel Romirez prohibits any union among airport workers, even though the Ortega government has encouraged organized labor for railroad and dock workers," Fuentes said proudly. "If something goes wrong here, like the last time a wheel fell off one of the fighters and it cracked up landing, we find out which mechanic is responsible and we take him out in back of the hangar and we shoot him."

"Does this work?" I asked.

"I do not think so." Fuentes shrugged. "The major overhauls of engines we send to Miami."

The mechanics arrived in two jeeploads, a real PO'ed crew, but we got the wiring and fuel selectors checked out by eleven that night while I scribbled a report for the Coronel. In my memo I also asked for authority to set up tight regulations on airworthiness and for permission to employ a good crew chief from the States.

I could have mailed the report or sent it by messenger in the morning to the Air Ministry office in the Government Palace, but what I did was deliver it myself—and pronto, because I knew Romirez was a night-blooming type who slept late mornings. I had heard that most of the serious business with the Coronel was done at the Hotel Mirado, where the Air Corps had the whole sixth floor and the Coronel had a five-room corner suite for himself. I went there.

The receptionist on the sixth floor of the hotel was an Air Corps corporal who carried a submachine gun cradled like a baby in his arms.

"What do you wish, Capitán?" the corporal asked.

"To see your Coronel, if you please," I said.

He consulted an appointment book. "Eleven forty-five is open," he said.

I said I would wait. I felt good about the two days' work I had turned in and I suppose some of the kick came from a feeling of being needed by the beat-up little airline, of coming through for them. There was also ambition, which is like a disease, not too different from gambling.

There were guards at most of the doors, and blue-uniformed officers chatting in the halls. Two of them swaggered past, giving me the arched-eyebrow stare and slapping their polished boots with riding crops. They had an arrogant way of walking very slowly with long, stiff-legged steps.

Quarter to twelve came and went, but the Coronel kept me waiting. I noticed girls going into different doors on the sixth floor. They were all too pretty and overdressed to be secretaries.

At twelve-thirty the corporal said, "The Coronel will not be much longer."

At one-fifteen: "The Coronel is sorry about the delay."

At two o'clock: "The Coronel will see you pronto."

I had my audience at two forty-five. The Coronel's suite was jumping. It was a party. There was a busy bar. Romirez sat in a high-backed purple and gold wing chair, like a throne. Four of the prettiest girls hovered close to their fat host. Armed guards were close, too, with Tommy guns half pointed at me. I bet myself the safeties were off.

Romirez was armed with a long cigar and apologetic about the delay. He waved a thick arm in the general direction of the gaiety surrounding him and said, "Affairs of state." And he laughed.

A soft chair was pushed behind my knees. It sat me lower than the Coronel. Somehow my report on maintenance procedures seemed insignificant now. I was tired from the long wait, and irritable, too, so I thought about the money Romirez paid me. That helped.

"Maybe you ought to read this," I said and handed my handwritten note to him.

"It is important?" He pushed at his mustache with a corner of the paper.

"Would I wait three hours if it weren't?"

"Have a drink."

"No thanks; I'm flying this morning."

He shrugged with surprising indifference for a man who had hired me for my alleged sobriety to replace a chief pilot who had turned lush.

Romirez read my report, but he seemed distracted by the sight of a couple dancing to bongo-drum rhythm coming from a phonograph. Then he said, "Thank you, Capitán," in a way that dismissed me.

"Will you issue orders for compliance with all bulletins I sign?" I asked, standing. "And let me hire a crew chief?"

I got no answer. His little black pig eyes were looking past me.

"We must have regulations for safety," I said.

"You issue them, then," he said.

"The crew chief?"

"Later. Later."

"I have a whole reorganization plan in mind."

"That is good—later."

A guard ushered me out of the great man's presence by another door. I caught a glimpse of some pornographic paintings on the walls and some acrobatic sculpture of the same type.

I went down to my room on the third floor. I had got part of what I wanted from the Coronel but felt uneasy about it. The airline's problems didn't seem to interest Romirez much. Well, wasn't that what I'd hoped for, a clear field to take over more LARC duties? I slept on that, but damn little, because our regular Thursday run to four little northern towns, mostly to move cargo, had a seven-o'clock takeoff.

First stop was Abenico, a cotton town almost due north of Santa María. Our manifest showed tractor parts, sawmill machinery, mining machinery, dynamite, cement, oil, grease, tractor tires, jeep parts, household appliances, cases of beer, cases of Coca-Cola, five-gallon tins of dried milk, medicines and other drugstore items, and two typewriters for the growing bureaucracy.

The country around Abenico was flat and dusty. Cotton was planted for as far as you could see, and good Christ, it was hot! I found out that the land used to grow beans, but the Indians, for whom beans were a staple, couldn't pay as much for them as the plantation owners could get from cotton exports—so no more beans, and empty bellies here and there. So what? Sweet potatoes grew wild.

We didn't unload much at Abenico because they had a road and trucking. A priest boarded the flight, wearing his flat-brimmed, round-crowned black hat and ankle-length black habit. The padre looked cool as can be. I couldn't figure that out as I wiped sweat from my eyes and neck.

Another passenger was an itinerant saw-filer bound for the lumber mill in Madera. That town didn't have a main street, just a cluster of weathered wooden, thatch-roof shacks around the mill, the much bigger overseer's home, and a fancy paneled lodge on stilts for important guests. Total population: 617. The landing strip had been bulldozed out of the forest of hardwood that gave Madera its name and excuse for existence.

We didn't carry a stewardess on this run, so Fuentes and I got some coffee at the mill mess hall. I looked at two acres of stacked timber and wondered aloud how it got moved out. Fuentes told me.

"Barges take it down the Río Norte to the sea, but unfortunately the lumber crosses the disputed border and it is heavily taxed," he said and grimaced. "We should fight those *chulos* and move Ruedo's boundary to the river, but our new government is weak; it does not understand the power of the Air Corps."

"Does Romirez want war?" I asked.

"It would not be a war," Ramón said disdainfully. "It would only be a border incident. Maybe twenty, thirty people killed, but we would take the Río Norte!"

"Who owns this mahogany forest?" I asked as we went back to the plane.

Fuentes smiled and said, "Let us not talk politics, Capitán."

I would have liked to find out if the northern landowners were the Romirez backers, and would have questioned Fuentes some more, but he had clammed up because another man had moved over to where we stood in the shade of the plane's wing.

The man was a swarthy mestizo and he was drinking orange pop. His clothes were good, but he wore the straw sombrero of the farmers. He waved his ticket at us. Fuentes took it.

"Thank you, Señor Congressman," Fuentes said.

The man gave his pop bottle to a barefoot kid, leaving a swallow in it that made the little fellow's day as he returned the empty to the mess hall.

After the man boarded the plane, Fuentes said, "That is Ycaza Lacayo." He spat dry with his lips and added, "That congressman pokes his nose into everything. He is one of those *comunistas* the new government encourages."

We fired up and headed southwest for Minas, which was located in the central range of mountains, where the gold had played out but where silver still kept the little town going. Ramón dug out the data sheet on Minas field. I absorbed the information with misgivings. Only eighteen hundred feet of lumpy dirt runway.

Ramón saw my frown and laughed. "This is nothing," he said. "Wait till you see the next one!" He also told me there was no radio and added, *"No hay gasolina."*

No radio and no gas was SOP for all these little back-country fields. I zigged and zagged around a couple of hilltops and put us down nose high with power, and that should have been that for any pilot, but then our troubles really began.

Ground facilities were so bad at Minas, Fuentes and I had to let ourselves out the front hatch on the folding ladder, get the ramp steps from beside the fence, put them under the door, open the door from the outside to let out the passengers, unload cargo, then unlock the airport shack, check cargo manifests, weigh the freight pickup, sell tickets, load the freight, and load and lock in the next batch of passengers, some carrying baby pigs or live chickens with their feet tied together. Then we ditched the steps again, climbed aboard on our ladder, started the engines, and had nothing to do but fly to the next village.

Cerro del Ángel was another mining town in the higher coastal range of mountains southeast of Puerto del Sol. When I saw the landing strip, I could hardly believe it. It had been carved into the side of a mountain. Regardless of wind direction, Ramón said, we had to land uphill and take off downhill. The data sheet told me the elevation was six thousand feet. I checked my altimeter and just shook my head.

"You want me to do it?" Ramón asked. "I have done it many times."
I didn't like the way he sneered. Anything he could do, I could do
better.

I didn't know where updrafts or downdrafts would be on the approach,
so I put us the hell down steeply in the column of air we were in. At
least I knew *it* was smooth. The Seat Belt sign was on, but I bet I put
the chickens and pigs on the ceiling along with our stomachs as I
peeled off like a dive bomber, down toward the end of the strip where
the mountain dropped off into space. How good the landing was going
to be depended almost entirely on the approach. I killed speed with full
flaps and pulled up the nose, power stalling to hit the spot on the strip
nearest the edge of the cliff. It was a whole lot like turning your car into
the driveway at ninety miles an hour and stopping before you knocked
the back out of the garage. I three-pointed us, gluing the tail wheel down.
We didn't bounce, but there was still real work to be done after the
touchdown. Control surfaces were mushy. I had to walk the rudder pedals
hard and use plenty of brake to keep us straight.

When we stopped with just enough room to turn, Ramón patted a
yawn. Cute kid.

Cerro del Ángel had a producing gold mine and could afford a single
ground attendant at the field, who Fuentes said was usually asleep or
drunk and useless, or just plain forgot what day it was. But this day
he showed, sober, industrious, and eager to please the new captain. He
even had a fork-lift to unload and load cargo for us. The machine had
come in by air and been assembled there.

It was a hundred in the shade, so I headed for a Coke in the shack.
It cost me ninety cents. If I had wanted rum in it, that would have
been an extra dime. The rum moved the long way around over unpaved
road from Vega to Matanzas and up the mountain trail, taking two
months. The government brand, called Espíritu de la Caña, could be had
for thirty-five cents a bottle. The ninety-cent Cokes were flown in, and
I saw a dozen cases of empty Coca-Cola bottles being loaded on our
plane for return to the bottler in Santa María. American mining engineers drink a lot of the stuff.

One of the engineers was coming with us, a homesick Colorado boy,
Pete Denning, who made good dough because he was good at blowing
dynamite. He drank a Coke with me and said he had another job to do
at the Lajas mine in the south and would fly with us soon again.

The congressman was still with us. He drank a Coke too and asked me what time we would get to the capital.

"Before dark," I said, not too politely.

"How much time do we have on the ground at Vega?" he asked. Vega was our last stop before returning to Santa María.

Fuentes butted in and said, "It is Capitán Hadley's first trip on this run, but not yours, Señor Lacayo. You know we only stop ten, maybe fifteen, minutes at Vega."

"All right," Lacayo said.

I went out to the plane and looked up and down the strip.

"We take off downhill and downwind, Capitán," Fuentes said impatiently. "We fly right over the edge of the cliff and pick up flying speed by diving into the valley."

I didn't like downwind takeoffs and said so. They all had to wait while I borrowed a metric rule from Pete, the engineer, and got a couple of wooden sticks off a carton of freight. One of the sticks I marked at a hundred centimeters. I didn't have a mason's level, but I went out on the field and held the measured stick as level as I could over the other one, that lay on the incline of the runway, and I measured the angle of slope. It was nearly ten centimeters, which equaled ten degrees. Some hill!

It was possible to lift off a DC-3 with minimum control at sixty miles per hour, and our ship was light now with most of the cargo delivered and most of the gasoline used up. I looked up the slope of the runway and calculated where I'd have to be airborne to make even a gentle thirty-degree banking turn away from the mountainside if I took off uphill and upwind. A turn would increase our stalling speed, but I wanted the wind on my nose.

The formula for figuring if I could get off okay went like this: The length of the run is equal to the product of half the acceleration and the square of the time. I got out my pencil and wrote it down—$d = \frac{1}{2}a \cdot t^2$. They taught us that in Ground School. It was taught to keep us alive, so why forget it?

At sixty miles per hour, we'd be moving eighty-eight feet per second, but there was a lot more to remember and to puzzle out in advance. At the six-thousand-foot elevation of this mountain runway I had to figure my true air speed by adding two per cent to my indicated air speed for each thousand feet above sea level. Then I had to take into account the slope upward, which provided a component of gravity working against me at the rate of thirty-two feet per second. Wind speed was in my favor, but heat, humidity, and poor runway surface were against me.

When I had all the numbers, including how long the strip was, according to the data sheet, I annoyed Fuentes to near distraction by pacing its length to be sure. Then I put on my sunglasses for one more look uphill at the rugged mountainside and said, "Let's go—*down*hill."

While my co-pilot gloated, I turned us around at the absolute uphill end of the strip, stood on the brakes, and really wound up the two Wasps before turning the old ship loose. Then we roared downhill and went off the edge of the cliff like a going-down elevator, but the air finally packed under the wings before we hit bottom. I wiped my hand sweat on my pants and let Fuentes fly us to Vega. It was flat country. I was through for the day.

The poor town of Vega spread like a running sore to the edge of the clearing we flew into. Flies buzzed lazily into the cockpit.

Here people lived in grinding poverty and squalor, too sick and weary to repair their hundred-year-old mud and plaster houses and ratty thatched roofs, too unaware now of the sour smells of pisspots under every bed, of garbage and burro road-apples in the streets. Here and there—sometime long ago—a woman had made a try with a piece of colored cloth in a window, or a pot of geraniums. A lost cause. The naked little kids with distended bellies and scabby impetigo were what really broke me up.

If Ycaza Lacayo was a Communist, this was the place to do his work in. I watched him talking to a shirt-sleeved Indian who had met the plane. They kept swatting flies and looking over their shoulders to be sure no one was close enough to overhear them.

Sugar cane was the money crop, and rum was the industry. The few who could afford to travel usually rode the twice-weekly bus to and from Santa María. The only one who had the price of the forty-minute air trip must have saved a long time. His whole family turned out to see him off. He wore his Sunday best and carried his guitar. He was a singer who had a nightclub job to go to in the capital. Arriving by air would give him class. He crossed himself a half-dozen times before climbing up the three ramp steps. His first flight. He was safe enough. I just hoped he never would have to go back.

Chapter 7

WE HAD flown a tight timetable. I was glad to see it could be done. Back in Santa María, Fuentes rushed to the phone to check up on Teddy while I went to the hangar to authorize overtime work on the other plane the next night when it got back from Las Piraguas.

Then I posted an order on the bulletin board in the Ready Room for Reynolds that his plane would be grounded until its fuel and electrical systems had been checked out. A note was waiting there for me. It was from Harry Donahue, an invitation to a cocktail party.

A hard day's work on less than three hours of sleep didn't leave me in a party mood, but after a long, soapy shower Harry's invitation sounded better. The uniforms I had ordered were hanging in my closet, also the white suit. I chose the civilian identity and, as I went through the lobby, I dragged my feet a little past the bar until I remembered they served cocktails at cocktail parties.

A brown-skinned, black-uniformed maid opened the door for me at the Donahue apartment, and almost at once I was greeted by a blonde as if I were a long-time friend of the family. She was Harry's wife, George. Yes, George—for Georgiana, I suppose. What the hell did a girl want to be called George for? Or Steve? Or Mike? Their names are Stephanie or Michelle, damn pretty names.

George led me across a terribly contemporary living room to a portable bar that was decorated with that American institution, a pitcher of martinis, made, I learned, with tax-free gin from the US commissary. It was a taste of home. I had one with George and then moved around, because I thought she gushed too much.

The other guests were all young American couples, not too different from the crowd Cynthia and I used to entertain or go to see in Westchester. The party laughter was liquor-loud, and damned if I could see what was so funny. Their talk about their hard life in Ruedo depressed me—the interminable conversations about plumbing breakdowns that took days to get repaired, all the different things that constantly went wrong in running a household in this broken-down little country, and, of course, the lazy Ruedans, the inferior workmanship of Ruedans, the dirty Ruedans, the corrupt Ruedans, the smiling Ruedans you couldn't trust. I didn't think any of them ever had it so good in the States. Their servants were six dollars a month.

Harry came over to the wall where I leaned with my drink and shook my hand like he was running for office. "Having a good time?" he asked and, not waiting for an answer, said, "Sorry we haven't any single girls here tonight." Winking, I thought, too extravagantly, he added, "But the married broads down here bear watching when a lone wolf shows up at a party. Stay out of the kitchen."

The wives he referred to were mostly aggressively blond. Their dye jobs were damn near an affront to the dark-haired Ruedanas. I wondered how brief my visit could be within the limits of politeness, but people kept coming up to me and asking the same question: "How do you like Ruedo?"

I got by with smiles and grunts because the American colony didn't really want to hear my opinion.

And a lot of these people had a way of saying, in one breath, "How-do-you-do-where-did-you-go-to-school?" They seemed disappointed when I said NYU, so after a dead pause I would add, *"Nights!"*

George passed some canapés to me, turning on her smile and that accent which is considered elegant in Greenwich because it isn't really affected after enough speech drills in Miss Something-Something's Country Day School. She reminded me of Cynthia. Was it also the goddamned worked-on feminine sweetness that once seemed so desirable during my leather-jacket days at the base? Had I been flattered when Cynthia wanted me and so many other guys wanted her? Well, I got her and got stuck with her. Cute girl, Cynthia. Everybody admired her. Everybody loved her. I got so I hated her guts.

I thought of the rawness, the sourness of Ruedo outside this slick apartment on Avenida Santa María. I thought of what I had seen in Vega, and before I realized it I was talking about it to some of the men. They listened to my first impressions of Ruedo tolerantly enough.

Daniels, a man in the coffee business whom I had met before with Sam Warren on the plane, had traded in Central America for years. He was full of advice.

"It does no good to try to get close to these people down here," he said. "You can't really get in touch. If you try, it will mix you up and it will hurt you. Just look at them the way you look at the strange trees and plants. They have their own life and don't want to learn yours."

It was obvious that the American colony kept to themselves. They worked at their jobs for American firms or the US government. They gave parties for one another, played lots of bridge, and read magazines from home. Their kids attended a small American school. They didn't even learn the language beyond kitchen Spanish to talk to the help. They were all going back to the States some day, sooner or later. I felt apart from them. I didn't know if I would ever go home again.

A Mrs. Cluette, with a hush-puppy accent, filled me in on what she called the Indian problem. "The Indians are strictly no-account, just like our southern niggers," she drawled.

Everybody laughed, and Mrs. Cluette told us that old bromide about Negroes being like children without any sense of responsibility, how when they wanted fancy yellow shoes or a new watch, nice things such as their betters had, they'd skip the milk bills to buy them, then probably hock their shoes when they needed money to eat. I heard how Ruedan Indians would work for money if they couldn't get away with stealing it, and how they'd never understand about saving money or investing it for the future.

"Hell!" I said, swearing too quickly because I'd been away from polite society for quite a while. "I've seen Indians who don't have a damn thing but rags and disease!"

I got a sharp look from a man who joined our circle with a fresh martini for Mrs. Cluette. He turned out to be her husband, Andy Cluette, the local AP Bureau man. He picked up his wife's conversation where she had left off, and his accent was all Dixie too.

"It's no damn use to he'p people who won't he'p themselves. When the new government came to power here, they tried land reforms in one of the provinces, and the Indians sold the land they were given to the first buyers and then bought flashy cars with loud horns, and they had no roads to drive them on. Let me see you do-gooders work on that one!

"Believe me," Andy Cluette went on, "if the Indians would only try to own houses instead of renting a couple of rooms or a shack in the cities, or instead of going native and living off the fruit and game in the jungle, they'd be building for their futures, gettin' a stake in their country. But they never do, with rare exceptions. That's why proprietors of businesses down here are always Spanish colonials and a handful of immigrants, including Chinese storekeepers."

We had a cocktail party forum going, and it attracted all the other men into a huddle near the bar. Mrs. Cluette joined the rest of the ladies, gathered in a far corner talking about babies, clothes, and the servant problem.

Harry Donahue disagreed with Andy Cluette, telling him he oversimplified things, and he needled the reporter about covering nothing but capital news and not getting out into the interior. "You ought to see the Indians Luke has seen in Vega," Harry said. "You'd understand then why Ruedo can't create a capitalist middle class when the low wage scale keeps most of the Indians in absolute poverty; and those with Indian blood are damn near ninety-eight per cent of Ruedo's population!"

Daniels, the coffee man, drew himself up and said, "My company pays wages to the Indians. It's money they'd never see otherwise."

"Nuts!" Harry said. He did love an argument. He waded into Daniels with facts about the Ruedan government's hundred-and-fifty-day work cards that forced Indian labor off little garden plots that were poor enough at best but worse for neglect after the men were away from them for half a year's work on coffee and cotton plantations, mines, or wherever they could get their cards stamped. These part-time members of the country's money economy ended up in debt to company stores and in city slums.

"American companies with branches down here don't sell our way of life to the Ruedans. We don't practice what you preach at home about free competitive enterprise. We foster monopolies here and have no social conscience."

"Neither have the Ruedan landowners!" Sam Warren boomed. He and his wife had arrived late. He slapped me on the back.

Harry was shouting, getting hot, "Damn it, we've got to cooperate with the democratic Ortega government on moral grounds or we'll get one of two worse alternatives—fascism or communism right on our doorstep. Talk is cheap. I'm trying to do my job when I talk about political liberty, economic freedom, and social justice down here, but it's like explaining sex to a eunuch! God knows, the Indians just understand beans and rice."

Sam walked away, muttering, "Politics!"

"Are there Communists operating here?" I asked, thinking of the congressman I had met on the plane.

Andy Cluette, who, after all, was a foreign correspondent, felt impelled to answer. He diagramed it, gave us half a dozen reasons why the

Communist ideology couldn't get far in Latin America. We could count on rightist stability because of: first, the low level of industrialization with a not very significant labor movement; second, the political importance of the military; third, the strength of Catholicism; fourth, the proud, stubborn individualism of the Latino, coupled with the traditional social status of the Indians and their white masters; fifth, the benign climate of this area and its natural abundance of things to eat that you can just pick off trees; sixth, and finally, the nearness of the USA and Ruedo's economic dependence on its big neighbor.

It sounded reassuring for the status quo, except for Harry's arguments. He wasn't underestimating the Communists' chances. Harry said that Ortega's party, called the Liberal Conservatives, wasn't moving fast enough with changes in the Ruedan way of life. The university crowd of propertyless mestizo professionals, the lawyers, doctors, engineers, and so forth, who were called extremists and radicals even by Ortega, were joining labor groups of farm workers and miners to form several splinter parties.

"The real Commies aren't numerous, maybe forty or fifty all told, and mostly the home-grown variety, but they know how to bore from within. We've also got to concede that the Soviets have sent some smart ones everywhere, including here. Notice, I said smart ones. They'll be technicians in radio and printing, geologists, agriculturalists. All of them propagandists. The sons-of-bitches will speak fluent Spanish, too, and marry native girls from poor families. They will have money to finance trips behind the Iron Curtain for bright young Ruedan men who are potential subversives, the ones with no family connections and who are bitter about having to take lousy jobs after getting a college education. And the Communists will actually help people at first along capitalistic and democratic lines, but their dirty work will get done. As Andy said, the Indians don't seem to savvy capitalism anyway, maybe because of the communal tribal life their people led before the Spaniards came. That worries me. It should worry you, because it leaves a vacuum that Reds can fill if we don't encourage US business investment here to provide more and better jobs, if we don't lend countries like this one money for roads, dams, power plants, even ordinary sanitation, or whatever will help them to help themselves to a better standard of living."

"I declare," Andy said, "you're one of those northern Democrats who wants a WPA for the whole cockeyed world. Is our country prepared to finance Ruedo's unemployed?"

"You got me there," Harry admitted. "As you know, President Ortega and his braintruster, Doctor Vidal, are up in Washington right now, trying to get some aid money or at least a loan. The way they figure, why should Europe and Asia get it all?"

One of Harry's servants came up to him and very softly said, *"El teléfono,* it rang for you, master."

Harry excused himself, and the party began to break up. A few of the men refilled their glasses, last ones for the road. The girls began new conversations at the door.

Daniels shook his head and got in another lick. "We can't raise wages on coffee *fincas* here unless they raise them in other parts of Central and South America. We would price ourselves out of the market."

Another man said, "Harry has defined the problem though, and I'd hate to see it solved by communism. A Commie government would expropriate our holdings. Look at what's happening to Mexican oil!"

"Don't worry about that," Andy Cluette said with conviction. "The Commies have no legal political party here as they do in Cuba and some other Latin countries. Section Forty-four of the new Ruedan constitution expressly prohibits any party of foreign origin."

Sam Warren joined us and said, "You don't even have to worry about the labor unions the Ortega people have encouraged. They went too far when they organized schoolteachers and renters. That will topple Ortega with a push from Romirez."

Harry came back, got me aside, and said, "Stay for dinner, you big lug. You're a good listener."

"I'd like to," I said, and I meant it. I guessed I could listen to him some more. He talked a lot, but I liked him better than I had when I met him in that bar.

"That phone call was from the Ambassador," Harry told the others, and the men waited to see if there was news. They had to respect Harry as the official voice of their government. What he could tell them might make a difference in their decisions in the morning—to buy or to sell.

"Schlomer needed me to decode a cable from Washington," Harry said. "They want the straight poop on what's going on in order to know how to handle Ortega and Vidal in Washington. The straight poop is just what we've been talking about, a socio-economic problem, but what will get attention by the State Department is the immediate power struggle going on between two camps of old landowning families, represented by Ortega and Romirez."

Harry sounded discouraged, but Daniels and Cluette laughed. "It's the the same old thing, Harry," Andy Cluette said. "They fight over who gets the keys to the treasury."

"Maybe," Harry said. "Maybe once more like that, but next time, or the time after . . ."

Then he spelled it out for us. If the budding democracy was doomed in Ruedo, it was because Ortega hadn't yet learned that in Washington he should talk about Communist infiltration. That was bingo. That was the way to hit the jackpot. But the few influential and vocal Commies were against Romirez and screaming for more democracy, while giving their support to Ortega. As a consequence, of course, Ortega, who wasn't even pink himself, but wanted to stay in office, couldn't recognize a Communist if he tripped over one.

The Ortega regime could win an election, if there ever was another election, but the guarantee of that was threatened. It had looked safe when the Army was put under Dr. Vidal and changed to the Federal Police without the second sons of landowning families among its officers, but some of the politics-by-force types had switched to the blue uniforms of Romirez' Air Corps. Now Romirez, a shrewd politician, could negotiate from strength and also be expected to smear Ortega with the Commie label. Therefore Ortega wouldn't get a dime's worth of aid from our government.

The good-bys finally got said, and it was a lot quieter in the Donahue apartment. I would have helped empty some ashtrays or carry out dirty glasses, but there were servants for that.

And dinner was certainly no trouble for George. She gave some orders to an Indian cook, who answered her two or three times with, "Yes, mistress," and it was all done. The food was good, too, plain American cooking, like at home. Lamb chops, peas, and potatoes. There wasn't one Latin American influence on the table. Somehow I resented it. I looked at the dark girl who served us, and she almost dropped a plate. She had thought she was invisible.

"We'll have to give another party, Harry," George said, "and invite Jane, that nice Mr. Bullard's daughter. He didn't come tonight because we're not important enough yet. He goes to the Ambassador's receptions."

"J. K. Bullard is down here surveying the possibilities of building a hotel for Connie Hilton," Harry said.

"What's his daughter like?" I asked.

"A dog," Harry said.

"It figures," I said. "What's wrong with the wine of the country?"

"Now *really!*" George said.

"We can't let you go native," Harry said. "There are only two kinds of girls down here, good girls and bad girls. The good girls you can't reach through the bars on their bedroom windows or take on a date without their mothers or *dueñas,* and besides, they're being saved for political marriages just like in the Dark Ages. The others? Well . . ."

"I thought the Spanish settlers who came here married a pretty Indian girl now and then," I said.

"Sure they did," Harry said. "You can see it in their color and facial characteristics sometimes, but they remain colonials through and through. No Spanish family ever lets its *daughters* marry Indians, or anybody else outside the club."

I wasn't planning to get married again, so I changed the subject. "I had a passenger today," I said. "One of the Commies we were talking about, a congressman called Lacada or something."

"He's no Red, Luke; not Lacayo. You shouldn't say things like that!"

"I heard him called one."

"That doesn't mean anything. Ycaza Lacayo is a congressman from Matanzas, a product of Ortega's democracy, and he's in favor of land reform, which may be politically left of Romirez, but he's no Communist. Everybody down here who is in favor of a living wage for the Indians, or against the government work cards, like Lacayo, is called a Commie. Don't you believe it. Of course, the actual Reds do support social and economic reforms, which confuses people, but Ycaza Lacayo stops short of the party line."

George had listened to her husband with rapt admiration. "Harry is very ambitious," she said rather inanely.

"I'm impressed," I said.

"Well, don't be," Harry said as he went to a sideboard for a decanter of brandy. "I'm just learning, just getting in shape for the main event. Ruedo is a warm-up game for me."

George got up and ran her hand through Harry's short crewcut, gave him a peck on the cheek, and went back to the kitchen to beat the cook or something.

Harry said, "Isn't she great? Comes from a fine family. Wonderful connections. Good education at Smith. Lots of nice *old* money. I really picked me a wife!"

I must have raised my eyebrows, because Harry went on the defensive.

"A career diplomat can't make it from here up through the ranks," Harry said. "George's father wants me to go back into law and into state politics at home. If I can help elect a president from Buffalo's Irish First Ward, I can skip a few steps all the way to ambassador. And I'd do a better job than old barrel-ass does here, a lot better job than that brewery owner who made a fat contribution in the last election."

Money talked, I thought; Schlomer's money, Harry's wife's money, Washington's money. Romirez' money was good enough for me. Smart money.

"You said I should meet the Ambassador," I said.

"Forget it. I was working then. I'm off duty now. Schlomer is doing as bad a job of representing the United States of America as is possible unless he were doing it on purpose. He's a baby in politics. He actually seems to like everybody. He is a sentimental slob with less executive ability than his embassy clerks. He belongs back in the McKinley era."

George returned from the kitchen to hear the last part of Harry's diatribe. She said, "Harry is trying to help Howard Schlomer."

"Yes, I am!" Harry said. "God, how he needs help! But all Schlomer thinks he has to do is give receptions and go to them. It takes a full-scale espionage operation just to keep track of his social engagements with Romirez. Those two get together ex officio and drink beer all night. It embarrasses the staff with the new liberals. Then Schlomer's wife overpays their gardener and louses us up with the old landowning families too. It's hopeless!"

I asked, "What's the background on my boss, Romirez? How did he get into aviation?"

"When it looked like Hitler was licked, Ruedo declared war on Germany and Japan and sent some military attachés to the States. Romirez, a captain then, chose the Air Force for his tour of duty. Our boys taught him to fly with tender, loving care, because he was a piss-poor pilot. But Fatso learned a hell of a lot about the logistics of aviation. Now he's got the best-organized air corps in Central America."

"This is the best?" I was incredulous. "I'd hate to see the worst!"

"Don't knock it," Harry said seriously. "It's potent. Romirez could have made general with it when he bought those P-51s, and there hasn't been a general in Ruedo since Sagasta."

"Who is he?" I asked.

"Fermín Sagasta is the ex-dictator, exiled in Mexico, sulking in his tent like Achilles, waiting for a call back to power that will never come."

"What was he like?" I was full of questions.

Harry was full of answers. "Sagasta was a typical strong man—ruthless, smart. He ruled twelve years. His nickname is *El Sagáz*. It means 'the sagacious one.' He still owns more good real estate in Ruedo than anybody else."

"My guess is he owns the stands of lumber up around Madera," I said, thinking of what Fuentes had been secretive about when I pumped him that morning.

"You guess pretty good," Harry said. "Coronel Romirez makes noise about invading the northern border, so he could be getting some financial backing from Sagasta."

My poker face must have slipped, because Harry said, "You got a guilty look on your kisser. Are you wondering if you're playing around with the wrong gang?"

"Well, yes, in a way."

Harry sighed, "Forget it, fly-boy. You've got a good job, and it performs a useful service to this country. Just keep your nose clean. Americans all over this part of the world are in the same boat. Just save your money. Maybe I got things somewhat overanalyzed tonight."

"Okay," I said. "I guess I like it here. I like the people."

"But let's not be naïve, shall we?" Harry admonished.

I hoped I wouldn't be, and then I explained why I had to say good night. I was pretty bushed and glad to be thinking of bed and of getting up early in the morning to run a good airline for ordinary folks who sort of reached me the way they looked up into the sky for the LARC planes. That was probably kind of corny, or what Harry called naïve, but it was just as genuine as my enthuisasm for Romirez' dough.

They saw me to the door, and I thanked them. Along with friendly so-longs and be-seeing-yous, George said, "Simply divine!" about nothing in particular.

Chapter 8

ON FRIDAY morning I showed up at the *aeropuerto* in my new uniform and let Ramón Fuentes know he could buck for captain's bars like mine.

I gave him the left-hand seat, because the way to get a bigger job myself was to bring him up to take over my flying duties.

Ramón took me through the cockpit check by the numbers; didn't miss one of the thirty-nine things to do and check before starting the engines. He barked orders while our four hands moved around over switches, levers, and knobs in a perfect duet. I hand-pumped hydraulic pressure and gave him the reading while he tried the controls for freedom of movement and then set all three trim tabs at zero. I called out that flap control was at neutral and also moved the landing-gear lever rapidly to neutral position in order to trap down pressure. Before he pushed the battery switch on—as we had no external power truck—I reported all electrical switches were off, radio off too, and I checked the circuit of the fire-detector system, testing the alarm bell.

"Autopilot?" Ramón asked.

"Off," I replied.

I told him firewall shutoff valves were open as I made sure the handles were down. We checked the parking brake, the No Smoking and Seat Belt signs, Pitot heaters, and cowl flaps. It was, as always, a busy time, but we were a smooth team, and Ramón liked bossing the action.

"Fuel-selector valves?" he asked.

"Main," I said.

"Carb air?"

"Ram," I said and asked, "Carb heat off?" forgetting for a second that I wasn't in charge.

Ramón's fingertips set mixture controls at idle cut-off, and the palm of his right hand cracked the throttles. Next was prop pitch controls to full increase. Then he checked manifold pressure.

"Fuel booster pumps?"

"On."

There are no less than seventeen explicit steps to starting engines on a DC-3, and Ramón didn't miss one. I was feeling pretty good about him as I listened to him check with Teddy on the intercom and heard him make sure the doors were shut and secured. Then he shouted out his window, "Props clear!"

I did the same on my side. We acknowledged the all-clear wave of a mechanic.

Ramón smiled as he held the starter switch for the left engine and watched fifteen blades pull through before he snapped the ignition switch on both mags. Nothing happened. His smile evaporated. He hit the prime, got a cough out of the engine and some smoke. Then it caught. He adjusted the fuel mixture to auto-rich. We both read the oil-pressure gauge as the engine idled at twelve hundred rpm. Ramón turned the booster pump switch off, and I told him hydraulic pressure was okay as I tested the flaps down and up.

The whole starting procedure was repeated without a hitch on the right engine. When both were turning over nicely, the mechanic pulled the wheel chocks free, and Ramón remembered to unlock the tail wheel before taxiing out.

As we rolled, Ramón called the tower and got the wind direction and velocity report, with clearance to take off from Runway 36. He was grinning like a fool and about to move the supercharger handle for low blower when I called him on not checking the zero settings on the compass, altimeter, air speed indicator, rate-of-climb, turn indicator, and other flight instruments. He gave me that annoying Latin shrug of indifference.

I got sore and bawled him out—and loud over the engine noise. "Damn it to hell, Lieutenant!" I yelled, emphasizing his rank. "You can't overlook one single thing in this procedure. Not one! You're going to get it one hundred per cent correct or stay co-pilot forever as far as I'm concerned."

"What is the matter, Capitán?" Ramón said. "You have fear?"

"You're damned right I have fear," I yelled at him. "Any flyer who hasn't got some fear of an airplane isn't going to be around long. These things can kill you. One little neglected gismo and you've had it!"

Ramón had a superior smile on his face. I didn't think I was getting through to him as he fingered the Saint Christopher medal under his blouse.

"Look," I said, "the captain is responsible for his plane, all of it, all its parts, all its gauges and gadgets. The lives of the people riding behind him depend on how thorough he is with the check procedures."

"Okay. Okay," he said, proud of using the Yankee word.

On the way down to the south end of the runway, he checked the brakes. The right wheel seemed to drag a little, and he looked questioningly at me. It was my turn to shrug. He was smiling again, happy. He loved to fly.

We scanned all the gauges. Oil temp and cylinder head temp were a little high, but in this climate what could you expect? The day was another scorcher.

At the end of the runway Ramón turned us into the wind for engine run-ups, advancing throttles on both engines and checking prop pitch controls at seventeen hundred rpm. He ran up the left engine to twenty-four-fifty and checked the magnetos, getting a minimum drop in engine speed. He did the same with the right engine and then very nicely double-checked mixture setting, supercharger, and fuel pumps. He got thirty inches of manifold pressure and smiled from ear to ear, while adjusting the friction lock on the throttles and ordering me to crank down one-quarter flap and lock the tail wheel. We were down to the wire now. He released the brakes. It was his airplane.

"All set," Ramón said.

"Roger," I said.

Ramón advanced throttles on both engines smoothly for maximum power at twenty-five-fifty, and we picked up speed fast. The tail came up at sixty miles per hour, and Fuentes used up some more runway letting her fly herself off at nearly a hundred. At his signal, my left hand dropped to reach the gear lever, retracting the wheels. Then, as ordered, I got the flaps up too.

Ramón reduced the power setting when we had a hundred and twenty indicated air speed in a normal climb, and he adjusted the cowl flaps. We were moving upstairs at better than a thousand feet a minute. He made a gentle climbing turn in the direction of Puerto, and I turned off the *No Fumar* sign.

I unfastened my belt and got up to leave the cockpit. I wanted him to have his big moment in the left-hand seat without teacher around to fuss him.

I had a *café puro* in the galley and showed off my new uniform to Teddy. She admired it with enthusiasm and little love pats, but I sent her up front with a coffee for "the capitán." She got the message. When she came back, rather quickly, her dark eyes were flashing.

"Ramón is very serious, very proud to be flying in your seat," she said.

"No hanky-panky with the pretty stewardess, eh?" I kidded.

"Not even a smile," she said, pleased as punch. "He was marking the chart and doing arithmetic."

"I'll be damned!" I said. "Ramón is figuring our ETA!"

"I think the man has stature now," Teddy said.

"I'll let you know," I said, and went back up front.

I sat down in the right-hand seat, picked up the chart, looked at the dials and did my own arithmetic. My figures checked with Ramón's, and later he was over Puerto del Sol within twenty-two seconds of his estimated time of arrival.

I took his orders on the landing too. He called out the check list precisely and accurately. Turning into the pattern, he asked for auto-rich mixture, carbs on ram. While still on the downwind leg, prop controls were set at twenty-three-fifty rpm, and we slowed to one hundred and twenty.

"One-quarter flap," Ramón said.

"Roger—one-quarter," I said.

"Gear down," he said.

"Roger," I said.

He had the booster pumps on as he turned base, and he called the field again and was cleared to land.

"Flaps down one-half," he said.

"Flaps one-half—roger," I said.

We slowed down some more. You could feel it like brakes. He put the props at full increase rpm and turned on final approach. On final, he called for and got full flaps from me. He held her over stalling speed, clearing the fence at about one hundred twenty kilometers per hour. His flare-out was smooth as silk, and the wheels touched down first with the tail low. I watched him stay on the rudder, holding back pressure on the yoke. The tail touched softly. He didn't rush the brakes.

"Nice landing," I said.

We took on full tanks of gas at Puerto, enough for all the way to Las Piraguas and to spare, which was another safety procedure Fuentes had to remember. We made Matanzas right on schedule, however, and got out on time too, Fuentes running the whole show.

As we came into Las Piraguas, Ramón's call to the field gave us word of a crosswind. He looked at me and raised his hands from the wheel. I kept my arms folded. He smiled again and went back to work.

Ramón had the good judgment to use only half flaps on final, and he crabbed down in the crosswind. He flew her onto the strip, maybe fifteen miles an hour faster than normal, making a wheel landing and holding the tail high for steering control, so she wouldn't weathercock. He used plenty of upwind aileron taxiing to the terminal shanty, and then we cut half a dozen switches. He killed the engine properly with throttles at twelve hundred rpm, using the mixture control idle cut-off.

I reached over to shake his hand. "Congratulations, Capitán," I said.

It was a check ride as good as any pilot could have given me in the States. Ramón could make night landings if he had to, and Ruedan weather would be good enough most of the time, so he could get by on his minimum instrument ability. By checking weather ahead, he could cancel flights if he had doubts about socked in fields. My only question, then, was about his judgment. I wondered if he'd understand that saying about there being old pilots and bold pilots, but no old bold pilots.

When the passengers had deplaned, I went down the aisle and saw Teddy waiting. I said, "Yes, Capitán Fuentes has stature."

"I think so," she said. She was waiting for him. The wind blew hard against her, outlining her fine, strong body.

I didn't have supper with Ramón and Teddy, although they asked me to join them. I didn't figure to beat Ramón's time again.

Once more I stayed in the lobby of the Gran Hotel and worked on the report. I also wrote a recommendation for Fuentes's promotion and put it in an envelope addressed to Coronel Romirez.

I worked another hour until the ideas ran thin and the sheets of hotel stationery got limp with humidity and the paper I hadn't filled with notes became a challenge I could successfully resist. A dark rum nightcap was what I needed and had, and then I went up to my room and to bed. But I couldn't sleep. It was hot and sticky. My room buzzed with mosquitoes.

I got up, turned on the light, and swatted mosquitoes, working up a sweat. It was a losing battle without screens or glass in the windows. I phoned down for ice and a bottle of Espíritu de la Caña.

After a long time, while I fidgeted, sitting on the edge of the bed thinking about the Club Zerape, which was only a couple of blocks away, the bellhop came. He was a Negro-Indian breed with a wise flat face like a monkey's. He seemed to sense my problem.

"You want a girl, *señor?*"

"No."

He put the tray with the rum bottle and ice on the bureau. He swatted a mosquito and said, "You need a lizard in the room, to keep mosquitoes out."

"Is that so?" I asked. "How are you called?"

"Mono," he said and laughed. It was the Spanish name for monkey. "I can get you a lizard to eat the mosquitoes, and a girl too. Pretty girl," he said.

"No girl." I had to smile. In this double-standard country a bachelor was permitted—urged, even—to seek adult recreation without a lot of nice-Nellie hypocrisy.

"You are sure? No pretty girl?" Mono insisted.

"No," I said again. "Just a little lizard to eat the mosquitoes."

"No girl?"

"No. What else has Las Piraguas to offer?"

"Hunting," Mono said disgustedly. "You can shoot the jaguar or the alligator. There is also fishing. Not as reliable as girls." His flat-nosed face split with a laugh.

"Where is the fishing good?" I asked.

"Downriver."

I built myself a drink, and he watched me so avidly I made him one in the extra glass he had brought.

"Mono," I said, "what kind of fishing?"

"In Río Culebra swim the *róbalo*—big ones. Also the *sábalo,* which you call the tarpon."

"You can get me a guide with a good boat?" I asked hopefully.

"*Sí,* in the morning."

"No, tonight," I said. "Go to him now. Tell him to prepare, so we can start in the dark before sunrise, when it is cool."

Mono's monkey face saddened. "It will be expensive to disturb *el guía*'s sleep."

"*Cuánto?* How much?"

"Ten dollars American."

"That is robbery," I said. I was learning.

"Perhaps it can be negotiated for seven." Mono shrugged.

"Three dollars," I said, as if losing interest.

"The gasoline is very expensive for the motor. The *sábalo* break many lines," Mono said.

"Five dollars," I said, knowing I was still being had.

"*Bueno,*" he said, and held out his hand for the money.

I got my wallet out of my pants in the closet and gave him duros that equaled six dollars, to pay for the rum and for his services too. He was grateful and backed out of the room bowing. Once more he said, "You sure you do not want a girl?"

"No," I said, less sure.

I lay back on my bed with the cold rum on the rocks held to my sweaty belly and I let the excitement come about the prospect of fishing for the two species that jumped when hooked. I had never fished in tropical waters, but I'd read about snook, as *róbalo* are called in Florida, and, of course, about the silver king tarpon. Once, when I had a flight to Ocean City, Maryland, I had shared the cost of a charter boat with three other guys and been lucky enough to get a white marlin. It was something I'd remember all my life. I regretted that I had left the photo of it behind, but I had left a lot of things behind when I came to Ruedo. I had cut and run quickly and traveled light. But I didn't want to think about that any more, so I thought about fishing.

After a while Mono came back to tell me the fishing trip was all set. And he brought the lizard, which was like the kind they sell at circuses and incorrectly call chameleons. The thing stationed itself, motionless, on the wall near the window jalousies, and damned if the mosquitoes didn't disappear.

I got up for another drink and a cigarette and to write a note addressed to Capitán Fuentes telling him to take the flight back to Santa María without me. I told him I would ride the Sunday and Monday local circuits with Reynolds and Lopez, and he could have the Mexico flight if Johnny Michaels was sober enough to ride with him or was not committed to some military flight. Then I left a call for four a.m.

I fished early and fished hard, trolling in the river with José, the guide, who found tarpon for me, but they were all rolling and not taking lures. Finally I caught a *róbalo* that couldn't put up much of a fight against the heavy tarpon tackle. When it got too hot on the river with the sun straight up, we came back and I divided the fish with the guide. The chef at the Gran Hotel cooked my share. It was very good. He called it *pescado bilbaína,* a Spanish dish in which the fish is boiled and reheated with a greenish clam sauce. It went well with several bottles of ice-cold beer. After lunch a tremendous feeling of well-being came over me, and I liked the way the heat of the tropical afternoon seemed to make the marrow in my bones come alive.

I tried a siesta in my room but was too restless to sleep. I phoned down for ice and stood by the window, looking out on the street. When a woman walked by, I stared at her as though I'd been away at sea for six months.

Mono came in with the ice I'd sent for. "You want a girl now, *señor?*" he asked.

"Yes," I said, choking the word out.

"It is natural," he said. "I will get a pretty one for you."

"No, *por favor.* Go to the Club Zerape and inquire for a girl called Carmen. Do you know Señor Salas?"

"*Sí,*" Mono said. "Fidel Salas is known to me, but this Carmen is no ordinary *puta.* She will not come here."

"Tell her it is the Capitán who wishes to see her," I said.

"I will try, Capitán, but it would be better if I got another girl." Mono shrugged and went out.

I stripped to my shorts and bathed at the corner sink, and then I lay on the bed and wondered if Carmen would come. I began to doubt it when nearly an hour had gone by. I had another drink and wondered what I would do if she didn't come. Would I go to the Club Zerape and pick up a girl? Then I heard a scratching sound. It was at the door, like a cat's claws on the wooden door. I went to the door and opened it. Carmen was there. . . .

About sundown, when Carmen had to go to work at the club, I offered her money. She said I had paid her too much for nothing the time before. When I insisted she said, "Whatever you wish, my Capitán."

That evening, sitting at the bar, feeling like a whole man again and feeding the toucan some *tostada* crumbs, I waited for Ken Reynolds. When he finally showed, he said he needed a drink—bad. Pepe Lopez had ground-looped them in Matanzas, blown a tire, and delayed the flight two hours.

"Wish you could get me another co-pilot," Ken said after downing his shot. "Pepe can't fly for sour owl turds!"

I had two days to find out for myself how lousy Pepe was. We would be moving cargo in and out of five small towns. I looked forward to seeing them, if not to washing out Pepe. Ken and I talked it over and decided to split the trips, so he could take Sunday off. I'd take the first two towns and then go along for the ride to three more on Monday.

The first stop, trans-shipping freight that came up river to Las Piraguas by barge from the Caribbean, was at the Pacific fishing village of Playa Blanca, where ocean freighters seldom stopped. Pete Denning, the mining engineer I had met up north, was our only passenger. He had a ticket to Lajas. We carried his dynamite and also new canvas for sailboats, some tools, and a marine engine. Marked *Urgente* was emergency Diesel fuel for the pueblo's single generator. They were so short of it lights were going out every night at nine. There were local jokes about the effect of this on Playa Blanca's birth rate.

Pepe Lopez flew us there. The best I could say was—we made it.

We were slightly delayed at Playa Blanca by a hassle with violently screaming shipping clerks about waybills on some cases of canned mackerel we were supposed to pick up, but that was eventually straightened out, and we took on some passengers, a whole family moving to Lajas, where digging in the mine was less seasonal employment than working at the cannery. We found room in the cabin for all they owned in the world —a hand-me-down bed frame, a broken chest of drawers, two lopsided chairs, a battered tin trunk, a parakeet in a cage, a guitar, and a black iron pot almost big enough to cook missionaries in. I didn't weigh all the stuff we loaded for that Ruedan family on the move. I know I undercharged them. I didn't do it just for them. It made me feel good.

At Lajas, in the mountains to the north, I said good-by to the family, and to Pete Denning and his dynamite and wished him well with it. There were lots of people at the airstrip, people who came to see the plane arrive and depart just the way they came to meet trains in small U.S. towns in another generation. The LARC plane with their country's colors painted on it was the big thing that happened every week. Many of the teenage kids who had never even ridden in a passenger automobile could comment learnedly on the quality of my landing.

Then we headed back to Las Piraguas. We flew pretty low, and the jungle was something to see from four hundred feet, so many different greens and shapes to the close-packed trees, some flowering red, others yellow or white, and an occasional dead tree like a bleached skeleton.

Pepe Lopez bothered me. Especially flying low, he bothered me. He was just the opposite of Ramón. Ramón could relax and fly like an angel. Pepe was tied up in knots. He knew his procedures letter perfect, but he flew with a mechanical, jerky technique. I wondered if I could relax him with some patient instruction, get him to feel the airplane and coordinate with a smooth, rhythmic touch. I tried to take the wheel, but he held on tight, rigidly. There were beads of sweat on his pencil-line mustache.

"Goddamn it, Pepe!" I yelled at him. "Let go!"

He dropped his hands in his lap and stared straight ahead.

"Now," I said softly, sorry about yelling, "take the wheel again, lightly. Follow through with what I do."

I began a series of gentle esses, coordination exercises, rolling and turning left and right, steepening the bank as we went. Our half-dozen passengers must have thought we had lost our minds, but they got a real fine look at the jungle when the plane rolled on its side.

As we zigged and zagged, Pepe seemed to get the feel, and no longer tried to sit straight but let his body lean with the bank of the plane. I eased off my control of the wheel and rudder pedals and let him take over. The little ball stayed in the center of the turn and bank indicator all through his turns. I said, "That's the stuff, Pepito."

Back in Las Piraguas and on the way to the hotel, I didn't think any more about Pepe or the airline. I thought about the feline Carmen. I thought about nothing else but how smooth her creamed-coffee skin was and how she enjoyed her work. All this tropical sun and heat can make a man crazy for a woman, which is the way the Latinos put it. No wonder they put bars on their daughters' bedroom windows.

The next day we flew up the coast to Palmas. More low flying, this time along the beach, sightseeing and scattering coveys of big pink birds. They were flamingos, and some flew close enough to be a hazard.

I gave Pepe another workout on coordination, but forgot to put the Seat Belt sign on and must have spilled a passenger into the aisle, because Ken put his head through the doorway into the cockpit and said, "What the hell's going on?"

I said, "I'm teaching this kid to fly."

"Christ!" Ken said. "He's already had more dual time than all the rest of the Ruedan Air Corps put together. He just can't cut it. He should be driving a truck!"

"Well, he's your boy," I said. "Either check him out or ground him."

"*You* ground him," Ken said. "I want to see that, big man."

I guess what we said didn't help Pepe's confidence any, because he bounced us good on the landing at Palmas. I wondered if I could trade him in on another co-pilot from Romirez' Air Corps. The Coronel could let his cousin kill himself in a P-51; that way he wouldn't take a load of passengers with him.

Palmas was at the mouth of another river, the Río Róbalo. In the days of the Spanish Main, Palmas had been a more important city than Santa María. The town had a sixteenth-century Spanish fort of hexagonal design, made of coquina-shell bricks and situated on a palisade overlooking the harbor. There were also a beautiful cathedral on the central plaza, and many Spanish fountains, Moorish arches, and statues, all with the fine patina of four hundred years of graceful aging.

We had lunch in Palmas at a tiled garden-patio restaurant and ate some wonderful tamales cooked in a wrapping of banana leaves that turned black in the process and steamed the soft corn meal and meat inside.

I took a walk on the crooked cobbled streets after lunch, because I wanted to look around this town of the idle rich and the idle poor. I heard soft guitar music coming from cool pastel patios, but gates of curled wrought iron kept me and the other uninvited from interrupting somebody's siesta. It was almost a ghost town, but I liked Palmas.

It was midafternoon before we flew our casual schedule west along the Río Róbalo. Our destination was the village of San Juan de los Prados, located on the point of land where the Río Róbalo was fed by another river from the north. We gave Pepe the landing to shoot, and he loused it up as usual, but we walked away from it.

This trading-post town had actually been founded only a few years before by a Chinese who gave himself the Christian name of the saint the padres eventually named the settlement for. His surname was Yick. We went to see him. He owed the airline money. We couldn't carry any more cargo in or out for him until he paid.

We found Juan Yick in a poker game in the back room of a Chinese chop-suey joint. The room had the only air-conditioning unit I had seen in Ruedo.

Fortunately Yick was winning. He paid us in cash. He looked to be anywhere between thirty and sixty years old, with one of those ageless Chinese faces and a full head of straight black hair.

The soft riffle of shuffling cards, the murmur of betting, and the richly soft clatter of chips on the blanket laid over the card table were almost more than I could stand. Ken and Pepe wanted to head back for Las Piraguas, but I couldn't see what the hell the hurry was, not if I could sit in for a few hands.

Juan Yick and another Chinese called Fat Chow welcomed some new money in the game. The other players were a prosperous-looking Indian answering to Pedro, and a Dutchman named Hans. They all agreed that, win or lose, I could pull out before sundown.

Mostly we played stud poker. With cards out in the open, the game displays a man's mathematical ability as well as his nerve or chicanery. These players had plenty of all those. It was a table-stakes game, but my five hundred duro stack of chips went up and down imperceptibly as I played pretty close to my vest, feeling my way.

On a side pot bet with Juan Yick, I called his bluff to win, and then I played deeper, getting to know how the money talked. I got called a few times when I had the hole card and that gave me some pots in the show-down. After that I ran some successful bluffs of my own and when I finally got caught, it helped to get raises and calls the next times when I had high cards back to back.

Ken tried to pry me loose from the table, complaining about the runway lights in Las Piraguas, but I told him to get lost. I was hot and hated to quit now when bets were getting bigger.

I had always worked hard for money, which was part of my reason for being in Ruedo; but I would never get rich because I was only a half-smart guy. I knew my job but never understood much about finance, so I gambled and I liked to plunge if there was a taker for a big bet. Poker is the best game if there are no millionaires up against you, because you bet as much against the money a man has as against cards. Knowing the way men react to the force of money is as much a help as luck.

We played some draw, too, jackpots, and I lost back some of my winnings, being too proud of flushes. The big winner was Juan Yick, who played recklessly from a big stack of chips. Pedro, the Indian, did damn well with an almost perfect poker face. I was better than even. Fat Chow was getting lousy cards. The Dutchman was a loser because he always bluffed a poor hand too strongly and got sneaky checking his good hands. Hans also drank too many rums to know what he was doing half the time, and he talked too much.

I learned from Hans that Juan Yick had started this settlement by first getting a stake in a Chinese laundry in San Francisco. After living on rice and sleeping on piles of dirty shirts for years, he saved enough to come down here and go into business for himself. Fat Chow was already running a general store in Matanzas or someplace, and he showed Yick the ropes. The way to financial independence was to invest in three items: first, a reasonably portable gasoline-driven 110-volt electric generator; second, a big electric icebox full of sweet soft drinks and beer; third, a juke box full of rumba records. That's what Juan Yick poured his savings into. Then he scouted the different rivers until he found a spot that looked good for a trading post. There was nothing but rain forest here at the fork of the rivers when he unloaded his equipment from a raft. He started the generator and the juke box and plugged in the icechest. When the music penetrated the jungle, out came the natives on foot and in dugout canoes, whole families three generations deep.

The very first day the Indians cleared the land for the Chinese and put up four stout poles with a thatched roof. Yick traded fairly and well for work, food, handcrafts, and gold in exchange for cold soda pop, beer, canned goods, and an assortment of five-and-ten-cent-store merchandise. A town had grown up around him in the steaming hot jungle.

That was the story Hans told, but he got quite drunk and sloppy with his cards. He seemed scared to bet against a gambler like Yick. Pedro worried him too. I worried Hans some myself. He just couldn't take a chance. The risk of losing big in trying to win big drove him to the bottle of dark rum, to conversation, and to a conservatism in his play that was slow death.

I was dealing when Ken and Pepe came back into the room.

I could tell right away there was trouble. Pepe splattered the room with Spanish too rapid for me to follow, but the gist of it was that some bombs had been exploded in Palmas and that the town was on fire.

Ken said, "A river boatman told us."

Juan Yick said happily, "They will need to buy supplies."

It annoyed me to hear the Chinaman thinking of business at a time like that, and the more I thought of Palmas destroyed, the madder I got. Nothing bad should happen to such a town.

I looked at Ken, who was shaking his head resignedly, and I wondered what we could do.

"Should we fly down there and take a look?" I asked.

"It will do no good," Pepe said. "Morning is soon enough to see what happened, and it will be safer."

"Safer my ass!" I said, "Why can't we take some stuff to them now? We could requisition some fire hose, buckets, first-aid stuff, food, maybe."

"On what authority will you commandeer such items?" Juan Yick asked. "I do a cash business or I know whose credit rating I am dealing with."

Pedro, the Indian, showed emotion for the first time, saying, "Will the government do nothing?"

Hans poured himself another dark rum and laughed at somebody else's hard luck.

I said, "I'll be responsible. I'll order the things."

"Your authorization is no good," Pepe said.

"Are there telephone connections to Palmas or Matanzas or Las Piraguas?" I asked.

"No," Juan Yick said. "No telephone at all."

"Damn it to hell!" I yelled at them. "A town is burning!"

"It's this chicken-shit revolution," Ken said, sighing softly. "I've seen it coming. They do it all the time in these countries. There's nothing you can do now, big man."

"The hell there isn't!" I said. "I'm going to take off and get enough altitude to raise Matanzas on the radio. They can telephone the capital and confirm a request to requisition supplies."

"Well, we can try," Ken said. "Let's go."

"Un momentito!" Pepe said, sort of snapping to attention. "I do not think I can permit that."

"Who the hell are you to permit anything?" I asked, pushing past him.

"I am Lieutenant Lopez, Ruedan Air Corps. That is who I am," Pepe said.

"Congratulations!" I said and kept on going.

"Watch it!" Ken said, going with me out of the Chinese restaurant. "He's Romirez' cousin, you know. Maybe that little prick planted the bombs himself."

"Jesus!" I said.

Pepe didn't try to stop us, but he didn't come with us either. We rode to the strip in a jeep and quickly cranked up the ship. A few minutes later I read Matanzas radio loud and clear and told them about the trouble. They relayed the message, and I got back a clearance to sign for whatever was needed, from Armando Ortiz, the Vice President himself.

I steered us over toward Palmas to estimate how bad things were, and when I saw the red glow in the night sky I felt a little sick. I thought I had seen a thing like that for the last time.

Back in San Juan, after a hairy landing guided by truck headlights, we loaded whatever we thought could help. Juan Yick was no philanthropist. The cheap Chink trader had me sign a dozen requisition lists and enjoyed the transaction.

At the last minute Pepe came with us to Palmas. Over the town the fire's rising thermals bounced us around. I didn't need landing lights to find the field. We unloaded into the grateful arms of the men of Palmas who had been fighting the fire.

Just about everybody in the town pitched in, forming bucket brigades from the river to the worst part of the fire. They fought the flames stubbornly to protect their cathedral, and they succeeded.

We stayed until morning, helping at the hurriedly set up first-aid station. Pepe shaped up pretty good helping, too, except that he kept saying the fire bombs were a people's protest against the Ortega government. It didn't make sense. Nobody I talked to was mad at the government, not mad enough to try to destroy their own town.

"Do you really think Pepe did it?" I asked Ken when we were alone, getting some rest in net hammocks slung from the wing of our plane.

"He could have set some time bombs when we were here at noon," Ken said.

"If he did it, it sure gives me a different picture of Romirez."

"Not me, Luke," Ken said sadly. "I've bummed around, flying in a lot of these two-bit countries. They're all alike. They all have these struggles for power going on, with bombings and riots started by one side or the other and often just to put the blame on the side that didn't do it."

In the morning we had a visit from the commandant of the small local garrison of Federal Police. He ordered us to pick up a platoon of reinforcements from Las Piraguas. He needed more troops to stop the looting. It was getting out of hand. I was surprised. The people had all seemed so friendly and helpful during the fire.

"It is a disaster," the commandant said sadly. "The poor people who finally realize they have lost everything feel it is their right to take from those who are better off. And some of the trouble is from Indians outside of the town who will kill you for ten centavos or for your shirt.

"It is my duty to defend private property in this jungle," the commandant said almost apologetically. He smiled a little smile with just his lips. "I will be wrong no matter what I do, the way enemies of the Ortega government will tell it."

That problem was his, not mine. I had helped all I could, and, of course, I would also ferry the troops. I did that. Then, back in Las Piraguas again, I had to get the delayed flight north on its way. I looked forward to flying in the high, clean sky that would somehow be nicely remote from trouble on the ground, but that kind of escape was made less than ideal by the wind that came up as the sun climbed in the sky.

Even while parked on the Las Piraguas strip, Ken and I both had to fight the controls. From occasional dead calms, gusts blew to over forty, maybe over fifty, miles per hour. Airports are always the windiest places, but this was ridiculous.

"What the hell goes on?" I yelled over the engine run-up and noisy rattle of wind buffeting.

"February is always the windy month," he said, eying the crazily twitching windsock on the hangar roof. "It's the wind they call *viento papagayo*. So help me it's a down-blowing wind."

Ken made the takeoff. He could fly a DC-3 as well as I could. It was no day to give Pepe another check ride, although I half hoped to save him. LARC needed every transport pilot we had, even a saboteur—if that's what he was—even that lush, Johnny, and partly trained Ramón Fuentes.

Once off the ground a plane handles all right in a wind, because it becomes part of the moving body of air, and drift is relative to the ground, which trouble, of course, can be fatal when you're too low.

Upwind at the end of the Las Piraguas strip are two big hills or little mountains, one to the left and one to the right. Taking off and maneuvering between them with wind drift to correct isn't easy. Ken Reynolds did it with our starboard wingtip nearly scraping the high, tangled treetops of the right-hand hill. I successfully overcame a mighty strong desire to take the controls. You just don't do that to a real pilot. I finally left Ken alone up front and went back for a cup of coffee.

I was leaning on the buffet with Pepe and Carlota when we ran into even rougher air over the mountains south of Matanzas. The turbulence got so rugged I had trouble balancing my coffee cup up and down and finally spilled some as we dropped deep and bounced back up sharply. The ship shuddered, making other cups rattle ominously in their tight aluminum galley shelves. Fortunately everybody was belted into his seat. I had to fight my way, hand over hand, from seat to seat, up the aisle to the cockpit.

I strapped in and let Ken stay with it. He didn't push the panic button. We did all that could be done to slow down, even dropped the wheels. Sometimes it was like riding a balloon, the way the updrafts hit us, and other times it was as though the bottom dropped out. There were falling jets of air all around the mountains, which scared the hell out of me, but I got more mad than scared thinking about trusting passengers to that Pepe in weather like this. I had taught a lot of kids from scratch, and I'd washed out better ones than he was. But I gave him another chance, the tough landing at Matanzas. Easy chances wouldn't prove anything for him. The best I can say about the landing is that inertia finally set in, and Pepe parked us with the nose into the wind to prevent damage to control surfaces, and he remembered the gust locks. He knew his procedures by the numbers; if only he could fly, I thought.

I went back to see how my passengers were. Lots of them, even

Carlota, had been sick in the paper bags. A wizened old Indian kissed the ground as soon as he climbed down the steps. I heard him say, "God is kind."

I kidded Carlota. "It's in airline regulations all over the world—a stewardess may not throw up during a flight unless it's morning sickness."

She looked meanly at Pepe coming down the aisle and said, *"Quién sabe?"*

We were so far behind schedule I canceled the flight to Puerto del Sol and headed straight for Santa María. It meant some disgruntled passengers had to lay over a day, and LARC policy didn't provide hotel or meal chits the way Stateside airlines do. We were a government monopoly.

I let Pepe fly again with Ken beside him while I tried to concentrate on my unfinished report. It wasn't easy. We were all over the sky. Pepe couldn't hold his altitude or his heading worth a damn. I guessed Ken was being rough on him and rattling him all the more. It was nothing personal, nothing to do with our suspicion of him concerning the fire bombs. It was just that we set a high standard for performance in a transport pilot. If he couldn't take a riding from us, he'd never face up to the strain of bad weather or trouble with the airplane either. He blew the landing at Santa María too, right in front of his uncle, the Coronel.

I saw Romirez and his guards near the fence as we taxied up to the ramp area. As soon as the doors were open, I kept my customer-service record perfect for the day by brushing past the passengers in the aisle in my hurry to let the boss know it wasn't my landing he witnessed.

"Coronel," I said as soon as I reached him, "I want to request that you transfer Lieutenant Lopez out of the airline service."

"Put it in writing, Capitán," Romirez said curtly.

"All right," I said, "but that's just a formality, I hope. The boy can't fly for me or Captain Reynolds."

"Your written request will be reviewed by the officer cadre," the fat man said. I knew he was stalling me and he knew I knew.

"What about Fuentes' promotion?" I asked.

"Approved," he said.

"Good," I said and pushed my luck, adding, "I'll have a report to present to you in a day or two, but I want to spend more time on the ground. Can you assign me a couple of Air Corps pilots now or let me pass the word up to the States that we're hiring?"

"I will think about it," he said distantly and changed the subject. "How did you leave things in Palmas?"

"We flew some troops in from Las Piraguas," I said.

"Brutal, pointless terrorism!" he exploded.

"Pointless?" I was aghast. "There has been a more pointless bombing and also looting. *That* is terrorism!"

"You do not understand." The Coronel was patient with me. "Ruedo has grown and prospered in its modern cities. Palmas has been left behind. Its people are resentful. They want government help. The government ignores them."

I was reminded of the poker-faced Indian saying, "Will the government do nothing?" I said, "Why throw bombs? Ruedo is a democracy, isn't it? The people can criticize the government if they want to in the free press and on the radio."

Romirez laughed as though I'd told him a joke, but his eyes stayed cold. He said, "Our republic is not so democratic as it looks, and yet I agree the trouble in Palmas was probably ill-advised. Very clumsy. Communists, no doubt."

He paused to light a long cigar. After exhaling a puff of smoke with evident satisfaction he said, "Vice President Ortiz is wringing his hands about this thing, without catching the Communists or whoever caused the trouble in Palmas. In Ortega's absence, he called the Congress into session and had the effrontery to hint that the bomb plot was some fiendish masterminding of the old Sagasta landlord clique. The implication was very sly. I was insulted. I walked out of the chamber."

"What will happen now?" I asked.

"Nothing. Absolutely nothing," Romirez said, looking at me sharply for persisting with my questions. "Nothing will happen until Ruedo gets a strong government to replace these political crybabies."

When Romirez bade me *hasta la vista* there was no warmth in his voice. Did he know I had used the plane's radio to get help to Palmas? Probably. I wasn't sorry I'd done that, but a cold trickle of sweat ran down my ribs.

Chapter 9

EARLY in the morning I got a phone call from Lieutenant García, one of the Coronel's aides. He told me that office space had been assigned to me in the Air Ministry wing of the Government Palace and that Capitán Fuentes would take my flight south—but with Lieutenant Lopez as co-pilot. Well, I rationalized, you can't win them all.

I'd been promoted. With the managerial job I wanted, all I had to do now was deliver the report I had teased the Coronel with. No time like the present, I thought. Shoulder to the wheel, nose to the grindstone, and when you kick, kick toward the goal. You can't call that nonsense when it works.

I knew Romirez wouldn't be in his office at the palace until late, not if he had kept his usual political court open on the Mirado's sixth floor most of the night; so I started shuffling the pile of papers that contained my recommendations on how to improve his airline. The report had grown to a fat document, and it was organized as to objectives, problems, and recommendations. It was formally addressed to Coronel Romirez as Minister of Aviation.

I put some finishing touches on it, sitting in my shorts at a little table in my room, with the jalousies open to catch the morning breeze. I became so engrossed in the work I let the telephone ring without answering it.

Paco brought me a big American-style breakfast and also a message from the hotel switchboard. It was from Harry Donahue to call him back. I didn't. It was time to head across the Plaza República to the palace. I walked there in the bright warm sunlight, pleased with myself and with the fact that it was February fifth and that New York was probably full of dirty snow and slush.

I was glad, too, that I had on a freshly pressed uniform, because it got the door opened for me at the *Ministerio de Aviación,* and not by the porter but by the receptionist himself. This male receptionist character wore a wing collar, a zoot-cut morning coat, and striped pants. He was lord of the lobby.

I told him I wanted to see Coronel Romirez and learned he wasn't in yet. That was all right with me because I wanted a good translation and typing job done first anyway. After explaining who I was and what work I required, I was taken by another flunky to the Ministry of Peace, where there was a secretary whose proficiency in translations from English was renowned throughout the palace.

After scooting ahead of me to open at least nine thick mahogany double doors in a labyrinth of cool marble corridors, the flunky introduced me to the girl who was secretary to the Minister of Peace. There were a lot of names used in the elaborate Spanish introduction, including mine and that of Dr. Luis Vidal, the Minister, and the girl's, which was Celia. I just stood there like a dummy, because the girl was the one with the cinnamon-colored tan I had watched across the hotel pool ten days before. I still couldn't say whether she was beautiful or not, but there was something she had, some quality I could feel more than see.

"*Mucho gusto,*" Celia and I both said at the end of the introduction, and then she held out her hand North American style and said with only a trace of accent, "Hi, Capitán Hadley. I hope I can be of some help."

I'm not usually tongue-tied, but I found it difficult to get a word out. I was conscious of my own breathing, and the way she affected me annoyed me. I guess it made me look stern, and she must have thought I was doubtful of her qualifications to help me with the report, because she quickly launched a big sell on her education, which included four years at Wellesley. That explained the oversize cashmere sweater and the Ivy League skirt that hampered her good points.

"Thanks," I said at last. "You'll do." I dropped my handwritten report on her desk beside her Underwood Noiseless. "I'd like to see the finished job in Spanish before I present it to Coronel Romirez, maybe in an hour if you can make it."

"Yes, sir," she said in a refined, almost prim way, and sat down at the typewriter and went right to work as though I had already left. I stood over her a moment. I noticed that her eyes never once left her work, and what wonderful dark eyes they were in a land of dark eyes.

Then back I went to the Air Ministry to see what my own office looked like.

Romirez had taken good care of me. I had been given a big office, befitting a very big boss. The thick rug on the floor and the high ceiling gave it a nice hush after the clatter of tile and marble floors in outer offices and palace halls. There were three windows with a fine view to the east across the university to the foothills. I could also see the gray stone prison, which looked like a feudal castle. On the wall behind my desk was a huge map of Ruedo. On other walls were framed photographs, one of President Ortega, who looked like a kind, jowly, and balding judge. Another photo, just as large, was of Coronel Romirez, scowling at me over his bushy mustache. There was also a rectangle on the wall where the paint hadn't faded from the sunlight. I wondered whose photograph had been taken down. Sagasta's, probably.

My office furniture was all dark mahogany and leather. I sank into a deep-cushioned, high-backed swivel chair behind my enormous desk and I could almost con myself into believing I had nothing more than a job to do at LARC. In a sense I could close one eye that saw any political nastiness and intrigue and keep the other on the strictly business aspects of the airline. I said to myself, live and let live. I had a good thing going in a job I found very satisfying. If Romirez got his kicks out of another side of the LARC set-up, who was I to criticize, much less jeopardize my own position?

In exactly one hour Celia was in the reception lobby. I went out there. She had the report neatly typed, double-spaced, and bound in leather three-ring folders. She had done two versions, Spanish and English.

"Muchísimas gracias," I said, showing off my command of her language.

"De nada," she replied, going along with the gag. She turned to leave.

I didn't want her to go. My throat felt funny. Breathing was difficult again. I quickly thumbed through some of the pages and called to her retreating back, *"Un momentito, señorita, por favor!"*

She turned and looked at me levelly, her eyes very dark. *"Sí?"*

I didn't trust my voice, but I said, "If it isn't too much trouble, may I have the carbon copies?" I was glad I thought of that. It brought her back a couple of steps.

"Of course, if you wish. I made carbons. I should have thought to bring them." She paused, deliberating. She didn't have a poker face. I could see her decide something. "I think, Capitán Hadley," she said, "that when you look through the report again, you may want to delay presenting it to the Minister of Aviation."

"Is that so? Why?" I asked. I held a pack of Ruedan cigarettes toward her.

She came back two more steps, shook her head "no" to the cigarettes, and glanced at the receptionist. My eyes followed hers. The man had his elbow on his ornate desk and his chin in his hand to steady his rapt observation of us both.

"They say he doesn't understand a word of English," Celia said, "but I wonder. Romirez pays him to tell what he sees and hears. We can talk better in your office."

"Sure. You bet!" I said.

I was proud to show off my office. I held the door open, and she went in and sat down in the straight-backed secretary's chair. I leaned against the desk on her side of it. She pointed to the report I had tossed on the desk.

"It could be a whole lot more complete, you know," she said coolly.

"Really?" I said, annoyed again and wondering how to put this girl in her place or, more truthfully, to get over the flustered feeling she gave me.

"Yes, really," she gave the word "really" an awfully white-shoe intonation. She had learned English surrounded by girls like Harry Donahue's wife.

"You have completely neglected the Mexico run in the report," she went on, "and haven't so much as mentioned the various political implications in the local operations."

I stood there and listened and hoped my mouth didn't hang open. "Okay, bright girl," I said finally. "I see I have my work cut out for me. You've been a big help. Thanks again. I'll present this report as a teaser of more to come, and when I see Romirez I'll put in a good word for you."

I grinned at her but I didn't get even a little smile in return. Verbally, I leaned on her harder. "I've had sweater girls working for me before, honey. Smith-cum-Katy-Gibbs girls in New York. And I'm not in the habit of telling them what I'm about in a business way, or maybe they'll know as much as I do and then take over my job or tell a competitor about it over cocktails or just have too much useless advice for me. Now scat—and bring the carbons!"

That readable face of hers showed a brief and honest fright and then some hurt as she got up to go. Then, the way her eyes turned smoky, I had the feeling her emotions would achieve hot, flushed anger before she went through all nine doors back to the *Ministerio de la Paz.* It would be something to see. I was disappointed when the carbons came back by messenger.

Romirez got in about one-thirty. I went to his office, and he seemed glad to see me. I leveled with him right off, skipping the dragged-out pleasantries which are supposed to precede every business discussion in Latin America.

When he finished reading the report, I got the job I wanted. It was plain to me that Coronel Romirez was happy to be relieved of a lot of work in the airline. He promoted me to operations manager, which in most respects was the same as general manager. He didn't shake my hand, but he gave me a cigar.

I sat back and enjoyed the luxurious smoke. I was *El Jefe* at LARC. I had the right to fly any route I wanted to or not to fly, as the case may be, and to assign the other pilots accordingly.

There was a sales manager named Martinez on the payroll, but up to now he had been in hiding, as far as I could tell. I hoped I ranked him, too, because I planned to make sales-promotion recommendations to Romirez, move in on every sphere of LARC activity the Coronel didn't personally direct.

The biggest items in my recommendations had been bought and the ante had been upped besides. I was authorized to purchase three more surplus C-47s converted to DC-3 passenger ships, and the Coronel also jumped at the chance to make LARC look big-time by buying a four-engine C-54, which the airlines called the DC-4.

The surprise was that he directed me to order a surplus B-25 as well. I gathered that the bomber was going to be Johnny Michaels' responsibility. Swell. One more reason the Coronel would have his hands full with the Air Corps and leave me alone to run the airline, but losing Johnny would leave me short a co-pilot, so when I pointed this out to Romirez he said he would assign Lieutenant García to me.

Then I said, "I've got to bring up a depressing subject—money."

"Money is depressing?" He seemed puzzled.

"No, I said that foolishly, Coronel. Only the lack of money is depressing." I was pitching him for a raise, so I smiled confidently.

Romirez reached for his pocket. "Here is money, then. Do not be depressed."

"I don't want another advance; I want my salary increased," I said.

"How much?" he asked, his small eyes getting cagey.

"Oh, a hundred more a week would be satisfactory," I said. He didn't blink at the amount. I wished I'd asked for more.

"You could use an advance on it?" he asked, slipping pink bills off his thick roll.

"I'll probably gamble it away," I said, reaching for the sheaf of duros.

"You will be deeply in my debt," he said with satisfaction.

"You could be right," I said, but I doubted it. I would earn the money. Romirez also promised me some of his staff to handle the paper work. I pitched him for an English-speaking secretary.

"How about that girl Celia?" I asked him.

"It is impossible," he said and laughed. Some of the damnedest things had a way of striking him funny.

"Impossible for *you* to fix?" I said as though I couldn't believe it.

"You do not know who she is?" Romirez asked, still chuckling.

"She is a secretary who knows English, that's all I know," I said.

"She is Celia Vidal, secretary for her uncle, the Minister of Peace," the Coronel said with a helpless shrug. "I cannot order her to report to this office."

"Oh, hell," I said. "Maybe we can borrow her until her uncle returns from his Washington trip." I was pressing.

"Some other secretary will do as well," he said, as if that ended the matter.

"Not without English." I was being stubborn.

"I do not want a Vidal in my department," he said just as stubbornly, his fat lips pouting.

I took one more stab at it. "My work is completely non-political," I said.

He thought about that. I could almost hear the machinery in his head sorting out the pros and cons. His small black eyes glittered briefly, and he came to a private conclusion with another laugh. "All right, Capitán," he said. "There is something quite disarming about a Vidal working in this ministry. I will ask her myself."

Then he dismissed me. I felt so high and mighty I went directly to the tailor and ordered another sky-blue uniform and a white dinner jacket.

Back in my office after lunch, I cabled the War Assets Administration about our interest in purchasing surplus aircraft. I also went through all the LARC flight records by months and weeks and days, sorting out passenger and cargo data southbound and northbound.

When Señorita Vidal reported for work later in the afternoon, we were polite to each other. There was plenty for her to do on the adding machine. Then I took the tapes of figures she handed me and made the numbers talk on rough charts and graphs.

I was all business, and it wasn't any act. Celia Vidal was just an efficient piece of office equipment as far as I was concerned, but we worked well together. It can be like that on a challenging job.

I kept the girl late working on the charts, and she got a couple of phone calls. Finally a guy came around to the outer office, to pick her up for dinner, I supposed, but I ignored him and dictated wires and follow-up letters that had to go out to the brokers and contractors who sold surplus aircraft engines and parts. After that, when Miss Vidal got sulky over keeping her dinner date waiting, I let her go and worked on alone.

When my ashtray overflowed with cigarette butts I called it a day, except I couldn't turn off my motor. In my hotel room I made sketches of how we could modify our present two DC-3s for cargo and rough passenger hauling. A good idea, I thought, would be some built-in block and tackle with pulley arrangements in the cabin ceiling for loading and unloading.

The next morning I could hardly wait to get to my office again. My head was full of plans to justify the nearly three hundred thousand bucks LARC would pay for new planes and the three-fifty a week they paid me.

On my wall map I marked our present routes and airstrips with colored pencils. Then I circled important settlements LARC didn't serve, even on the once-a-week basis. Miss Vidal was very helpful because she knew her country well. She circled Ruedo's centers of mining activity and important plantation areas.

We stood close together at the wall map and marked the roads and bridges, or lack of them, connecting the hinterland communities with the bigger towns. As I drew lines on the map my fingers touched hers accidentally, and I was acutely conscious of the contact, of her nearness. But I didn't think she was affected the way I was. Our eyes didn't meet. I only saw how long her eyelashes were, brushing her cheeks as she looked down at the map and inked in another farming area.

With some careful measuring I found that my plans would extend the unduplicated route miles of the line about threefold and really tie the country together with a network of transport that could bring all the people and their produce within a few hours of the capital. Some of the new stops I planned would be only ten minutes apart by air, yet that kind of service would replace all-day trips by oxcart on twenty-five miles of zigzag trails up and down mountains and over roads that were impassable quagmires in the rainy season. Miss Vidal was impressed and said so.

Then it was noontime, and Celia's boy friend was outside the office to take her to lunch.

About midafternoon I did get hungry, and my high-toned secretary came breezing in, conscience-stricken about her three-hour lunch to the extent of bringing back a box of sandwiches for me. I could only conclude she must have phoned to check on whether or not I had gone out. There was a container of strong Ruedan coffee, too, and the spread she set before me was a variety of open-face masterpieces of cold meats and cheeses. I was grateful, but I ate without missing a stroke of my pencil on a pad I was covering with notes.

The rest of the day went pretty much the same. Things I had learned in New York about marketing and sales promotion as well as my airline experience came in handy for developing further plans for LARC. I revised the timetable a couple of ways, with a Phase A schedule for the immediate future, utilizing aircraft we had, and a Phase B, that showed how two additional DC-3s and the DC-4 would provide increased capacity for passengers and freight tonnage.

The need for additional transport in Ruedo was so great I couldn't conceive of anything less than full loads, so I doped out how we could lower passenger fares and also move cargo for as little as five cents a pound and still show a small profit.

Miss Vidal offered to work overtime that night, and we got a lot more on paper for the supplementary report. I told her to call Paco at the hotel for food, and he sent over a tray with a covered casserole supper. She also phoned home, and I heard her lie about not being alone in the office with a man. While we ate the girl talked to me about the political importance of the airline in terms of rural economics. She told me how she could visualize air freight, outbound from the interior and coastal areas, carrying top grades of coffee, chicle, meats, fish, fresh vegetables, special ores; and the turn-around flights loaded with mining machinery, breeding stock, jeeps, farm equipment, cement, electrical supplies, refined food, clothing, and mail-order goods. The pile of notes on my desk grew, and at nearly midnight we were talking in terms of long-range proposals such as a plant for deboning meats at Matanzas to reduce shipping weight, and the installation of quick-freeze equipment there. Maybe a dehydration plant too. The girl's dark eyes glowed with enthusiasm, and I liked the animated way she spoke. It wasn't just the smiling soprano lilt to her voice that appealed to me, but the talk itself. A real conversation with a girl was something I hadn't had for a long time.

It didn't lead to anything but putting Celia Vidal into a taxi and dragging myself to my hotel room feeling tired, but with that satisfied kind of tiredness that comes after a job well done.

Friday morning I arrived at the palace early, ahead of my new staff of clerks that Romirez had directed to report to me—ahead of Miss Vidal too. I went right to work, and there were such stacks of paper around me that some of the new people, when they showed up, speculated that I had worked all night. According to what I overheard, I was going to be a slave-driver boss. Maybe I was, but I would work harder and longer than they would.

I got busy laying out the timetable for the printer, seeing what I could do with it as a business-getter when it was circulated among travel agencies and other airlines selling connecting service. The dummy I laid out had a couple of extra pages for some selling copy. I decided that a photo of Teddy and Carlota beside one of our planes would be a shot hard to beat even by airlines with a hundred stewardesses to choose from. Then I wrote a few lines about our dependable service and our American pilots, to counter any Yankee reader's chauvinistic attitude about spic incompetence.

A file of promotion material from United States magazines addressed to Señor Martinez proved useful. It urged Ruedo to place tourist advertising in their pages and contained survey reports on the growing tourist market, but much of it had never been removed from envelopes. I guessed that Martinez didn't care about what had been accomplished by Florida, British West Indies, Mexico, and Cuba. I decided to ask Celia Vidal some time just how political this Martinez' job was.

I knew what was needed early in the game for a country like Ruedo with an undeveloped tourist business. It was snob appeal. I was certain that publicity and advertising for Ruedo should begin with the appeal of discovery by those who could brag about it to their less venturesome friends, the ones going to the same winter resort year after year. The trick would be to make Ruedo *the* new place. It was happening, I read, to Majorca in the Mediterranean, among those who always went to the Riviera, and to Jamaica, among the regular Florida visitors. I would have to find some unique gimmicks, though. Mexico had bullfights, tequila, and mariachi music. Cuba had cockfights, girl shows, rumba, and rum. Most of the Caribbean places had deep-sea fishing and beautiful beaches. Unfortunately Ruedo could only say "Me too," unless there was some special attraction. It needed its own special drink or cocktail and its own native music. A hot-shot press agent might cause both to be invented, but meanwhile I thought maybe the fiestas, like the one I'd heard of coming up in Puerto del Sol, would fill the bill as a tourist come-on. I half decided to see that fiesta next week so the publicity mill could start grinding. For the next one, we'd send out gilt-edged invitations to key travel agents and influential magazine travel editors, providing them with a tour of Ruedo's attractions at no expense to them. We would let them be the first "discoverers," who would return home talking up Ruedo's charms to the clients and readers.

Meanwhile, the usual folders had to go out to the tourist trade. I scribbled what I could about the old Spanish colonial charm of Matanzas and Palmas, the modern architectural vistas of Santa María, the beaches and deep-sea fishing of Puerto del Sol. I got pretty fancy about the soft white sand of Puerto and convinced myself I ought to sample it personally.

I could have gone on dreaming up a scenic folder so gloriously picturing the beauties of Ruedo we couldn't afford the printing bill, but first I had to write a letter of particulars so agents could guide their customers intelligently. This resulted in a long look into the file of Intourist Regulations, and I found that Ruedo was a difficult place to visit.

Greedy, short-sighted Ruedan bureaucrats wanted American tourists to have eleven-dollar visas, purchased at Ruedan consulates in the States. Other requirements added insult to injury. One was a health certificate, including a blood test. I guessed they wanted a favorable trade balance on syphilis. Another was a good-conduct letter from the tourist's local police department, a nuisance to obtain and generally meaningless. I had one, and I was on the lam.

Federales everywhere with rifles and submachine guns didn't figure to make a tourist feel at ease. I had also observed that surly customs clerks could make a shambles of a visitor's suitcase. You were lucky if they didn't add a dribble of cigar ash or swipe something. Go ahead and catch them at it and learn that it was contraband you were smuggling. Finally, on leaving fair Ruedo, there was an embarkation tax levied in the mysterious sum of $1.68.

I gave up my attempt to write anything to the travel agents. Instead I dictated a memo to Romirez, recommending the repeal of the official obstacles to tourism. I stated that there were so few visitors anyway, the damn taxes and customs charges couldn't provide any revenue to speak of.

I also dictated a note to a friend of mine with Eastern Airlines in Mexico City, to hang onto a couple of bullfight tickets for me, as I expected to be there Sunday. I hoped the TACA airmail would reach him before I did.

When Celia brought me the neatly typed mail to sign and several pages of the expanded report, she brought me a cup of coffee too. She put the cup in front of me in a way that was without degrading subservience but with a certain deference and pleasure in pleasing a man that you'd never —well, hardly ever—get from an American girl, and I found it completely charming in her. I was reminded of the times she had matches for me and how she sometimes lit my cigarette, until she realized I often stuck one in my mouth not meaning to light it right away or forgetting to.

As a rule Miss Vidal wouldn't leave my office until dismissed. She would hold her shorthand pad ready and be quiet and respectful. This time I caught myself looking at her, really looking, mentally undressing her from the memory of how she looked in her bathing suit the time she had fascinated me across the hotel pool. Then I felt my face crease in the frown from the intrusion of a more realistic focus on the externals of a shapeless, oversized sweater she wore because the inside of a marble palace is as chilly as a tomb. It was the third different cashmere I had seen on her in as many days, and I guessed she had a drawer full of them.

I knew what cashmere cost, and my own money troubles from way back crowded my mind and made me swing my high-backed swivel chair so it faced the window instead of the girl. I heard Celia say, "Is that all?"

It sure is, baby, I thought. I realized that the incipient possibilities of a close office relationship were hampered by a strange new careful streak I was developing about money. I wouldn't risk my job now trying to mix business with pleasure. And the Vidal name was poison to Romirez. Besides, I didn't want to go up against the Vidal dough either. Of course, in the next quick second of thought, I also faced the fact that maybe I didn't stand a chance with Celia, couldn't score because she wasn't the kind of girl you could lay on the office couch. Then, too, there was that other guy who was always hanging around. . . .

"One more letter, please, Miss Vidal," I said, still staring out the window. "Please send it registered mail to Mrs. Lucas Hadley, Fernwood

Apartments, nineteen Westchester Circle, Scarsdale, New York. Got that?"

She didn't answer. I swung the chair back around to speak directly to her. Her face was down and intent on her book and pencil. I dictated rapidly a short and not so sweet note to my ex-wife, enclosing a bank draft for five hundred bucks and offering to make the same modest remittance quarterly if she would get the courts off my back by waiving the back alimony and reducing what was due to the amounts I proposed. I said I wasn't anxious to return to the States, so she could debate the relative value of getting a little something or nothing at all.

Then I said, "Thanks, Miss Vidal. That's all for now."

She gave me a level look, got up, and went to her desk outside my office. I could see her go to work, rolling paper into her typewriter. Good kid, I thought now. Appealing. Anyway, I would get used to looking at her, I resolved, and the longer I watched her, the more casual I would feel about her. Besides, hadn't I cut her off from me with that letter?

She glanced up from her typewriter and caught my eyes on her. Instinctively her hand checked her skirt, which, in fact, had crept up a little and showed some knee, pretty knee. She didn't blush or fluster. She hid the knee and kept on working, and then so did I.

There was plenty to do. I hardly thought about her at all for the next few minutes. Then she was standing in front of my desk again, but not speaking until I acknowledged her presence.

"Well?" I asked, busy with some papers.

Celia handed my letters to me for my signature and said, "Capitán Hadley, I know I have worked for you less than a week, but I have been in the government offices a year, and I had planned to start my vacation on Monday. I must be back by the time my uncle returns and . . ." Her voice trailed off softly with a sort of whispering quality. "I am sorry I didn't mention it sooner."

"There is still more to do on the supplemental report," I said a little harshly.

"Miss Valdez is studying English very hard," she said.

Oh, hell, I thought, Miss Valdez' English was worse than my Spanish. And she was such a bag.

"Where did you plan to go?" I asked.

"To Puerto del Sol," Celia said, her dark eyes picking up highlights and her hands making a little gesture of pleasure.

I wanted to see Puerto's beaches too, for business reasons. I said, "Fact is, I've got a flight into Puerto myself next week, and maybe I can stay over and borrow a couple of hours from you to look at the final draft of the report, to see if Señorita Valdez finished it okay. Where will you be staying?"

"At the villa of my aunt," she said, excited and happy to be going. She leaned over my desk and wrote the address on my pad. Then she added, "You should have reservations now, because the city will be very crowded for fiesta. You will need influence to get into the El Cortés Hotel."

Her face was quite close to mine as she still scribbled—a note to herself about the reservation. I felt something that didn't make any sense at all.

I said, "I have never seen anything of Puerto except the airport. I'd like to see the fiesta. Guess I can be there next Wednesday, the twelfth."

"That's Lincoln's Birthday," Celia said as she moved back from my desk, and it seemed odd, somehow, to hear about Lincoln in Ruedo, but of course Celia had been in the States four years. She gave me one of her wonderful smiles. With it she had a way of dropping her eyelids sort of shyly and then opening her eyes and looking at me as if for approval. It could have been a flirty trick, practiced before a mirror to make the most of her long eyelashes and all, but I didn't care. The smile stayed in my office until lunch time.

Then, as I went out, I grandly gave Miss Vidal the afternoon off so she could square away for her vacation. I felt in a holiday mood myself and went to the Hotel Mirado to be administered to by Paco at the bar. The airline had had me for the day.

Chapter 10

PACO wouldn't let me order my lunch. He smiled with a lot of white teeth in his dark face and said I was to leave the problem in his hands. He would negotiate with the chef, and I could expect to enjoy a Spanish *spécialité*.

I listened to happy voices mixed with splashing sounds coming from the swimming pool, but my mood had changed. I actually missed the office. It would have to be some lunch to fill up the emptiness that was bothering me again, not hunger but that feeling of hollowness in which there was both boredom and restlessness. Maybe it was a reaction from all the work on the report.

Suddenly the hotel dining room was full of engine noise. Once you have heard Rolls Royce Merlin engines winding up, especially coming closer, low and fast, and then pulling up in a climbing turn, you never forget it. Now it sounded like all nine of the Air Corps P-51s were overhead, and their shadows interrupted the bright sunlight at the windows with rapid-fire shade. Some people went to the windows to watch. I didn't. I just listened and realized that the planes spooked me, which was something new. Maybe it was just those particular Romirez planes.

When I was a kid in Long Island, I remembered, I was always running out in the street when I heard a plane overhead. I could identify them even then—the Fokker and Ford trimotors, the Army P-6 Curtiss Hawk that some guy buzzed our neighborhood in to impress his girl, the twin-engine Sikorsky amphibian that flew back and forth from the bay, and the biplane trainers from Curtis Field, also my favorite Douglas that test-flew engines for Wright from over in Jersey and made such a wonderful noise.

Airplanes had been everything in my young life, only we still spelled it "aeroplane" then. I collected pictures of flying heroes and talked about them constantly, the way other kids talked about football and baseball players.

Paco served me from a big pottery baking pot still hot from the stove, a mess of saffron rice, shellfish, chicken, and sausage all cooked together. It was really delicious food, but too heavy. Paco called it *paella Valenciana,* and I guess I wasn't appreciative enough, because my mind was far away. He went somewhere to sulk as I ate mechanically and remembered the model planes I used to make out of balsa and paper and powered with rubber bands. I was so proud to get the first Boy Scout merit badge in aviation in my county. I was going to be an aviator some day; that's what I told everybody.

I was sixteen in 1927, when Lindbergh flew the Atlantic. I stayed up all that May night, getting no more sleep than Lindy did, until the radio I was glued to announced he'd landed in Paris.

That summer I hitchhiked to all the nearby flying fields and hung around being a pest to those Godlike men in helmets and goggles. I asked endless questions, helped to wash planes, ran errands, and one fine day I raised nine blisters on my hands with a scythe, cutting down the summer growth of high weeds at the end of a field to earn my first ride. I was taken up in an open biplane with a blue fuselage and silver wings, an OX-5 Waco, and I could still see every detail of it in my mind. What a ride it was! The guy looped me, did power-off hammerhead stalls and snap rolls. My stomach was twenty feet outside the plane half the time, but it didn't cure me of my dream.

Even now a summery day like this could make me think of flying just for the fun of it. I wasn't supposed to be an executive, damn it! I was a pilot, what I always wanted to be, but what had happened to the old dreams to mix up their realization?

Well, for one thing, a fellow doesn't ever live alone. There are always other people who, without a word, can make his hopes and dreams seem selfish. My dad's fatal heart attack was in '29, when the crash wiped him out, the year I finished high school. I had to go to work in the paint factory to help out at home. There wasn't any money for flying lessons, so the Army Air Corps was the route for dreams to go, but applicants were required to have two years of college, and there wasn't any money for that either. I tried working days and commuting by train and subway to NYU nights, but that didn't last after the family house went for the mortgage.

Another guy in the paint factory had become an amateur boxer, the kind that got paid in watches worth ten bucks. I had handled him easily enough when we sparred a few times, so I tried to make some money the hard way too.

There were a lot of hungry fighters during the Depression, and I always remembered the ring as a place where I went to work. I couldn't romanticize pro boxing as a sport. Winning as well as losing was mean and dirty in that Coney Island abattoir, in St. Nick's and the Bronx arenas. Actually, I wasn't too bad at it, thanks to a long reach and some fast reflexes, but when I got on a winning streak it was because I got rough and tough. After I took my first low hard one and then a glove-touching apology that didn't put my strength back I did all the dirty stuff myself, and sometimes did it first. Could be that had a brutalizing effect that didn't go away.

When I got good enough selling paint, I hung up the gloves and didn't smell of wintergreen rubdown anymore, even though the sales meetings I spoke at were full of boxing figures of speech and our merchandising methods often as cute as any feint with a right. There were times we really didn't sell paint at all, just loaded up the dealers, and there were times, I remembered, when I doped out who the hell I, personally, was working for. My musclehead boss. I got ahead by giving him just exactly what *he* wanted, which occasionally was an ad with pretty artwork because then his wife flattered him, or his girl friend. That worked just like in the ring when you were getting licked in the late rounds and the boss was the referee. Then you put together a crowd-pleasing flurry of punches to bring them off their seats cheering, and more often than not the cheers worried the referee into not scoring too much for the other guy. Putting in usually useless overtime had the same effect as standing up in your corner between rounds instead of resting, even if it half killed you, to con the crowd. The referee might not be fooled, but he didn't want to make an unpopular decision. *Jesus,* but the winner's purse gets to be important.

Paco was tending bar. I sat with him and praised the lunch. He cheered up and kept the *cerveza* coming and tried to sell me on the local custom of shaking salt into the brew. I could take that or leave it alone.

My mother died of pneumonia in 1934, and since that winter I've never liked cold weather. I moved to New York and worked for an advertising agency as a copy cub. I shivered in a threadbare overcoat and began saving money for flying lessons. That summer two brothers stayed up in an airplane, a Curtiss Robin, for twenty-seven hours, refueling in the air. Then Howard Hughes flew his Special better than three hundred and fifty miles an hour for the world speed record. After that I even skipped lunches to put every spare cent into learning to fly across the river in Teterboro, New Jersey.

My instructor was an old-timer named Dan North who had an OX-5 Travel Aire for his students and a J-5 New Standard he went barnstorming with on Sundays. It must have been because I was so eager, but anyway Dan started taking me with him on the barnstorming trips. I used to get some stick and rudder time on the way to and from whatever small-town field we picked to work. I would earn the lesson and a ten-per-cent commission by hawking tickets to the prospects who drove in and parked on the edge of the field, most of them just out for a Sunday drive and curious about the airplane. Dan had souvenir tickets printed with a picture of his biplane on them, and a ride cost a buck. The Standard could haul four passengers at a time in the big open cockpit up front, so a five-minute hop around the field was profitable for both of us. Forty cents was my end. Sometimes I could sell a sport on a ten-dollar ride with a loop thrown in. This was easier when I put the pressure on a fellow who wanted to show off for his girl.

I wore a cheap pair of white cotton coveralls, a white canvas helmet, and a pair of second-hand goggles. The prospects thought I was a pilot, and I didn't mind.

If we didn't pull enough cars off the road with landings and takeoffs, Dan would buzz the neighborhood, hedge-hopping for a few miles around and finishing off with some stunts over the field. I always went along on those rides, because I plain loved the excitement.

To keep the suckers from leaving, I always showed them a parachute and announced that I was going to make a jump at five-thirty. When I had sold all the people I could convince that leaving the ground was not dangerous, or when the crowd got abusive about waiting for the parachute jump, since it was maybe seven or eight o'clock in the long summer evening, I would pass among them with my helmet held like a sack to accept their donations. Then I'd put on the parachute, which was a mildewed bag of rags that hadn't been inspected or repacked in years, and climb into the plane. Off we would fly into the sunset, never to return.

Dan wouldn't let me keep the ill-gotten proceeds of contributions to the jumper. He said it would be bad for my character, but that any time I actually wanted to make the jump I could have the money.

"Not with that chute," I would say.

"Whatsamatter? You got shit in your blood?" Dan would reply.

I learned a lot of stick-and-rudder pilotage from Dan North, but looking back, remembering how impressionable I still was at twenty-four, I might have picked a more moral guy to hero-worship. Dan could fly like an angel, but he had some hellish ways to make his money. Before I knew him, during Prohibition, he had flown a lot of cases of scotch across the border from Canada. The Standard had the room for it and also the wings and the power for amazing performance in and out of short cow-pastures. Later he worked the Mexican border, flying Chinese in. Dan North.

I can still hear him saying, "Luke, it was *good* whisky, not the stuff that makes you blind." And: "Luke, we gotta have laundries and chop-suey joints." And: "Luke, I needed the money."

Money. Always the lousy scratch, the rent money, the carfare, the eatin' money, and, most important, the gasoline money to fly again. At any rate, it wasn't money for its own sake, but money for essentials like getting up in the clouds. Dan made good dough and could have saved some for the future, but he blew it on a flying dream. Dan North always wanted to fly the Atlantic.

He couldn't get a backer because a lot of planes were dropping in the drink then, so he gave up on the idea of a Fairchild 71 and on his own financed a raft of special-sized auxiliary gas tanks for the Standard. I think what bothered Dan most was that a dame had made it solo across the big pond the year before, Amelia Earhart. He had to get the flight out of his system, but he cracked up the old biplane in a Newfoundland snowbank. He always said any landing was a good one if you could walk away from it, but he was quieter after that one.

In 1940 he joined up with the group of Canadians who formed the first Transatlantic ferry group to deliver Lockheed Hudson bombers to England. He disappeared in a storm over the ocean he always wanted to fly.

I poured me another beer and drank a silent toast to Dan, who had turned me loose for my first solo. It was in his Travel Aire, and I remembered how it felt the first time up there alone. How wonderful! If you've ever done it, you know it's one of the best times of your life. When I did it, I sang the whole time. "God rest ye merry, gentlemen," I sang—and hell, I never sing.

I put a lot of solo hours in my logbook, hours rented in open cockpits so noisy I had to sew powder puffs into the earflaps of my helmet. My face got sun- and windburned around the ovals of my goggles, and those were the hours I really *lived,* flying wired spruce and fabric-covered planes that were gone now: the Eaglerock . . . the Swallow . . . the Waco . . . the Great Lakes . . . and especially the Travel Aire. I went round and round the fields, countless circuits, polishing landing technique; my hands on stick and throttle learned to be light, gentle even, but not tentative or uncertain. There was a strength they learned, without roughness, a touch you had to have to ease a plane off the ground clean and smooth, to turn her true and land her greased on. And afterward I'd give my airplane a pat on the tail or on the cowling, an affectionate pat, unashamed of my fondness for her.

And I remembered a very special Ryan S-T-A, a low-wing open job with an inverted Menasco engine, a little beauty I loved to stunt the hell out of and the one the CAA examiner rode in with me and then gave me my license. That was in 1936, and a thousand pilot licenses were issued that year.

It was a happy, carefree time learning to fly cross-country, learning to navigate, sweating out the weather, and now and then taking up passengers illegally for hire, or students, including a girl everybody at Teterboro called Tailspin. She loved flying and flyers and proved it in the high grass across the field or in the deserted hangar at night and once up in the air in the thickly carpeted aisle of a five-place cabin Beechcraft, the stagger-wing biplane that a friend of mine named Artie had for charter. That time Artie and I took turns flying. It was important that we fly at an altitude* of at least 5280 feet so we could claim membership in the Mile High Club. We tossed a coin for first, and I won, so Artie swore he was going to loop us during the act. He started the pull up, and the girl and I had to hang on, though weakly from laughing so much, but Artie quit fooling around, because he knew I would do the same to him.

In 1937 I got my commercial license and Eastern Air Lines inaugurated its New York-Miami passenger service, but they said they didn't need me as a co-pilot.

I still had my copywriting job in New York but lived cheaply in order to continue flying on weekends. I didn't rent planes any more but put some dough into part-ownership of Artie's Beechcraft. Charter business wasn't too good, so lots of times on Saturday or Sunday it was just going out to the airport and wandering around inside hangars to visit the planes and sort of stroke their taut fabric-covered wings and smell the banana oil in the dope shops. Sometimes I helped the A & Es, and I remember what was cranky about each of the engines—the Wright J-5s, the Warner-Scarabs, the Jacobs, the Kinners, the Franklins, the Menascos, the Pratt and Whitney Wasps and Hornets.

Those were fine days, even the day I got fired by the agency. I had been delayed in Pittsburgh by weather. It wasn't the first time I had been two days late to work. I didn't blame them. I didn't care.

Then Artie and I had a forced landing with a broken oil line that retired our Beech. It was too unsprung for relicensing, so I found some work flying the little T-crafts and J-3 Piper Cubs that in 1938 were becoming popular because they were cheap to maintain. I instructed mostly and slept in the hangar. Sometimes I towed signs. I had dirty fingernails, a leather jacket, and a white silk scarf. I was a pilot. I guess I knew I was also some kind of bum. When the field was socked in, I began to read. I borrowed books and bought some too. I must have read a thousand. The weather wasn't good that year.

In March 1939 the Government Pilot Training Program got under way. I became a civilian instructor. In September I was in Cleveland with Dan North at the National Air Races when the news came that the Germans had invaded Poland. We stayed to watch Colonel Roscoe Turner win the Thompson Trophy for the third time in a Laird Special at 282 mph. I recall the speed because I was instructing in BT-13s, the Vultee Vibrators, that couldn't do half that. I never saw Dan again.

In 1940 I enlisted, but I got turned down for peashooters because I was too tall. So it was bombers for me, and I checked out in the Beech AT-10s. I didn't get operational, though, just wound up instructing again, this time in a brown suit. I was sent to Texas, and there was a girl in San Antonio who was part Mexican and she taught me how to dance and maybe planted some notions in my head about this part of the world.

After Pearl Harbor it was good-by to the Texas girl and a lot more good-bys the way we moved around. I got me a four-engine B-17 and a crew, and on my last leave before shipping out I also got me a wife.

I had to marry Cynthia to get her into bed, and I had to brag to her about the advertising agency job I had before the war when it was plain that I needed more going for me than the glamour of a first lieutenant's silver bars. I had to have a postwar future complete with station wagon, country club, and house in a right neighborhood. I admit I made myself think I wanted that stuff too, if it was a package deal. But I was disappointed when I unwrapped the part of the package my bride was in. She was a stiff in a white veil who had got all her kicks counting the wedding presents.

I was pretty sure I was going to my death without ever having gotten enough. I couldn't listen to the other guys rhapsodize about their last leave, even the unmarried guys, even the ones I knew were bragging.

Later, when I was dropping bombs on real targets the summer of '42, and when the ME-109s were shooting at me with real bullets, it got so flying wasn't the good clean fun it had been. Within a year I had that shuttle run over Germany from England to North Africa, and then the crew wasn't mine any more. I was theirs. I was their ticket home from the raids, and they took care of me like I was some kind of Seeing Eye dog. God, how I hated to be used by everybody—my crew, the Brass, *and* my wife. And so I pushed my luck with poker, got the use of something, if only the cheap money and the expensive money you earn fighting a war.

"Pilot to navigator, I'll raise you twenty bucks."

"Bombardier to pilot, it'll cost you that and another ten to stay."

"Co-pilot to all you bastards, I fold."

We called our B-17 the Wild Card, and one thing its crew needed was a gambling spirit. I dealt their war to them, but I couldn't stack the intercepters and the flak in their favor.

"Tail gunner, ante up!"

"Is that an order, sir?"

"Yes, damn it! Bombardier, you got openers?"

Sometimes on the long rides home from the target we bet on the weather. Up to then nobody had fixed meteorology, but if somebody had heard about salting the clouds with dry ice for rain he'd have tried it— probably Eddie, my co-pilot, who played a safe, close-to-the-vest game and lost anyway. He finally got his ass shot off sitting right next to me.

I hadn't been rotated home after twenty-five missions—not that I wanted to go home on leave just to go furniture shopping. But when it was finally over, the war seemed almost a pleasant memory compared to job-hunting with the ruptured duck pin in my lapel and the bickering, bitching time at home.

Cynthia had a friend at one of the big advertising agencies, Batten, Barton, Durstine & Osborn, who was going to hire me, but I was a flyer. Some people really are some one thing. A farmer is. A fisherman. A miner. I had to fly, or thought I had to fly, which is the same thing. I know I disappointed Cynthia. But that woman wanted to push me. I don't push. Sure, there were half a million pilots in America going at three for a nickel. Yet we weren't starving, except for love.

When I took a now-and-then job with a new air freight company flying a Non Sked C-46 up and down the coast, she could have come with me on the trips south. We could have had a ball in Miami. Instead all I had that was like love was the flying. Even when I got on with American as a co-pilot, it was all I had and I kept it close, with my mouth shut about it —that feeling of genuine affection for a lot of duraluminum riveted together in a marvelous way that responded to me when I treated it right. I couldn't help it if I didn't feel emotional about wall-to-wall carpeting.

Now this.

Now even this in Ruedo spoiled a little by some cockeyed compulsion to get my hands on more money. I wondered what had happened to my eagerness to fly and why I had painted myself into a corner behind a desk again.

I left the bar and walked back to the Government Palace. Reluctant executive or not, I was deep in my plans for LARC. There was figure work that had to be done, and I was disturbed by the answers to some of my addition.

I asked the Valdez woman to fetch the guy in the Ministry of Finance who was responsible for LARC's accounting on gasoline and other purchases for the airline. To my surprise the bookkeeper turned out to be none other than our invisible sales manager, Señor Martinez. Naturally, he had already left for the weekend. Well, I would just have to talk to him when I got back from Mexico.

When the sun dove out of sight early, as it did in these latitudes, I switched on the lights in my office. My staff went home, and I stayed fussing around. There was nothing to go home to—just a hotel room or another bar.

Saturday, too, turned out to be a nothing day. It was hot, so I lay around the pool and got a little more tan on the old torso.

To escape the worst of the afternoon sun, I got dressed and sought the cool of the Mirado lobby bar. I talked stupidly to a cat that rubbed against my legs. The blind man came in with his lottery tickets, and I bought one. What the hell, I hadn't paid any taxes in Ruedo. A paper boy sold me a copy of *La Hora*. The political news was innocuous enough. There was no criticism of the government, as far as I could see, but I didn't get the impression that the press was controlled or censored, rather that the editor played it safe.

I read the whole damn paper, including the coffee and cotton futures. I read that February eighth was the Saint's Day for San Juan de Matha, San Nicetius, Santa Elfieda, and San Esteban de Muret. I read the social notes on garden parties, bridge parties, betrothals and weddings, and about a cocktail reception for a Ruedan trade delegation at the French Embassy. I read about a buffet for women golfers at the Maya Country Club, given by the Minister of Justice. I even read the classified ads, including one that interested me about a Stateside refrigerator for sale by a family that was going back home.

I stared at my half-finished *mojito* and made circles on the bar surface with the condensation from the glass. It was my third or fourth drink, and it wasn't doing much for the dull feeling I had. Even the sunshine was monotonous. I scowled at nothing.

Then there was a voice in my ear. "You haven't called me." It was Harry Donahue.

"I forgot," I said.

He led me to the end of the bar, away from other drinkers, and asked, "What's new?"

It wasn't an idle question from him, so I gave him the straight dope. "We're buying some more airplanes."

"What kind?" He was the United States government collecting data. He looked into the backbar mirror, satisfying himself that no one was behind us to hear our talk.

"Four surplus transports, including a C-54. Also a bomber, a B-25," I said.

Harry whistled.

It was my turn to ask a question, one I hadn't seen answered in the paper. "How are things in Palmas?"

"Calm, according to official reports," Harry said, "but I doubt it."

"Why did they try to burn Palmas, Harry? Seems so pointless," I said.

"It's a pattern of terror," Harry said. "A few real fire bombs someplace make later threats more frightening. In the beginning, Palmas is a better place for trouble than here in the capital. The way they look at it, Palmas is far enough away to get fearful rumors started and make people worry about what's going to happen next."

"What do you think will happen next?"

"Something pretty big, I expect, because a foreign correspondent arrived from the States this morning on TACA. *Time* magazine man. Those guys usually know something."

"News must be dull at home," I said. "Maybe the correspondent just talked himself into a nice winter vacation on the expense account." I thought of the niece of the Minister of Peace, taking a vacation too. Miss Vidal wouldn't leave the capital if things were really bad.

I ordered another long, cool *mojito* and another of the same for Harry. With my nose in my drink I said, "I'm flying to Mexico tomorrow."

I thought that would change the subject, but it didn't.

"Fine," Harry said. "Romirez is going too. Find out if he sees Sagasta up there, will you?"

"What are you paying spies these days?" I laughed.

"I'm serious, fly-boy." Harry frowned. "We've got to know if fat stuff is working alone, or what. Romirez is the leader of the opposition, the strong man of the 'outs,' who has an important 'in' in the present government. He provides all the other 'outs' with *de facto* if not *de jure* power in Ruedo. The old president, Sagasta, might be using him. It's hard to tell, but I think Sagasta is behind the Coronel." Harry looked at me over his drink with a carom shot off the mirror behind the bar.

PART TWO

Part Two

Chapter 11

THE flight to Mexico was scheduled early for the aficionados who wanted to be in the plaza by four o'clock on Sunday afternoon. I didn't want to be late for my first bullfight either.

Pepe Lopez showed up to fly with me, showed up on time and contrite, apologetic even, because his uncle, the Coronel, had countermanded my orders assigning García to the flight. I was disappointed at missing a chance to check García out. I already knew Pepe stank.

I fidgeted in the cockpit when the flight wasn't called. From the baggage men loading our tail I heard of errors on the manifest, how some cargo from yesterday's trip had become mixed with stuff bound for Mexico. At least half of it was tagged wrong, but which half? At once too many officials got into the act, including the airport's *administrador* and the Customs *comandante,* each with his side order of underlings and his many too many pieces of paper requiring rubber stamps. They enjoyed public displays of temper over baggage, freight, government cargo, air express and mail, but after that was settled, a further delay was caused by the shipment in a crate of a fighting cock which had to be admired by the loading crew. Then I thought we were all set, but no.

Passengers waving their arms and shouting created a near riot because the flight had been oversold. Thinking I might be able to help, I went out to the gate and caught hell, mostly from disgruntled countrymen of mine. All the passengers were thoroughly PO'ed at having to reconfirm three times before flight departure: first, precisely seventy-two hours before flight time; subsequently, twice more at arbitrarily inconvenient hours and in person at the Mirado counter or the airport. It was obvious to me that ticket agents were taking under-the-counter money from some with late requests for space and then canceling the reservations of others on technicalities of reconfirmation. I didn't have the time or patience to read twenty-two time-stamped tickets, so my solution was three refunds and gratis transportation the following week. Even that wasn't an easy sale, and I decided to take it out of our so-called sales manager's hide. If I had my way, Señor Martinez wasn't going to be with LARC much longer.

At last every seat was occupied but two. The *comandante* told me they were being held for Coronel Romirez. We kept the rest of the people waiting another ten minutes in the sweltering airplane until Romirez arrived. He walked out to the plane from his Cadillac with a redhead on his arm, a somehow familiar-looking goregous redhead. Everybody watched them board.

When I found a cruising altitude with the most favorable winds, it looked as if we could make up for lost time, and I guessed we were high enough at nine thousand to trust Pepe with the controls. I went back to visit with the passengers.

Romirez had taken the window seat, of course. He overflowed somewhat in the redhead's direction, so she had her legs crossed out in the aisle, the one crossed on top showing more than the knee. The leg jiggled in my direction, making her gold anklet, under sheer nylon, glitter in the sunlight that streamed in the windows; the spike heels on her shoes were gold too. She gave me a not necessarily friendly little wave that flashed gilded fingernails. She was a gold-plated solid-brass chippy.

The legs I kept on looking at finally blocked my progress down the aisle, and I had already read the name, Lita, on the anklet when the Coronel grudgingly introduced me to Miss Lita Shelton. I grinned at her and took in a fitted suit of cool-looking pale green nubby cotton that went well with her shoulder-length red hair. She didn't wear a blouse under the jacket, and its deep V neck showed a lot of honey-tanned cleavage to where a black lace bra cut off the view. Her skirt was a slim sheath with a slit in the side, without which she couldn't possibly have crossed her legs.

"Capitán Hadley," Romirez said, "Miss Shelton is an actress from Hollywood." He said it with evident pride in the dame.

"That's nice," I said. I wanted her to know I had never heard of her.

"I'm working in Mexican pictures now," she said defensively or to explain Romirez. I didn't care. I guessed the Coronel's wife didn't care either. She, like other wives in Latin America, had the security of at least five kids at home and wouldn't be as jealous as the girls on the sixth floor of the Hotel Mirado.

My coffee break with Carlota was short. I went back to the cockpit as we headed into mountain passes and put a lot of air under our DC-3 because we would be better than seven thousand feet high when we landed in Mexico.

I felt pretty good when I saw the beautiful snow-capped cone of Mount Popocatepetl and knew I would get to the bullfight on time.

After we landed, a white jeep pulled up to our door and a fussy Mexican in a white uniform came aboard. Pepe called him the bug man. He was the public-health officer, and he went up and down the aisle with a spray gun until a fine mint-flavored mist settled over everything, but the few flies thrived on the stuff and buzzed happily.

By the time Pepe and I negotiated tie-down fees, permits, and tax payments, and cleared immigration and customs paperwork, our passengers had all departed in cabs. Romirez had left us, taking Lita with him.

My two bullfight tickets were waiting for me at the Eastern ticket counter in the terminal. I wondered why I had ordered two and supposed it was a habit a once-married man gets into. When I checked in at the Hotel Reforma, the clerk's eyes bulged at the *barrera* ticket I showed him and asked him to find a customer for. It was plain that a front-row ticket was as scarce at the hotel this late on a Sunday as it would be at SPCA headquarters. Then I took a shower and changed from my uniform into slacks and sport jacket. The air on the Mexican plateau was cool and fresh. I felt pepped-up and excited about seeing my first *corrida*.

Back at the front desk the clerk told me that a beautiful *señorita,* a *peliroja,* for whom he personally would have turned Mexico inside-out to find a ticket, had offered him three prices for one no matter where it was in the plaza.

I dug the ticket out of my pocket and tried to remember if *peliroja* meant what I thought it did. "Your customer is a redhead?" I asked. "And here in the hotel?"

"Sí, sí, señor; la peliroja es muy linda!" He kissed his fingers and rolled

his eyes and made a pass at the ticket I held just out of his reach across the counter. "But she is not staying at the hotel. Only I know how to find her."

He was a bandit. I had to laugh and give him a couple of pesos. "Where is the *señorita?*"

"At the bar," he said and had no further interest in anything.

Lita Shelton didn't see me approach in the dim light of the bar lounge. I sat down next to her very quietly. Her mouth shaped up a go-to-hell expression until I showed her my two tickets.

"Billetes para los toros!" she said, and her Spanish had no trace of American accent. Then she added, with New Yorkish intonation, "Front row in the shade, yet!"

I guessed maybe she *was* an actress. "Let's go!" I said.

The tunnel entrances are high up the sides of the deeply tiered bull-fighting stadium that is Plaza Mexico. To reach our first-row seats, right behind the *barrera,* we had to pick our way down a steep concrete stairway. Lita's hatless red hair, in a long, carefully combed pageboy cut to her shoulders, undulated with the rest of her as she went down the steps on her high golden heels. I followed her, frankly sort of proud of my flashy date. The Mexicans in the stands, watching her every step of the way, were articulately appreciative, as is their custom.

"Bless the loins of the mother that bore you," I heard one say to Lita.

A young Mexican in a tight-fitting black Sunday suit stood up, bowed, and said, "Would that I had been the tree that made the wood that made the bed that holds that shape."

Another insinuating voice: "Oh, *la peliroja,* to be your powderpuff or your rosary!"

Lita was wafted to her seat on waves of open and ribald admiration. I was about to compliment her myself, but delayed too long tipping the usher and renting two cushions. Another voice, so passionate it cracked on the verge of tears, won the *piropo* competition hands down, crying out, *"Te comería toda linda mujer, aunque tuiera que estar cagando flecos durante veinticuatro horas!"* Everybody laughed good-naturedly, including Lita, and then my redheaded woman was suddenly no longer as important to the Mexicans as what was about to happen in the ring.

Trumpets sounded shrilly. I felt the excitement crawl along the skin of my arms up to the short hairs on the back of my neck and then, as it got under way, I resolved to keep an open mind about the symbols of life and of death in the bullring. I knew it was not theater but the actual, through controlled, drama of real and mortal danger.

I must have appeared terribly intense to Lita, because I was conscious of her looking at me in a clinical way as she asked, "Are you going to be sick at the sight of blood?"

"I don't think so," I answered her, but I thought of the time I flew back from a mission vomiting in my lap because a dead man sat beside me with a big hole in him and the flak hits in front of us let in a two-hundred-mph wind that splattered blood all over the inside of the flight deck.

"If you get sick, just leave," she said. "I won't come and hold your head. I intend to see all six bulls."

The fight went on and didn't bother me. I was surprised not to be shocked by the bull's attack on the horses, but rather felt a pride in the bull's willingness to keep charging even with the sharp point of the picador's lance drawing blood from the hump in his shoulders, splashing his black hide with crimson from spine to forelegs. The bull actually seemed to get some satisfaction out of hitting something solid. If it had bothered me, I wouldn't have stayed and been a nuisance to the Romans in Rome.

Close in front of us two of the matadors fussed with their different capes in the alley between the stands and *barrera,* a protecting board fence. I heard them joke about being absolutely unable to spit. My own mouth was dry.

"Goddamned perfumed monkeys!" Lita said, curling her lips. I noticed for the first time that her eyes were a cold blue.

A trumpet blasted again. The bull moved out to the center of the ring as if he owned the place and dared anyone to challenge him. I was amazed that anyone did.

The thin, puny-looking torero slipped quietly out of the slot and walked unhurriedly toward the half-ton monster. He was just a kid, not a day over eighteen, wearing a fancy spangled lavender and gold suit and carrying nothing more than a pair of barbed sticks decorated with colored paper. He walked out with a loose-hipped, screw-you arrogance that hushed the crowd.

Lita said, "Cocky son-of-a-bitch!"

I glanced at the program, damp from the sweat off my hands. I read that the kid's name was Manolo Bartóleme, a matador who placed his own banderillas.

"Come on, Manolo," I said softly to myself.

Three times Manolo incited the bull to charge him by waving the sticks over his head, arching his back, and pushing his pelvis out at the menacing horns. Each time the bull charged, Manolo cleared the horns by inches, pirouetting like a ballet dancer and leaving the barbs stuck in the bull's lacerated withers. I clapped my hands hard and once found myself clapping longer than the Mexicans did, so I had to stare straight ahead, a little embarrassed by my enthusiasm.

Lita laughed at me and said, "Oh, brother!"

Kettle drums rolled, and the trumpet sounded for the next act.

Manolo strutted back to the *barrera* to be handed his *muleta,* a smaller, all red serge cape that could be held out square with a wooden stick inside it. He was also handed a sword. The kid saluted a head man up in one of the boxes and, after doing an about-face, he tossed his matador's hat over his shoulder to a pretty girl near us. It meant he was dedicating the bull to her. Then he strutted back to the bull. I heard Lita say, "Stuck-up little bastard!"

Manolo opened this phase of the fight with a series of passes, each one punctuated by an *olé.*

"This is called a *faena,*" Lita said, and behind me I heard knowledge-able Mexicans talk of the *derechazos,* the four *pases de rodillas* and the *molinete*—which gives you an idea of how technical bullfighting is. The regulars knew this stuff and talked it up just the way baseball fans at home buzz about hit-and-run strategy or a squeeze play.

The crowd called out, *"Música!"* and the band played the "Mexican Hat Dance" for Manolo as he worked very close to the horns. I held my breath.

Lita wanted a cigarette. I gave her one. She exhaled smoke, bored as hell. "You're really lucky," she said.

"Why?" I asked.

"Because it's your first *corrida* and it's going quite well. These things are usually a shambles, you know."

The bull's head was held much lower now, and he didn't look quite so proud with the large red stains of blood wetting his sides, so I could understand the feeling of sympathy for the animal that North Americans in the crowd gave voice to. But I also sensed something else about the bull—a quality, not of defeat but of uncertainty about the outcome of the fight that was suggesting to him in the late rounds he would have to get cute, have to make fewer wild rushes, have to box a little and watch for an opening to score a knockout. I felt that made him meaner and more dangerous than at the start.

Manolo made another pass with the *muleta,* fluttering it like a pendulum behind his legs, offering his body to the bull, but tricking the animal into hitting only the moving cloth.

The crowd exploded in unison with a sharp *"Olé!"*

Lita's breath came out in a sigh that sounded almost disappointed.

This happened again and again—the bull's horns stabbing close to Manolo's body, led by the passes of the cape, followed by the *Olés,* and the lip-curled hisses from the redhead. I didn't speak to her. I cheered my head off.

Then from behind the *barrera* a helper handed another sword to Manolo in exchange for the lighter one he had been holding. The young matador glanced quickly up at his girl, where she sat with his sequined dress cape spread in front of her and holding tight to his woolly black *montera.* She stared glassy-eyed at him in his tight lavender pants that didn't hide anything.

Lita sneered. "I suppose she'll have an orgasm when he uses his sword on the bull."

"What the hell is the matter with you?" I asked her.

"I just hate men," she said flatly, her eyes very blue and expressionless as a doll's.

"Sure you do," I said and hunched my shoulders away from her and watched the ring.

Fifty thousand people sat in such absolute silence that Manolo's voice could be heard as he flicked the *muleta* open again and called the bull to him.

"Ahhhhhhhh-ha, toro! Mira toro . . . ahh, mira bonito!" His tone was loving, cajoling. He arched his back and pushed the bit of red serge forward with just his wrist moving.

The bull charged, an ebony streak that blended with the red cloth and the lavender-gold of the man. *Olé!* was like a cannon shot from the crowd. Softly I half whispered another *Olé* to myself.

When little Manolo's feet moved at all, they moved toward the bull in slow heel-and-toe steps, one foot directly in front of the other. He swept the *muleta* low and forward into the bull's face, forcing him to charge again. He linked together a series of what are called natural passes, very slow and suave. He was on the brink of a triumph.

Then the young matador sighted along his sword blade at the bull as if preparing to kill, but the fans protested, shouting, *"No! No!"*

Manolo looked up at the crowd, pleased with himself and with the brave bull. He gave in to the fans' wishes and prepared to pass the bull again, but now the animal wouldn't move. So the kid moved toward the bull with inching little steps, his feet close together, moving until he crossed the angle of the bull's horns. Then he slowly turned his back on the bull and knelt, smiling up at the crowd. I felt like praying for him.

When he walked away from the dominated animal, he got a standing ovation, and the band knocked themselves out playing the "Hat Dance."

"He'll have to tip the musicians plenty," Lita said.

"To-re-ro! To-re-ro!" The crowd chanted the staccato three syllables. Manolo had given them tremendous emotion. Me too. I was shaken. Now it was building to the climax, this twenty-minute demonstration of life with courage, courage that was something more; call it courage with style.

He sighted down the sword blade again and lined the bull up straight by shaking the *muleta* under its nose. He was taking time enough to do it right.

"Matador!" a throaty Mexican voice said behind me.

Manolo was ready, still as a statue, the sword pointed to the spot high on the bull's shoulder hump, the *muleta* low to control the head— as Lita told me—so he could go in over the horns; a most dangerous time, and no wonder they called it "the moment of truth." But the *muleta* fluttered suddenly like laundry on a clothes line. It was a puff of wind that did it.

There were yells from the stands, *"Cuidado!* Look out! Be careful!"

Manolo shook the cloth to gain control of it but had to step back from an unexpected rush by the bull. He recovered quickly and with anger on his face he ran after the bull and led him into chopping, neck-twisting passes that fixed him in place.

"Ahhh," Lita said with some satisfaction. "It is getting windy."

A breeze had come up and freshened, blowing a small cloud of dust where the bull stood pawing the sand with a forehoof. Manolo ran back to the *barrera*. His helpers spilled water from an earthen jug on the *muleta*. He dragged it in the sand and stepped on it to make the sand stick and add weight to the cloth. I felt for him. A bullfighter and a flyer have something in common about treacherous winds.

Then Manolo prepared again for the kill, but when he went in with the sword something must have gone wrong, because the sword did not penetrate properly and most of it was left sticking up out of the bull's back. The young man shook his head with disappointment.

The fans, too, voiced their disappointment for him with a sympathetic sigh in unison.

Lita explained that the spot between the bull's shoulder blades where the sword must go is no bigger than a silver dollar, a difficult target. The rest is all bone. Also, the sword must go in straight and nearly all the way in to reach the heart.

Manolo tried again—and failed again. Twice more he tried, but the sword hit bone repeatedly, going in only a couple of inches and spanging out again, so the kid had to trot after it and retrieve it from the sand.

The crowd lost patience. They weren't with the boy any more. They whistled derisively, booed, and cursed.

"His *estoque* is just plain impotent," Lita said, and she was smiling now. "That fine bull is going to die very badly."

Again the weapon failed to go in, and then, on the sixth try, the sword seemed well placed and at least halfway in, but the bull stubbornly charged Manolo, bumping him back, making him leave his *muleta* draped shamefully over the bull's horn and nose. The animal shook his head and mooed until the cloth fell to the sand. A trumpet blasted a warning that the matador had only five minutes left in which to make his kill.

The three banderilleros closed in on the bull, surrounding him with their capes, teasing him to turn this way and that, hoping his movement would make the curved end of the sword twist into an artery. Instead it cut into a lung, bringing a gush of bright red froth from the bull's nostrils. The animal choked and bellowed and pawed the sand. He began to drown in his own blood, but he was not yet ready to admit defeat. Red-eyed with pain and hate, standing bravely, attesting to the wild strain that was bred into him, the bull simply refused to die.

One of the banderilleros dragged a cape across the hilt of the sword to pull it out. When this finally worked, he handed the sword back to Manolo, just a little disdainfully.

An American couple near us got up and started out up the stairs. The man was loudly disapproving. "I've seen my first and last toreador," he said. "It's just a lousy slaughter. The bull doesn't have a chance!"

I had to admit to myself that it was bad at this stage, but Jesus, what did he want—to see a man killed instead of a bull?

Again the young matador profiled with the *muleta* and sword, but the crowd yelled, *"No! No!"* Their loud disapproval was based on the observation that the bull's forelegs were wide apart, thus, I learned, closing the target between the shoulder blades. But the matador went in with the sword anyway and once more it hit bone, bent, and did not penetrate.

Manolo stood in front of the bull, hands on hips, cursing him and the milk of the cow that birthed him, also cursing his own mother's milk, which he wished had been poisoned. The crowd shared his second curse. So did whoever ordered another warning trumpet blast.

"I knew that *faena* was too good to be true," Lita said, giggling a little. "Now you're seeing the usual Sunday afternoon degradation. One more trumpet *aviso,* and they will send in steers to lead the bull out, and then, under the stands, they'll shoot it."

Manolo went to the *barrera* for another sword, a different sort of blade. It was stiffer and had a crossbar near the point. I heard it called a *descabello*. Others helped Manolo by spreading their capes flat on the sand before the bull, who lowered his head to sniff the cloth. With the bull's head down, the matador was supposed to make a short thrust into the neck behind the brain where the spinal column is near the surface.

At the precise instant that Manolo made his thrust the bull raised his head, deflecting the blade. The crowd moaned.

The bull backed into the *barrera* and his bowels let go. He mooed again and he coughed blood with his tongue hanging out, but he did not fall.

Again the two capes were slid under the bull's bleeding nose, and again he lowered his head. Again Manolo took aim. The fans screamed for him to do it now, but he hesitated, worried about his aim, and choked up. Too late he poked the blade and missed the spot. He poked again. Missed again.

Then the bull went down, hind feet first and then forefeet. He lay as if dead. I hoped it was over. Nobody liked this. One of the banderilleros slipped up behind the bull's head with a short dagger to sever the spinal cord for sure, but before he could do it the bull rose again, turning his wicked horns and making the man with the dagger jump back.

Seat cushions rained down onto the sand around poor Manolo. Lita threw hers and hit him. The kid turned with a pleading gesture to the fans who hooted his incompetence. High up in the cheap seats some rabid aficionados built a fire of paper programs.

The bull had to die. It is ordered that way from the first. Lita told me that in twenty minutes of fighting the bull gets an education, can eventually distinguish between the moving cape and the man. No bull could be fought a second time.

But this bull died hard. He stood there, so weary, and wanting his own death as much as the frustrated matador wanted it.

Tears streamed down Manolo's cheeks as he held the weapon, point down, over the bull's head and seemed to beg, "Die! Damn you, die! *Muere, bicho, por favor!*"

The trumpet was blown again to signal that time had at last run out, but just then the bull's head sagged and Manolo tried a desperate final stab. Mercifully, the bull's knees crumpled and he dropped sideways as though shot.

"*Malo! Muy malo!*" the Mexican behind me muttered. "Seven swords and four *descabellos!*"

"*Y tres avisos!*" another said.

A team of mules with gay ribbons on their harness came into the arena and towed the carcass away. The crowd applauded the bull and whistled and booed Manolo, who walked, head down, dragging his feet, back to the *barrera*. Sand was shoveled over the bloodstains and manure by red-jacketed *mozos*.

"Now, wasn't that lovely?" Lita asked.

The first three rows of Plaza Mexico were called the American sector of the city, according to Lita, but only for the first bull. I looked around, and she was right. Most of my countrymen were leaving, and many had already left when the first hemorrhage was induced by the picador. Now thrifty Mexicans moved into their vacated seats, having previously purchased cheaper seats with that expectation. Lita pointed out a few Americans who remained. Some were genuine aficionados, but others were queer ones from up north who had taken up this thing for queer reasons.

"Look at that one, Luke," Lita said, pointing at a type who looked as if he zipped his pants on the side. "The dear boy must really be shivering with ecstasy in the middle of all this raw masculinity. I can feel the maleness here too, but I loathe it!"

I caught the beer vender's eye and bought two Carta Blancas. It was just like Yankee Stadium, because he poured them into paper cups so we couldn't throw the empty bottles at anybody.

I took a swallow of the good pilsner brew and looked at Lita. She sipped her *cerveza* and was so pretty I wished she weren't so damn mixed up.

The trumpets sounded, and the second bull was let out of the gate. He was another fine black beast, but the second matador didn't show us the kind of cape work Manolo had. Of course there was the wind to contend with. But he tried hard and in the end he killed well with a single *estoque*. He launched his body over the horns, getting the sword in to the hilt while his left hand moved the *muleta* down and across his knees to his right, deflecting the bull's last lunge at the moment when both bull and man had an even chance at each other. As the man and animal separated, it was the bull that staggered, groping for the ground, and dropped over on his side, legs out stiff.

I felt wrung out, cleansed and made happy, by that ending, the way I've felt after putting a ship down smoothly in a bad crosswind.

A sea of white handkerchiefs was waving. I turned to Lita to ask her what it meant, but she just looked discontented and bitchy. To hell with her, I thought.

I watched this matador, an older, flat-nosed, dark-skinned Mexican, take a turn around the ring, holding up a severed ear he had been granted for his work. He was called Chico Vasquez, and he looked pleased with himself. Many cigars and a few bouquets of flowers rained down on him, also sombreros, which he scaled back into the stands. Occasionally a lady's fan or shoe landed on the sand as tribute, and then a tequila bottle skidded into the ring. Chico picked it up, drank or pretended to drink from it, and wiped his lips on his gold-embroidered sleeve. When the bottle was passed back hand over hand, drink after drink, among the fans, the one who threw it out got it back empty but didn't mind.

A pink brassière fluttered out on the sand, and Chico quickly scooped it up, kissed it appropriately twice, and blew a kiss to the crowd. They loved it. The high-pitched, rooster-crowing laughter of the Mexican Indians echoed in the stands.

The third matador had a *manso* bull, meaning its manhood was suspect. It refused to charge the horses and even ran away from the unfortunate fellow who had to cape it. Somehow the matador got through the ordeal with uninteresting passes, and the bull died with the second sword thrust.

The grumbling all around us about that bull quickly stopped when the next one came into the ring with a grunting, stomping rush. The sight of him was a shock like a punch in the stomach to me. He was bigger than the others and faster, and his horns were wider and sharper. The hump of his neck seemed swollen with pride. According to the program this black beast that stood so defiantly in the exact center of the ring was called Legado. It sort of meant "ambassador," Lita said. Ambassador of death was what he looked like.

He was Manolo Bartóleme's second bull.

The fans shouted their approval of the big bull, calling out over and over, *"Toro! Toro! Toro!"* as the animal lunged at the *barrera,* making the wood thunder as splinters flew.

Manolo was reluctant to come out and take Legado on. Hell, I didn't blame him, but the crowd was on him and began whistling.

Finally Manolo went out from behind the protecting wooden wall, holding his magenta and yellow cape squeezed into narrow folds in front of him. For an instant he dared to take his eyes off the bull and turned to look up in the stands. Then he spat on the sand, which proved something. He moved slowly toward Legado as if he knew that this was one in a thousand bulls that could make him great or kill him.

I wondered, though, about Manolo's reason for being in there with that bull. Was it a dream he'd always had as a poor kid of owning his own *rancho?* They said all bullfighters had to start with hungry dreams, and I wouldn't quarrel with that reason behind every good pro. But to face a bull like Legado when the poor days were just a memory—perhaps it demanded the sin of pride.

My own problems and goals seemed less as I watched Manolo move closer to the bull, holding the cape still squeezed narrow in front of his chest. He bit the collar of it and repositioned his hands. Then he arched his back and gave a little hop with both feet close together, bringing them down hard on the sand to attract the bull. The plaza was so quiet Manolo's voice could be heard, calling, *"Toro!* Ahhhhhhhh-ha, *toro mío!"*

The bull, Legado, charged from an unbelievably fast standing start. I swear he charged right through Manolo, but when that concentrated ferocity was past, there Manolo stood. He hadn't moved his feet an inch. The *Olé* that filled the Plaza nearly tore out my eardrums.

"He's going for all the marbles!" Lita said. "After this he gets any woman in Mexico or Spain. He gets Cadillacs. Everything. The works!" Her voice was disdainful.

"What the hell did he *do?"* I asked.

She took the handkerchief from my breast pocket and with her fingers adroitly demonstrated a pass she called a Veronica. "The pass is named for the saint who wiped the face of Jesus on the cross," she said.

Manolo took the fast charges of the fresh bull with a series of five more fluid Veronicas, all terribly close. After each pass and a shattering *Olé,* the bull skidded, trying to stop his rush and turn back quickly. I must have imagined a look of surprise on the bull's face.

Then with a lower, swirling pass I heard called a half, or *media,* Veronica, Manolo stopped the bull in its tracks and walked arrogantly away from it, receiving a standing ovation.

The trumpet called out the mounted picadors and Manolo led the bull to the first horse with a beautiful butterfly-like pass.

"Una buena mariposa! Capote bonito!" said the Mexican expert sitting behind me.

Legado hit the horse so hard that, even with the mattress padding hung on its side, the horse was turned completely around. The picador never got his lance into the bull's humped muscle, and, before anybody could do anything about it, Legado charged the horse again on its unprotected side. An upthrust of his horns into the horse's belly threw it down, half on top of the rider. Again and again the bull hooked and ripped, first right horn, then left, into the kicking horse's hide.

Manolo stepped in close and presented his puny body as a target to draw the bull away from the fallen horse. It was a wonderfully brave and beautiful thing to see.

Then the picador tried to get to his feet and scramble out of danger, but he was awkward with fear and tripped over his one heavily armored leg to fall sprawling on the sand. Legado must have seen this out of the corner of one eye, and he turned away from Manolo. In a confusion of many swirling capes frantically attempting to distract the bull from the picador, the half-risen horse became the target again and was shoved with a resounding crash against the wooden *barrera.* Again the fallen picador was half under the bleeding horse.

A red jacketed *mozo,* an attendant whose function in the ring is like that of a street cleaner, now had a moment of reckless courage. He leaped over the *barrera* and pulled the bull by the tail. He dug his heels into the sand and leaned back, pulling with all his might. When Legado suddenly backed away from the horse, the poor peon lost his balance and sat down foolishly. Then all the toreros rushed in with capes to cut *him* from the bull's view.

Meanwhile the horse regained its feet and, riderless, actually trotted around the ring with pink, ropelike intestines dragging in the sand.

"The horse doesn't feel anything," Lita said. "He's in a state of shock."

Besides, he's just a fugitive from the glue factory. Did you know that the horses are purchased in the States?"

I didn't say anything. I watched the *mozo* and the banderilleros carry the injured picador out under the stands.

"You know what? You laughed," Lita said. "You actually laughed when the *mozo* who pulled the bull's tail fell on his butt." Lita's tone was mocking. "We may make a pretty good Latino out of you yet!"

Chico Vasquez took his turn at making what they called a *quite,* taking Legado to a second mounted picador. Vasquez' movements seemed jerky and uncertain compared with Manolo's. His feet skittered, and his Veronicas were wide and safe.

The big bull hit the second horse, but this time the picador got his lance into the hump and held it there. Still the bull pressed forward as if it were only a pinprick, and shoved his horns into the padded side of the horse. Blood drawn by the lance ran down Legado's black hide, but he didn't flinch. The fans cheered Manolo when he motioned to the picador to ease up on the punishment.

Vasquez had left the ring, and more *Olé*s roared from the throats of the crowd as Manolo did a series of passes in which he withdrew the cape from the bull at the last instant by turning his body and wrapping the cloth around himself. These passes were called *chicuelìnas* and were performed so close that the bull's blood wiped off on Manolo's cape and on his suit of lights.

Legado was tireless. He turned to rush the kid again and again. There was a dreamlike quality to Manolo's classic art, and I still felt it was something more than courage that made him hang in there. The stands were silent while Manolo prepared to execute a different kind of pass.

Five yards away the bull was turning back as the matador held the cape to his hip with one arm behind his back, the other arm opening its now limited folds. Manolo's body was exposed. There was a languid flow of color when bull and man were joined, but the *Olé* was cut off in the first syllable. Manolo went high in the air like a rag doll—all loose arms and legs and upsidedown. *"Aiiii!"* was the animal cry of pain from the crowd.

Manolo fell lengthwise, face down on the sand, but he was scooped up by the bull's horns and tossed over the animal's head again to crash and lie still, his *montera* gone, his head with his shiny black hair and little pigtail cradled in his arms as though he slept.

The Mexican expert behind me said the pass was a *gaonera,* and he thought that maybe a gust of wind had partially deflated the cape, permitting the bull a glance at the true target.

Chico Vasquez and the other matador and the banderilleros ran out with capes to turn the raging bull away from Manolo's prone body.

Then I couldn't see as Lita leaned forward in her seat and cut off my view. Her blue eyes were wide and flecked with yellow and they never blinked. Her lips were drawn back, baring her teeth in what would have been a smile if it hadn't been so twisted. Her jaw worked in little biting motions. A barely audible dry chuckle came from deep in her throat.

I shouted at her, "Lita! For Christ's sake, *Lita!"*

I took her arm above her elbow and shook her. "Lita, snap out of it!"

She never heard me, but her unblinking eyes widened even more, making me look back to the ring.

The third matador had been caught on a horn and was stumbling to the *barrera,* pressing his groin with the palms of both hands to hold back the spurting blood that ran down his pants.

I heard Lita's hysterical cackling giggle, but my eyes were on that poor kid Manolo. He had evidently been trampled. His lavender suit of lights was partly covered with kicked sand. His two round buttocks in his tight pants were shining upward in the bright sunlight.

Capes had been left in the ring, scattered and torn, and as Legado turned again, he hooked one off the sand into the air. Both his horns were stained red, and then, as if to survey the scene of his victory, Legado stood still a moment.

Chico Vasquez made a timid, halfhearted attempt to move toward the great bull and get his attention. Almost under the bull's nose, little Manolo stirred and half raised his head.

The crowd screamed again, knowing Manolo had a better chance if he played dead.

Legado saw the movement, lowered his head, and charged again. His horns went over Manolo's body, but the broad, flat nose of the bull rolled the tattered, bleeding boy over and over.

Chico Vasquez and the banderilleros came closer with their flashing capes, but Legado ignored them. Twisting his thick black neck, he got one horn under Manolo and, lifting his head, had him on it. I could see Manolo reach his two hands down toward the horn where it went into his groin and up into his abdomen. Feebly he tried to hold his body weight off it, but the bull shook his terrible head and the boy revolved on the curve of the horn so it ripped and tore a deep circular wound inside his guts too awful to contemplate. And then Manolo was tossed almost into the arms of his rescuers, a red blotch of what had been a bullfighter.

Four men carried Manolo, making a stretcher of their arms, racing him to the *barrera*. One of his patent-leather pumps was gone, and there was a hole in the bottom of his pink stocking. Then he was out of sight. A doctor and a priest had him now, and there probably wasn't time for either.

And so Legado belonged to Chico Vasquez, but he couldn't do anything with him. Neither could the banderilleros, who got only one stick into him, and that down on his flank. With the *muleta* Chico's feet moved all the time and he resorted only to chopping, punishing passes from a safe distance, trying to get the bull's neck tired and low enough to make a kill and get it over with.

I'd had it.

"Let's go," I said to Lita and looked at her. She still had a crazy, fixed stare in her dilated eyes. The dry witch-cackle still came from her twisted lips. Her face had turned old and ugly, shrunken behind her pancake make-up. She didn't hear me; she didn't see me. It occurred to me to slap her, but I didn't, because she suddenly crumpled with her face in her hands, sobbing. I gave her my handkerchief. But she pushed my hand away and sat up, dry-eyed, looking at me blandly, completely composed. She had sobbed without a tear.

"Let's go now," I said.

"No, Luke, I told you I would stay. I'll stay for all there is."

"Why? Do you call what you do enjoying it?" I asked.

"You can go. *Go!* I want you to go," she said.

I didn't leave without her. I looked back at the ring. Chico Vasquez fixed the big bull on a spot with a neck-wrenching pass and, feigning bravado, turned his back on Legado to face the crowd, but he couldn't carry it off and took a peek over his shoulder. It was a good thing he looked. The big bull started after him, and all Chico could do was drop his *muleta* and run for the *barrera,* diving over it head first, just in time. Lita laughed.

Chico returned, sneaking out of the *burladero* slit with his sword and another *muleta*. Amid the catcalls of the crowd he quickly killed Legado with a cowardly stab in the side of the neck. More cushions flew. Lita threw mine.

The fifth bull was Chico's too, since he was the only matador left.

He urged the picadors to make four very deep and punishing probes with their lances. To the disgust of the fans it took him five sword thrusts and five more jabs with the *descabello* to kill. He got a tired bull for the last one of the day. They said it had been given a physic. He was still trying to kill the bull after two *avisos* when I finally dragged Lita up the concrete steps to the exit.

We left the plaza, quiet and subdued. I got us a taxi for an outrageous bribe. Inside it, with the windows rolled up against the sudden cooling after sunset that comes at Mexico's altitude, I sat back, still reacting to what I had seen but trying to sort my impressions and wondering if I would ever go back for more.

Lita voiced my question. "Well, Luke, you saw quite a show. What did you think?"

"I don't know yet," I said, "but I know I need a drink."

"I'll give you one at my place to thank you for the ticket," she said.

"Not necessary," I said, not feeling good about her and sitting way over on my side of the cab.

"Oh, come on," she said gaily. "I don't hate you any more for acting just like the men do down here about the *fiesta brava.*"

"You're pretty sick with your hate, Lita," I said, and I meant it kindly. "I'll drop you and have my drink at the hotel. Okay?"

"Don't be silly!" Lita said, "Be a good fly-boy and come out of your spin. I may even show you some of my town. It's your first time here, isn't it?"

I gave her a slow grin, figuring, what the hell, a night on the town alone was a lousy prospect. Besides, she seemed all right now.

Chapter 12

LITA's apartment was on the Calle Rodríguez in a good section of the city just off the Paseo de la Reforma. She handed me her key to open a hand-carved, big-hinged door about twelve feet high that opened right on the sidewalk. The huge brass doorknob was in the middle of the thick door panels, and it made me grunt to pull it open.

"How could you ever come home alone?" I asked, leering at her.

"My maid pushes from the other side, wise guy," she said, "but Sunday is her day off. That's really why I asked you to come."

"Just to open the door for you?" I asked, kidding.

"Now that's something I'll bet you're going to try to find out sooner or later," she said. She moved quickly ahead of me across a marble-floored foyer to another, smaller door that needed another key.

I opened this door into a little vestibule from which we stepped down through an archway into a big, comfortable-looking living room. There were thick Spanish wool throw rugs on the waxed squares of a red tile floor. To the left was a low five-cushion couch in front of a tile-edged raised-hearth fireplace, and, surprising to me, the walls either side of the entry arch were lined with books from floor to ceiling. The other end of the room was all glass, with sliding doors that opened on a walled patio garden. A horizontally split door near the fireplace proved to be a swing-out bar, and behind it was a small kitchen. The wall opposite was almost completely covered with oil paintings of Spanish grandees, except for two doors leading to bedroom and bath. I used the bathroom and admired the sunken tub that seemed to suit Lita better than those paintings I couldn't quite see her picking out. I guessed they came with the place.

Then Lita waved me toward the bar, saying, "Make us a couple of drinks, like a dear. A martini, very-very dry, will do me."

Telling me she would be only a minute changing for dinner, she disappeared behind the door flanked by two paintings of mustachioed Spaniards. I got some ice out of the refrigerator and built two martinis plus dividends, using practically no vermouth at all, and I chilled some crystal stemware by swirling ice cubes in the glasses on the polished top of the bar. Then I decided the cocktails would get watery if they weren't poured right away or warm if not consumed right away, so I took one to Lita's bedroom door and knocked. I heard the shower stop running.

"A for-dressing drink," I called to her.

It was the door to the bath that opened a crack. Her wet, naked arm came out, grasping. I took it by the wrist, very gently, and put the drink carefully into her hand.

"You are a dear," she said as the arm withdrew and the door closed tight.

Okay, baby, I said to myself, that's one point for you in the game you think we are playing.

I took my drink over to the bookshelves and looked at the titles. There were many novels and a number of more serious tomes, including some history and philosophy. I drank my martini thoughtfully, wondering if I didn't prefer dark rum now and the company of a dark-eyed girl, but here I was with a book-reading American gal who must be a little nutty. It all felt kind of good, though, which proves gin works fast.

Lita came out, showing me her empty glass. She looked great in a black wool dress of simple, clean lines, and with it she wore a bracelet that, if the diamonds and emeralds were real, made her a very successful gal indeed. Her red hair was piled up regally on top of her head. It went with her snotty expression.

"One for the road, Luke dear, and we're off to dinner," she said.

"Coming right up," I said and poured some of the dividend.

She sipped her martini appreciatively, holding it to her lips with two hands and looking at me over the rim of the glass. Her expression was either quizzical or daring, I couldn't tell for sure. I finished my short second cocktail fast.

Lita passed me her glass and said, "I can drink you under the table, if that's how you figure to play it."

I smiled evilly and mixed some more gin and ice, not measuring, and adding only a few drops from the Noilly Prat bottle. I mentally gave her another point and began to wonder how I would score and if I wanted to.

We were feeling no pain when at last we drained the pitcher. By then she had talked about her book clubs and a book on ancient Greek lesbianism she was reading, and also about what she called her career as an actress. I just listened like a good-natured slob, which was what she wanted. When she was ready to go she dragged a silver mink stole half on one shoulder. I tried to help her into it at the door, but she was very self-reliant and not the least bit cuddly. Three points for her now, I figured.

During the cab ride we talked restaurants, and when I vetoed the chichi places, it got so chilly on her side of the seat I didn't get to first base. The evening looked as if it might be a shut-out. But I liked the place she picked. It had a low-beamed ceiling, a stuffed bull's head over the bar, a *mariachi* trio singing and playing out-of-tune guitars. We ordered *tacos* and *mole* sauce. I sent a boy out to find some flowers for Lita, and he brought back a pretty corsage of tropical camellias. Then we began to have a good time. We drank the black beer and had a few laughs. Lita requested several *ranchera* songs I had never heard. One I liked especially was *Tres Días,* for which I tipped the trio. And Lita told me about the styles of the different bullfighters whose names were on the bullfight posters on the walls. I heard about Aruza and Procuna and wished I could see them fight. They had done such things as Manolo tried to do, and lived.

We were drinking our brandy and coffee at about eleven o'clock when the place really began to fill up with boisterous, happy people. Mexicans dine late. But by then Lita wanted to leave.

I told her I was ready to barhop to a half-dozen more places but not the usual nightclub.

"Oh God! A tourist!" she said, and we did look in on a couple of Spanish gypsy joints.

When she finally gave her apartment address to a cab driver, she looked very desirable over in her corner of the taxi. I paid her the usually expected compliment of moving closer. I got my lips an inch from hers, and she didn't move. She sat very stiffly, looking out the window.

I backed off and lit a cigarette. She wanted one too. Smoking filled up the time until the taxi arrived at her door. I wasn't sure of the count any more, but gave her four points to zero for me. It looked as if she had won the game, set, and match; that is, until she asked me in for a nightcap. One point for me.

She asked me to build a fire in the fireplace, which I did, using all the wood there was, while she told me how expensive wood was in Mexico. I didn't offer to buy her any. A second point for me.

Then she said, "There's some good brandy under the bar. 'Scuse me while I get into something comfy."

I almost laughed in her face. She was as corny as the kind of roles she probably played in the movies. The "comfy" line was easily worth two more points to me, and that made us all even. Funny thing, though, I didn't care much about winning. It was just a game.

I stayed off that casting couch of hers. I sat on the thick rug in front of the fire, poured brandy, and placed the two big brandy snifters on the raised hearth close to the heat. The brandy was Domecq Carlos Primero that I knew cost fifteen bucks a bottle in New York. Lita had expensive tastes.

She came out of the bedroom wearing a high-necked, square-shouldered, ankle-length golden brocade housecoat, a stiff, formidable armor, but I wasn't going to give her any points, because she had unpinned her beautiful red hair and she could make it move cleverly when she turned her head. She sat on the rug too, leaning back on the couch about six feet away from me. Gold threads in her housecoat danced in the firelight.

I looked at her with honest admiration and passed a warm brandy to her. She breathed into the snifter and talked. She talked a whole lot. She talked too damn much. How would you score that? I hoped it was still a draw.

Her voice got a husky, dirty quality from the brandy, and she told me about café society in the Federal District. I learned that government officials and the big businessmen were all supposed to have mistresses, because, as Lita put it, their wives were too sacred to take out to commercially social cocktail parties and night clubs. The wives stayed home with the children and servants and came out for church on Sundays or to visit relatives or for special fiestas. Same as in Ruedo. When papa had to entertain in town he required the social graces only a woman could provide; hence the excuse for mistresses, who were something like the geishas to the Japanese. The big deal right now, she told me, was to have more than one mistress—maybe two or three—all kept in nice apartments in nice neighborhoods.

"The girls are not always for sleeping with," she went on, "just to show what a big and successful man you are."

"Who pays *your* rent?" I asked, smiling to take the sting out of the question.

"You bastard!" she snapped back. "What a thing to ask me! You know damn well I'm an actress. I've had two good parts in Mexican films since I left Hollywood!"

"Okay, doll," I said. "I just thought you were protesting too much. I haven't seen your name in lights, and Romirez seemed awfully protective this morning."

"You can go to hell, Luke," she said. She got up and went to an ornate white chest and pulled open some drawers. She came back with an armload of movie magazines, some with Spanish mastheads.

"Look at these, goddamn you!" she said and flipped some pages of leg art in front of my face. The pictures were of her all right, with little on but sequined briefs and skimpy bras. She looked great in both green and brown roto layouts. I guess I seemed impressed.

Lita pushed up one sleeve of her housecoat and let the firelight bounce off the diamonds and emeralds she still had on her wrist. She shook them under my nose and sneered. "Darling, if I were selling it, you couldn't afford it!"

I had to give up a point, because she had me there. "I do all right," I said defensively.

"Like hell you do! I *know!*" she came right back at me.

I must have looked surprised. She laughed at me. Her laugh started deep in her throat and ended in the kind of giggle that upset me.

"Romirez is a big gossip," she said, still giggling. "He told me all about your love life, fly-boy. You don't do any good at all. You're the least-laid man in Ruedo. Why, the nice stable married types down here get it on the side twice as often as you do and three or four times a week at home besides."

We were playing rough and close to the goal line. Probably some penalties should be called, but no points scored. Then I got hold of my sense of humor and gave her some extra yardage by saying, "So you think you have my sex life all tabulated?"

"Damn right!" she said and got explicit. "Once with that stewardess who can't keep her knees together with anybody, a couple of times with a beige dance hostess who is a whore on the side. What a lousy score! When are you going to make a pass at your society-girl secretary?"

My mouth must have hung open. She had the straight dope.

"The Ruedano pilots gossip with Romirez," she confided. "They do it for laughs, and why not? They resent you. They're not about to be your buddies. What did you expect? They could even grow to hate you. But right now they know they need you, so they need some laughs at your expense to cheer themselves up."

"What do *you* do in Ruedo, in addition to keeping up with the gossip?" I asked her, trying to change the subject. "If you're such a big star here, why come down to Santa María?"

Lita seemed a little rattled for a second or two. She shifted her fanny to get more comfortable on the floor and she moved enough to make me aware of a bare leg that got out from under her housecoat. It was a nice-looking leg. But I wasn't going to look at it and give away any more points, not if I could help it.

I turned my back to her and stirred up the dying fire. I heard her say very slowly, "I go down to Ruedo quite often, Luke darling, and *why* is none of your business. Could be that I just like the Hotel Mirado. I saw you there once, at the pool. I sort of hoped you'd buy me a drink that day. We Americans ought to stick together."

When I turned back from the glowing embers I saw that her housecoat had parted below her neck. "Am I so hard to take?" she asked, breathing deeply and stretching her arms.

"Hell, baby," I said, "you're gorgeous and I'm overtrained, too, as you know, but . . ." I looked away. The game I was playing sure as hell fascinated me. Getting back some points was what I wanted most.

"But what? *What?*" Her voice was insistent.

"Lita," I said slowly, "you're kind of mixed up. Maybe I want to be the guy you met once who spent a few bucks on a show and dinner and didn't feel he was entitled to a payoff."

She gave me the go-to-hell smile and said, "All men are bastards, you included. You can't fool me. I know all the lines. *All* of them, you hear? Yours is just a stall to make me hot or something."

"Sure it is," I said and looked at the dying coals in the fireplace. "Sure, that's it. I want to heat you up, because the fire is going out and it's getting cold and you don't have any more wood."

Don't get me wrong. She affected me. It wasn't easy to get up and go to the bar for another brandy. I was glad it was quite dark, or she could have seen how she affected me.

"Don't bother to drink more brandy," she said. "They say it can't really warm you up. It's warm in bed, though."

"Go to bed, then," I said as I sat down on the hearthstone with my drink and leaned back against the warm tiles of the fireplace. "You go to bed. I'll see if they're right about the brandy. One more, and I'll let myself out."

"Goddamn you!" she screeched. "Goddamn you! Come to bed with me!"

I didn't move. She was on her hands and knees. She was like an animal. Her red hair was half over her face. Her lips pulled back, and she gasped through bared teeth. The housecoat fell open all the way. Suddenly she was all over me, wildly grappling with her hands and with her legs and with kisses like bites.

We never made it to the bed.

It was sex without joy. It was like a continuous compulsive scratching of an itch that made the itching worse. It was too much. But at last she slept—or, more accurately, passed out, snoring with her mouth open. I must have dozed off too, because consciousness returned dimly with the sound of a bell ringing. It sounded like a telephone, but it stopped.

The fire was just ashes and the deep ground cold of Mexico's winter came up through the floor we lay on. We shivered together. Then I laughed shortly.

"What's so funny?" Lita asked, waking.

"I just thought of a stupid game I used to play," I said.

Then the bell rang again. Lita became rigid in my arms. I rubbed my brandy headache and listened. It was a stubborn, incessant, pushing ring, over and over. It had to be the doorbell. Lita half sat up, cowering as if the ringing hit her with physical force. In the pre-dawn half-light we both listened to the intrusive sound, and Lita's eyes were strangely unblinking, the way they had been at the bullfight. With one hand she pawed the air foolishly over and over, as if the gesture would make the ringing go away.

"Who is it?" I asked her, but I couldn't get her attention. She couldn't even see me. Her jaw and bared teeth made that biting motion again. For the second time since I had met her I wanted to slap her. This time I did. It brought tears to Lita's eyes, and they ran down her cheeks in muddy trickles from her mascara. She stared into space, grimacing, her hand still making that spastic pawing motion.

"Who the hell is at the door?" I asked her slowly, so each word would register. I caught her hand and held it hard. I squeezed her twitching fingers, trying to get her to snap out of it. The doorbell didn't stop.

"Listen to me," I begged her now." Who is it? Who's got you scared like this? Tell me!"

"Him!" she said.

"Okay, now we're getting someplace," I said patiently. I knelt, facing her. I felt cold and ridiculous without my clothes on. The ringing went on.

"He'll kill you," she said as if she had just realized I was there. Her hand went limp in mine. The crazy look went out of her eyes, and she seemed suddenly composed.

"He'll *shoot* you!"

"Who?"

She didn't answer.

"Romirez?"

"No."

"Who? For God's sake, who?"

"Sagasta!"

The doorbell stopped ringing. The silence was almost worse. Lita had slumped forward, her red hair spilling over her knees. She looked soft and helpless now.

"He doesn't have a key?" I asked her in a whisper.

She didn't answer but rolled over on her side with her knees drawn up, her elbows down, hiding her now shrunken breasts. Her face was in her hands. Her skin was a mass of goose pimples. I put her housecoat over her and made my hand gentle on her shoulder.

Her voice came thinly through her fingers. "No key," she said. "I wouldn't give him a key. I keep changing the locks." Lita began to giggle weirdly, saying, "It's a small conceit of mine, a little hold I have on independence. No key for the man who pays my rent, buys my clothes, and gets me parts in dirty movies. He has to ring the doorbell when he wants in."

"What happens now, when you don't answer the door?" Christ! I had to know.

Lita just giggled.

"Come on, give!" I shook her shoulder. Nothing.

"Will he go away now, huh?" I asked hopefully.

Still curled up like a foetus, she was silent. Then the ringing started again. The doorbell was being poked with short jabs.

I groped my way around the living room to find my clothes without turning on a light. I stubbed my toe. It hurt like hell. My pants and jacket were in a rumpled pile near the fireplace. My shirt and my shorts were farther away, and damned if that didn't strike me funny. I dressed fast, really fast, while the persistent ringing filled the apartment. I felt a chill, and it wasn't just from the icy tiles on my bare feet. I had to get out of there. I stuffed my necktie in my pocket and sat down on the divan to put on my socks and shoes.

Lita had begun to tremble again. I shook her. "Is there a back door?" I asked.

All I got in reply was that miserable hysterical giggle which was more like a dry cackle in her tight throat. A driblet of saliva ran down her chin.

The doorbell rang and rang. I went looking for a way out. I tried the kitchen. No door there. Out in back the patio was surrounded by a brick wall twice as tall as I am and unclimbable. I thought of piling chairs on top of a table to get over it.

I went back inside to the bar and took a long pull direct from the brandy bottle. The bottled courage was running low too. I put a cigarette in my mouth but I didn't dare light it because maybe he would somehow see the flash of a match.

All of a sudden I realized that the ringing had stopped again. I was surprised to see Lita sitting up on the couch, looking quite normal. She had her housecoat on.

"Give me a cigarette, Luke," she said.

I carefully lit two and handed her one. She seemed relaxed. My hand shook, and she noticed it. Her eyes were mocking.

"Have you got a gun, Lita?" I asked.

"No," she said, but her eyes moved toward the bedroom door. Those pale blue china-doll eyes gave her away.

I went into the bedroom, and it was lighter in there. The windows had thick iron grillework bolted in place. No escape. I went through her night table. I found a small bottle with a prescription label, unscrewed the cap, and looked in it. It was half full of red capsules. I recognized them: Seconal. I had used them myself once for the twenty-five-mission shakes when sleep had seemed impossible. I put the bottle back on top of a little rubber finger cap. So she took them rectally. I guessed they were strong enough for lonesome nymphomania too. I hoped Sagasta would remember she was on the stuff. I wished he would take one. No, two. The ringing filled my head. I opened bureau drawers, poking through stacks of silk and nylon stuff, and then I found it. It was a .32-caliber revolver. Nice little gun. I broke it open. It was empty.

Back in the living room, I showed the gun to Lita.

"Bullets?" I asked hopefully.

She blew smoke toward me and got back her go-to-hell smile. "Nope," she said.

"I'm going out now," I said, trying to convince myself. "It would be easier if the gun were loaded."

"He'll kill you sure as hell. Sure as shootin'," she said and laughed at her lousy joke. "Down here they get away with it too. Did you know that?"

"Yes, Lita," I said. I knew. I had heard about Latinos shooting each other over girls. A crime of passion, they called it. There was no enforceable law against it. The police apparently didn't feel obligated unless it became a civil case, when the family of the deceased decided to sue the survivor for damages. Then the cops would go looking for the killer, usually after he had gone on a vacation across the border until his family could make a reasonable cash settlement out of court so the whole matter could be dropped. Yes, I knew that walking out into the Calle Rodríguez from the door of Sagasta's mistress's apartment was not calculated to be good for my health, not with him standing out there, very likely armed.

I waggled the pistol under Lita's nose. "No bullets?" I must have sounded kind of pathetic.

"Poor baby," Lita said. "Honest, I don't have any bullets. I wish I did, for your sake. For my own sake, I wish you could bump off that bastard!"

I didn't believe her. The doorbell started ringing again. He was leaning on it. Then it stopped again.

"You're wasting your time," Lita said. "I don't have any bullets for the gun. But I think it's safe to go now."

"How do you figure that?" I asked.

"I think he's gone now," she said, sort of thinking aloud, convincing herself. "After all those tries at the doorbell without getting an answer, he's got to give up, especially with his chauffeur out there in his car watching him. Sagasta can't let himself look like a fool, not in front of a servant. Word might get around that the big man is not the great lover, that he can't control his woman. Imagine what a story like that would do back in Ruedo, where people still flinch at the mention of his name. No, he won't hang around any longer. Not now. There's a little hotel near here with an all-night bar. That's where he will go. I think he will send his driver to a whorehouse to get him a girl and make a show of not giving a damn about me."

"So all I have to do is walk out of here," I said, looking at the empty gun in my hand.

"Sagasta will drink a double brandy," Lita went on, "and a lot will depend on whether or not somebody saw us together and told him. Even so, he won't let himself believe I'm out all night or that I have a man here with me. Too much ego. He will eventually assume I'm doped up and way past waking."

"You didn't seem too worried about being seen with me," I said.

"Oh, that's nothing," Lita said impatiently. "Fermín is very worldly, quite sophisticated, within certain limits. Now, you better go!"

"Okay," I said, backing away, still holding the useless gun.

"Hurry!" she said. I saw her frown, and then she said something that seemed to come hard for her. "Be careful, sweetie."

Before I could make it to the door she jumped up, grabbed me, and held me. Her body shook against me. "Luke, oh, Luke," she sobbed. "I didn't think I'd get you into something like this. Honest! He hardly ever comes here. He never came here before when Romirez was in town. They always talked politics all night. Believe me!"

I got loose and went across the living room fast. I looked back once and saw her face fixed in that wild, open-eyed trance. She was going to seesaw back into hysterics. That awful giggle started again.

I went out the door into the foyer and swiftly, on tiptoes, crossed the marble floor, and stopped dead at the big door to the street. The thought crossed my mind that this would be a crummy way to end up, shot full of holes on a street in Mexico where nobody knew me, where nobody would give a good goddamn.

Quietly I slipped the bolt back and braced myself to push the heavy door open. I knew he was still there—or had come back. I had only *hoped* he wouldn't be there, kidded myself into accepting Lita's explanation of his actions. Why should she care if I got it? I remembered how she had actually enjoyed it when the bullfighters were ripped open. How did I ever get mixed up with this crazy, sick dame anyway? *Jesus!* This was it. This was for goddamn sure and finally *it!*

Unless I came out very fast, unless I came out as a sudden surprise to him, unless I could get the drop on him with my empty gun, it would . . .

Then I *was* out. I was out in the middle of the sidewalk, waving the damn pistol around in the quiet gray dawn. The street was empty.

I laughed like a loon, but I was still so scared I ran three whole blocks before putting the gun in my pocket and slowing to a walk.

Chapter 13

I HOPED to get a couple of hours' sleep before going out to Aeropuerto Central and organizing the return flight, but I was awakened by a key turning in my hotel-room door.

"Go away!" I said, thinking it was an overzealous chambermaid, but the door opened and two men came in.

They were swarthy characters in identical dark pinstripe suits. They had pearl-gray snap-brim hats on. Both wore conservative light gray neckties on blue-black shirts and looked so much like movie gangsters I couldn't quite believe in them. However, the Luger automatics they showed me had a believable quality.

"*Buenos días,*" one of the gunmen said cheerfully. "You come with us!" His accent in English was terrible.

"*Por qué?*" I asked him why in Spanish to make it easier for him.

No answer.

"*A dónde?*" I asked him where.

He answered that. "*A la casa de* Fermín Sagasta." He gestured toward my clothes with his gun.

I felt awful to be caught after thinking I'd escaped Sagasta. The silent one kept his Luger pointed at me casually as I got out of bed and numbly reached into my B-4 bag for a clean shirt. I was careful to keep my hands in plain sight. When I peeled off my pajamas, they both began laughing. Something was a real knee-slapper. In the mirror I could see what was so humorous to them. There were two red welts on my collarbone from sucking bites, and my back was a mass of scratches.

"*Muy hombre!*" the talker said to the other one, and damned if I didn't feel a little proud. They joked together about passionate Mexican girls. I supposed Sagasta didn't have to tell them why he wanted me picked up.

I put my jacket on and reached into a side pocket for my cigarettes, but the quiet one got hold of my wrist and went into the pocket with me. His hand came out with Lita's empty .32. He made clucking noises and shook his head as he broke the pistol open, found it empty, and tossed it into my B-4 bag.

"A very small pistol and empty," the talker said. "My friend, you are loco to try to take us with so little gun."

They looked at me with mixed amusement and admiration. I knew it would do no good to tell them I had forgotten the gun was in my pocket, that all I wanted was a smoke.

They took me down the hall, one on each side of me. They were short men, and there was a moment before the elevator came when I thought I could bang thir heads together, but I went out of the hotel like a lamb being led to slaughter. All I could think was that this was a mess, a stupid, unnecessary mess, and I hoped Sagasta had the sense of humor his gunmen had.

They made me sit in the middle of the front seat of their long black Cadillac. The talking one drove. The quiet one crossed his arms so that his Luger pointed downward at my guts. The sun had risen, and the big car rolled smooth as silk through the city's morning traffic of trucks and burros. The gunman who was driving chattered almost like a tourist guide about the new modern buildings of Mexico which his country, Ruedo, was copying in Santa María. So they were Ruedanos and not Mexicans.

We did a lot of turning and climbing. I was told that we were in Chapultepec Heights, which was called Little Hollywood. Then we stopped at a gate in front of a curved drive leading to a Spanish-style mansion.

A gatekeeper unlocked the iron-spiked gates, and we drove in.

"Welcome to *la casa de* Fermín Sagasta," said my guide.

"It is very impressive," I said and meant it. There was a swimming pool beside the house, a greenhouse and stables too.

"It is nothing. You should see the villa in Puerto del Sol!" he said proudly.

The quiet one opened the car door, and I was beckoned to follow him past another Cadillac parked in the drive. I was taken to the front entrance of the house. They both put their automatics away in shoulder holsters and were so polite I didn't know what to think.

A butler ushered us into a great marble hall with a three-storey ceiling held up by gilt Corinthian columns. I was led up a wide, spiraling marble staircase past fabulous paintings and tapestries, past statuary on the landings, then over velvet carpeting into a huge library. The book-lined, drapery-darkened room had safari trophies: lion and leopard skins on the floor, an elephant's tusks on the wall, and the heads of horned African beasts I couldn't identify.

Lamps were on at the far end of the library. I was led in that direction by the talkative gunman. The other one closed the door behind us and leaned against it. No guns were in sight. Then what I saw was like a tableau. The three people in front of me seemed to have been arranged like waxworks around an enormous mahogany and leather desk covered with expensive-looking souvenirs.

Centered behind the desk sat a big straight-backed man in a black suit, wearing dark sunglasses. He had a magnetism that made me see him first, but from sheer surprise I did a double-take at Lita, sitting to the right of the desk. Sagasta must have come back to her door once more and got her. She sat with her knees crossed, in her tight green traveling suit, looking as cool as she had the first time I saw her. To the left stood Romirez, a wide expanse of loud hound's-tooth tweed over his bulging body. The glitter of his small black eyes was the only sign of life in him. All three of them looked at me in silence for what seemed an eternity but was probably half a minute.

Sagasta broke the silence. "You are most welcome, Capitán Hadley," he said with a deep, purring voice. "I apologize for the early hour. I sincerely hope it hasn't inconvenienced you to pay us this visit. I further regret the manner of bringing you here, Capitán Hadley, and if my *pistoleros* were discourteous, I shall punish them. Please be seated."

He pointed to a straight-backed chair in front of his desk. My legs were so weak I just made it.

"I am Fermín Sagasta," he said unnecessarily. It sounded just as though he had said he was God.

Sagasta gestured again, and Romirez sat down in his chair like a puppet collapsing when the strings are released.

Sagasta turned his dark sunglasses to Lita, who had not looked directly at me for an instant, and he reached over and patted her hand where it rested on her knee. His barely perceptible nudge got her to rise, kiss him lightly on his cheek, and jiggle her fanny out of the library. All three of us watched in appreciative silence. I was in so much trouble anyway, why ignore her? Fact is, I marveled that not a vestige of her hard night showed. With every red hair in place and her make-up on straight, she looked as if she had just left a beauty salon.

I also chanced a look behind me. My silent guide still leaned against the door there, eying the ceiling. The talking gunman had moved behind Sagasta, where he sat on an ottoman and proceeded to clean and oil his Luger.

The silence got pretty heavy. I had time to catalogue Sagasta's desk ornamentation: a model of a Spanish galleon, a Mayan jade statuette of a warrior god, a desk lighter shaped like a cannon, a Damascus dagger—for opening letters, of course—and a gold-framed photograph of four handsome young men. Someplace I had heard that Sagasta's wife was dead and his sons scattered in European and American colleges with their fancy sports cars.

Sagasta leaned back in his high-backed leather chair and, as if signaling us to relax, put his feet up on his desk. They were encased in beautiful hand-tooled black cowboy boots. He waved grandly toward a mahogany humidor, and Romirez took a big cigar and sat preparing the end of it while I stopped holding my breath.

"Again I must ask you to forgive me for the peremptory way in which I sent for you, Capitán Hadley," Sagasta purred. "I have been trying to locate you since your arrival in the city. You left an interesting trail: the Plaza de Toros, some quaint restaurants, the Hotel Reforma."

No mention of Lita's apartment. Not yet. His English had only a trace of Spanish accent, and his deep baritone voice had a hypnotic quality that must have once charmed the people of Ruedo. Nobody looked away when he spoke. He had no nervous gestures to distract you, just a quiet strength and great poise. His hair was as black as a fighting bull's, but I got the feeling that there was a lot of age in him, maybe sixty years, and mostly years in which he had practiced the use of unlimited power.

The sound of his voice swelled up and filled the room to the ceiling, and it ran down the walls of books and it flowed into the corners and under tables and chairs. I didn't pay much attention to the words, because they were only the usual Spanish-style warm-up of excessive flowery courtesy before the conversational main event. I was going to find out what he wanted of me when he wanted to tell me, not before. He would tell me ever so politely. I saw no point in getting fresh.

Then I heard him say, "You are working for me, of course."

I looked at him blankly, and in the gap he gave me I said, "I thought I was employed by the government of Ruedo."

"That is just a technicality," he said.

Romirez, who was an irrepressible laughing boy, couldn't help himself. He guffawed, but briefly. A flicker of Sagasta's finger stopped the Coronel's laughter as though a toggle switch were snapped. We were in silence again. The big man looked at me and waited. It was ridiculous waiting like that. It was demeaning. What did he expect me to say? I thought of him pushing Lita's doorbell and started to fidget, but I didn't say anything. My stomach rumbled. Not another sound. A whole minute went by before I finally opened my mouth and sort of croaked the first syllable of his word: "Tech—"

I was going to tell him that, technicality or not, Romirez had hired me on my flying record and promoted me on my business ability, and what did he mean by telling me I worked for *him?* He must have been waiting for me to speak only to interrupt me.

He did so with another oily apology. "Excuse me, Capitán Hadley," he said. "May I suggest that you learn something about our country of

Ruedo, and that such a study is incomplete—no, such a study is quite impossible without a genuine understanding of Fermín Sagasta. *I* am Ruedo!"

I just blinked at him.

"With your permission," Sagasta continued, "I will presume to advise you, in your own best interests of course, and certainly in the best interests of Ruedo."

Sagasta spoke gravely, as if my whole future and the future of Ruedo depended on whether or not I understood. "You are now the top man in Líneas Aéreas Ruedo Central. You are the *Jefe*. In your own country, in the United States, it is important to be the boss, no?"

I nodded. Who the hell could disagree with that?

"Now," he went on, "you have had a little taste of running things your own way in the airline, and it is a very stimulating experience, is it not? You have grand schemes for developing and expanding the business. That is good. Incidentally, this also tends to develop you, to expand your personality and your importance. Those are the logical and just fruits of your efforts. Eventually, however, such an experience changes you somewhat, not for the worse as some idiots suggest with regard to the corrupting influence of power, but, on the contrary, changes you for the better. Being the top man in any sphere of influence makes you more mature—even, if I may say so, makes you more attractive to women."

I wondered if he wasn't half defending his ideas about himself. And did his crack about women mean I still wasn't off the hook with him about Lita? It was hard to tell. There were only his carefully chosen words and that fine voice. No smiles. No frowns. No eyes to read through his dark glasses.

"As a favor to me," he said, "I want you to keep your position in LARC, but also please realize that it is I who make this position possible. The Minister of Aviation, Coronel Juan Miguel Romirez, is my man."

So that was it. I looked at the Coronel, who, out of uniform, was just so much suet in tweeds being melted down by the big dictator. Romirez was a breed of fat cat that had no political counterpart in my country. He was an official who recognized a chain of command that breached oaths of loyalty to the government.

Sagasta must have read my thoughts, because he added, "However reprehensible you think this may be by your standards, sir, I humbly submit that it is a political fact of life in the way we do things in Ruedo."

I said, "There is such a thing as responsibility to the people, the

voters." I was a little amazed at myself for interrupting him. He was too.
"I am responsible to myself!" he said with finality.

I felt responsible to myself too. So maybe I agreed with him in some basic way. It was a troubling thought.

His rich voice purred again. "After the recent unpleasantness in Europe, there was a fairly general repugnance for dictatorships. This spread to my country and resulted in my foolishly testing my popularity in an election. My mistake was to let the opposition help count the ballots.

"Ortega defeated me and now has four more years of a six-year term of office if I permit him and his idealistic professors to govern my country that long." He said *my* country" as though he really meant it was *his*. "I am spending an enormous personal fortune for the Ortega government's overthrow," Sagasta said proudly. "To me, money is no object. I will bankrupt myself to put Ruedo back on the road to progress and respect among American nations!

"Coronel Romirez is with me. Are *you* with me, Capitán Hadley?"

I wasn't ready for this question. My head was swimming with his sonorous speech. I was so tired. Hell, I was exhausted. I put a cigarette in my mouth and forgot to light it, but I didn't say anything.

"*Un momentito,* before you answer, Capitán Hadley," Sagasta said, covering my silence. "Please be certain your answer is a final commitment. You are either with me—or against me!"

I reached for Sagasta's cannon-shaped desk lighter and stalled for time getting it to work and inhaling a couple of drags. I realized that the very fact that I deliberated at all meant I didn't see Sagasta entirely as a menace. My government did business with Perón and Batista; so what was the difference? I was enjoying my job running the airline. He had me there. It would be easy to say: Sure, I'll go along—that is, if I could hedge a little.

"Señor Sagasta," I said, "there is a lot more I can contribute to making LARC a first-rate outfit, but I want it understood my participation is just a commercial one. I don't want any part of dropping bombs on people. I've had that."

"Ahhh, forgive me, Capitán Hadley," Sagasta purred. "Forgive me if I gave you the impression you would be involved in a military action. You would, of course, continue to take orders from the Minister of Aviation, Coronel Romirez, who also heads the Ruedan Air Corps, but beyond flying certain war material such as the cargo you will carry to Santa María today, you will operate strictly commercial transport flights."

"What war material?" I asked cagily.

"Your conscience can be quite clear," Sagasta said. "After all, you know, even food shipments are of military significance in Ruedo."

That wasn't much of an answer, and his logic was cynical, but so was mine. Wasn't the world full of rich and, hence, respected families whose fortunes were originally based on gun-running to whichever side had the price?

I must have nodded to him. Romirez beamed on me, cleared his throat, and said deferentially, *"El Presidente,* I knew I chose a good man when I chose Lucas Hadley. *Sí,* I know he will serve our cause well, just as the other *Norteamericano,* Michaels, does."

I thought to myself that the Coronel knew us both all right, knew our weaknesses too, but I made a little private pact with myself that Romirez would keep my job on the up and up or the deal was off.

Aloud I said, "It suits me, the way you've outlined it, Señor Sagasta. I want to run a good airline."

Sagasta stood up then and held out his hand to shake. I took the hand and found it strong. He turned to Romirez, and they pounded each other's backs in an *abrazo fuerte.*

Romirez was nearly overcome by this show of affection. *"A sus órdenes, El Presidente,"* he said humbly.

"Now, gentlemen, my only orders are to join me at breakfast," Sagasta said.

I felt so glad to get started on a gallon of coffee, felt so lucky not to have been fired, beat up, or even shot for being caught damn near in bed with the head man's mistress, that I had little spare concern for the decision I had just made to stay in Ruedo on Sagasta's terms.

Sagasta sat at the head of a long table in what he called his morning room. There were four other dining halls in the mansion, he told me, but this one was best for breakfast. I looked around, and it wasn't easy to define where the inside or the outside of the room left off. We were only partly walled in with glass and flooded with bright morning sunlight. Potted plants and ferns hung on chains along the walls. The room blended with a patio and an inviting free-form pool. Lita was out there having a swim when she wasn't posing that fantastic body of hers in a bikini swimsuit. After a while she put on a robe, came in, and sat at Sagasta's left. Romirez sat at his right, and I next to the Coronel. The two gunmen were stationed strategically at entrances.

Pepe Lopez arrived and greeted everyone in the proper pecking order for this deluxe barnyard. He saluted me last and sat next to Lita. I was glad to see him looking so cocky and rested, because he was going to drive the airplane today while I caught up on my sleep. Maybe I would even find out how well the Coronel could fly.

After a few polite comments to the servants about the ham and eggs, Sagasta began transmitting again for my benefit. I had no choice but to receive.

"The *caudillo,* or leader, is an old tradition throughout Latin America," he said. "It goes back in our history of colonization in a very literal way to the men on horseback who replaced the Indians' rulers. It is no surprise to the Indians and to the descendants of the Spanish *conquistadores* that might makes right. It is a completely acceptable idea.

"Our people," he said, able to make that great voice of his carry even while stuffing his mouth with ham and eggs, "are not capable of understanding an ideology such as democracy. Civil liberty is too abstract a concept for a fifteenth-or sixteenth-century people, for that is what most of them are."

Sagasta's dark eyeglasses reflected the sunlight like mirrors, and his face told me nothing of his feelings. There was no indication that he wanted a discussion of his ideas. He was making a speech.

"In a society such as ours, revolt is not always a matter for the underdog. Here it is a concern of the topdog also." He pointed skyward. "And in Ruedo today the topdog is the air power. The alternative is voters— and *what* voters! Stupid *Indios!*

"We are blamed by some of your countrymen, Capitán Hadley," he said softly, without animosity, "for cruelly exploiting our Indian population. We do it. It is true. I do not deny it. But to criticize us for it is unjust. It is perfectly natural for the strong to exploit the weak. Your country did it too, when you foolishly killed off your North American Indians and took their lands. At best, you put them in the concentration camps you call reservations. Moreover, the United States has enjoyed successive waves of immigration. There were the Negroes, brought in chains from Africa as slaves, then the poor immigrant Irish, the Germans, the Swedes, the Poles, the Italians, the Jews, and now the *Puertorriqueños.* You exploited each new shipment of immigrants as cheap labor, and you still do it. They are the ditchdiggers and busboys. We in Ruedo have no immigration problem, but we still have plenty of Indians!"

Sagasta permitted himself a rumbling, room-filling laugh that was contagious. The others laughed too, Romirez the loudest, and I felt a little ashamed for joining in.

"Ortega," Sagasta went on, "and especially his Doctor Vidal, think they can educate *los Indios*. I am sorry for such politicians. In my humble opinion the Indians will only make fools of them by being less productive on the farms and in the mines or wherever they are employed. In the end, the Indians will follow a strong man and turn on that silly paternalistic government.

"Hernán Cortés understood the situation perfectly from the first. His *capitánes-generales* knew that it was not enough to defeat a weak heathen people in battle. It was necessary to destroy their gods, to build a true church on the site of every pagan temple, and to capture their black souls as well.

"Of course, the godless Reds oppose the church. But in Ruedo, Rome is stronger than Moscow. One priest can control more Indian hearts and minds than a hundred Ycaza Lacayos."

That name again. Well, I thought, the congressman's reputation had traveled far. I tried to sort out my own impressions of Lacayo, who had seemed mild enough, and of the Indians. Some softness of my facial expression must have been visible to Sagasta.

"Don't feel sorry for the Indians, Capitán Hadley," Sagasta said. "They were a cruel and bloodthirsty race. They practiced human sacrifice. Before the Spaniards came they had a long history of treachery and ambush in war. Fortunately, they thought we were gods, successors to Quetzalcoatl, to whom gifts of gold and life had been sacrificed for generations. By the time they discovered we were all too human, Cortés had destroyed their will to resist. Their men became docile workers. Their good-looking women became the fertile gardens in which to plant sturdy Spanish seed and swell the ranks of the ruling class, who have always been outnumbered."

I felt I had to speak, but I couldn't come up with a rebuttal, just a question. "How come colonialism remains as a way of life, even though Ruedo has been free from Spain for so long?"

"Look at it this way," Sagasta said. "Countries down here are at a different period of political evolution from your native land, because North America was settled by the British, who in the sixteen hundreds had already limited their monarchs' powers at home with parliamentary government. Consequently your settlers proceeded to set up colonial legislatures for self-rule just as fast as they cleared the land. Spaniards, on the other hand, started colonizing two hundred years earlier in Central and South America, and at a time when absolutist rule was all they knew at home. They simply reflected the same kind of rule in the new world. It is a different heritage." He looked around at what was his, and the look included me.

We dawdled over coffee, and I glumly fiddled with an unlit cigarette. Romirez was surreptitiously eying his wristwatch. I finally got a light from him and then, for the hell of it, passed my pack of smokes to Lita.

"How was the swim?" I asked her. I meant to ask if everything was all right and couldn't tell if she got the message. Her blue eyes were as expressionless as glass buttons.

Sagasta watched Lita tolerantly, the way an older man sometimes will be vastly forgiving of a much younger wife or mistress. Maybe everything was just fine. He told her to go and get dressed.

"Lita is my best courier," Sagasta said to me. "My best carrier of messages between here and Santa María. She is my little pigeon. Soon there will be another message for her to carry back to me, so she must accompany you to Ruedo today."

I smiled and nodded and kept my big mouth shut.

"She was almost as difficult to find as you were, Capitán," Sagasta went on. "But no matter. You will all leave for the airport now. I will say good-by here. When we meet again"—he paused for effect—"it will be at the palace in Santa María."

No wonder they called him *El Sagáz,* I thought.

At the airport, when I checked the flight manifest, I discovered that all passenger bookings had been canceled, except, of course, those we were deadheading—Romirez, Lita, and our stewardess, Carlota. The reason was a five-ton cargo payload for which clearance had already been granted by Mexican customs. Pepe got the weather report and filed the flight plan, so I went aboard.

All but the four seats up front were folded against the windows, and the floor space was jammed with tied-down wooden crates about four feet long, a foot and a half square at the ends. The manifest said it was farm machinery, yet I was curious.

I closed the cabin door. With the machete we always carried, I pried a board loose from one of the boxes. It was full of excelsior padding. I pushed some of it aside. My hand encountered a smooth, round metal cylinder with fins in back. I knew what it was. It was a GP two-hundred-and-fifty-pounder, a general-purpose high-explosive bomb!

Well, I was an ammo runner now. *Forty* bombs! I'd asked for it. How did I feel? Kind of crummy. I put the lid back on the Pandora box.

I didn't trust Pepe with the takeoff, particularly not with that kind of load. I stayed on the ball despite the fact that my eyelids felt like sandpaper, and I got us upstairs and headed south. Then I just had to use one of the aisle seats for some sack time. The Coronel went up front to take my seat next to his incompetent nephew. At that point I would have turned over the controls to a couple of trained apes.

Lita was wide awake, which proved she wasn't human. "Will I see you again?" she whispered.

Maybe I should have said a plain no, but I told her I couldn't because I would be out of town—at the Puerto fiesta. Then I reclined the seat and went out like a light. I dreamed I was flying over an endless landing strip, a kind of heaven especially reserved for pilots.

Romirez woke me with a rough shake of my shoulder, telling me Pepe had begun the letdown for Santa María. I'd had a long nap. What I saw from up front was almost like my dream—the lighted Santa María runway. I took over. "Full flaps!" I shouted.

"Roger," said Pepe.

I wanted to touch down very gently with our explosive load because I had used up most of my odds long ago. For luck, I said, "Hold the left one!"

"Roger," said Pepe.

PART THREE

Chapter 14

WHEN I awoke it was nearly noon on Tuesday. I called room service and ordered a steak-and-eggs breakfast. The telephone operator said there was a message to call Señor Donahue at the United States Embassy. Harry would want to know if he was right about Sagasta's being behind Romirez. I decided to let him wait for confirmation of how smart he was.

Down in the lobby I picked up a newspaper and was about to head out to the taxi stand when I saw one of the Little Boy Blues of the Ruedan Air Corps waving to me. I was surprised when I recognized Pepe Lopez.

"How come you're not flying south today?" I asked.

"The flight was canceled," he said, unconcerned. "The Coronel has commandeered the plane for a special trip."

I frowned and started to move off toward the cabs.

"No, this way, if you please, my Capitán," Pepe said, and took my arm, leading me down the steps to the covered arches of the hotel's loading zone for private cars.

Under the outbound archway was parked a shiny cream-yellow Lancia sport car with the top down. Pepe opened the door on the driver's side and with a sweep of his arm gestured for me to get in behind the wheel.

Pepe ran around the front and then hopped into the other red leather bucket seat. "She is yours, this charming automobile," he said. "Here is a note from our Coronel."

I sat there caressing the wheel and holding the unopened envelope addressed to me. So this was the payoff, I thought, and wondered if it

149

was for what I had already done or for what I was still expected to do. A bribe was a new thing to me, and I didn't quite know how to take it, or if I would.

I read the note: "My dear Capitán Hadley, This little gift is a token of our esteem for your rare qualities, which we are so glad to have enlisted in our cause." It was signed, *"su amigo,"* and with an "R."

I turned the key in the token of esteem and listened to the wonderful Italian engine come to life. I had driven European cars while in England, so I knew how to shove the gearshift forward into first and let her go. The Lancia was a pre-war model, of course, and nicely broken in. There are no speed limits in Ruedo, so I let the engine wind up to over five thousand rpms on the tach as I shifted up through all four speeds. In less than a minute I had her doing close to a hundred and ten on a stretch of good road out to the airport, where Pepe Lopez wanted to go.

After dropping Pepe, I drove over to the hanger to check up on the Coronel's personal trip. Madera had been his destination—an errand for Sagasta, no doubt. Then I drove back to the palace, and there one of the guards took the Lancia to park it in the underground garage. I hoped he would be careful not to load it up with carbon by lugging it with insufficient revs.

I went into my office, thinking I could always return the gift. But that would certainly hurt their feelings. It would also make them question my loyalty. What the hell, I was in with them—up to my neck. Why be a jerk? Keep the car. Keep it. That's what I told myself.

At my desk I tackled the problem that had bothered me before going to Mexico, that of some high costs of operation which couldn't all be explained by our distance from the source of aircraft equipment and supplies.

I fussed and I figured. Maybe, I reasoned, keeping my job depended on my drag with Romirez and Sagasta, but how well I performed on the job depended on me. I could do a good job of work for them on the airline, make it a paying proposition, and then, I rationalized, perhaps my conscience would let me keep the Lancia and not worry too much about who was going to be bombed by those forty GPs I hauled down from Mexico yesterday.

From the available data in the files I estimated that our present DC-3s cost us sixty cents a mile for direct operating expense plus another forty-five cents a mile for fixed expenses. But even after I added allowances for depreciation, LARC's actual costs were higher than they should be.

I knew what money we took in. Our revenue seat miles were way above break even, the way I figured it, yet there were no profits. Why? And how come I couldn't find copies of all suppliers' invoices? Because somebody had to be padding the bills, that's why!

Miss Valdez told me that Señor Martinez was actually in. He would see me, I was informed, if I would go to his office. I went there fast, making a wake of slammed doors, breeze-scattered quadruplicates, and flustered bureaucracy. I busted into his office with fistfuls of paper in my hands.

"Señor Sales Manager or Señor Purchasing Agent, whichever you are," I said with plenty of sarcasm, "I have satisfied myself that LARC can be operated a whole hell of a lot cheaper with some competitive bidding on stuff we buy like gasoline and oil and tires and spare parts and ticket-printing and insurance."

I didn't sit down when he invited me to. I leaned over his desk and pounded the flat of my hand on the papers I tossed in front of him. Martinez flinched. He knew I had him cold—and for more than stealing stamps.

"I have written a report of this whole mess!" I said. "Coronel Romirez will get it today!"

Then, to my surprise, he smiled. "You are making this report of—er—leakage to the Minister of Aviation?" he asked incredulously.

"Yes, and it's not leakage. In plain language it's kickbacks."

Señor Martinez shrugged and smiled again. He offered me a cigar. He was the least worried man in Ruedo. And then it got to me, how naïve I'd been. Martinez was small fry, just the assistant graft-taker. I had hold of something big, something on Romirez himself.

"The information I have goes in my report," I said stubbornly. "There are legitimate ways of making money with the airline."

He laughed at me. "Then you'd better include this in your report," he said, going to a file cabinet and unlocking it with a key from a chain he carried. He flipped some indexed folders and pulled out a photostat, looked at it with satisfaction, and handed it to me. It was a copy of the purchase order and license certificate on the Lancia. It tied me to Romirez with a lovers' knot.

I walked out of Señor Martinez' office without another word. It made me sore to think where the five grand for the Lancia came from. Grafters! Me included. I swore it would snow in Ruedo before I'd ever take that car out of the palace garage.

Back in my office I had both sets of figures typed. They cost-accounted LARC operations with and without bribery, and went into the report. Romirez could take his pick. Five copies were bound in limp leather covers. In sealed envelopes, two copies went to the Coronel's office in the palace, one more to the headquarters on the sixth floor of the Hotel Mirado. I locked another copy in my desk. I decided to take the fifth carbon with me, remembering that I hoped to show it to Celia when I got to Puerto del Sol. It took a while to tear up my bulky penciled original draft.

Feeling very righteous, I left the Lancia in the garage and took a taxi to the hotel.

That evening I had dinner alone in the hotel dining room without even Paco to keep me company. I had learned how they call a waiter in Latin America, by making a noisy kissing sound with the lips. I had learned a lot in the short time I'd been in Ruedo. I could also figure in meters, kilos, and duros; soon I might even be thinking in Spanish, but I wondered if I would think the same thoughts as my bosses.

Paco came to work late, but in time to serve me a brandy.

"Qué tal, Paco?" I asked.

He gave me an answer in a silly rhyme: *"Febrero loco y marzo otro poco,"* he said.

If he was just going to philosophize poetically about the calendar, I thought I should begin patronizing another waiter. Funny thing, though, I was pretty short of friends outside of waiters, bartenders, and whores. I scowled and decided it had been a hard day on everybody, with a dry, gritty wind and a burning sun. There were going to be more days like this before the relief of the rains. A lot of tempers would get edgy before then. It was a crazy time, as Paco said.

Next morning I got up early and packed for a week's holiday in Puerto del Sol. I could stay away that long—and I'd earned it. My dinner jacket went into my B-4 bag, because you never can tell how things will go on vacation, and in a corner was Lita's little empty gun and the carbon copy of my report.

At the airport I fussed around with Fuentes and García like a mother hen. They had to convince me that there had been a thorough preflight check. It's not easy for some pilots to ride in a back seat. I was one of those.

I finally went aboard as a passenger with nothing to do but read all three newspapers. *La Opinión* carried Tass, the Russian news agency, and headlined an editorial against Truman's plan for aid to Greece and Turkey. It also carried election news of three cabinet posts for Communists in Chile, a Red senator in Uruguay, and a governor in São Paulo who was said to be a Communist. The front pages of the other papers made a big thing of Lincoln's birthday. As I read I discovered that Abe Lincoln was as much of a hero down here as at home, and not just among men of color. The cartoons and editorials showed a fine appreciation for the Lincoln ideals. I wondered if somebody mailed *La Hora* to Sagasta. Then I remembered that I hadn't called Harry Donahue back.

I also read about Vice-President Ortiz' speech inaugurating the university classes. The ubiquitous Ycaza Lacayo turned up on the speakers' platform too, as a former honor graduate, no less. He quoted Lincoln: "Let us have faith that right makes might; and in that faith let us to the end dare to do our duty as we understand it." These were beautiful and strange words in Ruedo, and I felt proud, which wasn't consistent of me, but that's how it was.

Apparently no politician could afford to miss that ceremony at the National University, including Coronel Juan Miguel Romirez, who denounced communism and speculated pessimistically on the mission to the United States by Ruedo's emissaries, President Ortega and Minister of Peace Vidal.

I never finished reading all of Romirez' remarks because I was interrupted by the boarding of passengers, all of them young and pretty girls. They squealed and giggled and screamed at one another, acting the way a crowd of twenty girls always does on an outing together. They piled into the seats, some kneeling on them and yelling over the backs. A few began singing happy folksongs. In the States you would have thought them a group from an isolated girls' school going by bus to a dance at a boys' school, but Teddy came up the aisle and told me these twenty girls were all whores being transported from Santa María to the fiesta at Puerto, where business would be brisker the next few days. She tried to make the girls fasten their seat belts, but they didn't pay any attention to her until the engines started, and then they all crossed themselves and said their beads.

At Puerto del Sol's airport gates there were at least a dozen guitars strumming and twice as many song-filled voices to greet the girls. I was made to feel welcome too. The whole town was on a party.

My ride down hill toward the beach was in a vintage '32 Dodge taxi. The driver said he just paid twenty-five thousand duros—two thousand bucks—for it. There were one hundred eighty degrees of play in the steering wheel. I couldn't watch him spin it on the narrow zigzag cutbacks or when he swerved around an unconcerned Indian riding a burro in the middle of the road. I concentrated on the scenery. Each turn provided another vista of deeply notched palisades, rocky coves, crescents of white beach, and shades of water from the deep blue over kelp beds offshore to the coastal turquoise and pale foam-crested aquamarine at land's edge.

Clinging to the hillsides and nestled in palm forests were beautiful pastel stucco tile-roofed homes. A color riot of flowers grew everywhere.

The driver proudly pointed out an extravagant villa on the hillside above us. It had five-tiered patios for its five levels of rooms. Each patio garden was irrigated by a manmade waterfall, the overflow from a swimming pool that was surrounded by Grecian columns and sculpture. The driver said it was the summer palace of the former president. I knew whom he meant.

The El Cortés Hotel was out on a rocky peninsula jutting from the end of a half-moon bay. Native stone was blended with colored brick to form arches and a covered terrace for each room in the hotel. One would be mine for a week.

When I checked in, I was told the room they had reserved for me was in back without a sea view. I was disappointed, but the town was crowded for the fiesta and I was ready to accept it when an officious guy who had to be the manager came up to the desk, did a double-take at my uniform, and nearly fired the clerk on the spot.

"Idiot! Moron! *Estúpido!*" the manager shouted. His accent was a guttural German. "Are you trying to ruin me? Incompetent! *Bruto!* Can you not see this officer is entitled to an ocean view?"

The clerk groveled and dissolved. He ceased to exist. The manager barked orders. Brown-skinned bellboys scurried. Two of them took my bag. My key was exchanged for another.

The manager turned to me, softening his voice to an unctuous hissing. "Capitán Hadley, welcome. I am deeply sorry for this inexcusable mix-up. Half my help has walked out to enjoy the fiesta. If you will be my guest at luncheon, it will afford me much pleasure. I am Rudolph Heinen, the Executive Manager. My friends call me Rudy."

The German had unaccountably annoyed me more than the viewless room had. I looked at him without smiling. He had a soft round face with big soft lips that curled sensuously. His eyes were pale blue, and his silky blond hair was getting thin on top. He wore an immaculate white linen double-breasted suit, and the pink flower in his lapel was fresh.

"I will look forward to luncheon," he said. "We have much in common to discuss. I was a pilot also, you see—in the war."

Without much enthusiasm I shook the short-fingered hand he offered and accepted his invitation, thinking it might be educational to lunch with a former Luftwaffe pilot who might have taken a shot at me.

In my room I found flowers and a huge basket of tropical fruit with cards from Rudy. Then I found an ice bucket holding a bottle of champagne with a card propped against it, also from Rudy. He had worked awfully fast.

The bellboys hung up my suits for me, opened the jalousied French windows onto the terrace, and stood by for orders. Before I could tip them, another showed up. He brought me an envelope. This was not from Rudy. I tipped generously so the word would spread that Room 204 gets service.

Then I read the note. It was from Lita: "I came here just to see you," she had printed daintily, and her room number was at the bottom. Lita was the last person I wanted to see. I wished I hadn't mentioned my holiday plans to her.

I drank some of Rudy's excellent French champagne and washed up. Then I drank some more of the bubbly and went down to lunch.

The hotel restaurant was out on the rocky promontory in front of the building and was completely walled in glass. The tables and chairs were white wrought iron. Double glass tops let you see the flowers arranged on the bottom layer. Rudy waved to me from a window table. He was a feverish bundle of Continental charm, who certainly knew how to order food, and criticize it too. He complained about the wine, so another bottle was brought.

The story of his life was a candid self-appraisal. He had learned to fly at eighteen. But it was not the flying, he told me, that made it for him in the early nineteen-forties. It was the uniform of an officer in Nazi Germany, especially a flying officer.

We swapped some lies about our exploits in the air, and it turned out we hadn't been in the same battles. He told me how he had been shot down over London on a night raid in a Heinkel. He related this without disappointment, rather almost with relish. "Germany was finished," he said gleefully. "I could tell because the food in the British prison was better than our officers' mess. Being shot neatly through the gas tank so I had to parachute down was the best thing that ever happened to me. In prison I could have books, so I studied business administration and hotel management. When the war ended I didn't go back to the Fatherland, and I never will, unless . . . But anyhow, I could go to Ruedo. The Sagasta government welcomed Germans with open arms. Look at me now!"

I told him he did have a sweet set-up.

"But sometimes I miss flying, Luke," he said, deciding we were first-name buddies. "Yes, Luke, I would like to fly again sometime. My good friend Coronel Romirez once offered to put an AT-6 at my disposal here at the Puerto field."

That sounded like the Coronel, I thought.

Over our small Latin coffees Rudy told me how the fiesta was building to a climax. "By tomorrow night, Luke, it will be an orgy. You must not miss a minute of it. Do not go to bed at all, at least not in your own." He laughed. "I am getting a little bored with dark-skinned girls. I hope your airline will attract more American tourists, especially those pretty blond secretaries." He licked his thick lips and leered at me, lowering his voice, "Send me some blondes if they show up in Santa María. Send me the frustrated ones. I show them a good time here and when I get them in bed, they cry."

I said, "How do you like redheads?"

"Marvelous!" he said. "Would you like some brandy? French cognac?"

I shook my head no and said, "There's a redhead here already. In Room Four-oh-five."

His face clouded. "You are making a joke, Luke. Not that one—not with a ten-foot pole!"

"Why not?" I asked, smiling at his obvious concern.

"My God! Don't you know?" He was incredulous. "She is Sagasta's mistress!"

Rudy was up on things all right. I thanked him for the lunch and said I was going to sample the beach.

While I was changing to swim trunks my telephone rang, but I ignored it. I didn't want to touch Lita with a ten-foot pole either.

The Pacific breakers were as pleasant to dive into as a truckload of dumping marshmallows. When I swam to the bottom beyond the surf I saw schools of brilliantly striped fish like those in a tropical aquarium.

Lying on the powdery white sand around Baía de la Luna wasn't allowed to be a dull proposition, either. There were bronzed entrepreneurs who wore straw hats with woven straw figures of birds and fish on them. They would sell you those hats too. And they'd rent you a straw mat to lie on, if lying wet in the sand was not for you. I didn't mind it. The professional beachboys would also rent you a chair in the shade of the palms that fringed the beach, if you wanted that. I liked the sun. They would fetch you drinks, too—the omnipresent Coca-Colas or the fancy drink I ordered. It was made with a fresh green coconut that one of the boys climbed a palm tree for, cut down, and opened with his machete, filled with ice and rum and served with three straws.

The beachboys also organized the rest of the peddlers. One was an old woman in a black shawl who sold reclaimed catsup bottles filled with a mixture of coconut oil and iodine for tanning. I bought some. Two kids had the music concession, just bongo drums and a cowbell, and they sang for tips. I paid for an encore. A man came around with an antique camera on a tripod. No sale. Another rented paddleboards and dugout canoes. Later, maybe. Everybody working the Baía paid the beachboys tribute, everybody except the two sweaty soldiers who patrolled the water's edge with rifles slung from their shoulders. Besides the soldiers there was something else different about this beach that I couldn't quite define. Then it hit me: it was the absence of children and their high-pitched noise. Every other beach I had ever been on had happy, sand-kicking, splashing youngsters. Not this one. The local people were forbidden to swim here with the tourists. I didn't feel that exclusive.

I swam again to wash off the *aceite de coco* and the sand that stuck to it. Then it was the best time of the afternoon on any beach, when the sun is low and most of the crowd gone. I just lay on my back and looked at the terribly blue sky and forgot everything but how good it was to be breathing the sea air and feeling the salt drying on my skin.

I was so absorbed in relaxing I didn't see Lita until it was too late to run. She was walking toward me in a bikini the colors of peppermint candy under an open knee-length white robe. She wore jeweled cat-eye sunglasses and pulled off one of those silly decorated straw sun hats to let her red hair move in the gentle breeze. She was a fine-looking woman. I could acknowledge that now without getting ideas about it. Then she was standing right over me.

"Hello," I said. "Any messages?"

"I wonder if you'll have any fancy patter in front of the firing squad?" she said.

"Is Sagasta going to shoot me after all?"

"Why didn't you call me?"

I ignored her question. I wished she'd go away.

"Luke!" she said. "I'm chasing you. Don't be a bastard."

She knelt in the sand and sifted it through her fingers. It was a studied pose, as if I had a camera and she knew what leaning forward did to the ribbon of the bra she wore.

"I'm not having any, thanks," I said ungallantly.

"You going to use that pitch again?" she half laughed. "I'm on to you. Let's go to my room; no, let's go to your room."

"What's the matter, Lita? Your room being watched?" I said, looking away.

She moved close, damn near straddling me, and she kissed me sensuously—maybe too sensuously, too soon. I don't know what it was.

"No dice," I said.

She was crying. It wasn't just weeping or a theatrical effect. It was a throat-squealing, half-angry crying like a child's. I didn't feel good about having this effect on her, and I wished she would stop it.

She got out a handkerchief and talked from behind it. "Luke, you don't know what I've been through! All my life! I've been kicked around by men all my life. Please, Luke, not you too!"

Oh, *Jesus!* I thought. She asked for it.

"I'm a Polack, Luke," she said softly, as if explaining. "Can you imagine what it's like to be a redheaded Hunky girl who matures at thirteen and tries to have a decent life on the wrong side of the tracks in Passaic, New Jersey?"

"How hard did you try?" I asked her.

"I tried—honest I tried!" she said. "Do you know how many times I've married?"

I didn't want to hear another life story today. "Don't tell me, Lita," I said as gently as I could. "Come on, I'll buy you a drink."

She shivered, as though from a chill, and didn't move. I wanted to get away from her and I wanted a sundown drink, so I left. I looked back once, and she was getting a coconut-oil rubdown from one of the beachboys. She had been dealt some difficult glands to live with.

I saw workmen setting up platforms on the beach for a fireworks display. They hammered and shouted loudly and were happy; it made me feel better just watching them get a kick out of life.

My telephone was ringing as I went into my room. Not Lita, again, I hoped. I picked up the French instrument and said, *"Hola! Dígame."*

"Capitán Hadley?" a voice asked, a girl's voice but not Lita's.

I felt a frown crease my face. "Yes, Captain Hadley speaking," I said gruffly.

"This is Celia Vidal. Hi! Do you like Puerto del Sol?"

Her voice was slightly hoarse, as if she had a cold, which was why I hadn't recognized it right off, but it still had some of its whispery soprano. Somehow her question made me really see Puerto's gemlike beauty beside the sea, and I wasn't frowning any more.

"It's a paradise," I said. "For the people who live here, heaven must be an anticlimax."

"Oh, you are right," Celia said.

Her cracking voice was so young and cheerful that I wanted to hear more of it. I hoped she hadn't caught cold. I said, "You okay? You sound . . ."

"I've been screaming at everything in the fiesta," she said. "I haven't stopped talking for a minute. And I shouldn't have called you. It was an impulse. I should have waited for you to call me."

"I was just going to call you," I lied. "I was going to ask the operator to find your aunt's number." Maybe I would have called her eventually. I don't know. Then there was one of those funny silences that can develop in a phone conversation.

"When may I see you? Dinner tonight?" I asked. "I have something to show you," I added as an excuse. I meant the LARC report.

Celia Vidal made eager noises about tonight. First she suggested the bar at my hotel for a meeting place, and I had a quick horrible vision of a scene with Lita there, so we got around to making a date to meet at a café in town in an hour. I supposed I wasn't too welcome at her aunt's villa.

"The Café La Ronda is right on the Plaza Pacífica," Celia said. "You can't miss it. It is a good place to watch the fiesta pass by."

Yes, I thought, it would seem as if we had met accidentally. We said good-by, and I went into the bathroom and showered. And then I had a small debate with myself about shaving again. It wasn't as though this were going to be a heavy date. I let the chin-scraping go and climbed into my tropical suit.

I looked at my watch. There was something about that secretary of mine. I remembered that Celia had been swell to have around the office, with wonderful dark eyes and a smile that made me smile recalling it. And she was a big help to me. I actually liked her, that was it. She liked me too, I guessed, but I was Captain Hadley to her—her boss, nothing more. Okay.

I dug into my bag for the copy of my report on LARC operations, bent the bound tissue carbons, and forced it into my side coat pocket. Something for Miss Vidal and me to talk about.

The café was like those in Paris that spill out on the wide sidewalks with little marble-topped tables, all packed closely together. It was overhung with paper lanterns and jammed with a festive crowd. I got some attention from the headwaiter, maybe because I was taller than most of his waiting customers and so obviously a *Norteamericano* who would have plenty of pink duros to bribe him to bring a table from inside and plant it among the others near the edge of the sidewalk. When that mission was accomplished, I sat down with a frozen daiquiri and watched for Celia to appear.

I spotted her before she saw me. She was wearing a pretty white dress. Her face, her bare arms and legs were that cinnamon tan I remembered. Her short black hair had a windblown look, but as though the wind cared very much what it did to her. I could see her large, almost black eyes searching the tables for me. I stood up, and her eyes became more alive.

I went toward her. She held out both hands in greeting. I took them and, not planning to, I held her hands tightly and pulled her close and kissed her lightly on the cheek. I was just that glad to see her.

I know she was surprised by the kiss, and so was I. Our hellos were kind of breathless. I think she said, "Hi!"

Back at the table, we just looked at each other; I smiling foolishly, and she smiling the loveliest dimpled smile with a mouth large enough not to need exaggeration by her lipstick. I was suddenly conscious of still holding one of her hands and let go.

"Daiquiri?" I asked her.

"Yes, love one." she said.

I couldn't catch a waiter's eye and didn't want to make that ridiculous kissing sound, so we talked. Just talked. Again, did I like Puerto del Sol? Yes, I liked it very much. And wasn't the fiesta madness? Wait and see! It would be *fantástico!* She told me that this was really the summer season, now, in February. Winter was the rainy season, which would begin next month. I told her that there must be millions of guys in the States who would change places with me even if they had to abscond with the money to get here; even if they got caught and shipped back to jail in a week, they would think it was worth it.

Celia told me about the fireworks we would see later, an annual display of rockets down on the beach.

No waiter came to our table, so I got up to go after the drinks. On the way to the bar inside the cafe I went into a telephone booth and called Rudy at the hotel to ask him the best place to watch the fireworks, the best place with a girl. He said that the most fun was from a boat out in the bay, and he offered to reserve two seats on a launch that would leave the dock at nine. To be sure, the launch had been sold out for weeks, but Rudy was a fixer. I was not to worry. We could expect to dine on the boat.

Then I brought our daiquiris back with me to the table. We talked some more, but Celia still called me Capitán. I didn't really mind that. I was having a wonderful time.

She got her sweet voice back and really talked quite a lot. I listened happily with my elbow on the table and my chin in my hand, and I looked at her. Her face was marvelous—so animated, so expressive. Her eyes and her lips showed the emotion of each passing thought, and what I liked was the way it was all focused on me. I swam in the effect of it.

"I am glad I can make you smile, Capitán Hadley," Celia said. "You don't smile enough. And you have a wonderful smile."

So I smiled, and it was easy. I told her about dinner on the launch. She was as happy as a kid with a surprise and she was very young, just twenty-four. She made me feel younger than I did when I was that age, a dozen years ago. I told her some things about myself, the way a man is always glad to talk about himself to a girl who will listen. But the story of my life she got was the expurgated edition. She didn't pry at the things I left unsaid.

We drank another daiquiri, and she told me about her family. The Vidals, I gathered, were the class of Ruedo, one of the two hundred Spanish colonial families that had a couple of centuries' head start on our DAR. Celia had a nice comfortable feeling about her social superiority and her old, old money, of which there was plenty. A hundred-and-seventy-five-thousand-acre *finca* was too big for me to imagine, but Celia was no snob. There she was, where she was and what she was, and there was nothing phony or artificial about her aristocratic status. Celia loved her country unashamedly, especially this seacoast town that was her home. She was proud of all the people of Puerto del Sol. It was more than *noblesse oblige*. She pointed out the handsome people to me as they passed by, mostly Indians, come to enjoy a fiesta holiday. These were a clear-eyed people. Their stomachs were flat, their legs straight and strong. They all had hair on their heads. They looked much better than New Yorkers do. Nothing about these Ruedans was flaccid or shrunken or bloated by living in an anthill city.

Celia and I walked to the *embarcadero* and out on the pier, swinging our clasped hands. We found the ribbon-and-lantern-decorated launch. It was about eighty feet long and had a lot of open deck space with tables and chairs for twenty couples. Our table was against the boat's rail, and we sat side by side. White-jacketed stewards served us a supper that was something between a Hawaiian luau and a Swedish smorgasbord. We sampled different cold dishes of fish from a buffet and some hot spiced meats and saffron rice prepared in chafing dishes at our table. We drank a cold white wine.

Celia ate with gusto, unashamed of appetite, tongue playing roguishly with her fingertips that held a wanted morsel, and she delighted in watching me enjoy the meal, especially a dish called *sebichi,* which was bits of raw mackerel marinated in lime juice with onion rings, diced peppers, and chunks of tomato and avocado.

"You know, Capitán Hadley," she said thoughtfully, "I have been a little afraid of you. Did you know that? You are a big *macho,* a very tough guy at the palace, but I'm not afraid of you now."

I wondered if it was my little kiss of greeting that made me seem tame to her and what she would think if I kissed her here and now, so I did it. It was a hard kiss I gave her, with one arm hugging her, a strong, affectionate kiss that I deliberately meant to surprise and rattle her, and to see if she would still call me Captain after.

Maybe I did scare her again, or shock her a little, even though other couples kissed openly during the fiesta. Anyway, she was a lot quieter after the kiss. I was too. I was more aware of the delicate perfume she wore, a fragrance that didn't hide the fine, clean scent of the girl herself.

We watched the fireworks, and they were spectacular. We ooohed and aaahed at the trajectories of color in the black sky and their reflections on the inky water of the bay, and we both jumped back a little at the sudden explosions that echoed from the cliffs behind the beach. It was kid stuff and it was fun.

A little after midnight the launch docked, and there were taxis waiting. I hailed an ancient Packard, and Celia gave the driver her aunt's address. We were driven through crowds of people in gay fiesta costumes dancing in the streets to guitar music and castanets. The taxi just crawled. We sat close together but not touching. We didn't say anything.

Then we arrived at one of those homes up in the hills I had admired when coming down from the airport, a coral-colored stucco building of three levels, clinging to the cliff face below the road and looking out on the sea.

I don't know how long the taxi had been stopped. Celia was closer to me. I don't know which of us had moved. I bent to her and put my hands on her dear little face and drew it to mine. She came closer without resistance. Her hands stayed in her lap. I kissed her quite gently full on her lips. A good-night kiss. A tender little kiss with her lips pushing softly against mine. It was nothing. It was meant to be nothing. But then her lips parted just a little and there was a kind of inward answering, a touch of lips so exquisite with sensation I'll remember it all my life.

What happened then was proper and orderly. I got out of the taxi and held the door for her. She came out and stood close to me. I was conscious of my bigness when she stood next to me like that, although she wasn't exactly a tiny thing. I felt very protective. There was also a little tightness in my throat. I steered her by her elbow to the door of the house. An old manservant anticipated us there. We said good night.

In the taxi again and headed down the mountain to my hotel, I wished I had said something about another date. I thought I'd better telephone her in the morning, and I wondered how early a phone call would not be too early or too late either. And I thought about the brief kiss I could still feel somehow. I thought about that kiss more than I had thought about a whole night with another girl for as long as I could remember. Then I deliberately thought about another girl—any girl, even Lita, because of what was aroused in me and because everybody seemed to be staying up all night in this town; and then I realized that I didn't want any other girl, that I was oddly happy the way I was and didn't want anybody else to intrude on that feeling.

Chapter 15

FIRST thing I did next morning, when the operator woke me from a dreamless sleep, was to ask for the manager. "Rudy," I said when he came on, "thanks for arranging things on the launch last night, but they wouldn't let me pay for anything. They said it was taken care of. Nuts to that. I want to pay my own way."

"Not a chance, Luke," he insisted. "You are my guest all the time you are in Puerto."

"Listen, you damn Kraut," I said good-naturedly, "I want to ask more favors of you, but not unless I can pay for them. I want some help right now, so put everything on my bill. Understand?"

When I finally got Rudy to agree to my terms I asked him to find me a car I could rent, also to line up a charter boat for deep-sea fishing tomorrow afternoon and to reserve an outboard skiff, one I could run by myself, the following day."

"Anything else?"

"Well, if it's not too much trouble, tell the kitchen to go all out when I order a picnic lunch sometime."

"But of course. And for two?"

I could almost imagine the leer on his face so I said, "Go to hell, Rudy, she's not your type."

He told me confidentially that Sagasta's redhead had booked space on the afternoon flight to Santa María. Good, I thought, and when I sent for the valet to press my white suit I found the carbon of my report still in the side pocket. I was about to throw it into my B-4 bag when I remembered how nosy Rudy Heinen was. So I took the report downstairs and saw it sealed and locked in the hotel safe.

After that I got acquainted with the ten-year-old Plymouth coupe Rudy had found for me, and drove it down to the market place. Humanity was so thick there I had to get out and walk in the cobblestone street. It was a nice crowd to be in, elbow to elbow, without needing to shove. I loved them all, their gentle courtesy, their coarse noises, their spicy smells, their bright clothes of primary colors. The *vaqueros,* down from the high mesa country in the direction of Matanzas, looked just like cowboys at home wearing tight denim pants low on their hips and colored shirts and neckerchiefs. Only their hats were different, flat-topped wide-brimmed Spanish Cordoban style. They rode their fine horses everywhere. Other men were wearing fancy long-sleeved shirts outside their pants called *guayaberas,* with many pleats and embroidery so stiffly starched that the shirts stood out from a man's naked chest and let the cooling breezes get underneath. I tried to buy one in a shop, but none had sleeves long enough. The shopkeeper promised to make me a couple in less than twenty-four hours, so I ordered them and learned they were considered formal dress when buttoned to the top and worn without a tie. I also bought a wide-brimmed straw hat, the kind the Indians wore. It worked like an umbrella in the sun.

Many women were dressed in peasant blouses and full round skirts with hand-blocked primitive designs. Some shopped while balancing baskets or white enamel washbasins on their heads. You could see what they had purchased—mangoes and melons, sweet cakes, sometimes a couple of dressed squab or a fish. Many carried babies easily on their hips. Hundreds of little kids were underfoot, each with a cooky or piece of fiesta candy. Happy kids, well-loved kids.

The market spread over three crowded blocks converging on the Plaza Pacífica. Many of the shops spilled out across the sidewalk into the street, and wonderful smells were everywhere. The pungent aroma of coffee getting a deep roast competed with the sweeter essence of cooking chocolate, but six steps nearer a fruit stall I could sniff only the fragrance of hanging stalks of green and red bananas and plantains. A dozen steps farther on were hemp rope in coils, and leather saddles, harness, and sandals with their special odor. Beyond was the scent of grated coconut and then the new-mown-hay smell coming from a rack of handmade straw brooms. The overpowering spicy reek of fresh-baked bread stopped me, and I picked up a small loaf. Following my nose next door, I bought some smoked sausage. I found a place to buy cold beer in bottles, and, of course, rum. I used an American dollar for the rum; it bought three bottles, and I received change. Man's inhumanity to man is carried to its most awful extreme in United States liquor taxes.

I walked with my bundles past a place where fowl were sold alive and slaughtered to order because there weren't many stores with refrigeration. I stopped beside the cool, sweet breath coming off the cart of a vender who sold crushed ice in paper cones. It was a great penny's worth made with pineapple and orange juice, sugar, and coloring. I saw fresh eggs in wire baskets packed with straw, pyramids of fruit and vegetables arranged in abstracts of color—green limes, red tomatoes, purple onions, peppers of all colors, white garlic bulbs, orange carrots. Packaged or canned goods were scarce. Dried beans were measured out in baskets, rice from burlap sacks, sugar-cane stalks were sold by the foot. Nobody would starve here, not even the flies.

Before getting back to the car I found a telephone in a *cantina,* and giving the Vidal name was enough to get the call through.

After some palaver in Spanish with a maid, Celia came on.

"Capitán Hadley! How nice! Good morning!" she said.

"Good morning, Celia," I said. "Did I get you up?"

"Oh, no. Tía Felisa and I have been out shopping already. There are so many interesting things to buy during the fiesta. We saw you on Avenida del Sol."

"You did?" I said inanely.

"I pointed you out to my *tía,* and she thinks you are very handsome. *Muy guapo* is what she called you, and she said you are very attractive to women, a terrible type to have for a husband." Celia laughed then.

I didn't think I was a terrible type for a husband, though I'd had a bad experience at it. Then I said, "Celia?"

"Yes, Capitán?" She still wouldn't call me by my first name.

"Celia, I understand that tonight is the night the fiesta busts wide open and that a girl without an escort has a rough time. Would you and your aunt be my guests for dinner and watch the parade with me?" I was amazed at my own voice, like a boy's, asking for a date so tentatively.

"That is very sweet of you, Capitán," Celia said. "I'm sure my aunt will be delighted. I am too."

"And tomorrow? I made some plans for tomorrow," I said so damned eagerly. "I'll tell you about it when I see you. And I got hold of a car. What time shall I pick you up tonight?"

"About six-thirty, Capitán. *Mil gracias.*"

I switched to Spanish too. *"De nada,"* I said. *"Seis y media."*

I was in high spirits when I went back to the old Plymouth. I drove out of town to do some sightseeing, dodging around lumbering ox carts with squeaky solid wooden wheels. When I ran out of cobblestone road, I followed a narrow, twisting dirt trail north between some farm land and the sea cliffs. It led along the ragged contours where the land lost or won its battle with the ocean. Up a rocky cactus-covered slope, I ran out of road entirely.

I got out of the car and scrambled up, beyond the cactus, through a jungle of palms to a clearing on some high ground with a view that surrounded me like a friendly hug, an *abrazo*. I breathed deeply and had a crazy idea. It was the one spot in the world to build a house.

It was tropical, yet without dampness, or hardly any, and no mosquitoes. The sea here, from all I'd heard, was a fisherman's dream of heaven, and it would be at my doorstep with no tide changes to wait for, no temperamental winds to louse up a cast or drive the fish down.

I wanted to walk in all directions at once to inspect my property. The rock-buttressed land held the sea at bay with a point into the breakers making a protected cove, a snug harbor, on the north side. About three miles straight across the water was another land spit pointing south, an island or peninsula, I couldn't tell which for sure, but it formed a lagoon assuring calm seas.

I circled all the land, a half-running survey. Then I sat down and put a cigarette in my mouth. With a stick I scratched the outline of a house on the dirt, brushing away pebbles for more drawing room, erasing here and there, and finally getting it right in relation to the land.

For some unaccountable reason I suddenly remembered the time when Cynthia and I were living together in an apartment in Westchester. It was winter, and we had to bang on the radiator to signal the janitor for more heat. I had dreamed then of getting away from that and coming down to the Caribbean someplace if only I could get a flying job there. But when I suggested it to Cynthia, she ridiculed the idea. Impossible, she had said. She wouldn't think of living with those savages. Or it was too hot. Or there were bugs and snakes. That was supposed to be the end of a henpecked husband's dream that violated rule number one of the American Housewives' Protective Society: There Is No Escape.

But here I was.

I walked to the edge of the little cliff and breathed deeply. I'd made it here. I was free. No, I was home. Home free.

The cliff down to the little crescent of trackless white sand was steep and rugged. When I got down, I envisioned having stone steps with hairpin switchbacks to reach from house to beach. I kicked off my loafers and felt the powdery sand with my toes and, so absolutely alone there, I dropped my pants, shorts and shirt in a pile and headed for the water. I swam far out. I rolled on my back and looked toward my sheltered beach and safe high ground where my house could hug the rocks and nestle in the shade of tall palms. I felt so good I wanted to shout and sing.

Back on the beach, skin tingling with salt, I pulled on just my pants, rolled them up, and went barefooted back to the car, where I picked up the beer, bread, and sausage—also my straw hat. I ate hungrily at the place where my crude attempt at architecture was scrawled in the dirt. I stayed there all afternoon and daydreamed about my house.

The best way to do this, I found, was to sort of go through a day in it. I imagined waking up with a high-beamed ceiling over me, the morning sun streaming in through modern high windows facing east with a view of the mountains. The walls of the bedroom would be bleached native mahogany, and the bed frame would be the same material and huge, made by local artisans who still knew how to carve wood. In no direction would my six-foot-four-inch body be deprived of room to stretch out. Beside me would be my still sleeping woman, and maybe my foot would touch hers to wake her and she would roll into my arms. I would marvel at the splash of her black hair on the pillow, the length of her eyelashes on her cheeks. My daydream mixed me up because the sleeping girl I saw, filled with pride in her, looked like Celia. It was *our* house in my daydream, but damn it, I hadn't started out to think about the house that way. And my feelings for this girl I hardly knew didn't make sense. I was frankly puzzled, but amused too. Had I fallen in love? Hadn't I made up my mind to be against that?

I smoked and poked at the house plan on the ground with a stick, made myself think hard about the house—just the house—trying to work my way out of the bedroom.

Cynthia and I never had the house she dreamed of. She somehow failed to make me see it and want it. But now look at me. Now I could think in terms of walls and a roof and things in a house, even drapery fabric if it came to that. It was a different sort of house in a different place at a different time, that's all. I even felt a little sorry for Cynthia, and it seemed too bad, the way things worked out. Oh, hell! The house! Concentrate on it, I told myself.

I had planned it as a rectangle, walled all around on the outside, open in the center, with a sunlit patio and small swimming pool in the middle. The pool would be that fine mosaic tilework that nobody could afford in the States. And it would be fed by a fountain with a sculptured mermaid, a sea nymph with good breasts, stained green by algae. Around the poolside would be the loggia's columns and arches supporting a contemporary steep dihedral roof, its wing span covered with old Spanish roof tiles, the interlaced, curved terra-cotta kind. Walls would be white plaster silhouetting black wrought-iron grillework. Shade plantings of cool green would grow under the arches the way I had seen them in Palmas, and three or four leaning coconut palms would grow inside the patio, reaching higher than the roof. Floors would be pleasing mixtures of flagstone, terazzo, and big square tiles. The living area would be an L, with the living room in front, facing the splendid Pacific sunset. The kitchen would be handiest in the corner, with a bar, of course. The house could grow around the loggia on the west side if we wanted it to.

Wait a minute! I said to myself, pausing at "we" and plans for expanding the house. Did I mean for kids and servants, a whole family ménage? Take it easy, Luke, I told myself.

I tried to think of practical problems such as getting the road extended, of some trips to Miami for engine overhauls, when I could arrange to smuggle in good electrical appliances; and, like the Chinese Juan Yick, I would probably need to run my own electric generator. My daydream bogged down in the worrisome consideration about whether or not there was good water underground for a well.

The sun was beginning to swing down toward the ocean when I left my sketch on the sand and went after the rest of my clothes on the beach, then back uphill to where I had left the car. I was unscrewing the cap on one of my bottles of rum when a brown-skinned Indian in what looked like white pajamas materialized from behind a cactus bush. Under a wide-brimmed straw hat like the one I wore, he stood absolutely motionless, saying nothing, but smiling. I had heard that the *bandidos* in the back hills of Ruedo were like him, smiling robbers and killers.

I couldn't think of anything to do but hold my hand out toward him with the bottle in it and smile back at him with all my might.

"*Gracias,*" the Indian said and took the bottle, up-ended it, and let a long gurgle of the stuff go down his throat.

When he passed the bottle back I took a big drink and didn't wipe the bottle first, which would have been insulting, and besides the alcohol was sterilizing. I held back a cough brought on by the straight rum and asked, "*Cómo está?*"

"*Muy bien,* and you?" he replied politely.

I spoke to him in Spanish, "I have been here all afternoon, *señor,*" I said, handing the bottle back to him. "I have come to care very much for this place. I would like to build a house here."

The Indian nodded understandingly and took another pull on the bottle. "It is good land, a beautiful laguna," he said. "I have my *casa* near here, up in the hills with a few goats, my burro, my woman, and my sons. It is good."

Back came the bottle. We were standing there getting fried and hadn't introduced ourselves. I said, "My name is Lucas Hadley. *Cómo se llama?*"

"I am called Curro Aboroa. At your orders, Don Lucas," the Indian said.

"Is there water here?" I asked.

"*Sí*, Don Lucas, but it spoils the rum," Curro said, winking.

"Not for the rum, *amigo*, for my house if I build here."

Curro reached for the bottle and nodded gravely. "*Sí, sí*, Don Lucas, good sweet water, but a man must dig for it."

"I will have to do much work, save much money to build a house here," I said.

Curro was taking another big swig from the bottle as I spoke, and a sudden laugh caused him to lose some of the rum. He got his laughing and swallowing mixed up so that he choked and tears came to his eyes. He passed the bottle back and squatted down Indian fashion, still shaken by deep chuckles. I tried the squat, but it wasn't comfortable for my long legs, so I sat down cross-legged. I bought myself another drink from the bottle, which was nearly empty.

"*Trabajar demasiado es malo*," Curro said. "You *Yanquis* work too much. Is a bad thing. Is not for Curro!" He punched himself on the chest. "I have no duros now, but sometimes I do have them and that is fine, but if I do not have them, it is all right. There is nothing I need that duros can buy except a new shirt and new fishing line, but soon the goats will have young and I can sell one."

Curro shook his head sadly. "*Yanquis* work hard all year to have some money for a few days in Puerto del Sol to fish and lie in the sun. I do not understand this thing," he said. I thought he understood very well, because he winked extravagantly and added, "I live in Puerto del Sol all year, Don Lucas, and can fish and lie in the sun without working."

Together we looked at the laguna, and we both knew he was right, but I knew I would still have to work to get the money for my house, and that it would cost even more than money. It would cost me a piece of my life away from there, time spent where I didn't want to spend it. I let out a sigh and offered the bottle to Curro again.

After I insisted, he finished off the rum and pointed with the empty bottle up into the foothills and said, "Where you see that little smoke is my *casa* and my woman preparing supper for me and my sons. As a favor to me, Don Lucas, come and eat with us. My house is yours."

I could just make out the small adobe hut snuggled against the hill-side. "I must see some people in town. I am sorry," I said. I wished I could accept this hospitality. "Perhaps I will see you at the fiesta."

"*Creo,*" the Indian said, nodding and smiling. "You will permit me to offer you a drink at the fiesta, then?"

"It will be a pleasure," I said. "*Hasta la vista.*"

I got into the Plymouth, and he stood watching me start it and back it around to head toward town. Before leaving I leaned out and asked, "Do you know who owns this land?"

Curro's smile vanished, and he spat on the ground. "Sagasta!" he said.

I drove back to the hotel, wanting that piece of land so much, and knowing it would obligate me some more to deal with Sagasta. I spat, out the window of the car.

Chapter 16

THE evening air was velvety soft as I banged the ornate brass knocker on the door of the big Vidal house. A manservant led me in, and then there was Celia.

I stared in speechless admiration. She looked absolutely lovely, and yet untouchable in her old-fashioned Spanish costume. It was an egg-shell white taffeta, yards and yards of it in a full, ruffled skirt that rustled like an intimate whisper with each step she took toward me.

"Hi!" she said, breathing the American greeting in a way that seemed quite special, and she murmured something in approval of my white dinner jacket. Rudy had advised I wear it.

Then I was introduced to Celia's Tía Felisa, whom I, of course, called Señora Vidal. She was a triple-chinned old gal with lots of bounce. Her fiesta costume was a traditional Spanish dress of black crepe, and her black lace fan alone must have cost a hundred bucks.

While I waited, the two women artfully draped their shoulders in long, elaborately fringed shawls and then the three of us were on our way to town in my rented coupe, crowded into the front seat. Señora Vidal, a conscientious *dueña,* sat in the middle and instructed me to stop at the town house of family friends. It was one of the tallest buildings, three stories up from the sidewalk, with three rows of iron-railed balconies etched against chartreuse stucco. Our host was Armando Ortiz, the Vice President of Ruedo, no less, and both he and the gracious Doña Elena, his wife, greeted us cordially. I was a little awed at first, but then proud when Ortiz proposed a toast of gratitude to me for initiating the relayed radio message from the plane about the Palmas bombing. Everybody drank to my health, including the *alcalde,* which is what they called Puerto del Sol's Mayor. I must admit I liked the attention. And I liked the way Celia looked at me.

Another guest arrived. His skin was noticeably darker that the others'. I recognized the congressman, Ycaza Lacayo. Ortiz greeted him with an *abrazo.*

Lacayo wore a dark, badly fitting business suit and seemed a little ill at ease, but he remembered me and we chatted. He told me he had just flown in from Las Piraguas and commented that the LARC schedules were more reliable since I took over the airline. It seemed to be my night for compliments. I began to think I was getting somewhere at last. It was a feeling that Ruedo had accepted me, a foreigner.

When we were all seated on a wide balcony overlooking the main street to watch the parade, Time was rolled back a hundred years. We could have been sitting in Seville in 1847. Some of the women wore their long black hair pulled straight back and set with high combs, topped with lace *mantillas.* They carried fans for their practical value—either for cooling or flirting behind. Many of the men wore the flat black or gray *cordobés* hats down over one eye, very dashing. But those men looked at Lacayo and me with amused tolerance. Maybe I hadn't come as far as I thought.

We were served Manzanilla, a light, straw-colored sherry imported from Spain. The parade we watched was something between that of a Chinese New Year and a Mardi Gras. Servants handed us confetti and paper streamers to throw, and we watched parties on other balconies contribute to a blizzard of color.

Celia and her aunt explained the parts of the pre-Lenten festival that traced back to the *ferias* of Spain's Andalusia. Lacayo was knowledgeable about the other things in the parade that were pure Indian in origin, the banners of animal figures, including cats, snakes, lizards, birds, and fish—the totems of almost forgotten tribes, tributes to gods from the dim past, gods grown too weak for daily prayers. The women avoided reference to objects carried on poles by descendants of the Mayans, things that were obvious symbols of ancient phallic worship.

Men rode past on some of the finest horses I've ever seen, and some were dressed in tight-fitting suits like those you see on Spanish dancers. Other horsemen in the parade were latter-day cowboys on silver-ornamented saddles, and they could damn near make their horses dance. A few girls rode sidesaddle on the horses' rumps behind their men, with their ruffled polka-dot skirts billowing. Ox carts rolled by, carrying more waving girls. Cartwheels were decorated with colored paper, and dozens of bells in clusters tinkled from the oxen harness. The air was full of gas-suspended green and yellow balloons, Ruedo's national colors. Then came mule-drawn floats of woven flowers of all kinds, thousands of hibiscus, the reds, pinks, and whites, and orchids, gardenias, dahlias, and gladiolas.

To the delight of the children, big-nosed, wild-eyed papier-mâché goblins zigzagged into the crowds lining the sidewalk. These were followed by marching bands with many flutes and drums. Finally there was a scarecrow figure of straw dressed in pants and a shirt and fastened with hundreds of firecrackers that were exploded without warning, scattering the crowds and sending blue smoke and cordite fumes up to our balcony. The blasted-to-pieces effigy was labeled Ortiz. The Vice President's reception ended on that political note. Romirez was blamed, of course.

The Vidals had invitations to the yacht club dinner dance, and I was to be their escort, which made me feel more like a guest than a host for the evening. Ortiz and his wife invited Lacayo to join them at the club, but he shook his head and smiled with very white teeth in his dark brown face.

"No, *gracias*," Lacayo said. "I have been asked by those people in the streets to see the dancing in the park."

In the Plymouth on the way to the yacht club, I asked Celia what she thought of the congressman. Her aunt answered me. "Ycaza Lacayo is something rare, a man of the people in government."

"I have heard him called a Communist," I said.

"I could not say," Doña Felisa said. "But my husband, also Ortega and Ortiz, all those in the new government, believe that many voices must be heard."

Celia changed the subject. "Capitán Hadley, I think I should have told you to obtain a traditional costume for the ball. I hope you won't mind being fined for not wearing one. It is the custom, just a hundred duros to buy fiesta rum for the poor."

From the sidelines in the club's ballroom I watched another carnival *paseo* of costumed people, but these were the gentry, and Celia and her aunt joined the procession of ladies in Spanish dress. There were comic trophies for the best costumes, and I was fined the hundred duros by a genial old man wearing an old-fashioned admiral's uniform of the eighteenth century. There were many other traditional and historic costumes, including an authentic helmeted Hernán Cortés, who marched in with a troop of soldiers armed with ancient guns and swords that were museum pieces.

We drank more sherry, and a smooth orchestra in dinner jackets like mine played tangos. I danced first with the plump Doña Felisa, which was expected, and then with Celia. My tango was elementary, but it was wonderful to hold Celia as close as the tango requires. Other men danced with her too, danced marvelously with intricate tango steps and with the Latin's passionate seriousness. She obviously enjoyed it, and I felt a jealousy which I had to tell myself was stupid.

There was a buffet dinner being served of pâtés, galantines, and roasts, but Celia begged her aunt to let us go to the park and eat from the stalls there. She wanted to be part of the fiesta mob scene and street dancing. I did too. It was finally agreed that all three of us would go to the park.

The Parque de la María Luisa had been a gift to the people from Sagasta, Doña Felisa explained, so the statue of him had not been removed, as had most others in Ruedo. It was a beautiful park with ornate fountains and formal gardens of tropical shrubs and flowering trees. Now it was lighted by bonfires, pitch torches, cookstoves, and strings of gaudy lanterns swinging in the gentle breeze.

Everybody was supposed to wear a mask until midnight, so we were surrounded by a good-natured crowd of celebrants and forced to purchase masks.

I walked between the two women, their arms linked through mine, and I got the feeling that the words "not permitted" that harassed the population at all other times were repealed for the duration of the fiesta. Disguised by masks both real and imagined, the people were acting out a daydream in which anything goes. The poor felt they had become rich. How poor had the isolated rich become? I think we longed to find out, the way moths break out of cocoons and seek the crowd around the light.

The smoky smell of roasting pork reached us long before we came to the deep barbecue pit of burning hardwood and saw the hundred or more little suckling pigs turning on spits. Some older women were ladling a red sauce onto the meat every couple of turns. My mouth watered. We got in line and were each served a generous slice on a dried palm frond. When the *salsa roja* burned my mouth like a blowtorch, Celia laughed, but her aunt told her I was *muy simpático* because I tried the hot stuff.

I liked Celia's aunt. She was what you would call a good sport and she got a lot of fun out of joining in some impromptu round dancing where at least fifty people held hands and circled right and left. But she said she missed her husband, who had gone to Washington with President Ortega.

I goofed out of one of the more complicated folk dances, and Doña Felisa stood aside with me, watching Celia really throw herself into it, holding her long white skirt up out of the dirt to do the intricate footwork. It was a moment of detachment for me in which I could see Celia clearly, and I realized with surprise that she wasn't quite beautiful, anyway not by the standards of illustrations in slick magazines, but somehow I couldn't take my eyes off her. If Celia knew what she had or didn't have, she didn't let it bother her. She glowed. When she danced toward me and took my hands and made me learn the crazy steps of the swinging country dance, I lost my objectivity.

We were breathless and laughing when the music stopped suddenly without warning, the way many native dances did, the way life did. Celia said, "It is wonderful to see you laugh. It is almost as if laughing is new to you. Have you been so unhappy?"

"Not any more," I said.

Celia's beautiful smile was all for me. We went hand in hand back to where her aunt stood. Doña Felisa was making her fan go like a hummingbird's wings, which seemed to signal annoyance. She walked between us to a stand where two old crones tended a caldron of boiling sea water full of lobsters and crabs. Each cost the equivalent of a nickel, and I bought us some, which we cracked with stones so we could peel and eat them with our fingers, dipping the sweet meat in a pan of melted garlic butter that was set near the fire. From a pushcart I also bought fried shrimps, called *gambas,* and we munched them as we walked until we got thirsty and stopped for a cup of pink fruit punch with rum in it.

We were invited into an awning-striped tent by some happily plastered people and asked to join a sort of fiesta society called Los Duendes del Puerto, the Ghosts of the Port. The initiation required us to drink a native red wine from a wineskin spout by holding it high above our heads. I feared for my white jacket, but Celia and her aunt, with more to lose, took the dare. The way they sort of bit off the stream of wine without spilling a drop meant they had had practice. My performance was game but not so expert. The spots on my jacket meant I had to pay for the wine. Our memberships in the Ghost society were confirmed by little silver medals pinned to us with great drunken ceremony, *abrazo* back-slapping, and singing. Before we could leave, a clanging of all the bells in Puerto, tooting car horns, and chaotic screaming signaled it was midnight— unmasking time. But it was not permitted to remove your own mask. I removed Doña Felisa's and Celia's white satin masks. Celia took my black one off. A kiss was a part of this ceremony, but Celia's was no more rewarding than the peck on the cheek her aunt gave me.

When we left the tent, I was glad to get out in the air again because I had begun to feel the day's accumulation of rum and wine. The three of us were kind of high. When we came upon a row of open-air gambling tables, the old excitement was there at the sight of spinning wheels, and my hand was on my wallet right away. In a kind of trance I bought a stack of chips to play a native roulette on rough wooden tables that paid twenty-to-one odds with four rows of five numbers each, plus the usual even money. The wheel was made of cork and spun on a peg inserted in a tree trunk. The croupier shot a dart at the wheel with a blowgun. I won a lot very quickly, which everybody thought extraordinary.

"The money they take in goes for charity," Doña Felisa said a little disapprovingly.

"Some of it does," Celia added.

"Help me lose it, then," I said, giving them handfuls of chips.

I played so recklessly, so stupidly, I was amazed at myself, but I felt the gambling fever break. I passed a crisis through odd, unwanted luck that had to run out, and I could finally walk away from the table with Celia on my arm, feeling it was better to be lucky in love, and I was beginning to wish we could shake the *dueña*.

The carnival crowd was getting even more uninhibited, more profane, more candidly dangerous. We saw a man lying on the grass in a bloody shirt, being attended as best anybody can be after a knife fight. These usually soft-spoken people, these regimented, apathetic people who the rest of the year more or less avoided one another, were very close now— too close. Quarrels caught fire from jokes that turned out to be insults, or from a girl who, having been handled by everybody in the dark bushes, was finally handled by the wrong one. So the fiesta ended badly for some.

The remarkable thing was that the people behaved as well as they did. Perhaps it was because most of their abuses in this annual escape from reality were in the name of love and extravagant brotherhood. The firecrackers that exploded at our feet were thrown with laughing violence, meaning no harm. The joy-shooting pistols just happened to have real bullets in them instead of blanks. Nobody could afford blanks. Too bad old Pedro was wounded. Too bad young Manuel died in an explosion of noise and color that nobody could stop until it ran its course to tomorrow's hangover and the Holy Days.

A marching band of musicians came down the path like an air-clearing storm. It started an orgiastic dance of thickly packed humanity that flowed like a river along the curved paths of the park and into Puerto's streets, a dance going someplace, its destination perhaps a half-mile away, and as completely impromptu as the dancers' choice of partners. We could have gotten on this dance almost as if we were boarding a streetcar, but Celia's aunt disapproved.

Above the singing and shouting I heard my name called—"Don Lucas! Don Lucas!"—and then I saw Curro Aboroa and a huge Indian woman coming toward me.

Curro pulled off his straw hat with a sweep of his arm and a deep bow that scraped the hat in the dust. Then from his shirt he pulled a bottle of rum. Curro twisted the cork loose with his strong yellow teeth and passed the bottle to me. He was sweating; so was his wife, whom he introduced as Marguerita.

I introduced Doña Felisa and Señorita Celia Vidal and took the proffered drink. Indian courtesy required that the men drink first and that no one refuse to wet his lips with the bottle. Doña Felisa faked it, but Celia didn't.

Curro and his wife didn't stay with us long. We were too dull for them, and Doña Felisa held her nose pretty high, sniffing as if *los Indios* didn't smell so good.

"Would you like me to drive you home?" I asked the Señora.

"Yes, Capitán, I am a little tired," she said. "But when I was Celia's age I could always stay up all night during the fiesta."

"May I stay up?" Celia asked her aunt with good timing and a special deference.

Doña Felisa looked at me before replying. It was a searching look. I must have passed whatever test it was.

"Yes," the aunt said. "I disapprove of these modern girls, staying out without a *dueña,* but if I desire progress like the right for women to vote, I must accept other things."

We found the Plymouth, and it had been decorated with colored paper streamers. It was a quick drive back up the hill to the villa, and after we said good night to her aunt and started down the hill again, Celia sat very close to me. I kept both hands on the wheel and concentrated on the difficult downhill turns. Doña Felisa had succeeded in making me feel responsible.

We left the car double-parked, and Celia led me to a narrow street of *cantinas* off the Plaza Pacífica where most of the fiesta had moved. She pointed across the street to a place with a blue neon sign.

"That's the Linterna Azul," she said, "an awful place, from what I have heard. I am not allowed to go there."

We could hear the music out in the street. It was all the sounds and rhythms I had heard in the Club Zerape.

"I have collected many records of the *afro son,*" Celia said.

I looked sideways at her. She was sort of half dancing on the sidewalk —small little box steps with a subtly sensuous movement to the beat of the drums.

"Let's go inside," I said.

"It is a bad place," she said.

"But not the music," I said.

"No, the music is very good," she said.

From the shadow under the night-club canopy a huge blue-black Negro doorman loomed up. He was sweating in a long coat that was loaded down with gold braid and brass buttons. When he spoke his accent was right out of Memphis, Tennessee. *"Bienvenida,* you-all," he said. "C'mawn in."

We went in, laughing. There was a small dance floor with a long bar on one side of it. Booths were on the other side. There were tables in back and also a stairway with traffic up and down. The musicians on a band-stand in the front of the hall began to play again, so we didn't sit down. The music was a kind of pre-rumba called a tango conga, with lots of accent. I put my right hand flat and firmly in the small of Celia's back and led her strongly, but it wasn't necessary to shove. She followed in-stinctively, and she had the movement. I hoped what I had been taught by Carmen would do, but Celia made me dance better than I knew how.

"You have learned very well, Luke," she said.

I wondered if she realized she had called me Luke for the first time, but we didn't talk more—just shared the insinuating rhythm that was beyond conscious thought but not wanton. It was disciplined; most passionate when most controlled. The deliberate arresting pause in the rumba stylizes it, gives it a connection of mind and body, an aloof I-know-what-I-am-doing-to-myself thing with gratification and denial all in four beats.

When the music stopped, I spotted an empty booth where a waiter was clearing off glasses and ashtrays. I led Celia to it and sat alongside her at the table.

I ordered rum and Cokes for us. Celia nuzzled me with her face at my shoulder. She did it softly, without being arch about it, and she gave me feathery kisses on my cheek. The feeling I had was one of mixed pride, elation, and plain gratitude, but I kept busy getting a cigarette package open, lighting two for us with matches from Celia's purse, and then taking a drink, and all the while doing what is called making conversation. I was sure Celia had taken on more liquor than she was used to, and I didn't mind feeling noble either, but my arm went around her—a reflex action.

Celia told me more about her collection of Latin American records and also about the albums she had bought in the States. She had a theory about the connection between Caribbean music and American jazz. "The only difference," she said, "is that our Spanish music was influenced by Negroes who got off the boat sooner than your Negroes who made their music in New Orleans. My uncle calls the new thing, the mambo, a madness and a national calamity. I think I like it. I hope they play—"

The lights went out. In the sudden darkness I heard a familiar voice cry out, *"Cuidado!"*

The warning had been for me—too late. There was a crash of splintering glass over my head. I pushed Celia down in the booth, partly under the table, shielding her.

There was a shout. *"Yanqui,* go home!"

Something like a punch hit me hard in the back and knocked the wind out of me. It was an empty bottle, and it lay on the seat beside me. Another bottle crashed into the table, and glass flew. I knew from the damp feeling at my collar that my neck was bleeding.

"Leave our women alone!" a drunken voice shouted.

Then the lights went on again and the orchestra started playing.

I half stood up, keeping my body between Celia and our attackers. "Are you all right?" I asked anxiously.

"Sí," she said, lapsing into Spanish. *"Y tú?* My God! You are hurt!"

Celia reached up and touched my neck, taking her hand away with blood on it. She didn't panic. "A scratch," she said, but then she stifled a little gasping scream, her eyes widening at what she saw behind me.

I turned and saw a half-circle of three dark-skinned men moving toward us from the bar. The one in the middle had a thin, gleaming knife in his hand. I felt Celia's fingers dig into my back. The music stopped, one instrument at a time, with a fading dissonance.

"They are loco," she said tensely.

We were in a hell of a fix. I had to get Celia out of there. I said, "Celia, they don't want you. When I move out of your way, make a run for the door and keep going."

"No, no!" she said.

"Please go!" I said, but she didn't answer and there wasn't time to argue. I gripped the neck of the empty rum bottle that had struck me without breaking. I broke the bottom off of it on the edge of the table. It made a vicious weapon. I held it out in front of me, waving it from side to side so all three of them could see it.

The hands of the other two men sort of flicked toward their belts, and then all of them held knives.

I used an insulting Spanish idiom I'd heard at the bullfight. *Cabrón* was one of the words. I called them cowards and told them they had only enough courage for attacking women and that they were lucky there were three of them to make it an even fight with me. I was loud. They slowed down their advance, but their leader in the middle kept coming on. He crouched over with his knees bent and both hands in front of him, an accomplished knife fighter.

I feinted at his face with the bottle. I shouted, "I will take that knife away from you and carve my initials on your ass!"

He slowed his creepy advance almost imperceptibly. The blade of his knife lowered a fraction.

The voice that had warned us from somewhere in back shouted again, *"El hombre es el Capitán y el Jefe por Romirez!"*

The man in front of me looked toward the voice. So did I. Dimly I saw a dark silhouette of a man standing in the shadows. It was Lacayo. I hoped my eyes said *mil gracias* to him, but I knew I had to keep on acting brave. I took a step forward. The leader of the three men stopped. The others faded back a step. I moved forward again and grinned gleefully at the broken bottle in my hand as if I'd enjoy using it. The leader retreated a couple of steps.

Lacayo was suddenly at my side, cat quiet. He was unarmed.

The three men put away their knives and their leader said, *"Perdon, Señor Capitán. Perdon Señor Lacayo."*

Somewhere in the crowd a voice berated Lacayo for protecting a *Yanqui* lackey of that *cabrón* Romirez. I collected a pretty limp Celia at the booth and then, with a defiant gesture, I was about to throw the jagged stump of my rum bottle at the feet of the men who had attacked us. Lacayo stopped my hand. His eyes weren't friendly.

"They hate you," he said dryly. He meant I ought to quit while I was ahead.

I dropped a pink bill on the table for our drinks, and we went out.

Two drunken American guys were stumbling out of a taxi under the canopy of the Blue Lantern. It was the only taxi in sight. I pushed them back inside it and pushed Celia in after them. Then I fumbled out a duro bill, a tip for the doorman.

"Buenos días, y'all," the doorman said. "Hurry back, hear?"

Celia and I got the giggles, repeating, *"Buenos días,* y'all," and I guess we were having a kind of reaction from the danger. In Spanish I told the driver to take us to the El Cortés. The Americans protested drunkenly that they didn't want to go there and I kept on speaking to Celia and the driver in Spanish. The Yanks thought I was a rude native. They didn't know I had probably saved their lives.

Chapter 17

IT WAS about three in the morning, so we hadn't been up till dawn yet. Celia and I sat in a dark corner of the Bamboo Bar at the hotel and drank lemonade, which was her idea and it tasted good because we were thirsty.

Seriously, I asked Celia, "Why do they hate me, hate Americans like me, I mean?"

She was silent, thinking.

"Is it because they are poor and think all Yankees are rich?" I asked.

"Yes—and for another reason also," she said. "Because you are *white!*"

That shook me up a little. Celia was white too. I would have to think about that some more sometime. I felt cold sober and not very amusing for my date who wanted to stay up all night.

"It isn't the end of the world, Luke," Celia said. "Ruedo has been a battleground before and something always turns up, like a better price for coffee or cotton. Please let me see you smile now."

A twisted grin was the best I could do.

"Luke, you were very brave tonight," she said thoughtfully, not in a way intended simply to flatter me; therefore, the compliment cheered me up. And I liked to hear her call me Luke, so I did smile a little. Her smile was such a big one it was catching.

Suddenly she kissed me full on the lips. There were people watching, and she was absolutely shameless the way she kept on kissing me. I hugged her and began to talk softly to her in a certain way that could make the kisses last and last and lead to more than kisses.

"These people here," I said lightly, "are sure we are having an affair or are about to have one. I think they are right, huh?"

She didn't answer the question I implied. I said, "My room is right upstairs."

"Do you want to very much?" she whispered. Her face was very serious.

To answer that, I kissed her again. I could feel the marrow melt in my leg bones. The people who still watched us didn't leer. They smiled as we got up and went out of the bar with arms around each other's waists. Their looks said, We are happy for you. It is a grand fiesta and love is a wonderful thing.

We kissed again in the empty lobby and we kissed going up in the elevator as if the sleepy Indian who ran it wasn't there. Celia didn't hang back at all in the corridor; then it was I who fumbled with the key in the lock of my door. I finally got it open, and she walked right in. I guessed she had had a very liberal education at college in the States.

I made us a couple of drinks from my room bottle of rum, but she didn't touch hers. She nibbled a mango from the bowl of fresh fruit Rudy had delivered to the room every day.

I sat on the edge of the bed and drank. She sat down beside me. Her smile had faded, and she said, "Luke, I'm scared." Just like that. "Luke, I'm scared."

I didn't get it. "What do you mean?" I asked and pulled her across my lap and petted her. She pressed my hand against her breast and climbed up into my lap to nuzzle my face with her nose. Her voice was so low and soft I couldn't hear her.

"What, darling?" I asked, kissing her eyes, her neck, her ear. "What did you say?"

She moved her face back from me and looked into my eyes and said, "I never did this before. I never was with a man."

"Oh, no!" I groaned. "Not that!"

"It is true."

"Really true?"

She nodded as if ashamed of it.

"My God!" I blurted and got to my feet, dumping her on hers.

"Don't you want me?" she said, dark eyes very wide. In the little light that came from the bedside lamp, she looked lost and hurt.

"God, yes. I want you!" I said angrily. "Do you really want to go to bed with me? Are you sure?" I asked roughly.

"I know I shouldn't," she said lamely, finally taking a gulp of her drink and putting the glass back on the dresser.

I put a cigarette in my mouth and went to the window. I stood there, cranking the jalousies open and closed.

"Give me a cigarette, Luke," Celia asked in a small voice from far away.

I put another cigarette in my mouth and found some hotel matches on a table. I lit the two cigarettes at once and inhaled the poisonous Ruedan tobacco. She came over to me and took hers from my lips, puffed on it, and then took the other one away from me too, and, pressing very close to me, gave me a very sexy kiss. She was clinging to me, clinging dumbly. I worked loose and turned back to the window and looked out at the sea that reflected the light of the false dawn.

"Look, Celia," I said, choking up so that the words came out hoarsely, "I won't seduce you." And then I had a nervous inner reaction because, hell, she was seducing me with kisses on my face.

I said, "Maybe it's just the excitement tonight—the fiesta. Let's forget it."

I felt protective and noble again. She didn't say anything, so I filled the silence. "Celia, we feel something for each other that's pretty wonderful. Swell. But let's leave it at that if you're a virgin. Let's say you just came up to my room for a drink and got a little carried away. I'm flattered. Now I'll take you home."

She said, "Excuse me, Luke." She went into the bathroom and closed the door. I stood by the window and smoked what was left of one live cigarette I retrieved from the ashtray.

Then I realized that the lamplight had gone out behind me, and I heard her voice saying, "Luke?" It was a question. "Luke?"

I turned and saw her in the dim pre-dawn half-light. She was standing there beside the bed with one of those huge Spanish bathroom towels wrapped around her.

I didn't move. I watched her pull back the bedspread and the sheet and climb in, still with the towel tightly around her. She pulled the sheet up to her chin. Her dark eyes were huge.

It's funny the things you remember. I remember her shy smile, her saying, "I don't know what to do." And I remember her curiosity and finally her crying out, "Help me. Oh, help me!" I hoped to God I was helping her, and I felt just as clean and noble helping her as when I had tried to protect her. Then there was her shout—so loud: "Honey!" Yes, that was the word, the American word, and so incongruous that I almost laughed. Over and over, with a frantic two-syllable rhythm: *"Hon-ey! Hon-ey! Hon-ey!"* And finally soprano sighs and tender lip-pushing, grateful kisses.

For a little while we slept in each other's arms. I woke first and marveled at her childlike breathing so close to my face, and then with my hands, very gently, and with my eyes in the light of the new day, I marveled, too, at her fine, clean-limbed body. Her waist was a two-hand-span nothing, making her hips beautiful. I put the flat of my hand on her firm, small belly, and that waked her.

"I knew I would love you," she said dreamily. "I knew it long ago."

It would have been so easy to stay in bed all day, but it was I urging to take her home so as not to compromise her reputation or make trouble with her aunt.

She got her clothes from the bathroom while I shaved, and the glass cut on my neck started to bleed again, so I was lavish with after-shave lotion, hoping it would disinfect. Celia kissed me and sniffed and teased that the lotion's scent drove her wild. We laughed like kids and stumbled to the bed, where we collected pieces of confetti from wrinkles in the sheets, specks of color that had clung to us during the fiesta and now had a happy significance for us alone.

When we left the hotel, the sun was higher than I thought it should decently be at seven-thirty in the morning. We weren't the only carnival revelers who had not yet gone home and were quite inconspicuous getting into a taxi to find where I had left the car. Then we located a woman selling coffee at a portable booth. Some people were still dancing in the streets, and the musicians would not stop playing so long as one couple could still dance. We stood with hot, steaming cups in our hands, and I looked into the dark eyes of this wonderful girl. We were silent. What could we say? Or what should we say? Except—I love you. That, I suddenly thought, should be said, if only as a compliment to the way things were, so I said it.

"I love you, Celia," I said, and it did not come out with as much difficulty as I imagined it would.

"Oh, tell me," she said.

I told her again. It had been a long time since I had used the words, but they got easier, being used. There in the morning sunlight and slightly hung over, I kept on telling her I loved her. And I was glad I had not told her before—had not said it in her arms, when it would have been easy to lie and believe the lie myself. But then I stopped because I really didn't know whether I meant it.

"I love you too, Luke," she said. "I love you very hard."

I was glad she wasn't being sophisticated and blasé about having gone to bed with me. Our coffee got cold, unfinished. Then I took her home. We didn't have to face her aunt, who still slept. I said I would call her. And we kissed good-by, a lingering kiss.

Immediately after leaving her, I missed her. I cursed at nothing, trying to clear the air. What was I getting into?—I wanted to know, and almost overshot one of the downhill turns, skidding the Plymouth crazily.

Puerto del Sol seemed charged with electricity. My batteries didn't run down. I drove to the *embarcadero* and walked around the fishing pier, smelling the good sea smells of oakum and bait. I found the boat that Rudy had chartered for the afternoon. The skipper of the thirty-foot Diesel craft told me there were sailfish out there.

The charter boat had a wide-beamed hull with a rounded mahogany overhanging stern. A flat cabin top, supported on thickly painted iron stanchions, was hung with green and white striped, fringed awnings. She was certainly a turn-of-the-century launch for bustled ladies and men in blue coats and white flannels, but I guessed you could catch fish from her because the two fighting chairs were on swivel posts and had well-worn brass rod sockets and removable backs in the seats.

I hurried to the hotel to telephone Celia. She said she had never been deep-sea fishing and was enthusiastic about the idea. She said she would bring the lunch. Time dragged until noon because a nap wouldn't take. I changed into white duck slacks and a T-shirt and bought some beer to take along. I also picked a flower for Celia, a big red hibiscus.

When Celia came to the dock, her aunt was with her. I swore under my breath and glumly shoved the red flower at Celia. Her aunt made a fuss in rapid, half-whispered Spanish when Celia put the hibiscus behind her right ear, which was supposed to let all the boys know she was spoken for. That cheered me up, so I grinned at her aunt. The older woman wasn't much for sun-tanning. She was wearing pleated culottes and a long-sleeved cardigan.

Celia had on a pair of pink pants, cut narrow like a *torero*'s, fitting her legs snugly and ending at her calves. There were straw sandals on her bare feet, and the tails of a man's white shirt were tied in a knot at her waist. Her straw hat had a turquoise band that came through the brim to tie under her chin and keep it from blowing off. She looked so good to me I hardly watched the big Spanish-mackerel baits trolling in the wake from our outriggers.

I didn't even see the tail fin of the sailfish following Celia's bait until the mate yelled, *"Pez vela!"*

The clothespin on the outrigger let her line drop back when the fish's bill hit the trolled mackerel. As the skipper changed places with the mate, he shouted, *"Atrás!"*—and the propeller went into reverse.

I reeled in my line to get it out of the way while I coached Celia step by step. *"Muy bien!"* the skipper said as I kept his hands off Celia's rod so she could set the hook herself, as well as play the fish and have all the satisfaction there is in the catch. I counted for her slowly to five, slower than I could have counted for myself if I had had the strike, and the line ran out. I urged her to watch the line so she would see as well as feel the action and learn it, and next time be able to do it alone.

"Now lower the rod tip. Point it toward the line," I said calmly. I watched the line run off the free spool. It stopped and my heart almost stopped. Then it started again even faster. I showed her how to brake the spinning spool a little with her finger on the side of it. That would prevent a backlash. I placed Celia's feet against the fish box in the stern and got behind her chair, swiveling it toward the rod tip. Unhurriedly, so as not to rattle her, I pointed to the little brake lever on her reel.

"All right, now, when you push that thing forward, you'll feel him very quickly," I said, as though it were nothing at all. "Get set to lift the rod sharply against a lot of weight."

She caught on. She did as I told her and didn't strike too soon or too late. When she pulled back, she hit the fish good and proper. The rod dipped and bent with the pull of the line.

"Hit him again! Jerk the rod up!" I said. "No, not so easy. Do it hard! Hit him sharply. Sink the hook into him."

"*La señorita es una gran pescadora!*" the skipper said, beaming. He said he had seen men freeze at such a time.

The big silver-blue fish broke out of the rippled sea, all eight feet of him throwing spray as he twisted against the blue sky, clear out, tail and all.

"*Oh! Oh!*" Celia shouted.

"Reel!" I yelled over the other shouts on the boat. "Hold the rod higher. Crank him. Don't give him any slack. That's it!"

The sailfish jumped again and again, arching his back, flashing his dorsal sail, plunging back into the water, bill first. Then he tail-walked, shaking his bill to free himself, and, after a long run, fell back sideways with a weary splash. But he wasn't through. I counted seven more jumps, the last only half out of the water, close to the boat, as one big eye looked balefully at us.

The sight of the boat sent him greyhounding away at an angle. I kept Celia's chair swiveled toward the line, and the boatmen backed down on the fish with power, to give her slack to reel in.

It was a happy boat. We were lucky. Lots of times you get only follows by the big sailfish; sometimes they will hit the bait with their swordlike bills but won't eat it when it drops back, and they can't be hooked. Other times, even when hooked, they are lost if the wire leader kinks and breaks during the jumps, or the hook tears out. But this one was *on!*

And then he sounded. He took the fight into the depths and sulked down there. I sat in the other fighting chair and with another rod I demonstrated how to pump the fish up, then crank in line while lowering the rod. I made her keep her arms nearly straight to let her back do the work in a rocking motion with the chair's backrest removed.

She fought the fish hard in the hot sun and ached properly, but she didn't suggest my helping her, and I loved her for that. It was her fish.

When the line seemed to melt off the reel spool with a hum of gears, the strength of that fish brought a look of awe to Celia's face. For a long time it was a stand-off. Neither Celia nor the fish gained an inch of line, and her hands trembled. I wiped the stinging perspiration from her eyes with my handkerchief and saw her lips quiver.

I got a cold bottle of beer from the icechest and held it to her lips and didn't tell her how much more hard work might be ahead. I lit a cigarette and let her have a couple of puffs on it. The sun beat down from an angle below the awnings and made the deck hot on my bare feet. When I looked around for my shoes, the mate dipped a pail of water from the blue-black sea and splashed it on the teakwood to cool it.

My watch told me Celia had been fighting the fish for twenty-five minutes when the monster gave her a break by doubling back toward the boat, coming up, too. I didn't have to tell her to reel in fast and keep tension on the line, but I couldn't help shouting, "Keep him coming! You've got him, darling! Don't let him rest!"

When the fish turned and circled, still pretty deep, Celia kept her rod high and let him tire himself against its strong flexing. When pumping, she had sensed how it is right to start cranking the reel before lowering the rod so as not to belly the line loosely but wind it all up tight.

Señora Vidal stayed back in the shade of the boat's cabin, and when I turned to look at her she said, "Such a sport is not for a woman."

Celia looked sideways at me, smiling happily. I knew she'd heard what her aunt said, because she said, just loud enough for me to hear, "If a big man is for a woman, what is a big fish?"

That was my girl. What a girl!

The angle of the line changed. "Look! He's coming up now!" I shouted.

"*Color! Color!*" the skipper sang out, looking down over the rail.

The mate and I looked too, and even Doña Felisa got out of the shade to look into the clear water to see the silver-blue torpedo that finned itself away from the boat about ten feet below the surface. It was a beautiful fish, almost too beautiful to take out of its element.

The surface broke about ten yards off the stern. The fish came only half out of the water, his sail open all the way. He was very tired. He slipped back beneath the waves, tail first.

The rest of it was a little sad. The beaten fish rolled on his side and the skipper could tow it to the boat by the wire leader. The mate reached for some cotton gloves that were pinned to the outrigger line.

"*Por favor,*" I said. "May I do that? You get the club."

I remembered how I had seen the boating of a marlin done without a gaff the one time I fished off Maryland, and now I wanted to do the dangerous part, to show off. I think I felt a little of what a bullfighter feels as I reached down over the gunwale, my body half over the side, and took the fish's bill in my two hands to heave his head up against the side of the boat to where the mate could club him dead. The great forked tail thrashed twice, and the huge body, all muscle, made the sword in my hands a thing that could kill me if I didn't point it past my chest, sort of tuck it under my armpit. The mate didn't miss with his billy.

Then a heavy line with a slipknot was passed over the fish to cinch up below the tail. The skipper and the mate hauled him aboard and lashed him across the transom, and we all admired the sailfish and toasted him and Celia with cold bottles of beer.

I was never happier over any fish I had caught myself. I made up my mind to have it mounted to see it always above the fireplace in the house I would build for us. It didn't seem at all strange to have such a thought now.

Celia was limp with that wonderful physical fatigue that doesn't make you feel anything but good, and I hugged her to me impulsively and kissed her eyes. Then I climbed up on the cabin top to look down at the fish that would never be quite so beautiful again unless the taxidermist was a genius. His colors and stripes faded as his hide dried black in the sun, but the wonder of him remained.

Celia climbed up top after me with sandwiches, hard-boiled eggs, and more beer. Out of sight of the others, we kissed more hungrily than we ate. We were happy beyond understanding. It was a fine day. It was the day of our love.

The crew put baits out again and, as we trolled near the edge of some floating seaweed, there was a strike on the line we insisted was Doña Felisa's. She protested, but my kidding got her into the fighting chair, where she reeled mightily, connected to a blue and chartreuse miracle of shallow leaping fish the skipper called a dorado. It's called dolphin up north. The blunt-headed bull of a fish was alongside the boat in less than five minutes on the heavy tackle, but Doña Felisa was content.

"I will cook him for our supper," she announced. *"Me gusta dorado."*

The lines went out again and Celia and I watched the trolled baits from the cabin top while her aunt took the shade again and dozed. The boat rolled as the afternoon wind came up the way it always does and I kept one arm around Celia. We whispered together.

"I feel as I always felt before," she said to me. "I thought I would feel different today, that I would be changed somehow."

I got out some cigarettes but had no more matches. Neither did she. It didn't matter because we kissed again.

"I think few people have such love," Celia said almost sadly.

"Perhaps there are many," I said, "but I never had it like this before."

"Was I . . . ? Did you like me in bed?" she asked.

"You were the best! You knew . . ."

Her face actually reddened under her tan. "Yes! Yes!" she said. "I am very bad. For a long time I imagined how it would be. I daydreamed. But with you I knew. And I knew it would be you. I knew it before you did."

We were necking on top of the boat under the wide sky, and Celia said, "Before, when I wanted you, I felt it all over me. Now I feel my love more in a certain place. Yes, *sí,* touch me there. Oh, honey, touch me!"

The mate cried out, *"Aleta! Aleta!"* A fin was following my bait. The mate pulled the line loose from the outrigger to drop the mackerel bait back toward the sailfish. When that didn't work, I reluctantly jumped down to the deck and reeled in fast, in spurts, sometimes dropping the bait back again to tempt him. The big fish just wasn't hungry.

I was skunked, and Celia was unhappy for me. But I didn't feel skunked when she smiled at me. We held hands, and Doña Felisa watched us, not altogether approvingly.

We'd had our fishing for the day and headed back to port. The poor were waiting at the wharf with their centavos for the unused mackerel bait or a few dorado fillets. We gave most of ours away, which was really expected, keeping only some of the dorado and a mackerel wrapped in newspaper.

Nobody ate sailfish unless he was starving. We got Celia's hung from a scale, its forked tail high in the air. It weighed within a couple of ounces of a hundred and thirty pounds. I signed an order form to have it mounted.

A photographer was waiting to sell his services for the traditional photo pose. He told Celia to hold the sail open, and she wasn't squeamish about touching the slimy fins. She asked me to join her in the picture. I did, and I ordered an extra print to be delivered to my hotel.

Chapter 18

I DETOURED to the market place on my way to the hotel. I needed cigarettes and hoped I could also buy myself a lighter at the tobacco shop, because I never seemed to have matches. I found the lighter all right and then went looking for the goldsmith's shop. What I wanted there was one of those ornately carved lighter cases the native artisans made for Zippo interior works. After I had picked out a beautiful one for less than twenty bucks, the man asked if I wanted my initials on it. I said okay and was given a piece of paper to write them on. Grinning with an impulse that was still kind of selfish, I wrote a name that would look fine engraved in script with lots of curlicues: Celia. I would give her the lighter and let her keep right on lighting my cigarettes.

While I waited for the etching to be finished, an interlude of fiesta entertainment was provided by Coronel Romirez with his P-51 squadron. All nine of Ruedo's fighters came over low in a formation a lot tighter than I would fly with those jokers. They broke into Vs of three planes each and did loops, slow rolls, snap rolls, and some low inverted flights over the beach. It was an impressively noisy show.

When the fighters wheeled back toward the capital to get down before nightfall, I took the gift lighter with me to the El Cortés, where I decided in favor of a swim in the pool over a nap. Most of the hotel guests sat around in front of the cabanas drinking. I dove in and floated around, letting the water support me and work out the kinks. Soothing guitar music drifted across the water. A fellow in swim trunks was playing well enough to be a professional, and I guessed he was, because when he went in for a dip he swam around awkwardly with both hands held out of the water so his calluses wouldn't get soft and ruin his fingers for picking the strings.

I rested for a few minutes on a wooden-wheeled chaise longue. My siesta was interrupted by a pear-shaped man in a loud sport shirt.

"I'm J. K. Bullard," he said, as if I was supposed to be overcome with the pleasure of his company.

I just grunted, and he brought a chair over and sat near me. I turned over on my stomach and thought maybe he'd go away.

"It's good to see another Yank down here," he said. "Old J.K. is going to fix it so there'll be lots of Yanks here soon. Yes, sir!"

I propped my head up and looked at him. I had heard Harry Donahue mention his name, and after all, I was interested in any development that would help business for LARC. He sensed this.

"I'm a promoter, son. Represent some hotel interests back home. Might build a big resort plant here. Lots of room for improvement. Got to get local money in it for political protection. Hedge against confiscation later. I'll set up a lease-back arrangement. But what I want to talk to you about, son, is getting in on the ground floor. Guess they pay you pretty good to run the airline, so you should be interested in an exclusive home-site plan I have. Gonna get hold of some choice beachfront land and develop it for winter homes, each one with an acre and its own swimming pool. It'll attract a lot of moneyed folks at home who are looking around in the tropics for the very best. No need for all of them to settle in the Bahamas and the Virgin Islands. No, sir! Can get you in on the ground floor. Might make you a special deal."

"What will I be then—a shill?" I said, nice and calm.

"Ha, hah, *hah!*" he laughed. "You're smart! I can see that. Old J.K. pays for everything he gets. Yes, sir! I want the airline's help. So, you're in at a special price."

I got up and dove back into the pool. I swam to the other side, wondering if the bastard had seen the same beach property I had. J.K. Bullard walked around to where I hung on the edge of the pool. He acted as if rudeness was what he expected of me and it didn't bother him a bit. He squatted down and went right on promoting.

"Son, I like you. We can work together. Have dinner with me and my daughter Jane tonight," he said, smiling with his too even false teeth.

"Got a date," I said and submerged, returning under water to where I'd left my towel on the chaise.

J.K. Bullard called over to me, "If you're dining with Rudy Heinen, I'll see you then. Fine fellow, Rudy; he could figure in my plans too."

Back in my room again I shaved for the second time that day, and I nicked my chin laughing into the mirror. I was happy. That was it. I could hear the guitar music through my windows and I laughed aloud again, thinking of the guy swimming no-hands. What a country! As if that caricature of Yankee get-up-and-go could change any part of it into Miami Beach!

I slapped on some of the after-shave lotion that Celia had teased me about. "Man!" I said to myself. "You really talked it up big today. You told her it was the real thing!"

"That's right," I said slowly, seriously. I started giving myself a hard time. "What's the matter? You ashamed of it?"

"No."

"You mean you're beginning to believe it yourself. Is that how it is? More exciting if it seems like the real thing, huh?"

"It's not like that."

"No? You're fooling yourself too, eh? You want to fool yourself to be sure to fool her."

"No."

"Really? Look, man, if she believes you, if she really loves you, you are a louse. If this is some kind of daydream you've pumped up and passed along to her for kicks, you are a no-good louse."

"No," I said again, but I was sore at myself. Something sure as hell was going on that I hadn't planned for. I decided I wouldn't be a romantic jerk.

When I got to the Vidal house and saw Celia coming toward me all tan and lovely and sweet in a peasant blouse and skirt, I scowled at her before I kissed her.

"Luke," she said, sounding scared, "Luke, you're so far away. Hold me, so I can get you back again." Close in my arms, she whispered, "I love you very hard!"

There it was again, that word, and she didn't even say it like a cliché. I was still sort of annoyed to find I *was* in love. But you can't go on fighting a thing like that. You can't hide it from wise old eyes like Doña Felisa's either. She was downright abrupt with me when she wasn't smiling quizzically. We sat at the dinner table eating a salad course of *sebichi,* which Celia herself had fixed from one of the mackerels because she knew I liked it. Celia's eyes and mine seldom strayed apart. Smart guys, don't knock it if you haven't tried it.

The broiled dorado was beautifully prepared and served. I praised the cooking when what I really wanted to do was shout across the table to Celia that I loved her. I also told them how full my thoughts were of Ruedo, especially here in Puerto del Sol. I tried to make Celia and her aunt understand how I felt about it, praising the blue skies, the blue sea, the music, the people, *all* of it.

Then all of a sudden I got sick of the sound of my own voice telling them tourist stuff like I'd written in the LARC folder. I was afraid I was still being a phony. I wanted so much to be on the level about love—about everything. But to keep on hiding what I mistrusted about my own motives, I attacked theirs by making a couple of observations about their country that weren't so flattering. I noticed the two women exchange looks with arched eyebrows when I compared my good impressions of Puerto with my reactions to the slums of Vega and Abenico. With a little shame for not having said it to Sagasta, I made a case for my own country's equality of opportunity.

"My husband happens to believe in such a goal," Doña Felisa said testily.

I shut up. I didn't say what I thought—that it looked to me as if men like Dr. Vidal were still part of the old power oligarchy that wasn't giving up its feudal social structure. But what bothered me wasn't really politics at all. It was something personal and mixed up with my feelings for Celia. Maybe I felt frustrated by the girl's aunt, who had only tolerated me up to now. But why sit there and take it? Resentfully, meanly, I even thought that the goddamned fish dinner I'd praised came from a kitchen with four Indians in it, but all I said was, "You can't hold back progress much longer. The Indians have accepted the airplane; next they'll want their own refrigerators with plenty of food in them. One way or another, they'll get them! We've got to give them some hope, before it's too late!"

"We?" Doña Felisa asked sarcastically.

"I live here now," I said.

"It is not for you to interfere with our ways," Doña Felisa said sharply. "To us you are only a *visitador*. You are a mercenary employed by Romirez!"

Now it was out in the open. She had said it plain enough. I was on the wrong side.

"I apologize," I said. "I had no right to speak as I did."

"Oh, that's not true!" Celia said. "If Lucas Hadley means to live in Ruedo, he brings something good to our country from his; I know because in North America everyone is outspoken, free to say what he thinks." She turned to her aunt, adding, "This man says much that needs saying here. And I told you he was very aware, very sensitive."

I was grateful for Celia's praise, but as a guest I had got out of line.

Her aunt's smile was deprecating as she said, "Capitán Hadley has a big heart"—she used the fine-sounding Spanish phrase, *un gran corazón*— "but he is very foolish if his heart rules his head. The opinions of the responsible old families count for more!"

Celia lowered her head, getting more of a message from her aunt than I could infer. Doña Felisa sent the old servant she called Jorge for brandy with our coffee. Then she said, "The ruling families of Ruedo have scores to settle among themselves, Capitán Hadley. My husband's brother, Celia's father, was murdered by Sagasta. Yes, murdered! Everybody knows this, but it cannot be proved. Celia's mother, poor soul . . ." Doña Felisa patted Celia's hand and continued, "Celia's mother was simply driven out of her mind."

"She lives with my aunt as I do," Celia said calmly. "My mother is very melancholy. She has not gone out of the house for almost five years. Let's not talk about it."

Over brandies, Doña Felisa talked politics. She told me she had met Mrs. Roosevelt during one of the First Lady's extensive travels and had been inspired to take an active interest in Dr. Vidal's work. She agreed that my country was a good model for democracy, and it was this that had prompted her to urge Celia to attend college in the States, but she said it was too soon to expect Ruedo to compare favorably with the United States in political, economic, and social progress. But progress was being made. The republic, since Sagasta, was called a scandal by the Romirez faction, and Celia's aunt thought some criticism was probably justified because things occasionally got out of hand. There were perhaps too many political parties and front organizations. The labor unions were growing too strong and ambitious. Ortega's and her husband's party, the Liberal Conservatives, had trouble in the Congress with radicals who shouted slogans mixing socialism with peace, and sovereignty. Debates on agrarian reform in which Ycaza Lacayo participated were said to be very emotional.

"All is not black and white," Doña Felisa said. "At this moment, as you know, *El Presidente* and my husband are in your country begging for money. If we get financial aid, the Socialists and Communists will say we have succumbed to the dollar *imperialismo* of the *Yanquis*. If we fail to get assistance, the Romirez people will shout about the government's weakness or its acquiescence to the left wing. But, of course, we are all Ruedan patriots!"

Celia took one of my cigarettes and, looking at her aunt proudly, said, "My *tía* is very intelligent. If only more *Ruedanas* took an interest in politics the men would not make such a mess of things, but most women in my country still think only of their complexions, their homes, and their children."

She waited for a light while I patted myself for matches, and then I came across the gold lighter. I lit her cigarette and my own and then slid the lighter across to her.

"It is beautiful!" Celia said admiringly and then she saw her name on it and cried, "It is mine!"

She showed it to her aunt, saying, "Tía Felisa, look! Is it not grand? A gold lighter! What a lovely gift!"

The *señora* was only as impressed as politeness required. She probably had solid-gold doorknobs all through the house.

"We must not talk any more politics during the fiesta." Celia scolded her aunt prettily. "Perhaps the old ways were best. Maybe the Indians' native ways are better than what we teach them. Many still have the freedom to do as they please. They have no responsibilities. The one you introduced to us, Luke, the one with an enormous wife, he is much more free than we are."

"Curro Aboroa is one of the lucky ones," I said. "I envy him a little. You know, I haven't heard of any psychiatrists down here. I think it is because the ego gets satisfaction in these countries. You are all polite to each other. And you women are—well, more womanly. I don't think I will ever see a henpecked husband in Ruedo."

"All our men, even the poorest, act like proud *grandes*," Celia said.

"Maybe things will work out," I said hopefully. Damned if I was going to say anything else controversial.

Doña Felisa said, "We intend to make progress, and we shall if the United States provides help and not interference."

I nodded, and Celia's aunt permitted our escape from the table to the patio.

In the seclusion of low-hanging branches from a red-flowering poinciana tree we kissed as though we had been separated for a year. Then Celia lit our cigarettes with the gold lighter and said thank you for it again with more enthusiasm than it was worth.

I asked Celia to come down to the pier in the morning alone. I said I had rented a small boat and we could have a beach picnic. She whispered that it wouldn't be easy to get away alone and began looking toward the door, worrying that her aunt might see us.

I resolved to play up to Doña Felisa, but when we went back inside she wasn't there, not even to say good night to. The old watchdog butler, Jorge, saw me out. Celia could only blow me a last kiss from behind his stern back. Then I was outside alone, but keeping a hope alive for our picnic.

Chapter 19

JORGE'S wife, Juanita, was a housemaid with Celia's interests at heart. She conspired presumably to spend the day at the fiesta livestock show and horse races with Celia, so we had our day together after all. I took my girl to my special laguna where we beached the outboard skiff and we swam and collected seashells and made love. There was the kind of sweet nonsense talk that comes after, and it was then I proposed to her. Maybe in a more serious moment I would have gotten a plain yes or no, but the way it was I couldn't be sure of her answer. Yet when I told her about my house plans and we climbed the bluff together to see where it would look out at the sunset, I felt she wanted it to be our home.

The dark came quickly then, and I built a beach fire of driftwood and we finished what was left of the picnic lunch the hotel had fixed for us. There was a big bunch of purple grapes, and Celia would fill her mouth with them until her cheeks bulged, and then crush them for the juice, like a wine press, swallowing everything, even the pits. I tried it, but always had to spit out some pits and skins. She told me how her father had scolded her for eating grapes that way, the way peasants did, and I heard about her childhood. It sounded fine and wholesome, though a little over-privileged, with her own pony and all. Celia wanted children, and I did too—with her. A little baby from our love would be the dearest thing, and I didn't feel any panic about the fact that it could happen because we had been careless. Or was it carefree? That, I thought, would make her my wife pretty quick.

We were snuggling together close to the fire with no thoughts yet of going back, and I told her how the laguna somehow gave me roots and dreams for the future. I didn't ask her again in so many words to marry me, but that's what I meant and I believed her answer was in her eyes. She paid me compliments I regarded as outrageous and squirmed at hearing, but I like them too, about how my eyes were the bluest she had ever seen, probably from looking at the sky so much, she said, and about my hands being expressive like an artist's, but strong and kind of beat-up.

When the moon rose behind us, she moved out of my arms.

"Hey! Where are you going?" I called as she ran down the beach in the moonlight.

"Come, I'll show you!"

I caught up to her, and she pointed to the moon. "Look," she said, happy with a discovery. "Look from here! See where the moon is now?" With my face pressed close beside hers, I looked at the upside-down boat of a quarter-moon, the different way the moon is in this latitude, and it shone above the curve of a leaning coconut palm.

"When a palm tree bends so," Celia said, tracing the trunk's lines with her finger, "when it bends down and up again like a hammock, it is good luck to see the moon just above the curve where one could rest. There is an old Indian saying that you are supposed to look at the moon just so and make a wish and it will come true."

I looked and wished for her love forever.

"Did you make a wish?" she asked.

"Yes, but I don't believe in it," I said unnecessarily and in spite of myself.

"I will believe in it for you," she said seriously.

"I believe in what we are together," I said and hugged her tight. A little land breeze made the palm fronds rustle like crinkling paper. It was a soft, considerate breeze, carrying sweetness in the air from the flowers on the hill. We made love standing up as long as we could and then I picked her up in my arms and carried her back to the fire.

Later, when we were listening to a piece of damp wood hiss in the fire and to the calls of tropical night birds, we heard the surf begin to pound on the other side of the rocky point, and I thought of running the boat back in the dark and began to worry a little about it without speaking of it. Celia seemed worried too, about being late, I supposed, and about what her aunt would say. The whole day had gone by with twenty-minute hours.

I packed the boat and killed the fire with sand. We launched the skiff and waded around it, turning its bow to sea to get water under the motor so I could start it. I had it idling before we climbed aboard and while drifting out in the laguna I rubbed Celia's feet with a towel and she grabbed one of my hands and kissed it. No woman had ever kissed my hand before. I was a little embarrassed, but when I tried to take my hand away she held it tight, and there was a kind of wonder in the way she squeezed it and kissed it again.

"Luke," she said very seriously, "I think you are a man who is often close to danger. Will you do something for me?"

"Sure, what?" I asked. I'd do anything.

"Wear this," she said, slipping the gold chain from her neck and over her tousled short black hair. Dangling from the chain was her Saint Christopher medal, a very old and beautifully worked coin. "It was my father's. It was blessed in Rome and—"

"Thank you, Celia darling," I said, matching her solemn tone. I certainly wasn't going to debate the medal's power with her. I'd wear it even if it hadn't helped her father. "You keep them on all the time, don't you?" I asked. "Even in bed and in the shower?"

"Of course, silly. Now you can get this boat back safely, and when you fly you will be protected always. But be careful too, won't you?"

I was very careful rounding the point, quartering the chop. I sat on the back seat, working the outboard tiller, and Celia sat on the deck, leaning back against my legs with her head in my lap. I stroked her hair with my free hand and said, "I love you," over and over, but my voice was drowned out by the motor noise so she didn't hear me, but it didn't matter. The thing was, I did love her.

I drove Celia home, picking up Juanita at the park on the way. Celia's old Indian confidante scolded her cheerfully, and when Jorge let us in the house he hushed us with a finger to his lips. I could hear a voice in another room and it almost floored me. It was Romirez'. Then, of course, I knew it was the radio.

Celia's aunt was sitting in front of a big old-fashioned console radio and frowned at my presence. "Luke met us and took me swimming," Celia said.

Doña Felisa paid no attention to the explanation. She leaned forward, listening to Romirez' speech.

In a voice dripping with sarcasm, Coronel Romirez was saying, "I spoke today from the floor of the Congress. What I said is in the newspapers, but it is not my fault that all of you cannot read. The Ortega government has been slow to build schools. So, *mis amigos,* I will tell you now what I told the congressmen, your so-called representatives who represent only themselves.

"There has been no word from Washington," Romirez continued. "No official word has reached us, those of us in the government who stay in the capital and try to govern Ruedo while the President and his Minister of Peace are on a holiday in North America, while the Vice President enjoys the fiesta in Puerto del Sol."

Celia's aunt winced at the reference to her husband.

Romirez raised his voice. "I will tell you why there has been no news from Ortega and Vidal. It is because they have *bad* news. These emissaries are reluctant to tell you that they have failed you. They will not return to Ruedo with the *Yanqui* dollars. And how could they fail where the representatives of other countries succeed? Everybody knows that the United States must provide economic aid to other countries or go under. It is not the North American's generosity but his own internal economic necessity that keeps dollars in world-wide circulation to buy United States goods, and yet—"

"Not true!" I blurted in defense of my country.

"Shhh!" said Doña Felisa, leaning closer to the radio.

Romirez' voice had lowered to a conspiratorial tone. "Do you know what your fine Congress did when I told them this afternoon of the failure of the Ortega-Vidal mission? You will not believe it! It was incredible! I saw it with my own eyes and I could not believe it. They did not shout with anger. They did not cry out for new leadership. No, good people of Ruedo, your congressmen just shrugged and went on talking of other things. Some talked about their plantations, of their cotton, of their coffee, of their lumber mills, of their gold mines. They talked of the produce of your labor, of your sweat, that is sold to the United States for much less than it is worth while you continue to receive starvation wages, while your children go without schools, while the United States denies us aid for schools, for roads, for bridges, for dams and power plants for industrial development. Another congressman, that godless Red Lacayo, actually insisted we must continue without aid from the *Yanquis*. This strange type also glories in your poverty, your misery and disease—for another reason. He wishes you to have a new savior, one named Stalin—God forbid!

"Then do you know what I told those congressmen? I reminded them that their constitutional powers are temporary. Yes, temporary! The law of our land says they can govern only with the consent of the President. I told them that we can do without them!

"And one thing more. I told these temporary congressmen that we ministers would hold the President to account and that if the other ministers will not join me, I will challenge Felipe Ortega myself! Alone I will stand before him and call him unfit to be President. I will demand that he resign!

"I promise you, *amigos,* I swear to you, people of Ruedo, I will give you strength and leadership in government—even if I must seek the presidency myself!" There was the sound of cheers in the background. It could have been a recording of crowd noise from a football game.

Romirez' voice was now choked with emotion. *"Sí, mis amigos,* I will seek the presidency myself or for someone more worthy. My voice will not go unheard. *Salve a tí, Ruedo!"*

The radio lapsed into a hum and Doña Felisa reached for the switch to turn it off. She looked at me crossly. "Capitán Hadley, now what do you think of your Minister of Aviation?"

The woman's caustic tone brought Celia to my defense. She turned to her aunt and said sweetly, *"Tía mía,* Luke runs the airline. He does it very well. He is not a political person. We must not blame him for Romirez' actions."

"I am sorry," I said lamely.

"We are sorry too," Doña Felisa said. "We are sorry that my husband and Felipe Ortega failed to get aid or even a loan from your country. It seems a pity. We are only two million souls. We need so very little!"

As her aunt sighed resignedly, Celia said, "The United States helps so many other countries. Why not Ruedo, Luke? We are closer. We are near the canal too."

They hated Romirez, but he had got to them. He was still one of them, and I was not. My country had let them down. So they were putting me on the spot. I said, "Maybe my government sees other places as more troubled. In Europe, in Asia, for instance . . ."

I looked at them in their nice clothes that were purchased on flying trips to Paris couturiers or to New York's Fifth Avenue shops. I looked at the jeweled pin on Celia's cashmere sweater and the rings and bracelets Doña Felisa wore, and at their soft hands that the rough hands of servants had protected. I was in love with Celia Vidal and I admired and respected Doña Felisa, but I felt a rising resentment at their view of my country as a rich uncle.

"Nuts!" I said into the silence. It startled them.

"Nuts!" I said again, and then I blew up. "Look, I'm not going to apologize for my country. And I'm not going to apologize for myself, either. We're not always right, we Americans, but we're not always wrong, either. We mean well nearly all the time; you've got to give us that."

I felt I had to get through to them. More patiently I said, "I came down to Ruedo to sell my services to the highest bidder in the airline business. It happened to be your Minister of Aviation. Now I'm finding out that there isn't much difference between a fast buck and a dirty dollar. I don't like finding that out, but I still don't know if I am unhappy enough about it to stop taking the money. And neither are you! You and lots of your friends and Ortega's friends among the planters, as well as Romirez' friends, were quick to plow up their bean fields and plant cotton when the price was right for cotton. You never gave much thought to the fact that the people who work the fields and cotton gins are bean-eaters."

I got pretty heated. I said that even the English had an austerity program to help themselves get back on their own economic feet, but not the rich Ruedanos. The people who owned everything in Ruedo, I reminded them, got a guaranteed eight per cent on investments in their Banco Federal. They were surprised to hear that in my country an average of five per cent on money was lucky—no guarantee, in fact, quite a few risks. Their profit on Ruedan farms, mines, and lumber was something like fifty per cent, and they paid no taxes to speak of. And they seldom plowed back any of their profits into expansion of a business the way corporations did in the States. If they did, I explained, they could build their own dams and hydroelectric plants, expand their own industry with more available kilowatts to process raw materials themselves instead of shipping them north. I tried to make them see that they could create more jobs and more consumers with such an investment, and that they wouldn't lose a single damned duro in the long run, that they could ultimately earn greater profits through greater sales volume.

"There would be more taxpayers too—a middle class," I said, "a solvent society of better-educated people in between your present ruling class and the Indian peasants—also growing opportunity for everyone willing to work to better his life, even the poorest Indian."

"Such an idealistic concept can't succeed here. Not yet," Doña Felisa interrupted me petulantly. "Any new group of our people that achieves money and property tries to prevent those still under it from rising to its status. That is an unfortunate Latin characteristic. New strong men are always taking power, some of them Indians."

That sounded more like Sagasta than the Liberal Conservative party. I was confused.

Celia said, "It should make sense to give everybody a share in the government through economic and political democracy, but you don't know our people. It's a mistake North Americans always make about our poorest ones. You don't know how lazy they really are, how stupid they can be, and how something for nothing—even something stolen—appeals to them."

I tried to answer that, without sounding like a know-it-all, by telling them the pattern was clear, that Communists exploit poverty to advance their political ends, that the reactionaries answer the Commies with more suppression, which in turn seems to justify and perpetuate communism. I had spoken louder than I meant to. My tone of voice had shocked the Vidal servants into a frightened-eyed huddle in the doorway. Their sense of security was also linked to the status quo. They had jobs as long as the Vidals never got up to go into the kitchen for a glass of water. Maybe Celia and Doña Felisa didn't even know where the faucet was. The Vidals had an intellectual appreciation of democracy; extremes of left and right in Ruedo troubled them, but they wanted to blame anyone except themselves. They criticized American companies for exploiting their land.

"My country may not be perfect," I said, "but there stands the richest country in the world, because its free competitive enterprise system worked in the best interest of the most people. It was a wilderness two hundred years after the Spaniards colonized Ruedo. Maybe the United States should share its wealth with you and the rest of the world, but I'm damned if I can see why. Too much foreign aid is just plain charity—and you don't need charity. Besides, you end by resenting us if we give it anyway. Well, I resent the fact that millions of ordinary families in my country pay higher taxes than the Vidals to ship those filthy, despised Yankee dollars all over the world, and they don't have servants. Those American taxpayers scrub their own floors!"

Celia's aunt couldn't grasp what I said. Her knowledge of the United States was limited to a few blocks within sight of Bergdorf's. I sensed it was time to knock it off. "I've been preaching to you," I said. "I have no right to. I guess I got a little worked up when you looked at me as though my country had left you in the lurch—as if, somehow, the people in the States owed you something. I never even thought they owed me anything!"

I was finished talking. I sat there and didn't look at them. I looked at my hands between my knees and felt slightly lousy.

Señora Vidal got up and without a word started out of the room. At the door she turned back and said, "Lucas"—she had never called me Lucas before—"I was only being sorry for my husband, for Celia, and for myself. Now I am sorry for you too. Truly sorry."

I knew what she meant. I had started to see Ruedo clearly and, in the process, had started to take a look at myself. Seeing yourself as you really are can be a painful experience, especially when you don't measure up to the high standards you set for others.

I hadn't told Celia and her aunt that all hell was going to break loose and that Sagasta was behind it. And I hadn't said I would break with those who wanted to be dictators. No, I had told the Vidals that Ruedo's troubles were their own fault and fussed about big-deal monetary matters on an international scale—an easy out for me. Who the hell did I think I was?

Celia broke in on my silent pondering. "And I have complained that you did not think politically!"

"You know I still don't," I said morosely. "Damn politics and politicians all to hell!"

Celia's dark eyes held tears ready to drop. I went over to her chair and held her on my lap like a baby. Her cheeks were wet, and she was trembling.

"I wish there were a plane tomorrow. Tía Felisa must be anxious to get back to Santa María. We should meet my uncle at the airport when he returns from Washington."

"I can fix that," I said, glad I could do something for her. I stroked her hair and gently rubbed her back and shoulders. My lips were pressed softly into her hair. I said, "I want to take care of you."

She nestled in my arms. I felt vastly protective. Then she shuddered briefly and tried to smile, saying, "I must go to confession, and I dread it."

In this I was not her protector. She seemed suddenly far away from me, leaning on some other, greater strength. I said, "You have nothing to confess." It wasn't the right thing to say.

"I have sinned," she said.

"That—that is—" I stumbled over words. Her belief in sin was impossible for me to grasp. I said in a rush, "It is I who—" But I didn't feel guilty.

"No, Luke darling," she said, and then her voice and her touch were trying to comfort me. "Not you. You had much less to do with it than you know. I knew I would love you, almost from the first. I was a surprise to you."

"I love you," I said.

She didn't say anything.

"I love you very hard," I said, the way she had said it.

She squeezed my hand. "You will stop loving me, Luke. Some day you will stop. And then you will talk about our affair with your friends. But please don't laugh, Luke. Don't laugh about it."

"I will never stop loving you," I said.

"Yes, you will stop," she said. "You will have a lot of girls, and you will forget me too."

"No!"

"You are very good, Luke. I will not forget you."

We heard Celia's aunt calling her from another room. She got off my lap. I got up too, and I kissed her once more. It was a different sort of kiss. It was affectionate, and it didn't arouse her, or me either. It was like a good-by kiss.

I left her fixing her lipstick.

Chapter 20

I HAD to call Las Piraguas and shift the schedule to get the plane up here for a run to Santa María on Sunday. I finally got through on a pretty shaky long-distance connection and talked to Ken Reynolds. I told him we could make more money with the extra flight out of Puerto now that the fiesta was ending. He said he'd bring the flight in by ten-thirty in the morning.

I checked at the hotel desk again to see if the sailfish photo had come. It hadn't.

It was very late, but I got Celia on the phone. "I'll fly you tomorrow," I said and told her the flight time.

"I am glad, Luke," she said, not sounding very glad.

I asked her if her photo had come, and she said it had arrived early in the morning, that it was wonderful, that I looked handsome in it, but she still seemed oddly distant. I had to ask her if she loved me. After a long wait I heard her say almost inaudibly, "Yes."

The sound of a primitive congo group playing folk music in the street reached the windows of my room. The last night of the fiesta was beginning to jump. I guessed a lot of people hadn't listened to the radio. Hell, they didn't have radios.

"Celia," I said, "come out with me. We'll go dancing."

"I can't."

"Why not?"

"My aunt needs me. She is very distressed."

"I need you," I said, but it was no use. I said, "Good night, my love."

I went down to the LARC ticket counter in the lobby and crayoned an announcement on the back of a Pan American poster about the special ten-thirty a.m. Sunday flight to Santa María. Reservations would be on a first come, first served basis, so I penciled the names of Señora and Señorita Vidal on top of a new reservation form.

Then I went to bed, but I couldn't sleep. I thought it was the Saint Christopher chain around my neck that disturbed me. I removed it. The night had become quiet—no more fiesta noises. The people had backed away from one another, withdrawn to their solitudes, their shut-off lives, until next year. I listened, hoping for one single firecracker, one song. Nothing. Celia seemed far away. I didn't sleep for a long while.

Church bells woke me in the morning, and I put the medal back on. I dressed and went down to inquire at the desk again about my photo. *"No hay nada aquí,"* the desk clerk said and didn't give a damn.

It was only eight o'clock, so I still had time to see my laguna once more. I telephoned Celia to see if she would come with me. One of the servants explained that the *señorita* and Doña Felisa had gone to mass.

Then a message came from the airport that the flight was delayed and wouldn't get in until 1300 hours. I posted the clerk at the LARC counter about it, and he told me we had a full load plus stand-bys even if the flight came in empty from Las Piraguas.

I went up to my room and packed. Dressed in my uniform, I went back down to the lobby and paid my bill. I also left a note for Rudy thanking him for his hospitality and asking him to check into the missing sailfish photograph. I had time to spare, and since the Plymouth rent was paid through the day anyhow, I drove it to the market and wandered around the quiet open-air stalls. I didn't know what I was looking for until I saw it, a fine old piece of Mayan sculpture three and a half feet high, a pre-Columbian carving of a woman with breasts like two ripe casabas. The two hundred pounds of jade alone were worth five times the hundred bucks I paid. Bargain or not, my purchase was big enough to be a commitment, like a down payment on the laguna land that had to be mine and Celia's. We would build our house around the Mayan goddess. Curro Aboroa could keep her for me.

I put the sculpture on the car seat and heard the church bells very close by. Hoping to see Celia, I drove past the cathedral. No luck.

When I saw smoke coming from the chimney of the Aboroa hut, I felt as if I were coming home. I guessed the fat Marguerita was fixing lunch. I hoped she had patted an extra couple of tortillas.

It was a tough climb uphill with the jade goddess on my shoulder, and I was glad Curro saw me coming. He and two barefooted youngsters ran down to give me a hand. The four of us shared the load.

The adobe hut of the Aboroas had welcome written all over its walls in flowering vines. *"Su casa,"* Curro said simply. I was invited to a hearty lunch of tortillas and cheese and beans.

Curro's Indian eyes twinkled as I told him about the house I wanted to build. He brought me paper and a pencil. These were proud possessions, although none of the Aboroas could write. He wanted me to draw my plan for the house.

I sketched it and explained where I wanted the sun in the morning and at evening. Curro knew the sun's angles in each season and also where the drainage was when it rained, and where a well should be dug in the high ground to feed a network of gravity cisterns to the plants and trees which, with proper planning, could provide color every month of the year. He told me where the cactus should be rooted out and where to start the bougainvillaea, which grew so well near the sea. Outside, he showed me his purple gladiolas, white and pink oleander bushes, red and orange hedges of single and double hibiscus, lavender dahlias, white mariposa, and orchids in hanging pots. Curro also pointed out leafy plants of different shapes and textures, such as anthurium for the background to frame the colors, and the cat-tongue plant and the various crotons with their green leaves striped by splashes of canary yellow and orange as gaudy as the jungle birds that would live among them. He talked, too, of exotic scents from wild gardenias, tuberoses, mimosa, jessamine, and orange blossoms. The Indian's sensual pleasure in all growing things was perfectly natural.

We looked at his trees. Short plump bananas on a fat stalk hung from a palm handily near a window. Curro's almond trees would have nuts ready to pick next month. Their thin branches drooped with heavy pods and large waxy leaves. Clusters of papayas, still green but the size of footballs, clung to a thin tree-trunk beneath an umbrella-like spread of branches. Mangoes were already ripe, the yellow fruit hanging like huge bunches of grapes under bayonet-shaped leaves in the trees.

With a borrowed burro, my friend said, he could transplant more trees for my shade and food. He would see to it that all I had to do was reach into branches for bananas, coconuts, almonds, cashews, figs, oranges, tangerines, and limes. The Aboroas lived like this already and were anxious to share such a life with a neighbor.

I needed Curro's help, and he needed a burro, so I gave him the money to buy one. He took the duros a little sadly, and I knew there was now something between us that was spoiled. He began calling me *patrón.*

Impulsively I said, *"Amigo,* I want to do a thing for you, something with my time and my head, just as you are doing for me. When I live here, please let me teach your sons to read and write."

He looked at me for a minute without speaking, his face impassive. Then he asked, "Don Lucas, is it a good thing, this of reading and writing?"

"I believe so," I said, before I had thought about my answer.

Then I thought about it. Would a hold-out primitive Indian family with its unstudied ways of conforming to nature be helped by books? What did they need to read, beyond the messages in the earth and the sun and the sea? Clearly books would not help Curro or Marguerita now. They had it made. But how about the youngsters? I looked at the boys' bright, intelligent faces.

Curro's older son had simply been called Niño; the younger, Chico. They were twelve and nine years old. To Sagasta they were his peasants, but to themselves they were young princes of their realm. Did they need to know that books contained as many doubts and questions as answers and facts?

I remembered the titles of books in the little second-hand library I had collected and had left behind—the books bought at the rate of one each payday. I recalled how I had started to buy them when I was only a little older than Niño and trying to learn what there was in the world other than the part I stood on. In my mind I saw my bookshelves, the back bindings facing me and grouped according to their geographical origin. Oddly, I seemed to remember the poets first, including England's Blake and Donne; from Germany, Heinrich Heine's verses; from France,

Rostand and Saint-Exupéry; and from my native land the poetry of Walt Whitman, Robinson Jeffers, and all of Hemingway, who to me was a kind of poet.

Would experience with such printed words help Niño and Chico? What was my responsibility in giving them the skill to read? Their degree of involvement in society was at a minimum, but eventually the city would grow and reach out to them. Unless they moved farther up the coast, by the time they were men they would certainly need to know how to read the directions on a can of motor oil.

"Sí, amigo," I said. "Your sons will find it a good thing to read and write." God help them, I thought, if they ever read a Sears Roebuck catalogue.

"Why did you leave your country, Don Lucas?" Curro suddenly asked.

"I am not much for countries, amigo," I said, "just people. My country, right or wrong—that kind of nationalism that is called patriotism just doesn't sit well with me any more. Finally a country is a place with a soil, a sea, a climate you can like or dislike—and also it's more than a place; it's a way of life too. Some of all that in North America is not for me now as I grow older. I like this country better. It is very hard to talk about, but it is true. I like you polite, brave, lusty people. I like the air. Maybe it is like falling in love, the way I feel about Ruedo."

Curro nodded. I must have said it all right.

After the hasta luegos, I drove back to the El Cortés, where I left the Plymouth. Then I signed a receipt for my envelope in the hotel safe and was disappointed again at not getting my sailfish photo. I picked up my luggage, and went out to the airport in a taxi. There I did the things I had to do before the flight—checked the weather and filed the flight plan.

Passengers began arriving. I saw Celia. I appreciated her with my eyes. If you saw her on Fifth Avenue waiting for a bus—only she wouldn't be waiting for a bus but rather having a cab hailed for her by the doorman in front of the Pierre—she would deserve a second look. No matter how many times I saw her, she did something to me, and I knew it would always be so.

Inside the terminal shack I looked at the reservation list and saw that Jorge's and Juanita's names had been added near the bottom. Higher up I saw the names of Vice President Ortiz and his wife. They were returning to the capital with Romirez' speech still ringing in their ears.

The plane was in sight and letting down, so I went out on the little porch of the terminal shack and watched. More passengers had arrived. J. K. Bullard and his daughter were there, also some Ruedans I had seen at the yacht club.

Some fancy luggage was late for weighing in, and I heard a guttural accent behind me. It was Rudy, insisting he had a reservation.

I turned and said, "What's the trouble, Rudy?"

"This idiot clerk of yours didn't put my name on the list," he snapped.

"We have more than a full load here already, and probably some through passengers from Las Piraguas. Why leave today?"

"That's my business," he said sharply. His boutonniere was gone; so was the manner of the gracious hotel manager.

"We have a full plane," I repeated, thinking he was SOL.

"I don't care!" Rudy shouted at me. "I made a reservation by telephone. I can't help it if your system broke down; I'm going on this flight!" He stood scowling, his arms folded across his chest, his feet apart with weight back on his heels.

"Take it easy," I said. "We'll work something out." I thought he was lying about his reservation, but I owed him something. "Your space will be confirmed," I told him and went inside to write his name on top of the list. I knew it wasn't fair to do that, but it was accepted practice in bigger airlines than LARC.

The plane was touching down on the strip when I walked over to Celia. I wanted always to go up to her whenever I saw her and to greet her by touching her gently and kissing her, but I just put my hand briefly on hers, and this time I was not rewarded by her special smile the way I wanted to be.

Yet she did say, "Hi."

"Hi," I answered, completing our ritual greeting. I stood there a moment longer, trying to catch her eyes, but she was way out of focus, or maybe I was. I suffered.

When the plane taxied up, I excused myself. As soon as the steps were in place I helped open the doors, and Carlota came out to say good-by to the deplaning passengers.

"How many staying on?" I asked her.

She referred to her clipboard and said, "Eight going through, Capitán; fourteen off here."

I had nearly thirty people ready to go, including stand-bys, and, of course, I was going. Now came the difficult business of calling their names in the order their reservations were made. The clerk did the actual list-reading from the porch of the terminal shack, while I talked things over with Ken Reynolds and Pepe Lopez, who had come out to stretch their legs. We stood in the shade of the wing and smoked.

There was a general groan at the end of the list-calling. Only one of the Vidal servant couple's names had gotten under the wire—Juanita, but not Jorge.

Doña Felisa summoned me. She looked at me as if we were ten billion light years apart. I was the man who ran the airline, which is to say I was something like a headwaiter in her eyes at the moment. She would try to bully me now and, this failing, she might try to bribe me.

"Capitán Hadley, you *must* do something! It is imperative that we all return to the capital today," she said.

"Your servant could go on tomorrow's flight."

"No, I feel responsible for him. We all go—or we all stay!"

I didn't quite see the logic of that and dragged on my cigarette, stalling. She was adamant.

"I'm sorry," I said.

"I insist!"

"It is a matter of weight and safety."

"Nonsense!"

I gave her a tired smile.

"You can ask someone else to stay behind," Doña Felisa said. "If necessary, offer someone money."

Pepe Lopez was near enough to overhear her request. He called me aside. "Let's take the old servant and get going, Capitán," Pepe said. "I looked over the passenger list. There is a whore you can easily bump so Doña Felisa can have her butler with her."

"You're kidding," I said, but not too righteously. After all, it was my fault that old Jorge got scratched. I'd added Rudy's name.

Pepe said, *"I* will speak to the *puta."*

I followed him to where the girl stood alone in the shade of the porch eaves. I didn't want Pepe to get rough. When we got near her, she pulled at the edge of her *rebozo* so that her face was half hidden. I thought she was acting awful damn shy for a gal in her profession.

"There is a mistake on the list," Pepe said ungallantly. "You have lost your seat on the plane to Señora Vidal's servant."

"It is not possible," the girl said softly.

Pepe laughed. "How can a whore know what is possible in the social order of Ruedo? Take yourself back to Puerto *hasta mañana."*

I said, "Cut it out, Pepe. If you won't tell her what we want, I will."

"Qué pasa, Capitán?" The girl asked, her voice muffled in the scarf.

"It's like this," I said. "We can only *ask* for your seat, as a favor, but Señora Vidal has offered to pay something so her servants won't be split up."

"Cuánto?" she asked, her voice rougher.

"A reasonable amount," I said. "Will you take fifty duros?"

"That is no money at all now that the fiesta has made me rich, but it is more than I can earn today. Look!" she said and pulled the scarf away from her face.

Somebody had worked her over good. One eye was puffed closed and blackened. Her lips were split and swollen. A cheekbone had an ugly purple welt.

I got out my wallet and gave her a pink fifty-duro note. She took it and spat on it. "Because I was nice to a *Norteamericano*," she said, "I have enemies among my own people here, but perhaps they are satisfied with the hurt they have given me, so I can wait another day to leave." Then she laughed bitterly, saying, "No man in Santa María will pay to see this face so quickly, and besides, the men in the capital now seek other excitement killing each other."

"Muchas gracias, Señorita," I said after she ran down.

The pilots' boarding was the signal for the passengers to say their last good-bys to friends and get aboard too. I held two seats together for Celia and her aunt.

When they were seated, Doña Felisa at the window and Celia on the aisle, they took rosary beads out of their purses, and Doña Felisa said, "I saw you give that woman some money; let me repay you."

"It was nothing. Please," I said, shaking my head.

"Thank you, Luke," Celia said.

"De nada," I said, and wished we could really talk to each other instead of this way, but I had to get up front and fly. I gave her hand a squeeze and felt the prayer beads in her fingers. There was no answering pressure from her hand.

I went up front with Ken. Pepe deadheaded. I took over the controls. With Celia in the cabin, this flight was going to be all mine, but I must have looked glum.

Ken said, "Something eating you, big man?"

"Yeah," I said, leaving it at that. Why should I tell him my love life was loused up because I wore the uniform of the wrong side? I wanted to court Celia fast and furiously. I wanted to send her flowers. I wanted to hire guitar players and serenade her under her balcony. I wanted to buy her a diamond ring. But I wanted to keep my job too.

I maneuvered the plane with a banking turn on Celia's side so she could see our special laguna beach. The cockpit door to the cabin was open, and I looked back, but she was intent on her rosary.

When we had our cruising altitude, Rudy came up front and poked his pudgy face between Ken's and mine. "Would you mind if I flew her for a few minutes?" he asked.

"Against regulations," I said, making the regulation up right then. The German was a respecter of regulations. When he went back to sit down, he left the door to the cabin open, and I could look back and see Celia again. Her purse was still in her lap, and her hands still held her beads. Her lips moved, saying Hail Marys, but sometimes she would stop, and a hand would dart into her purse and come up with a mirror and comb and she would poke at those wonderful short waves in her hair; then the beads again; next a lipstick; back to the beads; then a nail file; once more the rosary. Pretty mixed-up prayer. As if she finally felt my staring, she looked at me. I got a little smile. I went back to flying and smiled to myself.

"You're a man of many moods," Ken said.

"Go to hell," I said, still smiling a stupid shot-in-the-head smile.

Two P-51s came out from Santa María to escort us in the last ten minutes of the flight. They flew close with wings tucked in behind mine, almost poking into our cabin windows. Once they made a good show of changing places, one rolling up and over us, the other under. Those Ruedanos could fly, all right.

When we were down and parked on the apron I was impatient to re-join Celia, so I opened the forward cargo hatch behind the cockpit, planning to drop down before the passengers had all deplaned from the rear doors. I stayed right there, though, because I saw Celia, her aunt, and the servants heading away from the plane in a hurry. They weren't looking back for me. They went directly toward a black pre-war Cadillac limousine that had driven out on the field. Ortiz and his wife followed them. There was a chauffeur at the wheel, and a man was waiting outside the open car door.

I stood there and watched, feeling a little like an eavesdropper but unable to turn away when Celia and her aunt kissed the man who was standing there. He was too young to be Celia's uncle.

PART FOUR

Chapter 21

IN MY horn-tooting taxi on the way to the Hotel Mirado I looked out the window at the changes in Santa María. Many store fronts were boarded up and padlocked. Some of them looked as if they had been broken into and looted. One was burned out. Near the Plaza República there was a bus on its side and a lot of broken glass on the street. On the corner of Calle Quintana a bloated dead horse was making a meal for a hundred flapping buzzards.

"*Qué pasa?*" I asked the driver.

"*Quién sabe?*" he replied, looking straight ahead with glazed eyes. He knew what was going on, all right, but he wasn't telling it wrong to anybody if he could help it. He just blew his horn and charged on.

The heat was very sticky after Puerto del Sol. I undid another button on my shirt and tried to question the driver again. "What's been going on?"

No answer. He stared into space and carelessly, almost languidly, avoided collisions with other cars at the last possible split second. I tried again. "Riots?"

"*Sí, señor.*"

"Who started it?"

Again no answer.

"Was it the students?"

"*Sí, señor,* it was the students."

I was having more success with leading questions. "Where are the soldiers—I mean, are the *federales* keeping order?"

217

"Sí, señor, the *federales* are keeping order."

"Has the President returned from Washington?"

"No, *señor,* the President has not returned from Washington."

I sat there in the back of the taxi looking at heat waves shimmering on the rooftops and on the street, and wondered at a feeling of waiting for evil. I wished the heat would break.

At the hotel I went directly into the lobby bar for a drink while a bell-hop took my baggage up to my room. There were little clots of men huddled over tables, whispering and looking over their shoulders. Paco was busy serving, but when he saw me I got a table against the wall. He could be very practical about things like that. Now my rear was covered; my flanks could take care of themselves.

"Qué tal, Paco?" I asked.

"Malo," he said, not whispering. He was a foreigner like me. We could talk together without incrimination. His white teeth showed in a wicked grin. "The *revolución,* she is bustin' wide open, Don Lucas. It is so bad I can smell her now. It has a smell all its own." He held his nose. "It is the smell of fear—like rotten eggs mixed with piss and—"

"Do you smell it on me, for Christ's sake?" I interrupted him.

"Only a little—but on myself as well. It is not shameful. How we act with this affliction is more important. Do not disappoint me by ordering whisky or brandy for your courage."

"A daiquiri, then."

He winked. *"Un doble."*

Before he came back with it I was paged for a phone call. I rushed to the booth at the end of the bar, sure it was Celia, but it wasn't. It was Ken Reynolds. He said he was at my office in the palace, that Romirez had suspended LARC's scheduled operations, and that I'd better come right away because there were a hell of a lot of people waiting to see me.

I said, "All right. I'll be right there," but I telephoned the Vidal home first. Jorge said the *señorita* was not in. He said he would tell her I had called. I swallowed my drink fast and tipped Paco big, telling him where I would be if another telephone call came.

In the waiting room outside my office all the chairs were filled with Americans. Harry Donahue was there talking to them. I spotted Mrs. Cluette, Sam Warren, J. K. Bullard, a lot of familiar faces. The Valdez woman was all upset and shrill about working on Sunday just because these people wanted help with reservations for flights out of the country.

"Call Señorita Vidal," I said to her. "Ask her to come down and help."

I went inside my office and found Ken there. I pointed to the lettering on my door. *"Privado* means 'private,' " I told him.

"I had to see you first," Ken said.

"I should see Donahue first."

"I'll be quick, big man," Ken said. "Just long enough to tell you I quit."

"Wait a minute, Ken," I said. "Take it easy. Breathe through your nose, will you? I need you. Who can I get to replace you now?"

"Don't worry about it, boss. Anyway, maybe they're gonna replace you." His voice was edgy.

"Come on, spill it, Ken," I said, with the voice of authority I had learned how to use in the service.

"It's this way," he said. "I've worked in these four-bit Latin countries longer than you have. I know the signs. I know when to move on. There are lots of flying jobs opening up in South America—better ones, with more opportunity for side money in a little smuggling. I don't like it here any more. And I think there's a bullet here with your name on it too. I don't want to be the dead innocent bystander."

While Ken talked, I went through the mail on my desk. It was a rude but sometimes effective bit of office procedure for the boss to use on a subordinate. I also hoped to find something that would give me a rebuttal. I did.

"Ken, look," I said and held up some papers. "These are memos and requisitions signed by Romirez. The C-54 gets here tomorrow. The Coronel had some ideas of his own. We're going to inaugurate a flight to Miami with one stop in Mexico. That run is yours if you stay. It can be profitable. You can smuggle in air-conditioners, all kinds of stuff."

"When do we start the Miami service?"

"Tuesday the eighteenth, day after tomorrow. Just domestic flights have been canceled."

"Then that's what this crowd is here for. Word must have leaked out."

"What do you say?"

"I'm the only guy with four-engine time besides you." Ken sounded like he was buying.

"Right!" I said heartily. "You're my four-engine man."

"Okay, I'll fly your DC-4 out, but I won't guarantee to fly her back from Miami. She's my ticket out of here. Maybe you ought to be on her too."

"Why are you so damn worried about me?"

"Luke, you're too ambitious for your own good. You are playing both ends against the middle."

"How's that?"

"Hell, everybody knows you got pally with the Vidal girl. That family is poison to Romirez. Maybe she's just a broad you're laying, but Romirez no like. So now I think he has big plans for that kraut Heinen. I saw them together a little while ago."

I thought for a minute, then I said, "Ken, I'm in love with Celia Vidal. You married a gal in Bolivia, didn't you? You know how it is."

"It was in Colombia, and it was different. She didn't have a powerful family. You marry the family down here."

I remembered what a problem Celia's aunt was. I said, "Maybe you're right, Ken. Thanks. Now I've got to talk to Donahue. And thanks for taking the flight."

. "*De nada,* big man; remember what I said."

Harry came in and shut the door on Sam Warren's booming voice outside, but not before I heard Warren call to me, "You know me, Luke, I gotta see you next."

Harry looked at me sadly. "Hello, fly-boy. You're going to have a busy evening. Lots of our countrymen want out." He half sprawled in the chair in front of my desk.

"Are things that serious?"

"Boy! You *are* green! Romirez is going to blow the lid off this country, and I don't think he or Ortega will get it back on again. Now you got to tell old Harry if I'm right about who will put the lid back on and nail it tight."

"Who is your choice?"

"Sagasta."

"You approve?"

"Approve, hell!" Harry jumped to his feet, and walked up and down my office. He shook his finger at me. "Luke, you're in this thing some way, and I'd be damned careful if I were you. It's a dangerous game you're playing. As a friend, let me tell you to straighten up and fly right."

"You once told me not to worry about my job."

"I didn't tell you to get involved politically!" he shouted.

"Tell me how to stay out, then!" I shouted right back.

"Mary, Mother of God, I can't," Harry said more softly, "except to tell you to leave the country."

"The hell with that noise," I said.

"Our government makes the same kind of mistakes you're making," Harry said, "but we *have* to stay here. Our policy is in favor of peace and order and anti-Communistic, but we try not to meddle. We're neutral-against or neutral-in-favor-of some of these governments, however—and every damn time we take a position in one of their imbroglios, we wind up having supported the wrong crowd."

Harry looked at me so unpleasantly I asked what his beef was with me for getting some of the loot the hard way compared to his friends Sam Warren and J. K. Bullard. I asked him how he thought a lot of fortunes were originally made in the United States—and when I mentioned the munitions business I let it out that I wasn't above hauling a load of bombs in from Mexico. Harry gave me an awfully disapproving look.

"You and I aren't reformers, Harry," I said. "Let's not be goddamned hypocrites either. If the two hundred snobs who run this broken-down country want to belt each other around because my country didn't increase their allowances to pay for their servants, *let* them!"

"Just so you get yours, is that it?" Harry was scornful.

"You *married* your dough," I said in anger. "I'll be some other kind of whore."

He swung at me. I didn't blame him. I felt sorry for him because it was such a wild punch. He rushed me, and I pinned down his arms in a clinch.

"Knock it off, Harry," I said, waltzing him around into a wall. "I'm sorry."

He relaxed, and I guessed it occurred to him how bad it would look to the people if he came out of my office sporting a fat lip. I let his arms go.

He finally said, "You shouldn't have said that, even if I do say it myself. You need a friend, fly-boy."

"Then don't preach to me."

"You're a one-month expert on Ruedo, Luke, but you sure as hell don't know it all. By the way, rumor has it you hobnobbed with the Vidal and Ortiz people at the fiesta. Could be you're thinking of marrying a rich dame yourself." He laughed. "My guess is you discovered that some of these people down here are nicer than others, even if they are loaded. Right?"

"Right," I said and I smiled. "I'm in love with Celia Vidal." I was telling everybody.

"You poor bastard!" Harry said.

"What do you mean?"

"If you're serious, if you really want to marry her, I feel sorry for you, that's all."

"I'm serious as hell!" I said. "I'd marry her tomorrow!"

"But you won't get the chance, fly-boy. She's spoken for."

"Not so I noticed," I said, but I had a sinking feeling, remembering again the fellow who met the plane, the one Celia and her aunt kissed; then, too, I had a recollection of Celia's gentle brush-off before I left her aunt's home, a deep freeze later on the telephone, and again at the Puerto field the next day. What I thought was the real thing was turning out to be just a quickie vacation romance.

"Señorita Vidal won't get married without her folks' permission, her aunt's and uncle's. That's how it is down here," Harry said. "And all Americans are going to be mighty unpopular in Ruedo for a while—you especially, when Doctor Vidal gets home and sees that blue uniform."

"If I take the uniform off, I'm out of a job," I said.

"That reminds me," Harry said, "what about the rumor that LARC will get its DC-4 this week? Any chance of a quick run north out of the country?"

"We take delivery of the aircraft tomorrow," I said with my mind elsewhere. "It should be in shape for a turn-around right away, so *LARC* can start service to Miami no later than Tuesday." I grinned at him cynically. "I ought to be grateful for the revolution because we'd go broke on the Miami run without all those ticket sales out there in the waiting room."

"You really don't care how you make a buck, do you?" Harry said and nudged my conscience the least bit. "Well, you can book a seat for my wife and Mrs. Schlomer—first class. And let me tell you one more thing. The Ortega government isn't out yet. The President and Doctor Vidal get back tomorrow. They still have the *federales*. It's no army, but it's a pretty tough outfit. And the people have had a taste of democracy. They won't roll over and play dead. Besides, you can't occupy a country with airplanes."

"Could be Romirez will get licked," I said. "But my job ought to be like the civil service. I can work for his successor just as well."

"You know," Harry said, "I think that's how come Fatty got the idea for a Miami route. Sure, it's a big thing these days for every little country to have its own flag airline and go international with it, but approved landing rights in Mexico and Miami also provide a handy escape route if his revolution fails."

I picked up my phone and buzzed the Valdez woman. "Have you reached Señorita Vidal?" I asked.

"No, Capitán, but Doña Felisa says her niece has resigned this position."

Well, she didn't need the job.

Harry had gone over to the window. He motioned for me to join him there and pointed over the top of the university toward the gray stone building on the hill. "You know what that is?" he asked.

I nodded. Everybody in Santa María knew the prison. It was a building that could be seen from anywhere in the city, a constant reminder of authority. They even floodlighted it at night. I had walked past it once and seen paper cups lowered from narrow window slits on bits of string tied together, probably raveled from the prisoners' clothes. There were penciled notes on the cups begging for cigarette money. I had put a few coins in them.

Harry's voice hammered at me. He said that our government couldn't get its citizens out of that jail during the Sagasta regime. We put down the big stick since the second Roosevelt's treaty of non-intervention.

"You get yourself arrested in this country, and we won't land any Marines for you," Harry said. "Oh, I'll make a few polite inquiries, but I won't insist on your release. I'll sort of try to get you a fair trial, but you can be convicted in the courts even under Ortega by judges who have read no more law than my aunt's cat. A dictator can suspend civil rights altogether and jail you for imagined political offenses. It all adds up to the fact that sooner or later you're going to have to drop either Romirez or the Vidal girl. I don't know why I bother to tell you this; others will tell you soon enough. *You* can't be a neutral here."

I grinned at him, but I felt uneasy. I offered him my hand, and he shook it. I walked him to the door.

As soon as it was opened, Sam Warren shoved through. It was a broadshouldered, bull-necked, pot-bellied shove. He tossed his panama hat on my desk and hollered, "Now you look here, Luke, I want first-class reservations on your first flight out of Ruedo for me, my wife, and four kids. We'll have a lot of luggage too."

He shouldn't have said that about the luggage. I decided to handle him strictly by the book. Without cracking a smile, and calling him *Mr.* Warren, I said that excess baggage was ninety cents per pound and might have to follow on a later flight.

Sam Warren got a mite quieter and offered me a cigar. I decided to be pleasant to him for exactly two minutes. He had lowered his big body into the chair Harry had used. "Sure, Captain, I understand about loads and all," he said, smiling expansively and winking, "but I've got some very special luggage, so how about giving it a priority listing as freight if that's the only way it can go? I've always found that we American businessmen can get things done in these countries. You know, a little percentage here and a little there is all it takes. I'll bet you have a nice deal with Romirez. . . ."

I peeled the band off his percentage cigar. It was a fifty-cent Upmann, but I thought I ought to tell him I came much higher, that maybe an Italian sports car could buy me.

We both smoked up a cloud of blue cigar smoke, at least looking like conspirators, and he winked again and said, "Did you know it is unconstitutional in Ruedo for government and military personnel to conduct private business? Of course that law is interpreted as applying only to those below the rank of *coronel* or minister. Furthermore, no business whatsoever is done in Ruedo without a license or permit from the government. Ain't that slick? I'm much obliged to them for giving me exclusive sales rights for most of the United States export goods I represent. My God, Luke, if I had competition, I'd have to go out and sell, maybe reduce prices!

"It's been getting complicated lately, though," he said, wiping his red neck with a huge handkerchief. "Some of Ortega's people give a businessman the old run-around. In theory, Ortega has delegated authority to his ministers, yet if I see the Minister of Commerce, he says he has to check with *El Presidente.* If I say, 'Nuts, I'll see *El Presidente* myself, direct,' Ortega then tells me to go see the Minister. A businessman like me really prefers a strong man in power here, a man like your boss, Romirez. He's a man who doesn't evade decisions. Yes, sir, I remember under the old regime I always knew where I stood. You can bet businessmen will be glad to see this Ortega bureaucracy and his pinko friends kicked out. Meanwhile I'll take my family to Miami for a holiday till it's over."

Sam Warren pushed himself up out of the chair a second or two before I was going to look at my watch. In some uncanny way he had figured out his man and taken just two minutes of my time. I smiled and said,

"You'll get a phone call about the flight's departure time, Mr. Warren."

"Call me Sam," he said, "and thanks. I'll tell Romirez how helpful you were. Say, before I go, let me know what I can bring back from Miami for you. Okay?"

"I'm very busy, Sam," I said and opened the door for him. He pumped my hand.

And then I saw the rest of them. They were like spoiled children about who was entitled to be first in line.

J. K. Bullard had a story for me about a five-man federal police squad swooping down on his office, throwing all his employees out on the street, and putting wax seals on his company files. "That's the end of Ruedan Hotel Development Corporation for the time being," he said resentfully.

"Anything incriminating in those files?" I asked.

"Only that I had negotiated with Sagasta because he owns some of the most attractive real estate in Puerto del Sol. Goddamnit! I hope Romirez kicks hell out of those Ortega bastards!"

I didn't have time to visit with everybody. We got the whole crowd booked and ticketed in assembly-line fashion, with copies of the passenger list forwarded to the hotel ticket counter, the airport, and to Ruedan immigration and customs departments. I had the rest of Sunday afternoon off.

Back at the hotel, I tried again to reach Celia, but old Jorge, who answered the phone, was no help. I felt a pang of jealousy, which is a feeling that makes you ashamed of it when it comes like that.

A few tourists were hanging around the Mirado lobby, not doing any sightseeing today but still recognizable by their cameras in leather cases, by their sunburns, and sometimes by their paper match supply that hadn't run out. Some approached me timidly, because of my uniform, to ask about flights out of the country and then became hard to shake when they learned I was a countryman.

After a while I went up to my room, showered, and once again called the Vidal home. When I got the same 'No, not here,' from Jorge, I wrote a letter. I wrote a love letter. I even thought of quitting LARC as I choked up with the go-for-broke emotion, and it was difficult to keep my letter from pleading. I sent it with Paco in a taxi for a small fortune. He was instructed to give the letter only to Celia herself or to the maid, Juanita.

Chapter 22

THERE was no damn use sitting around in my hot room eating my heart out, so I finally went down to the lobby bar, disguised in my *guayabera* shirt. I kept looking around for Paco to return from his errand. From what I overheard at other tables, the Mirado had turned into a rumor factory.

"The United States Senate is recommending punitive trade barriers, cutting the quota of imports of cotton and coffee from Ruedo to zero."

"A bomb has been planted in the Pan Am plane carrying Ortega and Vidal back to Ruedo!"

"Vice President Ortiz has fled the country after selling every state secret to Romirez!"

"TACA and Pan American are cutting off service in and out of Ruedo, overflying Santa María until things get back to normal."

"A Communist-inspired general strike is scheduled to start at noon tomorrow."

I wondered if the truth, whatever it was, would sound as weird as the rumors. Then I saw Paco bringing me a daiquiri. He put the drink in front of me and leaned close as he wiped off my table. "I tried, Don Lucas, but could not prevail upon the butler to call the *señorita* or the maid to the door. I had to give the letter to him."

"Was his name Jorge?"

"Christ in His agony! We did not introduce ourselves. He was a *viejo,* very stubborn. Know him?"

The old one would be Jorge, all right. He would deliver the letter—to Doña Felisa!

Paco could tell I was displeased and he hung around trying to make amends by lighting my smokes. Then he nudged me to call my attention to a big, soft-looking American moving toward my table. "A snooper," Paco said. "Be careful what you say to this one. He is a *periodista,* a correspondent for *Time* magazine."

"Hi, skipper," the man said to me, standing over my table. "My name's Ben Green. Mind if I join you?"

I nodded to an empty chair. It was too soon to be rude.

The reporter's calculating eyes looked me up and down. "See you took off your uniform. Hope there's a story in that—otherwise I'll have to keep vacillating."

"The uniform is airline, not Air Corps," I said. "I'm not ashamed of it. I just want some privacy."

"Well, that's hard to come by when you're the famous Ca-pee-tan Hadley, Romirez' right-hand man, American adventurer, soldier of fortune, et cetera."

"Is that how you're going to write it in *Time?*" I said. "I'm not all that romantic."

"Oho! Your waiter tipped you off. Had dinner yet?"

I agreed to eat with him, but in the hotel, because I wanted to stay near the telephone.

"Expecting a call from the boss on the sixth floor?" Green asked.

"Not particularly."

"What's good to eat?"

"I'm going to have shrimps and rice. They have a dozen different ways of flavoring the rice. I trust Paco to order it right."

When Paco came back, Ben Green ordered two shrimps and rice, a daiquiri for me, and bourbon whisky for himself, which put Paco's eyebrows up, because bourbon traveled a long way and was the most expensive drink in town, more costly than scotch, which came in as ballast in British merchant ships. When the drinks arrived I raised mine to his expense account.

"Salud y pesetas," he said, which is what Spaniards say.

"You know the language?" I asked.

"Can't read it or write it," Ben said. "But I know enough *palabras* to get by speaking broken Spanish—all in the present tense, though. If anything of importance happened yesterday or is going to happen tomorrow, I'm dead. My communications all have a vital sense of immediacy."

We got along pretty well through a couple more drinks and dinner, which Paco served from a chafing dish.

Ben didn't pry. In fact, he didn't seem to care about listening to my views. He dominated the conversation, telling *me* what was happening. He mostly played the story for laughs, kidding the pants off comic-opera Ruedo. Romirez was referred to as "that fat Fascist" and compared to Mussolini, because the Coronel made the planes run on time. Ben dropped names like Quent and Ed, his buddies at the Overseas Press Club, with whom he had discussed this nickel revolution only a week ago. Of course, they had it all figured out from 39th Street. Smugly, he let me in on it.

"Here's what you've got," he pontificated. "The Haves and the Have-Nots—the Bad Guys and the Good Guys. Only there's a switcheroo like in Spain's Civil War. The Good Guys are not the Outs revolting against a tyranny to kick out the evil Ins; it's the other way around. Now what I want to know is, why the hell are the Bad Guys winning so easily? Why aren't the natives restless?"

I could have told Ben that the jungle is full of fruit and yams, the rivers are full of fish; that it's too damn hot to fight. But he didn't want to hear from me, so I heard a lot more of his brand of middle-aged bitterness that was endlessly contemptuous of everything that wasn't "the good old days," meaning 1930s. I heard, too, of his bleeding heart over the Lincoln Brigade in Spain, which he covered in '36. Ben was tolerant in a patronizing way about his employer. At least, as he put it, the magazine would put Ruedo in the world spotlight of public opinion.

I sat there quietly, hoping he would go away, wanting to phone Celia again. I was without pride. Miserable.

Another voice cut across my faraway thoughts. "Howdy, Luke. Howdy, brother Benjie." It was Andy Cluette's Southern drawl.

"Join us," Ben said to his fellow reporter. "What lead you cabling?"

"Nothin' tonight," Andy said. "I'm waitin' for the President's return tomorrow."

"That way you'll be a stringer in this jungle forever, keed," Ben said disdainfully. "There's a thought piece here—like how can the big shots who run this beat-up country sleep nights? How come they live so graciously, eat and sleep so well, without their goddamned consciences bothering them?"

More drinks came, bourbon for them, another brandy for me. Andy Cluette raised his glass and said, "Here's to old foreign correspondents, who never die; they just become associate editors!"

"Will one of you bastards answer my question?" Ben pouted.

"Why don't you ask Ambassador Schlomer?" Andy parried.

"How does *he* sleep nights?" Ben blurted. "Look, you guys, I'm serious. What's behind the apparently civilized façade of a ruthless ruling class that brutally subjugates and exploits the masses here?"

"Well-l-l," Andy drawled, "I declare, that's an interestin' question, even if it sounds kind of rhetorical."

Then the two reporters explained the answer to each other, Ben using Freudian terms such as "psychic denial." The families who supported dictators were said to practice a kind of group amnesia. I wanted to say that they weren't all like that, not the Vidals. Not Celia! Where the hell was Celia?

"I guess it's somethin' like back home in Alabama," Andy said. "The gentry there don't rightly seem much aware of the lynchin' and civil-rights problems. It is kinda amazin' what you can sweep under the rug. Shovin' the truth at the leaders here, too much too soon, makes 'em mad, gets their denial workin' overtime. They start arguin' the philosophy of absolute truth. I tell you it's no use. Their minds can accept truth, but their pride can't. These are a proud people. Make no mistake about that!"

I said, "Some of the Ruedanos are damn nice. They've treated me fine."

"Apparently they have, Luke, to get you into one of their blue uniforms," Ben said, sneering. "How's your denial workin'?"

"No complaints," I said. I was lying.

Andy turned to me and said, "Luke, thanks for gettin' my missus on the Miami flight. Except for the Pan Am special comin' down tomorrow with the President, I hear the other airlines are bypassin' Ruedo."

"That a fact?"

"Yeah," Ben said and got up to go, leaving money on the table.

After Green left, Andy Cluette said, "Ben's good, but he always wants to hang a label on people. I'd rather cover the action, not the analysis. Right now I wish somebody would blow up somethin'. The double-domed stuff really ain't my dish."

"What do you hear from Harry?" I asked, changing the subject.

"A no-comment interview is all," Andy said. "Harry is busy, though. That young diplomat is no pipsqueak like most of our State Department kids. I've learned a lot from him."

"So have I," I said.

"Stick close to him. You may need him before this thing is over."

"You could be right," I said.

"Another word of advice," Andy said, lowering his voice. "Just remember the smartest bastard of them all is a guy they call *El Sagáz*—the Sagacious One, Fermín Sagasta."

"I agree."

"You've met him, then?"

"I think you tricked me into admitting that," I said.

"You don't have to be too ashamed of it," Andy said thoughtfully. "A lot of good people have made mistakes with him before, and most Latin strong men have had good beginnings—Perón, Batista. You got to judge these countries by their own history, not ours. Even Simón Bolívar, the Great Liberator, was his country's first military dictator. He said, 'As long as our fellow citizens do not acquire the talents and virtues which distinguish our brothers to the north, a radical democratic system, far from being good for us, will bring ruin upon us.' Bolivar died in eighteen-thirty. So, what else is new?—as Ben would say.

I was thinking that maybe the revolution wouldn't get too rough. They had lots of experience with revolutions down here and knew how to keep them contained, a manageable size. It could be all over in a week and nobody too much the worse for wear. Then Ruedo would be a sleepy, fly-buzzing tropical country again, and Celia and I would be together.

I left Andy then and hit the sack. During the night I heard an explosion that rocked my bed a little, and, as I turned over before falling asleep again, I felt the Saint Christopher medal I'd decided to wear slide coldly across my chest.

Chapter 23

THE enormous crowd at the airport was a surprise to me. It looked as if the whole town had turned out to greet President Ortega and Dr. Vidal on their return from Washington.

Except for the bombed-out food market I had seen on the way from my hotel, which explained the noise in the night, there was nothing to indicate that a revolution was going on. There were no drawn battle lines. *Federales* were the only troops at the terminal.

I had decided to wear my uniform. It carried some authority and opened some paths through jam-packed humanity. My destination was the Air Corps Ready Room in the terminal, where I hoped to find Coronel

Romirez. I wanted to talk to him about the Miami flight and hoped to find out what else was cooking.

I would have made it there, too, except that the Pan Am Connie carrying *El Presidente* suddenly appeared over the field. I decided to wait and see Ortega and Vidal.

The *federales* lined up all along the two sides of a red carpet which ended where the unloading ramp for the dignitaries would be. The guards held their rifles vertically in front of their faces.

It was a funny sort of crowd, not cheering or anything. Somebody had organized a dozen schoolchildren who were listlessly waving little green and yellow Ruedan flags. The few women who had come to the airport seemed bored, and the men looked as if they would stand for hours in patient, resigned docility.

The Constellation landed and taxied slowly up toward the ramp but had to stop short of it because some of the crowd suddenly ran in front of the props. This necessitated an awkward attempt to realign the red carpet, which failed, as too many uncooperative feet stood on it, despite the urging of the federal police. Then, without the carpet, the ramp was moved and the *federales* honor guard formed a new line.

When the door of the plane opened, two microphones were handed up the steps to the returning President, who began to speak over the public-address system and Radio Ruedo. It was a nervous, apologetic speech. He had bad news. He was heckled by strident voices hidden in the crowd. People began to push and shove against the police line, muttering complaints about Ortega. I wished there were more than two platoons. When the President said something that wasn't too complimentary to the United States, he got a cheer, but then the PA system developed squeaks and static. Ortega cut short what he had to say. I felt sorry for the bald, jowly man who was president of a nation that was about to blow up in his rather petulant face.

The man behind him on the steps had to be Dr. Vidal. Celia's uncle had a thatch of white hair and a white mustache. He was a thin man with a melancholy look and stooped shoulders. Seeing him, I looked back along the cordon of guards to where two black Cadillacs waited. Three women emerged from the cars, carrying bouquets of flowers. I recognized Celia, of course, and her aunt; the other woman was probably Señora Ortega. People grumbled that Vice President Ortiz and his wife should be there and weren't.

As the landing party started toward the waiting cars, something awful happened. The lines of *federales* wavered and broke. Hot-eyed, angry faces poked up where guards had been. They shouted foul invectives and they spat. They spat into the faces of their President and their Minister of Peace. They spat saliva they must have hoarded for an hour, and they spat with fiendish accuracy. The women carrying flowers caught the spray.

I got so mad I started pushing forward. I had no plan, but I knew I was going to sock somebody.

The spitting became epidemic. The Ortegas and Vidals tried to hold their heads up proudly, but finally it was too much. Heads down, they ran then, toward their cars. The shatterproof glass windows withstood a couple of flying rocks, but were foamy with spit. A half-dozen motorcycle escorts of federal police revved up noisily around the cars, and off they went.

Then the remaining *federales* marched stiffly out toward the gates but couldn't hold their marching order. Soon they too were wiping spittle from their faces and uniforms. Unlike their leader, they struck back, but their rifle-butt reprisal against the crowd had only the effect of making it more hostile. The *federales* finally escaped in trucks.

The crowd didn't melt away the way crowds usually do when what they've come to see is over. They gathered around leaders referred to as students, though they looked to be in their thirties.

I was trying to complete my delayed trip to operations HQ when I heard some slogans shouted. One of them was, "Down with Ortega, the whipping-boy of North American gangsters!"

Stacks of banners and placards were delivered by dirty little men and quickly passed around. This part had to have been organized beforehand. One banner read: "Workers of Ruedo, Unite for Peace, Socialism and Democracy!" Romirez couldn't have written it. Another hand-lettered sign carried the words: "Down with *Imperialismo Yanqui!*"

The shouting got louder and had more cadence. Feet in soft straw sandals stamped a drumming rhythm, and usually soft voices became howls. And so a crowd became a mob.

I finally made it to the Air Corps Headquarters and found Romirez talking on two telephones and barking commands to an orderly at the same time. He waved me into the ready room, hung up both phones, and said around his cigar, *"Hola, Capitán. Cómo está?* How was the vacation?"

"Wonderful!" I said, which is what you say automatically.

He dispatched the orderly and offered me a cigar. The deep, soft leather chair I sat in, the good Havana cigar, and then praise from the Coronel about my report, made me wish times were better in Ruedo.

"I was in the palace office last night," I said. "I booked the first Miami DC-4 flight solid. Americans mostly. They think there's a revolution coming. What do you think?"

He smiled, but his eyes stayed hard, and he said, "No, I wouldn't dignify it with the name of revolution—not unless Ortega or Vidal does something stupid. It is just a change of the palace guard."

"What about the mob out there?" I asked.

"Oh, that!" He laughed. "A few demonstrators—students and Indians with nothing else to do for excitement, some Communists who are good at such things. They will march on the palace. I have ordered rum punch to be ready for them along the road, so they will learn to shout '*Viva Romirez*' and they will throw a few rocks. Nothing more."

"That crowd was rough on Ortega and Vidal. That spitting business was disgraceful," I said.

Romirez laughed again and said, "*El Presidente's* speech was too short, no? When it started to go well, one of my men put a canary in the PA system. Ha, ha! The people are angry at the Ortega administration for its failure in Washington, and now the administration is provoked at the people for the spitting. It is marvelous. And Ortiz doesn't show up. People start asking questions. Marvelous! When stones begin to fly at the palace, and perhaps at the home of Vidal also, the *federales* may club a few heads or fire a couple of rounds into the air. That will be fine. There are always dead and wounded when police interfere with rioting. That will do more harm to the Ortega cause."

"Is this Sagasta's plan?"

My question wiped every vestige of merriment out of Romirez's black eyes, leaving a hard glitter. I wondered if perhaps Sagasta's servant had begun to think he was master. I never got an answer because speech was suddenly made impossible by the noise of a flight of P-51s taking off.

Romirez whipped up the venetian blinds and stood at the big ready room window, watching the fighters zoom into the air. "They are a symbol of my strength, which is the strength of Ruedo," Romirez said with pride. "They will fly low over the capital and spread the roar of Romirez through every window. No one would dare to spit on me!"

I knew I should get to a telephone to call Celia, warn the Vidals of the mob.

"When the new DC-4 gets here," Romirez said, "I want you to show the plane to the people of Santa María. Fly it low over the city, all four engines making a wonderful big noise. Also, when Capitán Michaels gets here, the people must see the new bomber. I wanted to show the B-25 off this morning, but Michaels is late. Well, no matter, my fighters have a first-rate commander now. You must have met Major Heinen when you were in Puerto."

"Major?" I said with surprise. No wonder Johnny was late. I guessed he would be sweating out a massive hangover. The goddamned kraut ranked us both!

"*Sí,* Major Heinen, the German, is very good with a P-51," the fat man said. "He checked out at dawn and showed us things I had never seen the planes do before. He told me they are not too different from the Me-109s."

It was news to me too that the bomber had arrived. I asked where the crew was that ferried it in, thinking I might hire another pilot. I learned they were returning to the States on the Miami flight.

"Tomorrow?" I asked.

"Why not? A Ruedan plane flying normally to the United States at this time will make a favorable impression."

The Coronel's telephones began ringing. I waved a salute while backing out of the office, and just then Johnny Michaels came in, looking like warmed-over death, his gray hair matted down with water. He must have been soaking his head under a faucet.

In the terminal waiting room I went to the first phone booth and called the number I had learned so well. This time I got past the old Jorge who answered by telling him it was a matter of life and death. Doña Felisa came on the line, her voice icy.

"There is more trouble coming," I said, "a mob. They're headed for the palace and maybe for your home."

There was a pause, then, "*Gracias,* Lucas, *muchas gracias!*"

"Please let me speak to Celia," I asked.

"You must stop bothering the girl, Capitán," she said curtly. I was Capitán again, out in left field.

"What do you mean, bothering?" I asked. "I haven't spoken two words to her since—"

"Please do not call her again. Now, *adiós*."

"Wait!"

There was no disconnect click. I said, "I want to help. I'm coming over."

"No, you must not. My husband will not permit it. He has spoken to Celia. He is very disturbed about you."

"He'd better get more disturbed about the riot," I said. I was getting sore. "I'll come over to talk to him."

"He will not see you. He is very busy. It is useless to come."

"Señora Vidal," I said, making my voice very calm, choosing my words with deliberate care, "I must see Celia. I am coming to your house."

Her Spanish became shrill and partly unintelligible to me. Some of what she said had to do with the United States refusal to aid Ruedo. A Washington official had said that if Ruedo was wealthy enough to buy five aircraft this month, the country didn't need help for other things. It was all my fault. I wrote the plan for buying more planes. Then, suddenly, there was a soft voice on the wire saying, "Luke? *Luke?*"

"Celia, darling!" I shouted. "I love you!" I blurted it out like a schoolboy.

"Oh, Luke, no. You mustn't love me. Oh, Luke!"

Her voice did something awful to me, it was that different. It seemed to be pushing me away.

"What is the matter?" I pleaded.

The line was so quiet I had the horrible feeling for a second that she had hung up.

"Celia?"

More silence.

"Luke, I'm going to be married."

I heard the words. I heard them, but I didn't want to believe them. I didn't want to believe the feeling of the bottom dropping out of the world —the feeling that I hung in space with only the thin telephone line connected to my love. I couldn't speak.

"Good-by, Luke."

"No!" I shouted. *"No!* Celia, please! I must talk to you!" When I heard a clicking on the connection, I was sure that this time Celia had hung up, but I said, "Celia? You still there, Celia?"

"Yes, Luke!"

She was still there. It was a miracle. Every nerve-ending in me was sensitive to the slightest change in her voice, and I felt it change as if she had leaned toward me just a little.

"Celia, I'm coming over to see you."

"You mustn't. Don't come here, Luke. *Please* don't," she begged.

I had a wild, a crazy hope. "Meet me someplace, then."

"Maybe tomorrow."

"No, right away!"

"All right, but we must be good."

"Yes, where?"

"There is a music shop, the big one on Calle Quintana near Plaza Libertad—you know it?"

I grunted.

"I will be in a booth there listening to records at one o'clock." Her voice had that whispering quality. I guessed her aunt was nearby, trying to overhear.

I said, "Thank you, Celia," and I wanted to say more, but then the line was really dead.

Now I had to think of some way to get out of flying the DC-4. I found Romirez in the *cantina,* pouring coffee into Johnny.

I waved for a *café puro* and sat down with them. I talked about turn-around problems on the plane, the things to square away before the Miami flight tomorrow. I hit on an idea he liked that would supersede in importance a low flight over the city.

"We've got to paint the green and yellow colors on the new plane," I explained. "It will take time for the paint to dry." I looked at my watch. It was nearly twelve.

Romirez pouted over not having the big four-engine ship rattle dishes in town, and I thought for a minute I wasn't going to be in that music store at one o'clock, but then I suggested we radio the ferry crew to buzz the town on their way in.

Romirez smiled big, and I was off the hook. He went back to discussing maneuvers Johnny should make in the B-25 over Santa María rooftops.

I went to the communications room and talked to the ferry crew on the radio. Those Yanks thought I was nuts but agreed to make the low run. Then I instructed the ground crew at the hangar to check the DC-4 squawk sheet; also to do the paint job.

Before I left the field I saw Pepe Lopez join Johnny and head out toward the B-25 for a check ride. I guessed that no-good Pepe would like the way the bomber's tricycle landing gear handled, but I didn't wait to see them get into the air.

It took all the muscle my blue uniform and captain's bars could imply to talk a taxi driver into a trip to the city. On the way, streets were virtually deserted in the dazzling bright noontime, but not for the usual siesta. I could almost feel the stares of people who were awake and watchful behind closed wooden jalousies on their street-side windows. All shop windows were boarded up. It was as if a hurricane warning had come.

The closer to the city we got, the more vulnerable our lone taxi seemed. The driver must have thought of snipers' bullets, because he slouched way down in his seat. If I had shouted *"Viva* Ortega," he would have disappeared utterly. I began to think Celia wouldn't be able to keep our date. I worried about her.

The driver stopped where the streets narrowed, and we saw people running ahead of us as if they were trying to catch a moving train. The mob cut us off from the Calle Quintana and from the hotel as well. After I paid the fare, the taxi sped rapidly in the opposite direction.

On foot I made it to the old Plaza Libertad, where elements of *federales* were setting up road blocks and an officer was passing out live ammunition. I went on toward the music store, just in case. The DC-4 came over then—low and loud, as I'd asked. As the noise of its four engines faded, I heard a more ominous sound. In the direction of the palace I could hear the mob as one awful voice. It was coming closer. The sound of thousands of marching feet echoed in the narrow Calle Quintana. My heart pounded.

Then I saw it. I say *it,* not them. It was a thing like an ugly prehistoric lizard blocks long, writhing and stamping and screaming insanely. From a hundred yards away I felt too close to this force that smashed windows and bent lamp posts over as if they were made of tinfoil, that trampled its own fallen members to death. I would have run, but I was standing in front of the Casa de Música. The shop's show windows were boarded up, and the glass door was covered with a heavy wire mesh. My finger reached through the screen to ring the doorbell. It was five minutes after one.

A nervous proprietor opened up for me. It was my uniform that got it done. His waxed mustache twitched. His eyes watered. Could he help me? No, I could find the records myself. He locked and bolted the doors again and went to hide among the plastic table radios.

I wandered down a narrow aisle between tables stacked with *los discos populares* and eyed the listening booths that lined the wall. I didn't see Celia in any of them and wasn't surprised not to.

The street outside was running over with an orgy of hate. The building shook. They went past, thousands of legs running from one body.

I started to put a cigarette in my mouth, and my hand shook a little. Then I threw it away as I heard a phonograph playing faintly. The music was Benny Goodman's record "Don't Be That Way." In the back of the store was a booth I'd overlooked. Through its glass door I saw a short-cropped head of black hair bent over the record-player. It was Celia, all right.

She opened the door of the booth for me. I slipped inside, and we were in each other's arms just like that.

Breathlessly Celia said, "Hi."

"Hi," I said.

Then she talked fast and a little crazily about nothing but records. The riot had scared her, but she made it go away with talk about Goodman, Glenn Miller, Jimmy and Tommy Dorsey, and Arty Shaw. It was a conversation game. We got all the good names out, including Woody Herman, Count Basie, Duke Ellington, and Bunny Berigan.

"When I was in college in the States, swing was a whole new world to me," she said. "I loved the big bands!"

Then the record stopped playing and she stopped talking, so I kissed her again and we didn't pay any attention to the silently spinning machine.

"Did you get my letter?" I finally asked.

"What letter?"

"Never mind," I said. "I guess the messenger didn't get to your house." I knew better, of course. Her aunt probably had the letter. Well, I wasn't ashamed of it.

When I saw the proprietor sneaking a look at us, I put another record on, not caring what the label said. The record turned out to be one of Berigan's. Incongruous music. The whole setup was incongruous. There was a riot in the streets, and we listened to swing, and Celia asked, "Am I pretty?"

She didn't wait for an answer but quickly said, "I can get a hundred *piropos* if I go walking in the plaza, but I think the men here are just more gallant."

"Not today they aren't," I said. "Today they spit on people and tear up the streets."

She frowned, but she was practicing what the reporters had called denial. If she ignored the riot, it would go away. "Ruedanos indulge a girl's silly vanity with flattery," she said. "But what do you ever say to me about my hair, my eyes, my . . . Nothing! You never even tell me I look nice!"

She was wearing a suit, severely chic, a crisp material the color of black coffee. It looked great with her tan. I could have said so. Instead I asked, "This guy you say you are going to marry, he pays you pretty compliments?"

"Yes! yes! yes!" she said, smoldering. She worked herself up into a fiery snit.

I had to wrestle her to kiss her on her hair, her eyes, her nose, and I said, "You look very nice." When I kissed her on her mouth, she bit my lip so hard and her teeth felt so sharp she came close to scaring me. As soon as I got my lips free, I said, "You look gorgeous!"

"Where are we going?" she asked in a small voice.

"Let's go to my hotel," I said on impulse.

I felt her shiver a little, and some of the light went out of her face. "It's ugly, Luke, sneaking into a hotel room."

I didn't say anything.

"When I left the house," she said, "Tía Felisa said, 'You think you know what you are doing, but you are wrong. You do not know.' And she said, 'I cannot tell you because you will not listen. You will find out for yourself.' "

"Your aunt is a fine woman," I said.

"She is very angry with you, and so is my uncle," Celia said as she lifted the playing arm of the phonograph and slipped another record on the spindle. It was another Bunny Berigan thing, and the sound of his trumpet filled the booth. Celia turned the volume down and muffled the vocal of "I Can't Get Started with You."

"I love you," I said, and the song lyrics seemed so appropriate.

She made a face. She said, "I have thought so much about us, Luke; I even dream about you when I'm in bed alone and I almost hurt with wanting you, but it is wrong. We shouldn't. We have no right."

"I love you," I said again; I was a great conversationalist.

"I love you too," Celia said, "but it is very complicated."

We sat apart in the booth, just our hands touching. I didn't know what else to say. When the record stopped, Celia put another one on. We didn't listen to it.

"There were many people at the cathedral yesterday, because of the coming Holy Days and because of the trouble," Celia said. "Then I went to confession, and it was so disappointing! I thought I had committed such a big, terrible sin! When I was in the States the Irish priests preached so sternly about the evils of lust that I went into that hot, stuffy wooden box very repentant. I prayed, 'O, merciful God, forgive me!' but I believed I should get a very severe penance to do."

"What happened?" I asked with the curiosity of a non-Catholic for such things.

"That's just it, Luke," she said. "The father seemed in such a hurry, so mechanical. 'Make a good act of contrition,' he said, as if it all really bored him."

She took a pack of Chesterfields from her purse and said, "Look, Uncle brought them."

I borrowed the gold lighter and lit our smokes. Mine tasted very mild after the dark native tobacco I'd become used to.

Celia exhaled vehemently and said, "I cried; I actually cried. That priest said to me, 'Say three Our Fathers and three Hail Marys'—that's all, and I was out of there. 'Repent, confess, and be absolved,' that is what I was taught, but I didn't feel absolved. . . . Oh, Luke, I remembered stories about how in old Spain when a girl went against God's law the people would spit on her as they passed her on the street. And then that awful thing happened at the airport!"

"I know," I said.

We were quiet a moment. Then she said, "My *tía* told me that love is not a sin, that love is happiness and sacred, but that hiding it guiltily is wrong and makes you miserable. How right she is!"

Celia put her head against my chest, and I comforted her too. I loved her with all my heart.

"What did you say in the letter?" she asked, her voice far away.

"It was a love letter."

"Oh, no!" she breathed, and then, her voice half smothered against my chest, she told me there was a young man whose family were old friends of her family, a young man she had always expected to marry, and I even felt I could give her up for *her* happiness if that was was it would take.

"Let's go, Celia," I said. "If we can find a restaurant that's open, we'll have some lunch, and then I'll take you home." I was so self-sacrificing the music should have been "Hearts and Flowers" instead of Berigan's brass gliss. We left the booth, and I bought a Bunny Berigan album for Celia so the proprietor wouldn't throw a fit.

There were a few people on the streets, looking normal enough, which was reassuring. The mob had run its course. Santa María had recaptured the lazy quiet of siesta time. We walked until we came to a restaurant with its canopy being replaced over the sidewalk. I steered Celia inside, where it was dark and cool. There were no other customers. I chose a booth in back and could have sat beside her on the curved banquette, but I kept the table between us.

Celia said, "My tía was still trying to run my life for me when you telephoned this morning. She and Tía Luis were greatly surprised that you would give us that warning—grateful, too. To them you are the wrong kind of man for their niece. A *Norteamericano* is bad enough—but a Romirez man!"

A still scared waiter scuttled out of the darkness, eying my uniform with misgivings. I ordered two frozen daquiris, a party drink, but it was no use trying to make a party of it. I was a glum glutton for punishment. I said, "All right, you are going to be married. Who is he?"

"He is a boy I have known all my life, Luke. He is a *fine* boy," she said as if trying to convince herself. "My uncle and aunt adore him. He is right for me, and he loves me very much."

"Do you love him?"

"I thought I did—once. Before I met you I did. And he knows I am different since Puerto del Sol. He is very jealous, but he tries so hard to be understanding. He lectures me about you, and he is right, of course. His words make sense, but my feelings are all mixed up."

"He knows me, then? Do I know him? Is he the one I saw meet you at the airport yesterday?"

She smiled gently. "Yes, he came to the airport and he knows you, but I don't think you know him."

The waiter came with the drinks, rum snowballs in stemware.

"Are you going to tell me his name?" I asked.

"Not now, Luke. I'm afraid you will beat him up or something else terribly American."

"Is it all right if he does something terribly Latin, like shoot me?"

"No, no, Luke, he isn't like that. Let's not talk about him any more, even though I will marry him and have five children."

I sipped my drink and decided that I had been a fool.

"I love Carlos—*there,* you have his name!" Celia cried. "I *do* love him! Why can't I feel for him as I do for you? He is good to me, but not like you. It isn't right to love both. I must be insane! Do you think I am insane?

When I heard your voice on the telephone, it was just as though I went crazy. When I knew I was going to see you, I imagined how it would be when you touched me and I was on fire. I felt the fire in my legs and in my mouth. Nothing could stop me from seeing you."

She held her face down, not looking at me, not touching her drink. "I don't want to hurt Carlos. I can't bear to hurt him. But I don't feel guilty when I am *with* you," she said, and looked up and tried to smile.

"*We* can get married," I said, "be together always."

"No, it is not possible," Celia said.

I wanted another drink and made the kissing sound with my lips to call the waiter, but the radio he was listening to at the kitchen door had all his attention. Finally I got up and went over to him. I heard some of a radio newscast. I only half listened. I had my own troubles. But I heard that the *federales* had been unable to cope with the mob which had given Romirez the appearance of leading a popular revolution. But something the Coronel hadn't planned on had happened. Most of the violence was directed against the United States. Dr. Vidal was quoted in an angry, defiant statement that the nation would not pay a single duro for the damage to the United States embassy. I had a wry thought that the doctor must be very upset about me.

The announcer said that Colonel Romirez regretted the stoning of the United States property and especially the burning of the American flag that took place in front of the embassy. I could see his play to Ambassador Schlomer. Romirez, with Sagasta's coaching, also had the sense to know that the mob had once more become separate human beings, full of guilt and shame for their nine dead and forty wounded, so his message didn't exactly scold the people and went on to ease their consciences with praise for their patriotism. Weird politics. I shook my head.

Then the news announcer quoted a bulletin from the palace about the mysterious disappearance of Vice President Armando Ortiz and his wife, the Doña Elena. So that wasn't a rumor now either.

When the drinks were finally made, I carried them back to the booth, remembering how I had carried our first frozen daiquiris to the little table in Puerto's sidewalk cafe. I slid onto the seat beside Celia this time and put my nose into the lime-sweet snow and rum.

"We can never be more to each other than we are now," Celia said.

I concentrated on my drink.

"Why don't you look at me?" She pouted. "You are miles away!"

When I did look at her, she said, "Now I am aware of myself as a woman, and nobody ever made me feel this way before you, but I suppose you affect lots of girls this way. It is just a rotten trick you have." Her voice had anger in it.

"Let's talk politics," I said.

"Order another daiquiri," she said. Her second drink was gone already.

I managed to catch the waiter's eye this time, and when he came over I ordered double frozen daiquiris and asked for the menus.

"I don't want lunch," Celia said.

"Dos daiquirís, solamente," I told the waiter.

We didn't talk any more, and the only sound in the place was the electric blender making the drinks. When we tried them, they were even colder than before, freezing our mouths and teeth the way hard-frozen ice cream did when we were kids. But no kids ever thawed out their lips the way we did. We kissed passionately right there in the booth. Other people were coming into the restaurant, but we didn't stop kissing, except to drink.

"Salud y amor," I said, raising my glass.

"Y tiempo para gozarlas," she responded, meaning "and time to enjoy them." It was a Spanish toast that made tremendous good sense.

I left money on the table to cover the drinks, picked up the record album, and led Celia out of there, feeling that, maybe, life was going to be good again.

Outside, the heat hit us as if a furnace door had opened. We stayed in the shade of the canopy, and I saw that traffic had resumed, so there was a chance for a taxi, but I don't know if I hailed one or not, because Celia turned toward me then and reached up on tiptoes to kiss me. Her tongue did something erotic. Her eyes were wide open and full of promise.

I put my arms around her, and we missed two taxis in a row. Then one stopped for us, and we stumbled into it. I gave the driver the name of my hotel, and Celia's eyes rolled upward as our mouths joined. "I want you!" she said. "I want to be *under* you!"

The taxi pulled up in front of the Mirado.

"I can't go in there," she said, moving out of my arms.

"I know," I said. I had known all along. The hotel was a stupid idea.

"I didn't feel this way in Puerto del Sol," she said nervously, taking a scarf from her purse and putting it over her head. It partly hid her face from Ken Reynolds, who was coming down the hotel steps toward us.

Seeing that Ken wanted to talk to me, I told the driver to wait.

"Take me home," Celia said sharply.

"In a minute," I said and then spoke to Ken through the window of the cab. "What's up?"

"I have a message for you, Luke," Ken said. "You were paged so often, I took the call. It was important. One of Romirez' boys said the Coronel wants to see you right away at the cockfights."

"What for?"

"How the hell do I know?" Ken said and backed off. He knew I had a problem in the taxi.

"Are you going?" Celia asked. She'd heard what Ken said.

"I must, I suppose."

"Honey, no!"

I looked at her, and suddenly there was more separating us than a few inches of back seat in a taxi. Romirez' name could do that. Celia's eyes lowered.

"You don't really love me," she said.

"You know I do!"

"What else can I think?" she said, reaching toward the door. "I'll take another taxi. You need this one to rush to your Coronel." Her eyes flashed angrily.

"Oh, hell, Celia," I said gently, "I have a job. The airline is in a mess— canceled flights, all kinds of trouble. I have responsibilities."

"Your dirty job is more important to you than I am," she said.

"I'll come right back. Please wait for me here. We'll have dinner together."

"No!" she snapped and told the driver, *"Vaya!"* The taxi moved away from the hotel. Instantly she was in my arms, clinging. "Hold me, Luke!" she commanded. "Don't ever leave me!"

"Never!" I said happily.

"Stop working for Romirez, then. For me."

"All right," I said, and meant it. I cared that much—really *cared.* "I'll see him now and tell him I'm through."

"Just don't show up. Don't go to him, and that's the end of it." My Ruedana love could be like a bossy wife too, and make me like it. "Oh, damn politics!" she said, as I had said it once. "Let's go to the States together." Her voice was pleading.

"Yes," I said. "Whatever you want." I wasn't anxious to go to the States. It might be a mess, I thought. Then the B-25 roared overhead, making a low pass for politics. The thunder and vibration of it filled our cab. Celia took my hand and kissed it. It still embarrassed me a little when she did that. I took my hand from her and kissed her on the mouth. The bomber's roaring passed, and Celia leaned back in the seat, her face going softly dreamy.

"No," she said as though she had thought about something, "whatever *you* want is what I want. We will stay in Ruedo."

"I still want to help the airline," I said. "LARC is more important than Romirez."

"You are so good, Luke, honey," she said. "You have to see that pig. I know you must. You just can't hide. Go see him."

"I'll tell him I resign," I said.

"I think you are wonderful."

"You are wonderful."

"I am crazy!" she said, and then she gave the driver orders to return to the hotel.

We went into the Mirado together, and I found her a table in the lobby bar. I gave Paco instructions to take good care of her, and then I went up to my room and changed from my uniform into slacks and a fresh *guyabera*. Before I left I had a quick drink with Celia and when I got up to go I bent over and kissed her softly on the cheek. *"Hasta pronto,"* I said.

"Adiós. Go with God," she said. "Be careful, angel."

I had time to think in the taxi going across town to what the driver called the *palea de gallos*. It was serious thinking about what had happened and what was going to happen. I knew I was very lucky. Never mind about Carlos, the poor guy. I was the one man Celia had let know her, with nothing held back. I had it all and I had to be worthy of it, because a woman hardly ever gave it all to any one man, never to two. I wouldn't lose it, not in any way. I was on my way to do something she wanted me to do—to tell the fat would-be dictator I wasn't working for him any more.

Chapter 24

THE *pelea de gallos* was in the slum section on an unpaved street full of naked little kids playing in a mud puddle for its bit of cool relief from the hot sun that dipped toward the horizon. I entered by an archway in a whitewashed brick lattice wall through which the poor children could watch their daddies gamble away the grocery money.

I found myself in a shaded patio paved with intricately meshed odd-sized pieces of colored flagstone but dirt-tracked. There were two tunnel-like openings from the patio to the arena, from which I heard the deep rumble of male cheering.

The place had a faint chicken-crud smell. Some roosters were in stacked cages along the patio wall. Other birds were tethered to iron rings cemented into the floor, and some were held in arms by men who owned them.

I didn't see Romirez in the patio and hesitated about going to look for him inside. A cockfight was nothing I wanted to see, not even the last one on the program. I could wait until he came out looking for me, and I thought of what I would tell him. I'd say: All right, I've had it. I don't like being part of your revolution. I quit. . . . No, that wasn't strong enough. Well, maybe the right words would come when the Coronel showed up.

Shouts of changing odds came from the tunnels, and I knew that if I went inside I could get a bet down on one of those roosters, but the urge wasn't strong. Soon an Indian came out holding a dead cock by one foot. He was a loser with nothing left but a tough stewing chicken, its head down, dripping blood and scattering feathers. The last fight was over, and the crowd poured from both tunnels. Still no Romirez. I thought of Celia waiting.

I was about to leave when a man came directly toward me from the street through the archway. He picked his way through the crowd as if he didn't want any contact with his spotless white suit. He had a vaguely familiar face. Then I recognized him as the same fellow I had seen with the car at the airport, waiting for Celia when we got back from Puerto. So this was Carlos.

I stood waiting for him. And I looked him over. It came to me that I had seen him in the same kind of tropical whites hanging around the palace, perhaps once or twice outside my office, to take Celia to lunch or to dinner. It seemed a long time ago. As he came closer I could see he was stocky, thick through the chest and arms. He walked on rather heavy legs with a self-assured stride. I guessed him to be about thirty. He had a good face, with fine upper-class Spanish features, but not tanned, as if that color was for the mestizos and the tourists. I couldn't like him.

He smiled at me with even white teeth. "Permit me to introduce myself," he said. "I am Carlos Caldéras."

"You are a friend of the Vidals," I said, holding out my hand. "Any friend of theirs . . . *Mucho gusto.*"

He ignored my hand. "I am also the fiancé of *la Señorita Vidal,*" he said curtly.

I retrieved my hand and used it to fish out my cigarettes. I put one in my mouth without offering him one, and then I put both hands in my pockets.

"Well?" I said.

"It is I who telephoned you," he said sadly, eying my unlit cigarette.

"That was cute," I said. "Now that you've got me here, what?" I asked roughly.

My unlit cigarette fascinated him. He was trained in courtesy, and I could tell he itched to give me a light.

"I want to talk to you," he said and got out his own cigarettes, in a beautiful flat gold case. He bit down on one, got out a gold lighter, and lit mine and his. We both snorted smoke. The patio was now completely empty, and it was getting dark.

"The Vidals cannot trust you," Carlos said. "You are a Romirez man. And they cannot trust you with their niece. You break the rules of this country, and that is not to be forgiven. You have broken the rules of your own country, too, señor. You are a bad man."

"Is that what you got me out here to tell me, Charlie?" I was getting sore.

"Partly," Carlos said. "The other part is to warn you. You will stay away from Celia. *Claro?*"

"Nuts!" I said. "Celia is in love with me." I said that slowly, pushing each word at him.

"Don't speak of Celia that way to me!" Carlos said, angry now.

He unbuttoned his white coat to show me the Luger in his belt. A Luger is a lot of gun.

"I am not armed," I said. "Are you going to shoot me? Crime of passion, I think you guys call it. Get away with it, too."

"I would like to shoot you, señor. You require shooting, but Celia . . ." He made a gesture that told me I owed Celia my life. Good for her!

Carlos buttoned his white coat over the gun, but his tone was still threatening. "I have another way to deal with you, since you will not heed my warning. It is quite a simple plan and it will be equally effective. I know you cannot go back to the States because there is a warrant for your arrest there. You are a divorced man," he said with disgust, "and a divorced man who owes much alimony. That is why you are here in Ruedo."

"I can go back," I said, "for a price." I didn't sound convincing.

"But you do not have that price, señor," Carlos said. "If you go back, they will throw you into prison. I know."

"I don't plan on going back."

"I can send you back, Señor Hadley. Did you know that?"

I dropped my cigarette, ground it out with one foot, and looked hard at Carlos Caldéras. I didn't scare him.

"*Sí*, señor, in my position at the Ministry of Peace, with my police connections, I can sign a paper that makes you an undesirable alien in my country because you are a fugitive from justice in yours. I can arrange your extradition and will be glad to see you put on the flight to Miami tomorrow."

I was cornered and didn't like the feeling. Carlos flicked his cigarette past my shoulder and glared back at me. He hated me all right. I didn't really blame him. He loved Celia too. But Celia loved me. She wouldn't let them kick me out of the country.

"You'd better ask Celia," I said. "She'll fight your plan with her uncle." God! I thought, now I'm hiding behind a woman's skirts.

"We don't ask for the opinions of hysterical women in this country," Carlos said disdainfully.

He had me in a spot. He had powerful friends in the government, lots of influence. Well, I had some too.

"Charlie," I said, "you better hurry down to your office and do that paper work on me real soon, because if you wait another day there may not be any Ortega government."

He blanched a little at that, so I pushed my luck. "You've still got a gun, Charlie, but Romirez won't like it if you lean on one of his boys."

As if to punctuate what I'd said, there were sudden shots out in the street close by—four shots and then silence. It could have been just joy-shooting. It happened like that here, but the way things were, you couldn't be sure.

Carlos drew his Luger from his belt and looked around the now quite dark patio. One of the deep shadows moved, and we heard the scrape of sandals on the stone floor.

Three men shuffled into view. One of them was a flat-faced Indian with a walrus mustache who held a long-barreled revolver. The others had machetes. They muttered together in a dialect I couldn't understand and squatted down on their heels, watching us.

"What are they saying, Charlie?" I asked.

There was relief in his short laugh. "They say you look like a rich gringo. They think you won money at the cockfights."

Carlos turned to the Indians and said, *"Buenas noches, señores, su gringo rico está aquí."* He pointed to me.

I said, "Fingering me for these bandits will save you all that paper work, Charlie."

"Sí, señor." Carlos smiled. "You have just met with a regrettable accident."

Carlos stuck his gun back in his belt and bowed his way out of the patio. The Indians didn't stop him. Out of the dark, probably at the archway to the street he called, "Too bad you didn't wear your uniform, isn't it?"

My mouth went dry. No smart cracks came out of me, but I wanted to say: Stick around, Charlie, so you can tell Celia how I died. But he was gone.

The Indian with the mustachios exchanged his pistol for a machete from one of his friends. He came at me slowly with the point of the blade held straight out. I thought, what the hell did these Indians have to kill me for? They could take my money and let me go, couldn't they? I held my wallet out toward the advancing Indian. But no, they didn't work that way. My knees got so weak I could just manage to stand there. If I could get my legs back, I'd run. Oh, *Jesus,* how I'd like to run!

In the shadowed patio, with just starlight above, with the sound of a dog barking in the distance, with the tropical night's heat settling down like a velvety mantle, with my dearly beloved Celia far across town, this was the end. The lousy end.

I wished I could make a fight of it somehow, but I just stared with fascination at the point of the machete coming closer. It reached my stomach. Twice before I missed getting it from people who wanted to kill me. Now no forgiving Sagasta, no Lacayo to save me. Third time's the charm. I tore my eyes away from the blade and looked into the flat, blank face of the Indian. My hands sweated as I felt the machete dent my stomach skin without breaking it, the Indian pushing it very slowly. He stank sourly of rum.

I knew then—and it was a kind of revelation—that there was nothing to do but try to die bravely. But I was ashamed of my legs when they wouldn't let me have that final dignity. With the blade digging at me all the time, I went stumbling backward until the rough plaster wall scratched through the back of my shirt. That's how I knew I was still alive.

I looked into the Indian hoodlum's face. I saw every detail, including the pimple on his low forehead under his wiry black hairline that nearly met his bushy eyebrows. His flat brown face with his mustache that grew heaviest down along the corners of his lips was without emotion, certainly without pity. He held the machete point just where my ribs separated. I waited. In the core of my fear—with sudden horror—I felt the overpowering need to piss. Oh, Jesus, I thought, I'm going to wet my pants and disgrace myself. I wanted to stand on one leg and then the other. I concentrated on keeping the valve closed.

Through a yellow- and gold-toothed smile the Indian spoke for the first time, "I am going to separate you from the world, gringo," he said.

He caressed the machete blade with his left hand. "This is death, gringo. I will weep for you. I will light a candle." His voice actually had kindness in it. There was a sudden welling of genuine tears in his cowlike brown eyes. Then, abruptly, he laughed. It was one of those high-pitched, hysterical Indian giggles.

A trickled drop of urine escaped from me as the blunt machete point pushed deeper.

Then the Indian addressed one of his friends. "What were you saying before, *amigo?* It was poetry. Tell it to the gringo so he will feel better about parting with his money and his life."

The Indian who was crouched on his haunches in dirty white pajama-like clothes began to recite in a singsong voice: *"No tengo tabaco, no tengo papel, no tengo mujer,* Goddamn it to hell!"

The three of them laughed.

Then I yawned. It was the involuntary symptom of fear I'd often seen among passengers on planes when the air gets rough, but the Indian's eyes opened wide with surprise. I let myself yawn in his face. I put the back of my hand to my mouth as if I was bored as hell.

"See?" the leader said. "It is nothing to die. It is nothing to kill, also."

He prodded the blade deeper. It hurt, but the point was too dull to cut much. It sort of bruised my belly that was swelling from a full bladder.

Then he stepped back a little and withdrew the point. He held the machete down and scratched his crotch with the pommel. Okay, I thought, so instead of pinning me to the wall, he was going to chop me down. I wondered if I'd instinctively duck or try to parry the blade—maybe get at it somehow, but I was almost sick with nature's need.

"Con su permiso?" I asked politely and I zipped open my pants and slowly and deliberately urinated against the wall. I half expected to be clobbered from behind, but the Indian stood there with the other two Indians on either side of him and didn't move.

When I finished, I zipped up my fly and felt so relieved I grinned. The Indian couldn't help himself. He grinned back with his gold tooth flashing and said something to the others I didn't get. He prodded me with the point of the machete again, but as if in fun. The other Indians came closer to watch.

"Muy hombre!" the leader said. *"Macho!"*

"Sí, Chamorro," the others chorused.

"Muchos cojones," the leader, called Chamorro, said. "I like him for blood brother."

He laid the machete alongside my cheek. The cutting edge was razor-sharp.

"I will make my mark on him," Chamorro said.

He drew the blade down on my left cheek in a sawing motion, and I felt the skin split. Blood ran into the corner of my mouth. With the back of my head against the wall I couldn't flinch if I wanted to.

One of the other Indians said, *"Bueno, pero él es un gringo rico. Dónde está su dinero?"* He still wanted my money.

I handed him my wallet again. I didn't have much in it—two or three hundred duros. My blood brother took the bills and returned the limp leather. It was a lot of money to him. I wiped my face with my handkerchief while they still stood around, not sure what to do next. Chamorro's pants bugs bothered him. He scratched again and returned the machete for his pistol. He broke it open, blew through the barrel, and said, *"Pasa."*

"Gracias," I said and stumbled toward the arched exit from the patio.

Street lights weren't working, and I knew why when I kicked some broken glass near a lamp post. It must have taken those four shots to do that. So Chamorro was a rotten shot. *Now* I knew it.

I headed for the Hotel Mirado on wobbly legs, holding my bloody handkerchief over my cheek. Where the streets got less crooked and less narrow, I saw a patrolling police jeep. They saw me too, and ordered me to halt.

The corporal wanted to see my papers. I handed him my wallet, and he seemed sorry to find it didn't contain any money. I told him I had been robbed. He read my visa papers and pilot's license, moving his lips. Then he addressed me as Capitán and told me there was a curfew, but not for officers. He also offered me a lift to my hotel. I asked his name and thanked him when he delivered me to the Mirado.

"*De nada,* Capitán," the corporal said.

"*Buenas noches,*" we both said. Everything always had to be done politely.

I raced into the lobby bar. Celia was gone.

Paco handed me an envelope and a glass of straight rum. I read Celia's note:

Luke,—I couldn't stay unless I was ready to stay forever. I wanted to, because if I ever loved you before, I love you now more, and will dream of life where we are never parted. Thank you for everything you have given me. It is so difficult to know what to say, but I can say I love you very hard and know what I am saying and know that you are still very close to me always. I will keep that feeling in me. I know that. Understand me as only you can, and we will keep a certain amount of happiness around us in these bad days. No matter what! It is very hard on you, I know, because you never expected me in your life and I knew I would love you from the beginning.

Do not worry. Ruedo is very old and strong in ways you do not yet know. This country will come out all right again and, God willing, we both will, too. But some of Ruedo's ways are not good for us. That is part of being in this world and not in heaven. If circumstances neither of us can help separate us, it is not the end, my honey. It is just off the main road, and even if parting seems unfair, remember we each know how to make the other happy. Keep me in your heart as you are and always will be in mine.

The note was signed with C, and there was a postscript: "I took the record album and will say I went shopping. I am the only person in all Ruedo who will play your country's music tonight and love a *Norte-americano,* though it hurts me."

After I went to my room, disinfected my cut cheek, and put a Band-Aid on it, I read Celia's letter again. It had an ambiguous quality. In a way, it sounded like good-by. Besides, she still lied to her aunt. I meant to worry far into the night, but, yawning, I remembered my lucky escape from Chamorro and slept.

Chapter 25

I WOKE up with the sun, reread Celia's letter, and found more hope in it. Maybe it was just the bright new day, but now her words made me feel so good I even sang "Siboney" in the shower.

I had to go out to the airport to see the Miami flight off; then, of course, to see the Coronel and resign; or, if I was really lucky, I would see his successor from the Ortega camp and not have to resign. In that case, I would have to stop Carlos Caldéras from deporting me. However, it was hard to be optimistic about Ortega's chances, so I decided to wear my uniform for the last time. After inspecting the healing cut on my cheek, I also decided that this was a good day to start packing a gun. I dug out the .32 from the bottom of my B-4 bag, the gun I'd swiped from Lita, and put it in my pants pocket. I still needed ammunition.

I needed breakfast too, so I called Paco up to my room. When I showed him the gun, he laughed.

"You are a big man with a very small gun, Don Lucas," Paco said.

"It's enough gun," I said, "but it needs bullets."

"This is a big-gun country," Paco said. "Little bullets will be difficult to obtain, but I can do it. I will send them to you in a box of cigars. Where will you be?"

"At the *aeropuerto*," I told him, and then we haggled about the price and he also took my order for ham and eggs. I wanted a two-fisted American breakfast.

On my way through town in a taxi I saw the front wall of an office building had been blown off. I could see into each office as if it were a stage setting. The desks, chairs, filing cabinets were all in place. I must have slept soundly, I thought. I hadn't heard the blast in the night.

"Who did the bombing?" I asked the taxi driver.

"*Quién sabe?*" he said, shrugging.

"Anything on the radio?"

"*Sí,* on the radio Romirez blames Ortega and Ortega blames Romirez."

We were barely on the highway to the airport when we hit something in the road that threw me against the ceiling of the cab. The driver nearly lost control of the car. We stopped to look back. Across the road a concrete pipe more than two feet in diameter had been half buried in a ditch cut through the asphalt. Some troops were stationed beside the obstruction with rifles and a machine gun. They were laughing at us and waving us on. I was surprised to see they wore blue uniforms. Every eighth of a mile there was another half-round of pipe across the road. The driver called them sleeping policemen. They would slow down any mobile army's attempt to rush the airport.

At the terminal there was hysteria close to panic. Miami-bound passengers wanted the plane and all the baggage searched for bombs. I told them Romirez was as worried about losing his new DC-4 as they were, and to relax.

Ken Reynolds put his South American wife and two babies aboard, and he told me he wasn't coming back. We said good-by, and he wished me luck. I didn't tell him I was quitting too.

Johnny Michaels and I managed to persuade one of the American ferry crew, the co-pilot, a kid named Dave Carter, to fly back with Fuentes and join LARC as a captain. He liked the look of our uniforms, and, of course, the dough, and very probably the excitement.

Funny, I thought, I wasn't getting the airline out of my system—still worrying about the crews, even though I sort of had my resignation in my pocket.

I got a wave from Harry Donahue, who had come down to see his wife off. Then Coronel Romirez, who watched the departure, asked me to go to his office at the palace. It was really an order. Well, I wanted to see him too.

The Coronel kept me waiting in his outer office the time it takes to smoke two cigarettes, and when he let me in Rudy Heinen was there with him. Rudy's uniform was new and sharply pressed. They both faced me from the Coronel's side of the desk. Romirez' beady eyes fixed on me like a target. Rudy had a haughty expression on his face and he folded his short arms across his chest. They both gave me the silent treatment. I was on the carpet, but I didn't know why.

"The hell with this," I said. "You've got something on your minds, then spill it, but it won't make much difference to me, because I'm turning in my suit."

The Coronel deflated a little, as if his blubber had sprung a leak, and the heat went out of his eyes. Rudy turned and whispered something to him.

"You can't resign!" the Coronel suddenly shouted. He hadn't lost his voice; he just needed Rudy's prompting.

"Why not?" I asked. I felt like telling him to take his job and shove it, but Rudy was whispering again and Romirez was looking mean.

"Capitán Hadley, I have some questions to ask you," Romirez said, not shouting, but taking a United States Army .45 from his desk drawer and laying it down with the barrel pointing my way. I remembered then that gangsters couldn't resign, either. The only way out of the rackets was in a cement overcoat at the bottom of a river. All of a sudden I lost my short, pleasant sense of freedom.

From the same desk drawer the Coronel came up with a photograph, a glossy eight-by-ten. He tossed it to my side of the desk. It was the missing picture of Celia and me with her sailfish.

I looked at Rudy's triumphant expression and said, "You son-of-a-bitch!"

The German unfolded his arms, and his right hand dropped to the flap of his black leather pistol holster.

"We will not call each other dirty names," the Coronel said.

Rudy's face went pink.

"What does this mean?" Romirez asked, tapping the photo with a fat finger.

My fuse was burning short, but the little gun in my pants pocket wasn't loaded. "It means your Nazi friend is a sneaky son-of-a-bitch, and if he'd take off that gun I'd beat the hell out of him."

Rudy's face went from pink to red, and his hand twitched at the flap of his sidearm.

"Capitán, por favor!" Romirez said placatingly. "Señorita Vidal was your secretary; I arranged that myself, but—"

I prefaced my answer with a short laugh, picked up the photo, and said casually, "This means I went fishing in Puerto del Sol with my lovely secretary and she caught herself a pez vela, lucky girl."

"Coño! I can see that!" Romirez said, shouting again. "What am I to think such contacts of yours mean politically?"

"Oh, politics again," I kind of drawled. "Well, it means you have an overzealous spy in Rudy here. He is probably after my job and thought this picture was a dandy way to get me in wrong with you. So fire me. I quit anyway."

Romirez grunted, dismissing my answer with an exasperated wave. "At Puerto," he said, "you were seen in the company of Señora Vidal as well, the wife of my enemy. You visited their home. You were also the guest of the despicable Ortiz. Señorita Vidal spent the entire night in—"

I interrupted him. "Don't listen to a hotel manager's gossip. During the fiesta many decent girls stay up all night. As for the girl's aunt . . ." I shrugged. "How can you avoid a *dueña?*"

Romirez sneered and stroked his mustache. "If you made pillowcase conversation with the daughter of a traitor who paid for his crimes against the Sagasta government, it is conceivable that you betrayed me. There is much you could tell—about the bombs you carried from Mexico, for instance."

"I didn't tell the Vidals about the bombs," I said, and it was the truth, though it didn't make me proud.

The Coronel fiddled with his .45 on the edge of the desk. "I can put you under arrest and keep you in prison forever," he threatened. "I can send you to the wall. I can have you tortured to get the truth. Think, *hombre,* before you answer me. Have you plotted against me with the Vidals?"

Rudy smirked. I felt my face go grim. The honest answer was no, but he hadn't accepted it. I hesitated. Sure, I had called the Vidals to warn them of the riot. So what? Celia didn't even know about Romirez' graft on the airline. I discovered that after she left for Puerto, and I hadn't shown her the report. Then I smiled, remembering the evidence I had kept.

"No, I have not plotted against you. Not yet—whether you believe it or not," I said. "And you can't scare me with threats!" I sounded confident. "After all, I did some damn good work for LARC, the organization plan and all, but our agreement was no military action. I don't think you'll keep your end of the bargain, so I quit."

Romirez got the message. He wiped some sweat off his face. But Rudy persisted. "My Coronel, this man is in love with the Vidal girl and he knows too much. How can we trust him?"

"Leave that to me, Major," Romirez said to the German. "You may be excused now; I will speak to the Capitán alone."

Rudy didn't like this turn of events. His pouting face showed it, but he walked out stiffly.

When the door closed, Romirez said, "Now, Capitán, we will understand each other." He put his .45 back in his desk and waved me to a chair. "Why do you wish to resign?" he asked almost quietly. "You have a good position here, no? What will you do?"

"I don't know yet," I said. I didn't.

"Do you think I am going to lose in this crisis with Ortega?"

"You could," I said without malice.

The Coronel smiled and pushed a box of cigars at me. I took one, and he said, "Don't be a fool. Ortega is finished. It is just a matter of time."

We both worked at the cigar wrappings in silence for a minute. Then Romirez said, "Your fine report and plans for LARC . . ." He stopped speaking to bite the end of his cigar and study it. "How many copies of it did you make?"

His question told me a lot. I felt something like a chill. I had left my copy in my B-4 bag. Why hadn't I put it in the hotel safe? Hell, he probably could get that open too.

"There are six copies," I said, exaggerating by one.

"Ahhhh," the Coronel wheezed, rolling his cigar around over a match. "That would leave one copy unaccounted for. We have been through the files in your office, and your hotel room was searched this morning. With mine, there are five. That is all Señorita Valdez says she typed."

"There was a first draft," I said, wishing I hadn't torn it up.

"Does Doctor Vidal have it?"

"No," I said truthfully. "I have never met Doctor Vidal."

"It *is* only the girl, then?"

"Rudy is right about one thing. I do love the girl."

"The doctor and Ortega could use your report against me," Romirez said. "It contains incriminating evidence in the budget analysis."

"Yes."

"You can't give it to them if you are dead!"

I managed to say, "There are ways."

"*Sí*, there are traitors everywhere. The Communists have a strong underground—and they take no bribes, no little graft while they work to steal the whole country. I can see how they would cooperate in the matter of your report."

The Coronel's eyes got that look of the executioner in them as he added, "When I have disposed of Ortega I will hunt the Reds down like roaches from under the rotten floors of his administration. But right now I am helpless against their intrigue until other things are accomplished first. You were smarter than I thought to hold out an extra copy of that evidence. It could embarrass me right now. You force me to make a deal with you."

"What kind of a deal?"

"A short-term deal. In a day or two the sixth copy of the report can't hurt me."

"So you won't shoot me now; you'll shoot me later. Is that it?"

"No, no, you are a valuable pilot, a smart administrator. I can use you. If you know what is good for you, I think you will not resign and you will not betray me. Am I right?"

I felt trapped. Cravenly I nodded and looked dumbly at the photo of Celia and me that still lay on his desk.

"Major Heinen does not need to know anything about my reason, but I want him to witness our deal," Romirez said and then shouted for the orderly and sent him to fetch the German.

Rudy came back, still pouting.

"Major," Romirez said, smiling, "Capitán Hadley and I have an understanding. He will continue as *Jefe* at LARC, but he is forbidden to see the Señorita Vidal again, unless"—he paused, and his black eyes seemed to twinkle merrily at his thought—"unless, of course, he can persuade her to marry him before tomorrow."

That was a hot one! I wondered what he was getting at now.

"What's the rush?" I asked. "Why today?"

"In another day she may be in prison with the other Vidals. I may have her handcuffed naked to a common criminal. I am not playing games. But you may see her today or tonight and find a priest if she is willing. Tomorrow morning you will be needed for a flight to one of the other cities, and you can take her with you as your bride, but she must be separated from that family. Otherwise you must never see her again. *Claro?*"

It was clear all right. I nodded again, hating myself for agreeing and remembering I had come to his office to resign. I opened my mouth to say something brave and shut it again. There wasn't any sixth copy of the report.

"I am a regular Cupid." Romirez laughed and held his fat stomach. He was the goddamnedest Kewpie doll yet. Genially he added, "You see, Capitán Hadley, it is just as Fermín Sagasta said, 'You are either for the revolution or against it.' Nobody in my employ can make me look bad the way you did playing around with the Vidals—not twice, anyway. I never tell anybody anything twice. If I start doing that, I lose security and control." The hard glitter back in his eyes warned me that he still didn't trust me. Why should he? He would be right to watch me like a hawk or else get rid of me. All I could hope was that the report would continue to worry him, unless I could hope for an Ortega victory too.

I let him think I was for him all the way, saying, "I see both DC-3s are here. I'll be ready to fly when you want me."

The fat man smiled at my renewed interest in his business. "Regular service is canceled only temporarily," he said, "We can get back in operation next week, and then the new government will start expanding LARC according to your plan. The other three aircraft should arrive in a day or two."

"Swell," I said, sounding enthusiastic.

"All the flying done today will be bombing runs," Rudy said. He seemed elated and a little nuts.

"Oh?" I said.

"*Es verdad,*" Romirez said. "We'll blow up the railroad to the sea and also the road to Mantanzas. That will cut Santa María off from food. There is not enough refrigeration here to make eating in the capital very good for long. I will call our bombing a reprisal for Ortega's bombings and, as long as I can hold the airports, my planes will dominate the cities. The *federales* will be hated for their uselessness. Then they will come over to me with new officers."

I stood there with a frown on my face. Food was a weapon in Ruedo all right. It was a sure bet that the food market bombing had been the Coronel's. And I wondered why he told me so much. Maybe to test me.

"You approve?" Romirez asked.

"As long as I don't have to drop the bombs," I said. "That was our agreement."

Rudy snorted. Then the orderly was at the door, saying there was a messenger with a package for Capitán Hadley.

"Bring it in," Romirez ordered.

From the orderly I intercepted a heavy package wrapped in brown paper, the shape and size of a cigar box. I had forgotten about the damn bullets. Paco's messenger must have followed me from the airport.

Rudy pointed to the package. "Perhaps that is the kind of bomb he wants to use," he insinuated. "I still don't trust him. If he will not participate in the military flights, he should not keep the position as *Jefe* of the airline." It was out now, what the new major wanted—my job.

I unwrapped the package and opened the lid of the cigar box so only I could see the contents. The top layer, at least, was certainly cigars. I offered them to Romirez and then Rudy. They shook their heads in refusal. Romirez was still smoking. Luckily Rudy didn't want one. I closed the lid on the box. I hoped the orderly would forget how heavy it was. Sweat ran icily down from under my arms.

I said to the Coronel, "You gave me a job to do. You put me in charge of LARC, hoping I would make it run better, make it grow. I didn't let you down. I've flown every damn mile of the routes myself. I've looked into every detail in every station. You've got the improved performance records and you've got my plans. I don't want the credit. It's yours. You pay me enough. But I don't need any help from your Kraut major or any crap about my motives at this stage of the game on account of not making any bombing runs. That was not part of the deal. Sagasta agreed."

"*Absolutamente!*" Romirez said. "You may go now, and good luck with your courting the Señorita Vidal." He laughed.

I reached for the photograph on his desk. "I'll take this now, if you don't mind?"

"Not at all." Romirez laughed even harder.

I walked out of his office and wondered how safe I really was. They could be playing cat and mouse with me. In my office I found the week's paychecks had been signed by Romirez but postdated. They couldn't be cashed until Friday the twenty-first. That was another way to buy three more days of loyalty.

The staff was nervous and full of questions about the future of their jobs. I tried to reassure them, but my heart wasn't in it. I left for the Mirado.

In the hotel men's room I loaded the .32 with blunt-nosed bullets from under the cigars and put the pistol back in my pants pocket along with the extra rounds. I wished I hadn't been cute about carrying Lita's gun when I probably could have requisitioned an Air Corps sidearm. Then I gave the cigars to the porter, went into the lobby bar, and looked around for Paco. He was nowhere in sight. After choking down a sandwich I went to the desk and inquired, "*Dónde está el Paco?*"

The clerk made a spitting gesture and said, "What can you expect from a Cuban? He has simply disappeared."

Then I heard martial music—the drums first, followed by bugles and flutes. With everybody else from the hotel lobby, I went outside and watched the *federales* parade. Vidal had apparently ordered this show of strength. His columns of helmeted marching soldiers carried rifles with fixed bayonets, but some of them were out of step. Too many looked like scared little boys dressed up in uniforms. They sweated a lot and unbuttoned their tunic collars. Crowds on the street didn't cheer much.

When the parade had passed, there was a general rush to the bar. My uniform received some hostile looks.

Once more parade music reached the bar. We all thought the *federales* were marching back, so we went out front again to watch. But there were shouts of surprise when we got outside and saw not the *federales,* but a parade of Air Corpsmen.

Coronel Romirez had somehow marshaled an impressive reply to the other parade. His men marched more crisply. Their sky-blue tunics stayed buttoned, and most of them rode in trucks and jeeps. Mortars and machine guns were mounted on the rolling stock, too. The people lining the curb cheered more than before.

Then the Air Corps band stopped playing. Having reached the Plaza República, the parade became a military maneuver. Marchers broke ranks on the double, formed eight-man squads, and took positions that challenged the palace, the federal police barracks, the business section, and even the hotel where we stood on the front steps gaping. Trucks ran up on the sidewalks, and we could see belts of ammunition ready to feed into the machine guns as they were swung around and aimed at rooftops, doorways, including ours, and other strategic targets. All this was done quietly and efficiently. Not a shot was fired. The question was, where the hell had the parading *federales* gone?

There was another rush back to the bar. We were six deep, shouting drink orders to one frazzled bartender. Mine was for a couple of ounces of bravery called Fundador brandy. After the first gulping swallows we were all quieter and noticed that the radio had gone dead. Now, staring stupidly at that little plastic box behind the bar, we really felt cut off. The worst thing was no news.

Then the radio stuttered back to life. "This is Radio Santa María. This station has been occupied by the Air Corps. Publication of newspapers has been suspended until further notice, and all official news will be issued on this frequency. The first bulletin has just been handed me. It reads: 'Coronel Juan Miguel Romirez has declared a state of siege exists in the capital city.' I repeat, 'Coronel Juan Miguel Romirez has declared . . .'"

I put down my glass of brandy and decided that if I was ever going to see Celia again, I'd better see her right away. I had to run up the three flights of stairs to my room, because the hotel elevators had stopped running. Something had happened to the city's power supply. Dripping sweat, I unlocked my door and found everything turned upside down. My room had sure enough been searched.

I quickly packed my B-4 bag, tucking in my log book, passport, the sailfish photo, and Celia's letter. Now I was ready to move out fast and for good, if I had to. But I kept my uniform on. It would provide more freedom of movement around the town, since it was on the winning side.

I could hear the P-51s in the air, and then the floor heaved and the building shook with the WHAM!-WHAM!-WHAM! of a train of 250-pounders going off with delayed-action fuses. This was no dry run. Those GPs I'd carried from Mexico must have done their ugly work on the Matanzas highway. I hadn't warned anybody. Romirez didn't have that on me.

The next blasts were farther away, and the shock just rattled things a little. That would be the railroad getting it.

Another, different engine noise roared close enough to my windows to get an involuntary cringe out of me. It was the B-25 coming back from the railroad target. Johnny was up there, and Pepe. My LARC co-pilots were bombing hell out of surface transport.

I threw my packed bag on a chair and went downstairs. Everybody was drinking as if it was going out of style. I had another brandy. It was two o'clock in the afternoon.

I spotted Harry Donahue buying somebody a drink at one of the tables. Sooner or later I would have to face him, as well as my conscience, about those bombs, so I went over. Besides, I needed some reliable information about the Vidals before I went blundering across town after Celia.

The man drinking with Harry scowled at my uniform. It was Ycaza Lacayo.

Harry said, "Hello, fly-boy." Turning to Lacayo he said, "Shake hands with Luke Hadley. He's not really Air Corps. He runs the airline. And, Luke, this—"

Lacayo interrupted the introduction. "We have met," he said, and his dark, hairy hand reached toward mine. I got a firm handclasp and a piercing look from eyes that burned in a swarthy mestizo face.

Harry looked up and said, *"Uh-*oh!" He had spotted Ben Green heading toward our table.

The correspondent sat down and fastened onto Lacayo.

"Rhymes with Ohio," I said, like a wise-guy.

Ben ignored me. "There's been a police rebellion," he reported. "During the bombing the *federales* mutinied. Those gutless wonders left fourteen of their own dead in the plaza. The revolt was led by a"—he looked at his notebook—"Capitán Jesus María Roblés Padilla. He charged that the Ortega government is dominated by Communists. He named you in particular, Señor Lacayo. Nobody knows where Ortega is, or Ortiz either. Vidal and his family have taken refuge in the Chilean embassy."

"Where is the Chilean embassy?" I asked Harry.

"On the Paseo del Campo, near the park," Harry said. "You going there?"

"If I can," I said.

"There are still some Loyalists sniping from rooftops," Ben said. "In that uniform you'll get your ears shot off."

The radio behind the bar crackled with another Romirez proclamation. He had suspended constitutional rights.

"It was a short war!" Ben Green said.

The agitated radio announcer also spoke of a Sargento Molina's secret police staff. We learned that counterrevolution would be punishable by death. Incitement to terrorism would be punishable by death. The proclamation ended with *"Viva la revolución!"*

Lacayo said, "The firing squads are waiting for me. I will also go to the Chilean embassy."

"There are guards across the street, but they seem to be leaving the hotel alone," Ben said.

Lacayo coughed a sort of warning as he observed people at other tables listening to Ben. The dark politician cupped his lips with a hand and half whispered, "It is to create a false sense of security. The hotel is the open mouth of a net into which counterrevolutionaries will swim. I suppose they know I am here and let me live awhile as bait for my *compadres*."

"It has been too easy for Romirez," Ben said disgustedly.

Lacayo spat on the floor and said, "I have been trying to explain it to Señor Donahue and I have hurt his feelings. If I tell you what is happening, you will not write it, or your magazine will not print it. It is hopeless!"

"Try me," Ben said.

Lacayo shrugged. "All right," he said guardedly. "This situation is the fault of the United States. In many ways. President Ortega and Doctor Vidal know it, too. I think they tried to explain the problems of Latin American countries when they were in Washington, but they were laughed at. To your State Department, our emissaries were just visionaries from a picturesque little country hardly anybody can remember the name of. The great big United States thinks it has all the world's intelligence in its Pentagon and speaks grandly of something called "Hemisphere Defense." United States military missions come into Central and South American countries and provide guns and planes which are really obsolete and have no strategic value against the presumed common enemy, the Soviets, but do, in fact, give dictators the means of keeping their own people down."

Lacayo glared at us. He spat on the floor again. Now he didn't care if his voice carried to nearby tables. "How naïve do you think we are? United States military equipment has helped to strip us of the freedoms it was supposed to defend against communism. I laugh in your faces!"

But Lacayo didn't laugh. He put his head down on the table and wept real tears in a very Latin upheaval of emotion.

Harry said, "Lacayo and the liberals have got to work peacefully to restore the constitution and democratic process here—even if only in a limited way under the new government. Sagasta permitted elections before, so there's hope."

I remembered I had read Lacayo's quoting of Lincoln in the paper and told this to Harry and Ben.

"I am a student of Lincoln too," Harry said. "Remember he said that there is no grievance that is a fit object for redress by mob law."

Lacayo heard that and raised his tear-stained face, passionately declaring, "Lincoln did not know our grievances or our mobs. I have recruited my mob army of freedom fighters, and we will triumph."

Lacayo pantomimed holding up a rifle to his shoulder and crudely spat imaginary bullets. His eyes burned with hate.

Harry pushed Lacayo's hands down. He spoke patiently. "Abe Lincoln said that among free men there can be no successful appeal from the ballot to the bullet, and they who take such appeal, he said, are sure to lose their case and pay the cost."

"You quote him well," Lacayo said. "But we have no honest ballot here. We are not free men in Ruedo. If Lincoln were alive, I think he would march with us and perhaps sing the 'Internationale.' "

"He was a God-fearing man, a praying man," Harry said. "Lincoln would not march with Communists!"

"As for God"—Lacayo snorted—"He too must be on the side of the landowners. Political correctness, to the Church, is merely to be anti-Communistic. That lets the Fascists in. The Church disowns me as a Red, so I disown the Church! As for communism, to me its evils are only scare stories *Yanquis* tell. I have first-hand knowledge of United States imperialism. The Communists didn't have to invent it. Romirez destroys democracy with United States airplanes. If Russia offered me or Ortega aid now, how could you blame us for taking it?"

Nobody at the table answered. Ben was making notes. Then he offered cigarettes and treated to a round of drinks. Lacayo didn't smoke. His drink was a non-alcoholic lime and soda. Ben said, "I guess I got a clean beat on Andy Cluette, but I'd like a quote from you, Harry."

Harry said, "Have you asked Schlomer for a statement?"

"You're a diplomat, all right," Ben said. "Now *give!*"

"Well, be sure you spell my name correctly"—he laughed bitterly—"with an 'a' in Donahue."

"Let me have something controversial," Ben said.

"That's what you're getting, pal," Harry said and launched into it. "If we had a press attaché here, he'd stick to what are called the facts at hand. He'd say, 'We must support law and order. Our country requires stability here.' But I'll have my say about the problem, and it goes a hell of a lot deeper than the intrigue and violence you see on the surface here. Now, I don't agree with Ycaza Lacayo about everything—his attitude toward the Church in particular—but his complaints about our people are somewhat justified. For example, we haven't exported our free economy system. Too many of our own people in business here favor monopoly. Unfortunately we don't pick up the passports of our citizens operating down here, the ones who before the war sold scrap iron to the Japs, who were the five-percenters in Washington after that, and who now don't deplore the grafters in Ruedan politics when they sew up exclusive deals. We haven't even scolded these men. Hell, we've called them VIPs and had them to tea at the embassy. The next thing our government will do is ship a lot of aid dollars here to be administered by a guy who never leaves the capital, never knows the real problems of the people. Old Ruedan families with government connections, and some United States firms too, will do a bigger business on more favorable terms with American taxpayers' dough, while poverty and misery will continue on the plantations and in the mines owned by less than two per cent of the population. No, we can't win a social revolution by writing a check and forgetting it. There is no surer way to insure an underprivileged people's hatred in the long run than to give them a few bucks or even food or shoes. After the food is eaten and the shoes worn out, they are as bad off as before. What downtrodden people all over the world want and need for their self-respect is decent jobs to earn their own food, their own shoes. This means giving them equality of opportunity—equality with us, regardless of the color of their skins!"

Ben scribbled in his notebook.

Lacayo gripped Harry by the arm and pounded his back. *"Eso sí que es!* That's it!" He said vehemently, "Help us to help ourselves! Send us your technicians. Show us your ways. If they are truly right, they will work, and we will be the best friends you ever had!"

"There!" Harry said, pointing to Lacayo, "Does this man sound like a Communist to you?" He gave Lacayo an embarrassed look. "Honest to God, I don't know. Everybody who is critical of the government here or at home gets called a Red. I tell you that right now there are people at home in the States cheering the Romirez victory. The dumb bastards will call it a victory over communism. They'll shut their eyes to the rest."

Harry looked at us sadly and said, "In the good old USA, it is a time of disillusion, a time of cheating in classrooms, of shaving points in basketball games, and of finally graduating to making fast bucks in business, in labor, and in government. The words 'crook' and 'politician' are almost synonymous, and hardly anybody cares. A patriot is a square. A hero is a fool. A guy like Lacayo, crying out in this wilderness, is a bum to be ignored. The fact is that Ycaza Lacayo makes an interesting contrast to our own dishonesty—maybe our underlying cowardice too. Some of his people can see that, so no wonder we are hated when we think we should be loved. I think, so help me, if we fight another war, the people we have become, we could lose. How about that? We could lose!"

"I'll be goddamned!" Ben Green said, and he wrote fast for a minute in silence. Then he got up with a nod to the three of us and left.

"That was pretty strong, Harry," I said.

"I haven't even started on *you!*" Harry said and lowered his voice to a conspiratorial whisper. "Now that Ben has gone, I can tell you what you've got to do. Stay away from the Chilean embassy. Stay away from the Vidals. I'll give Lacayo protection, even *ex officio,* if necessary, but you keep in good with Romirez long enough to hijack one of his planes and fly this patriot inland where he can get a counterrevolution organized."

"What?"

"You heard me!"

"Then what was all that pious advice about peaceful democratic processes?"

"For publication, fly-boy. Romirez and Sagasta can't be stopped by turning the other cheek. Will you make the flight?"

"You must be out of your ever-lovin' mind!" I said, shaking my head. This is all I need, I thought.

"You won't do it?" Harry asked scornfully.

"I'll think about it," I said evasively.

"You want to be paid?" Lacayo asked.

That was an insult and I knew it, which meant I had undergone some kind of change in attitude since I landed in Ruedo, but I hadn't changed enough to say yes to Harry's crazy plan.

Harry waved a waiter over for another round, and I saw it wasn't Paco. Paco hadn't shown up.

"I've had a few," Harry said with his nose in his brandy glass. "I just hope what I said still goes when I sober up, because you know something has happened to us, don't you? No guts any more. No loyalty. No wonder Lacayo doesn't respect us. But if we help him before the goddamned Reds do, that might make a difference. Romirez hasn't got all Ruedo. So, Luke, you could fly this man out of Santa María. That could be a big favor to your own country and you'll probably be thanked by having your United States citizenship revoked. What do you say?"

I couldn't look Harry in the eye.

"No, you won't do it, fly-boy, because you are messed up good. You're going to stop and think pretty soon that you've sat too long at a table with this Lacayo guy. You're just going right on seeing where a dollar can be made or where a girl can be laid. Hey, that rhymes!"

"*Yanqui* go home!" Lacayo said softly to me.

I looked at him over my brandy glass. He was reminding me that he had saved my life in Puerto.

"Luke," Harry said, "I was at the embassy yesterday during the riot. It moved me to see a mob pull down our flag, wipe their asses on the Stars and Stripes, and burn Old Glory in the street! Luke, listen to me! They burned the American flag in the street! Can we let that pass?"

I got up from the table and went to the phone booth, where I looked up the number of the Chilean embassy in the directory. The radio behind the bar blasted out another bulletin listing the names of state criminals who had been arrested and those who were still at large. One name was Ycaza Lacayo. I didn't hear Vidal's or Ortega's names.

When I got through to the Chilean embassy, it took the switchboard there a hell of a while to understand I wanted to speak to Señorita Vidal. The next voice that came on was one I didn't like. It was Carlos'.

"Charlie," I said, "you should have got that paperwork done sooner or you should have done your own killing."

I heard him gasp. For a second he must have thought he'd heard a voice from the dead. Then he said, "No matter, you are finished with Celia, bomber pilot!"

"I didn't fly one of those planes," I said.

"Perhaps that is so," he said, "but who will believe you?"

"Celia will believe me. I can prove it!"

"Did you wear your uniform today?"

"What of it?"

"Enough. You are an enemy. You did not resign as you told Celia you would. You will never see her again."

"Who is going to stop me? You?"

"She will stop you. We are engaged to be married."

"I don't think so. Put Celia on."

"No, *señor*."

"Call her! I'm going to keep on phoning until she talks to me."

"It will be useless."

There was a click on the line. He had hung up. I had to go over there. I had to beat hell out of Charlie. I had to marry Celia right away too, as the Coronel had said, and then fly her to Matanzas or some place. She'd come, if I was going to be a hero—if I was going to fly Lacayo out too. But I hadn't really decided to do that.

I stepped out of the phone booth and saw Harry and Lacayo watching me. I looked away from them. Harry got up from the table unsteadily, took Lacayo's arm, and they went out of the hotel. I followed far enough to see that there was a small American flag on Harry's government car, parked at the door. He would keep Lacayo safe. I leaned against the wall and listened to a guy in the corner of the lobby bar start picking out a mournful tune on his guitar.

Chapter 26

I STARTED for the stairs and nearly bumped into Rudy Heinen.

"I have news for you," he said, not unfriendly.

"Yeah? What about?"

"Your friend the waiter. Paco is in prison."

"The hell he is!"

"Don't you want to get him released?" Rudy asked solicitously.

"You're damn right I want him out of jail. What did he do?"

"Don't you know?"

"How the hell would I know?" I said, but had a sinking feeling about the bullets I had Paco get for me. Everything was counterrevolutionary now.

"I have some influence," Rudy said, tapping himself on his shoulder boards. "I can get your little friend released, if he is innocent. Why don't you help?"

I wanted to do what I could for Paco. "Let's go," I said. "Next thing you'll be running the prison. You could make it a regular Buckenwald, Rudy. That's coming up in the world from running a hotel."

"You may call me Major when we get there," Rudy said, leading me to an Air Corps jeep. He spun the wheels as we took off.

At the prison gate our uniforms didn't prevent our being searched for weapons. Rudy and I were relieved of our pistols. The sight of mine brought a smirk to Rudy's lips.

When the great iron gates of the prison clanked behind us, I lost the feeling I had of being just a visitor. Two guards dropped ten-foot-long hardwood crossbars as thick as railroad ties across the crack where the gates met, and linked the bars to brackets with chains and padlocks. I had come to get Paco out; I hoped I'd get myself out.

We were escorted across a cobblestone courtyard to a gray stone wing of the prison where an arched entrance yawned. In the dark and damply cold tunnel our footsteps echoed hollowly. A bare electric bulb of insufficient wattage showed a turn into a side corridor past barred cells that stank of urine. At first I couldn't see well enough to know if there were people in the cells, but when my eyes became accustomed to the nearly total darkness I saw huddled lumps of humanity on the bare stone floor, men so cowed they seemed to be trying to hide by shrinking inside themselves as turtles do, their heads pulled grotesquely down between their shoulders. Poor Paco, I thought.

At the end of the corridor, through a thick iron-strapped wooden door, was a sort of office. The guard left us there.

Two men uniformed in olive drab sat behind a green metal desk—a sergeant and a corporal, by their stripes. They rose and saluted us. The sergeant wore a black beret and glasses, and his salute was limp.

On a low three-legged stool in front of the desk sat the flat-faced Indian who had wanted to kill me with a machete the night before. Chamorro's half-closed brown eyes moved slowly from the floor in front of him over to where our feet were, and then up our legs to our faces. Looking at me, his eyes showed a flicker of recognition.

"Is this the man?" the sergeant asked with a thin, lisping voice.

"*Sí*, why should I deny it?"

The sergeant pulled his gold-rimmed glasses down on his nose, licked his lips, and, consulting a notebook, read: "You saw him at the *pelea de gallos* just after dark last night. He was accompanied by another man identified as Señor Carlos Caldéras. You watched them for some time. They were engaged in a friendly discussion. Then Señor Caldéras left. Do I have it all correct?"

"*Sí, correcto.*"

"Nuts!" I butted in, speaking to the Indian. "Tell it right, *hombre!* You and your *compadres* came into the patio at the cockfights to make yourselves big heroes by robbing and killing a gringo. Caldéras had a gun on me, and he gave me to you to chop down with your machete. Why don't you tell it the true way?"

The Indian's yellow teeth showed in a half-smile, and he scratched his crotch.

Rudy said, "This is better than the photograph, Luke. Now we have a witness that you have been consorting with the enemy."

"Lies," I said. "You tricked me to get me here. What about Paco?"

The sergeant flipped some pages in his notebook and, adjusting his glasses again, said, "I do not think Chamorro lies. The Cuban corroborated some of this testimony."

"Paco?" I blurted. "Where is he? Let me talk to him."

"You make no demands here," Rudy said, and I saw him signal to the corporal with his eyes. That one had somehow slipped behind me. I felt hard hands grab my right arm and twist it violently into a hammerlock. All I could think was: This is for the birds! I stomped backward with my shoe. At the same time I heaved my arm free. The corporal howled. As he rubbed his shin, I backed to the farthest wall and wondered why I had trusted a Romirez deal.

The sergeant was furiously stabbing at a buzzer on his desk and fluttering his other hand. Another guard showed up. After a palaver in Spanish, one of them led Chamorro away. That left three of them facing me.

Rudy said, "Sergeant Molina has an official order for your arrest signed by Coronel Romirez."

I was thinking fast. Hopefully I said, "I'll bet it was signed when you first showed him the sailfish photo. He didn't sign it since this morning. The Coronel doesn't know a damn thing about this so-called evidence involving Caldéras. I insist on seeing the Coronel!"

Molina laughed. It was a silly falsetto laugh. He said, "The next thing you will want is a trial."

I got my cigarettes out and patted all my pockets for matches. I was disgusted with myself for not having any. Now I couldn't use the smoke to help me act unconcerned. Sergeant Molina handed a box of wax matches to the corporal with a nod, and the corporal came over to me with a light. So they were going to be nice to me. Watch the tricky bastards, I thought.

Rudy said, "Our evidence is more or less circumstantial. It would be much better to have your confession."

"I have nothing to confess," I said as calmly as I could.

Sergeant Molina unrolled a canvas tool kit on his desk. "This is how we conduct our interrogations. Look," he said and caressed a hinged iron clamp that was grooved to fit five fingers and had a chain to hold the wrist. "It fits the hands so nicely and makes it easy to use these tongs when we bend back your fingernails one by one.

"Look at this, too. These little batteries put enough current in this copper wire so that I must wear rubber gloves to hold it against your inner ear. None of my patients can ever keep their balance afterward. They keep falling down and vomiting. It is most amusing to see them."

I was getting a lecture on torture from him while Rudy just kept that goddamned smirk on his face and the corporal looked at me blank-faced.

The leather-thonged whips, the blackjacks, and the knives Molina pushed aside as too crude for words. His soft, thin-fingered hands picked up some thin slivers of bamboo. "This trick we learned from the Orientals. I think you gringos call it the hotfoot. Bamboo is stronger than wood and can be made sharper to drive it in deeply under your toenails. Also, bamboo conducts heat much better."

My hands began to sweat.

"And *this!*" The fairy bastard was almost drooling as he showed me a length of steel wire and made a loop of it. "This is just a guitar string, but it can be looped around a single testicle to pinch it up in the sack as a target, and then I put a single steel ball-bearing in the finger of my rubber glove and stretch it so I can snap it at the *cojon.*"

I almost felt it.

"Over and over I can snap the weighted finger at the testicle until it is pounded to a pulp."

Oh, Jesus!

"An accomplished *torturado* like me has no use for the cumbersome wheel and rack that Cortés brought from Spain. The modern equipment provides more exquisite results."

Molina wet his lips and turned to Rudy. "I think he will talk now, Major." He sounded disappointed.

"I don't know what you think I can tell you," I said, my voice croaking a little in my dry mouth.

"We want to know what Vidal is plotting," Rudy said.

"I don't know."

"You are in on it."

"No."

Rudy sighed and signaled to Molina with his pale eyes.

Molina shrugged and opened his notebook again. "When you are through telling us about what Vidal has in mind, we will ask you about the plans of Ycaza Lacayo. No one keeps a secret in this place."

Molina took off his beret and ran his thin fingers over his completely bald head, put the beret on again, and picked up a long mattress needle from a fold in the canvas roll. "I have never had the pleasure of working on a *Norteamericano,*" he said sadly in a singsong high voice. "I have heard they are not as proud of their *cojones* as Latinos, so perhaps this needle is better. I can insert it under your chin and drive it slowly upward with taps of a hammer, a centimeter at a time, through your mouth and up into your sinuses and finally into your stubborn brain. You will speak as we wish in spite of yourself, if it doesn't drive you insane or kill you too soon. That is the trouble with it. You might die too soon."

He discarded the needle and picked up a piece of leather that looked like an eye mask except that one eyehole was fitted with a brass ring.

"I think this will do it better because there is no risk of your dying on our hands before you talk. I can keep you balanced on the fine line between pain and unconsciousness much longer."

In his other hand he held up a long scalpel-like knife with a buttonhook curve at the end of it. He lisped, "We will strap your eyes so one of them will bulge prettily and just a touch of the blade on the nerves of the eye will bring excruciating pain. Have you ever had a cinder in your eye? Of course you have; so you know what to expect, but if you fail to tell us what we want to hear, I can remove your eye altogether."

They were through playing games. The corporal was pointing a big automatic at my belly. Molina's buzzer brought back the guard, who kicked the little three-legged stool toward me and then lifted a pair of handcuffs from a nail on the wall. My eyes took in every detail of what went on. I wondered what I would tell them. I didn't feel very brave.

The guard came toward me. My hands were fists. "Turn around and put your hands behind you," he said.

"Just a minute," I said.

"Yes?" Rudy said. "You are conditioned to speak already?" His voice was contemptuous.

"I have no reason to protect Doctor Vidal or Señor Lacayo," I said, which wasn't true. "I simply don't *know* anything to tell you."

"That is a shame," Molina said, lisping. "I have the most fun with those who don't know anything. Finally they make up things to tell."

The guard moved closer. They will probably kill me, I thought. If I have to die, I ought to take at least one of them with me.

Again the guard said, "Turn around."

I could hurt him, I knew. I just wished it were Rudy or Molina coming within range. The blank-faced guard was a dumb, unfeeling butcher. If I hit him, so what? I turned around.

The iron handcuffs clicked shut on my wrists behind my back. A little shove, and I was sitting on the stool, the guard tying my ankles to its legs. The corporal put the leather thing over my eyes and pulled its straps back across my ears. Rudy held the corporal's gun. Molina crouched in front of me with the buttonhook knife, his glasses steaming up.

The leather pressed the ring of brass hard into my eye socket. My head ached. Molina waved the knife close to my bulging eye. I saw it in a kind of blur. Then red rockets and a stab of pain that made me grind my teeth. Both eyes blurred with tears and I saw nothing but swimming colors.

"That was just my fingernail"—Molina's girlish voice.

The ring pressed harder. Shooting stars. Pain like a sinus headache in a diving plane. I tried to squirm back, but two men held my head. Voices. Voices far away and indistinct. Noise in my head. Clammy sweat all over me. Brain-piercing pain in my right eye again. I yelled. Damn me, I yelled!

The pressure was removed. Oh, my eye, my eye!

"He doesn't know yet what happened to his eye," Molina was saying. "In another second it would have popped by itself from its socket like a skinned grape."

My hands in the iron cuffs convulsed with desire to reach up and soothe my eye. Did I only imagine tear-blurred purple vision in it?

I heard Rudy say, "Tell us what Vidal plans to do."

"I don't know."

The leather went tight again, and the ring plucked at my eye, letting me know it was still there. It felt full of sand. It felt as big as a basketball. I was all eye. Agony. What did I know that was worth taking this punishment for? It seemed as if I were running frantically through my brain, looking for something—anything to tell them. But I blacked out. I was far away and comfortable for a few seconds or longer. When I regained consciousness my world was still narrowed down to my eye. Then I was going out again. I knew it. I hoped so. But I didn't. The threshold of pain goes up with experience. I was afraid I never would pass out again.

I hardly knew it when the leather and the ring were again taken away. The imprint of their torment stayed with me. The lid on my right eye wouldn't close, but I couldn't see. Nobody held my head any more, so I leaned forward and tried to rub my eyelid shut against my knee. It felt puffy, huge. Gradually the pain subsided to a great ache. I had no sight. They had blinded me!

"We have the following information," Molina said. I could actually hear the notebook pages turn.

"While in Puerto del Sol from February twelfth to sixteenth," Molina read, "Hadley was once seen in the company of one Lita Shelton, a woman known to be close to the Romirez movement. It is possible that he may have been seeking information to give to members of the Ortega government. For example, we know that Ortiz had knowledge that Coronel Romirez' cousin, Lieutenant Lopez, was responsible for the fire bombs in Palmas. Capitán Hadley, did you tell that to Ortiz?"

"No," I half sobbed.

A notebook page flipped. Molina's voice: "Since returning to the capital on February fifteenth, Capitán Hadley's movements have again been of a suspicious nature. He sent a message to the Vidal house by one Paco Gonzales—Cuban, aged twenty-three, employed as a waiter at the Hotel Mirado. This same Paco obtained ammunition in secret for the subject. Hadley has been seen again in the company of Señorita Vidal, and, in fact, did entertain her at his hotel the afternoon of February seventeenth until he left to keep an appointment with the girl's fiancé, who is an official in the Ministry of Peace, one Carlos Caldéras. The latter meeting was witnessed by the Indian, Chamorro. Only an hour ago, the subject also was seen conferring with Ycaza Lacayo, a congressman from the province of Matanzas who is known to be counterrevolutionary."

"It's stupid," I muttered. "Why don't you have it in the dossier that I have also been seen in the company of one Major Rudolph Heinen and one Coronel Juan Miguel Romirez?"

"You are impertinent!" Sergeant Molina half screamed. "You are also a spy!"

"If you weren't so queer, Molina, you could see my relationship with Señorita Vidal is a romantic one and my contact with Caldéras something he himself rigged out of jealousy."

"And your espionage for Ortiz?"

"It wasn't espionage! I suspected Pepe Lopez of starting the Palmas fire, but I didn't tell Ortiz."

"You sent a radio message to him for aid to Palmas?"

"Of course. Why not?"

"What were you plotting with Ycaza Lacayo at the Hotel Mirado today?"

I had to have a quick answer for that one. "The congressman was the guest of the magazine correspondent, as I was, as the United States attaché was. We just talked."

"About what?"

"About politics—what else is there to talk about, for Christ's sake?"

I could see Molina now with my left eye. My right eye was swollen shut

—if it was there. The sergeant leaned back against his desk, trying the buttonhook knife on the edge of his thumb. Rudy sat in the sergeant's chair behind the desk. The other two covered the flanks.

"Perhaps I should detain the correspondent," Molina said to Rudy and looked into his notebook. "Benjamin Green can be arrested, but I think Paco Gonzales is the key to this. I will make the Cuban talk. I think he will be a great talker compared to this gringo."

The corporal took another pair of handcuffs off the wall. He and the guard followed Molina through a door. Sergeant Molina carried the leather eye-press.

When the door shut behind them, Rudy said, "Romirez was too trusting. I am convinced you are dangerous to the revolution."

And to you, I thought. Well, anyway, it was good to know I had the Coronel fooled.

A thin scream came through the closed door, a terrible, less-than-human sound. Had I made a noise like that? Then the door opened and Sergeant Molina minced in, holding a tin plate. In the middle of it was a brown eye with the white all lumpy and bruised. He held it under my nose, and something crawled up the inside of my throat.

"It is one of Paco's eyes." Molina tittered. "If he will not talk now, we will take out his other eye. But if *you* talk, we will stop."

Why was Paco holding out? What could *he* know? The brave little guy! By God, if he could hold out, even at the price of his sight, he didn't expect me to spill anything to save him. I shook my head.

Molina shrugged and went back through the door, and this time he didn't close it. From maybe fifty feet away, a mumble of voices and then another high-pitched, awful scream. Molina came back with the tin plate. There were two eyes on it. I looked away and gagged.

"Why? For Christ's sake, why?" I asked, my voice cracking.

"Because Paco only wishes to talk to a priest, that's why. But they all die unshriven here."

"You can save him, Hadley," Rudy said.

"We all die," I said, but I wasn't ready to—not here.

"Death is something to be desired by my patients." Molina giggled as he went out of the office again, carrying the tin plate.

"What is your rotten sadist going to do to him now?" I asked Rudy.

"The usual thing."

Then I heard it and tried to jump up, but the stool, tied to my feet, tripped me. I fell on my face. I lay on the stone floor, hearing the strangled sound of a man crying and begging. Over and over, the crying: *"No! . . . No! . . . No! . . . No! . . . Aiiiii!"* Then silence.

I lay there, tangled in the stool, thrashing around like a madman, until I realized Molina was standing above me with his frigging tin plate. I knew what was on it now, but he had to show me.

"These are his testicles I cut out," Molina said.

I felt an involuntary tightening of my loins as his voice went on over me: "The *cojones* are the symbol of manhood to the Latinos. They hate to see them go. They will often tell me anything rather than sacrifice them to my steel ball or my knife. Of course, an emasculated gringo like you— I don't know."

I found my voice. "You *son-of-a-bitch!* You *rotten son-of-a-bitch!*"

"Is there something you wish to tell us now?" Molina asked as he put the plate down on the floor near my face.

"Yes! You are a rotten son-of-a-bitch! Hear me? A son-of-a-bitch!"

"That is all he is going to say now," Rudy told Molina. "I think before you cut off *his* nuts he should see his boy Paco."

Molina protested. "Nothing is to be gained by that."

"Let's try it," Rudy said. "Hadley may crack when he sees—"

"No, let me work on him with the steel ball," Molina said.

Rudy didn't like being crossed. *"My* way!" he shouted.

They held a conference. Molina was against bringing Paco's body to me because he did not want a mess in his office. He was also against untying me to take me to the other room. "Forget about the dead Cuban," Molina said shrilly.

Rudy was a stubborn German. "No!" he shouted. "Show Paco's body to the Capitán. He will talk then."

"I am in charge here!" Molina whined.

"You forget yourself, Sergeant!" Rudy yelled, red-faced. "I am *Major* Heinen! The Capitán is *my* prisoner!"

"In *here,* Major," Molina said sarcastically, "the prisoners are mine. I myself will take the Capitán to see his dead friend!"

Rudy took a knife from Molina's desk, and it flashed down, cutting my ankles loose from the stool. Then the German ordered the corporal to unlock my handcuffs.

"No!" Molina shrilled.

My hands were free, and I was swinging from the hip. Oh, *baby!* It felt good all the way up my arm to my shoulder and down to my feet when my fist landed on Molina's face. His glasses were smashed. My knuckles were cut by the shattered glass. The fist had a life of its own. It moved again, lightning-fast, and I felt the bone in Molina's jaw give.

Rudy had goofed when he had my handcuffs unlocked—but maybe not. Maybe he knew what he was doing. He just watched Molina sag to the floor and didn't point his gun at me. Before the corporal and the guard could get over their surprise, I busted through them like a football lineman and made the open door. I knew the door was in the wrong direction, but in the second I had, it was the only way to go. A fast man can run a hundred yards in ten seconds, so it was no surprise to me that I got at least thirty feet between me and those ghouls in one second.

Nobody followed me. I looked around with my one good eye in the dim light and realized I was trapped in a dead-end corridor. Through the bars into a cell I saw a nude man lying on a table. It was Paco, and he had his eyes. His dead brown eyes stared up at the ceiling, but he'd died too late. The other things were gone. His life had run out of that wound.

I threw up. I did it mechanically, without losing control. Between the times I retched I made myself look again. Paco's body was chalky white and rigid. He looked as if he had been dead a long time. I wondered what the hell the poor little bastard had been up to to get it like this. It must have been more than the errands he ran for me.

I moved along the corridor to another cell and vomited again, straight out, right through the bars. I splattered a pile of bodies that were stacked like cordwood. Their heads were toward me, faces upward. Chamorro lay on top.

Where the Indian's eyes had been were two clotted holes with dried bloodstreams running down his cheeks into his mustache. The gold tooth was gone from his gaping mouth. He had been castrated too. Chamorro had told me it was nothing to die. He had just done it the hard way.

The office door opened wide behind me, letting more light into the corridor. What I saw then left me hanging on the vomit-slippery bars. Sticking out from the pile of bodies were two faces I recognized—those of Armando Ortiz and his wife. An eye was missing from each face. I could imagine how Molina had passed those in front of each spouse to get his information. Knowledge of Romirez' complicity in the Palmas fire had been Ortiz' death warrant.

Then Rudy was standing beside me. He held the pistol at his side.

I said wearily, "It isn't Buchenwald, but it's quite a show."

"I saw Paco's body also," Rudy said.

"Molina fooled you too," I said.

"*Ja!* Now let us get out of here, my friend."

"If you are my friend, Rudy, I don't need enemies." I held my handkerchief to my throbbing eye.

"All right, not your friend, then. Think of me as an ally. I freed you, no? Now I also know too much. We both have to get out of here. If you didn't hit Molina hard enough, it won't be easy. I don't want to shoot the head of the secret police."

Rudy led us back to Molina's office with the corporal's gun ready, but the two guards didn't bother us. They were helping Molina out the other door. "We are taking him to the hospital. His jaw is broken," the corporal said ruefully. "There are slivers of glass in his eyes."

I was glad. It was a feeling of satisfaction that came ahead of the rationalization of an eye for an eye. The corporal and the guard held Molina up by his arms and paid no attention to me at all. Then I brought my foot up like I was going to make a place-kick ninety yards. My size-twelve shoe caught Molina squarely where he had it coming. All three of them went down in a heap as their queen screamed.

Full of a sadness for the human race so deep I can't say yet what it meant, I followed Rudy down the corridor and stumbled, one-eyed, out into the prison courtyard.

Rudy and I got our guns back from the guard at the gate. If the guard noticed that I hid my eye, he was unconcerned. The slow process of removing the padlocks, chains, and crossbeam allowed time for Molina to appear, still supported by his men. They made no outcry.

Rudy drove us away in the jeep. "Your eye will be all right," he said, not unkindly.

I felt a big sigh of relief in me but I didn't say anything.

"Sergeant Molina likes his work too much," Rudy said, as if to himself. "But men like him are a necessary means to an end. We have so little time to get the information we need."

"It doesn't always work, though, does it?" I muttered.

"No, torture is a funny thing," Rudy philosophized. "The more we try to make some stubborn people talk, the more they resist us. It is the law of opposite results. I suppose it was like that with the waiter, Paco. I was distressed when you pushed us so far. I would have felt bad about you. Well, I didn't let Molina do that awful thing to you."

"Your better nature got the best of you," I said.

"I don't know what got into me."

"Why do you act the way you do, Rudy Heinen?"

"I wish I knew—yes, I do know. You were never a kid in Germany under the Nazis," he said defensively.

"Sure, blame somebody else."

"I *am* taking you to a doctor."

I didn't feel I had to thank him. We rode on in silence. My eye hurt like hell. "Please," I said after a while and hated myself for it, "please, where is the damn doctor?"

"Here!" Rudy said and skidded the jeep to a stop. The lurching hurt, and I made a sound.

The German had that smirk on his face again, and one hand patted his breast pocket. "I have Molina's notebook, so you won't try anything against me."

I sat there, almost too weak to get out of the jeep. My hands shook, and I felt a wave of nausea. I gripped the door and made myself jump over it. I held onto the little core of hardness left in me and hoped that it wouldn't turn to jelly. Then I swore at him. I called him every filthy name I knew, but it wasn't enough to get my self-respect back.

Rudy's hand plucked at mine where I leaned on the door for support. "What are you going to do now?" he asked.

"I'm going to see the goddamned doctor!"

"I mean after that."

"I don't know—get drunk maybe."

"Remember, you have a cargo flight tomorrow."

"Yeah," I said, and I also remembered I had Romirez' permission to visit the Vidals once more. "Maybe I'll get married," I added.

Rudy's eyes narrowed. "There is something—something I do not understand in the Coronel's wishes about that, but you may have to make a deal with me too."

"Go to hell!" I said.

"Listen," he insisted. "The head of the secret police can make his fortune by allowing a few rich prisoners to escape. It is to be expected." He said that flatly, as if allowing for a foible of human nature. "Now with Molina's notebook, I can also bargain. This is no war. The shooting could be all over by tomorrow. What good is an Air Corps command then? I want the airline. I want your job as general manager of LARC. It won't cost you any cut in pay. You can still run Operations and Sales—under me. Why not? After all, your politics is still the dollar, isn't that so?"

I blinked my good eye at him and didn't have a answer ready because a lot of things were mixed up in my mind. Maybe he was partly right about me.

"It's a deal, then?" He expected agreement.

"You've got all the high cards," I said, and I felt my lips tremble. The ache in my eye was unbearable.

"So!" he said, concluding the matter, but he had to rub it in. "When we make horrible examples of those who resist us, others fall into line."

Rudy had to be wrong, I thought. Wrong. But I was having a shivering reaction, the way you do after a close call in a near-fatal accident. It was a bad moment, much worse than the night before after Chamorro's machete. It was a time for a drink or a pill or a kind word. My internal shakes were as bad as that time after flying through heavy flak and landing with two engines burning. I hadn't been paralyzed by fear while in action—only later, back at the base, and even then it didn't show too much on the outside. Now, some distance from the prison and that pile of bodies, I was so scared I almost cowered, yet my mind was working. I rationalized that agreeing with Rudy at this time wouldn't be surrender, just buying some time. I needed time to plot something and to nail him. There had to be some way—even from behind. I'd cold-cock him the first chance I got.

In a nice even voice, I said, "So long, Rudy."

He drove off.

A minute later the doctor was asking me what had happened. I told him I had been in a fight.

"It's this revolution!" he said. "Hot tempers all day. I have treated four gunshot wounds and two knifings, but you are on the right side, Capitán."

Pride or something helped me control my twitching fingers while he lanced the mouse on my eye and put his mustached mouth on it to suck out the fluids. He spat in an enamelware basin and angled the little mirror strapped to his head to reflect light as he probed around with sticks wrapped in cotton.

"It will turn black and blue, Capitán," the doctor said, clucking. He put a big wet compress on the eye and also put some iodine on my skinned knuckles. His fee was a hundred duros.

As I paid him he told me had heard on the radio that Romirez had scheduled a six-o'clock meeting with Ortega and the ministers, granting them amnesty to confer at the Maya Country Club.

"All the ministers?"

"Sí."

There were no taxis on the streets. I walked to the hotel. It was six o'clock when I got there.

Chapter 27

I WENT up to the bar in the lobby and stood there wondering what to do. My hands trembled, so I put them in my pockets. I was the guy who wasn't going to get involved. Now I was not only involved, I was in the middle. I was cordially hated by both sides. And I had it coming.

A new barman stood in front of me, waiting patiently for my order. He politely refrained from mentioning my bandage, but I hated him. No, I just missed Paco. I couldn't even think what I wanted to drink.

"Capitán," the bartender said, "we have the whisky of your country, but is very expensive."

"All right," I said.

He ducked under the bar and came up with a bottle of Old Crow bottled in bond. He carefully measured a two-ounce shot and shook his head sadly. "Twenty whole duros," he said, shaking his head. *"Quiere agua?"*

"No water," I said and tossed it off. It had the remembered shock and flavor. I reached for the bottle before the bartender could hide it again. *"Cuánto por toda la botella?"* I asked.

In shocked disbelief, he said, "Two hundred duros!"

I sorted the pink bills out of my wallet and let them flutter to the dark mahogany bar, the equivalent of sixteen bucks. Then I took the bottle of bourbon by the neck and started for my room.

It was an old established American institution to get drunk when things look dirty black, like when you lose a job or the night before your marriage. If this was going to be my pre-wedding bachelor party, I was glad to have American whisky to get properly drunk on.

In my room I took off my soiled uniform and sat on the edge of my bed. I slipped the chain of the Saint Christopher over my head and put the medal in my wallet. My eye hurt. I hurt deep inside for Paco and also for me, because I was alone and because there was no word from Celia. And how the hell could I call her and tell her of Romirez' ridiculous proposition? Ridiculous!

I never let the glass get empty. I sipped and poured and sipped and poured, and I was making progress.

I had been in Ruedo just a month. It seemed like years. In the beginning I had felt right at home. Latin America can hit you that way—or the opposite way. Maybe a lot depends on why you're there. I had been running away. But sooner or later you have to stop running and turn and make a stand, if only to face the things in yourself you have been running from. I had decided to make my fight or make my separate peace, whichever it was going to be, right here. Ruedo had offered me a kind of hospitality, and a guy doesn't square himself away on a desert island. He does it with other people around. In my case I had preferred strangers for this, as long as somebody had to watch. Trouble was, they didn't stay strangers. One had loved me; others waited in line for a chance to kill me.

Oh, hell. Don't think about it. Concentrate on the whisky.

I looked owlishly into the emptying bottle and I thought I was looking into places I never had seen before. I didn't like what I saw. I poured a stiff one and was drinking it down like medicine when the telephone rang.

I looked at the instrument and didn't pick it up until I thought it might be Celia.

"*Dígame,*" I said.

"Hello—Luke?" It was Harry Donahue's voice.

"Yeah," I said, getting some more of the hundred-proof bourbon down.

"Have you decided anything?" he asked.

"I think this phone is bugged," I said.

"Sure it is," Harry said. "But right now everybody wants to be friends with the USA. Get me? Hey, my spies saw you go in and out of jail. Glad you made the round trip. Everything okay?"

"I'm not sure," I said and put my glass on the floor and then I tipped the bottle over it. Leaning over made my eye throb and brought the nausea back.

"I wanted to ask you if you've given any thought to that proposition—"

I knew what Harry meant. "Don't ask," I said.

"You want business, don't you?" His words were cryptic, but I got the meaning. He was talking about flying Ycaza Lacayo out. Maybe he also meant paying me.

"The hell with that, you cooky-pusher," I said.

"What are you doing? You don't sound right."

I felt like laughing, but it would hurt to laugh. So I just smiled a small smile because somebody was worried about me. Oh, no, he wasn't. He was worried about his precious passenger to wherever I was going in the morning. "I'm getting drunk," I said. "Very drunk."

"You yellow bastard," Harry said.

"That's right," I said and lifted the glass from the floor and took a big swallow and coughed.

"We've got to help them," Harry said.

"Screw them!"

"I mean it. This is a real test."

"Of what? Of who? *Whom?*"

"Of you maybe. Of me too. Maybe of our foreign policy."

"Baloney!"

"You got me there, but I know what's right. So do you. Trust your instincts."

"My instincts say, screw 'em!"

"You got a radio in your room?"

"No, it's a cheap room."

"I'll call you back, then. There's going to be news. I've got to catch it. Romirez got all the ministers to meet at the Maya Country Club. Very fancy get-together. They are going to vote on a junta."

"Vidal go there?"

"Sure. Vidal, all of them."

"Not Ortiz!" The drink had made me incautious.

"You *know* something, Luke? Tell me."

"Nah!"

"You won't help?"

"Why should I?"

I hung up, not wanting any more of Harry's self-righteousness, and I looked out the window through the distortion of the nearly empty brown bottle. It's getting very drunk outside, I thought, and I thought about the Maya Country Club, where Ruedo's government was being auctioned off. I had never been there, but once when my LARC job looked like it was going to go very well I'd thought about buying a membership. It was a swanky layout. Two swimming pools. Dances. Celia and her society friends went there. She must have gone there with Carlos lots of times; danced with him; necked with him on the way home in his car. Goddamn it all to hell! She was the only passenger I wanted to take someplace in the morning. Romirez said this was supposed to be my wedding night!

I picked up the telephone to call the Chilean embassy, but I didn't. There was no use calling the Chilean embassy if Dr. Vidal was going over to Romirez. There wouldn't need to be any cargo flight tomorrow. All Ruedo would capitulate. I asked the switchboard for the bar and ordered another bottle of whisky, and that went sour too. They didn't have any more, so I ordered a bottle of dark rum. Damned if I was going to wait between bottles, needing a drink. I'd have the second one up in the room before the first one was finished. If I was lucky, it might come in an hour—without Paco, that is. Poor Paco. Too bad he can't vote for the new government, Harry! So I don't want to know how the election returns come out at the Maya Country Club. I took a drink from the bottle. Never mind the glass. I had it going good now.

The phone rang. I spoke aloud to it without lifting the receiver. "Don't tell me about it, Harry. I got troubles of my own," I said.

I examined my bottle, which had been a fifth and was now a smaller fraction. I'd had enough of it to make the working of fractions in my head difficult, but I finally figured that I had an eightieth left. I deliberately set about polishing it off to get my brain short-circuited so I wouldn't think anything, especially not about all the trouble I was in now. Trouble.

"Of my own making, Harry. Bad trouble," I said to the ringing phone. "Something must have happened to me in the war."

"Sure it did."

"Who said that? By Christ, something happened to everybody in the war. Quite a few got dead. How about that, Harry?"

"Some heroes, too."

"I am quite a nice guy in some ways, but I'm no hero. Sagasta's at the door, ringing his fool head off."

"Damn it, you are no hero."

"But I'm quite a nice guy."

"In some ways."

"I have *muchos cojones,* like Chamorro said. I am allowed to keep them until Sergeant Molina castrates me."

"You didn't want to get involved."

"I didn't want to get in love, either."

"And now you are alone."

"All alone by the telephone."

Ring . . . ring . . . ring . . . ring. That damn Sagasta! It was an outrage! I stood up and glowered, breathing fire. Now I was as well hung as that bull up in Mexico, and if I was cut and bleeding, like that bull, my wounds had made me mad. The ringing was the trumpets in the plaza where the bull had to be killed in twenty minutes or he would be unkillable as he learned to distinguish between man and cape. Maybe it was like that in a man's life. By the time he can tell reality from illusion, it is time for him to die. And still, a good brave bull doesn't run from it, or wait for it; he goes in for it and sometimes, though rarely, he wins.

I picked up the phone. "Hello, Harry," I said.

"Hello, Capitán Hadley?" It was another voice. It was Carlos Caldéras.

"Le' me shpeak to Celia," I slurred.

There was a pause, then Celia's sweet voice saying, "Luke, we need you. Help us! Please come now!"

I didn't even think. I said, "Where?"

"The embassy of Chile. Hurry!"

I staggered a little. I wanted to tell her I loved her. I wanted to know if she loved me. But all I said was, "Celia, I will be there as shoon as possible." I got those words out pretty good.

I put the phone down carefully and pointed myself toward the bathroom, kicking the empty whisky bottle out of the way, making it roll across the floor. I went into the bathroom and deliberately stuck my finger down my throat. The result made me feel a little weak but not quite so dizzy. I soaked my head under the cold-water faucet. I dried my face and puked again involuntarily. I had done a lot of vomiting for one day. I repeated the cold-water treatment.

I'm definitely getting older, I thought, looking into the bathroom mirror, and the wet bandage on my eye has got to go. The adhesive came off with some eyebrow, and I saw the damnedest black eye I ever had, only it was green and purple, and split. I put a Band-Aid over the cut part. I didn't look so hot for my wedding.

You're kidding yourself, I said to myself. That isn't why you're going to her. You've got about as much chance of marrying her as—as— The reason you're going is because you care. That's it. You really care for the girl. And that's what counts.

Two strong black coffees later I headed for the palace with a plan forming in my head.

When I got there I called out to the guards, "One of you get my Lancia out of the palace garage. *Pronto!*"

They saluted and cut a man loose for the detail because I stood tall in my Air Corps blues.

I drove the Lancia very fast through the streets of Santa María and out toward the park where the Chilean embassy was. Sure, some of the whisky was still working in me, but the breeze with the top down helped. I chewed on a dead cigarette and I didn't think, except about each downshift and when to steer with the throttle, drifting the corners. It was no use thinking more about how things were. Now I was doing something. I was driving well, the way drunks are positive they do. I was going to my girl's rescue. In the process, I might even help Lacayo. He fitted into my plans now. I grinned, wishing I could tell Harry he was right after all. The way I felt about that Irish bastard was something like the way it is after a ten-round fight when you are evenly matched and can't do much with the other guy because he takes your best punches and smacks you right back in the gut, and you pound away at each other till you're arm-weary and a very deep hatred for him changes, round after round, to what is very like love for a man at the end when, bloody and battered, you get to hug and cuff each other after the bell, willing to concede he won it.

In the park my headlights speared a gang of dark-skinned men, maybe twenty of them, in the road. They waved machetes, pistols, and a few rifles. I leaned on the horn, pedaled the clutch, and snorted the engine as if I meant to ram them. They opened a path just wide enough for me. Some of them leaned into the Lancia cockpit as I went by. One slapped the car with something. A couple of guns went off. Maybe at me. I don't know. They were hoodlums using the revolution as an excuse to shoot up the town, probably to settle a few personal grudges.

The Chilean embassy was floodlighted, and the iron gate in front was guarded by *federales*. I talked my way past them and the gatekeeper and then tooled the car up a curved driveway to the entrance of the mansion.

The Chilean butler opened the door for me, and the Vidals' old Jorge was with him. I was escorted to a large sitting room off the main hall that had a three-story ceiling and an enormous crystal chandelier.

Doña Felisa greeted me and introduced me to her husband. White haired Dr. Vidal didn't look as impressive close up as he had from a distance at the airport. There was something too pinched and thin-skinned about him. I noticed his forehead-creasing frown and the way his eyes half closed as if against pain when he shook my hand, but his lips smiled.

Celia came in through another door—with Carlos. She didn't say "Hi" this time.

Celia held out her hand to me. I shook it stiffly, wanting to take her in my arms.

I shook hands with Carlos Caldéras too, and what I wanted to do was belt him one.

The amenities over, Dr. Vidal got to the point. "Where do you stand, Capitán?"

There it was again. I knew where I stood now, but I had a funny habit. I gave him an evasive answer. "Where do you think?"

"I think he is with Romirez!" Carlos said. "I do not trust him!"

"Talk to Major Heinen," I said. He curled his lip, so I added, "Listen, Charlie, you don't like me. I don't blame you exactly, but I think you dislike me enough to—"

He cut me off. *"That* has nothing to do with this!" He didn't want them to know he'd left me to be killed yesterday.

Celia moved from his side to mine. She touched my arm and said, "We must not fight among ourselves." Her voice was honey compared to Romirez', but the words were the same.

"Those troops outside," I said to the doctor, "are any of them still loyal to you?"

"Not the ones still in uniform, Capitán, but some have taken them off rather than serve the new regime." He frowned with distaste at my Air Corps blues.

"What happened at the Maya Country Club?" I asked.

"You have have not heard it on the radio?" Celia asked.

"No."

"Betrayal!" the doctor said, "Ortega's position was weakened without the presence of Ortiz. Romirez said the Vice President had left the country. It is hard to believe. The Coronel has been very clever, very thorough."

"He isn't that smart," I said. "He follows Sagasta's orders."

"Es verdad?" Dr. Vidal asked, horrified.

"It's the truth," I said.

"Then we are truly lost," he said.

I looked at them with sympathy and said, "I saw your friends, Ortiz and his wife, dead in the prison."

"Oh, Mother of God!" Doña Felisa cried.

Caldéras asked, *"How?"*

"The worst way," I said and looked away from him and his stupid question.

"Your eye!" Celia said, touching the plaster gently with a fingertip. "Did they do this to you?"

"It is nothing," I said, the way heroes said it in the movies.

"It *is* nothing!" Carlos said. "You must have talked, or you would have no eyes!"

Then I hit him. I knocked him down.

It was not a nice, gentlemanly thing to do in that elegant embassy sitting room in front of good, gentle people. My God, I thought, I'm cracking up, losing all self-control.

I picked Carlos up off the floor, dusted his coat, and said, "I'm sorry." Like hell I was.

Nobody else said anything. That Charlie just dabbed at the trickle of blood at the corner of his mouth.

"It is incredible!" Dr. Vidal said, and he was talking about what had happened to Ortiz, not Caldéras. "Why would they do that? It is not done. Latin American governments have a way of changing. By giving the outgoing regime amnesty, the new ruler assures his own safety when his time comes."

"I always knew Romirez was impossible!" Doña Felisa said, "You are in grave danger, my husband." She put her arms around him.

The doctor wasn't panicky but he said, "I must get out of Santa María."

"Out of Ruedo would be better," I said.

"No, I will be safe in the country, perhaps near Puerto del Sol, where I have friends. I must stay in Ruedo to help fight this thing," the doctor said calmly.

"We need your help, Luke," Celia said.

"The road to Matanzas may still be passable," Carlos said.

"It was bombed out and there will be soldiers covering it," the doctor said sadly.

I knew what they wanted. They wanted the same thing Ycaza Lacayo wanted. I was their way out.

I said to Dr. Vidal, "Please, sir, I would like to speak to Celia a moment—alone."

He looked at Celia. She said, *"Con su permiso, Tío Luis?"*

He nodded okay, but Carlos protested. "Anything you have to say to her you can say in front of me and the family."

I wondered if he really wanted me to deck him again.

Celia's uncle said, "We will withdraw for ten minutes. I must speak to the Ambassador, to thank him." His word was the law.

The three of them went out and closed the double doors behind them. I looked at Celia, but there was no invitation in her eyes. My throat was hot with heartburn. I didn't feel well at all. I sat down for the first time since I had arrived.

Celia sat on the arm of a chair across from me. "Luke?" she questioned. "What is it between you and Carlos? I mean, it is more than me."

I put a cigarette in my mouth and offered her one.

She shook her head impatiently and said, "I am going to marry Carlos. I told you before."

"You told me you loved me. You wrote—"

"I love *him!*"

"All right," I said, but I had to ask her, "Like it was with me?"

"I don't know. No, I don't think so. I knew him a long time before I knew you. . . ." Her eyes were pained. There was a resemblance to her uncle. "Carlos hates you so!" she added.

Well, I thought, I hate him pretty good too, and I hated to think of him with her. It couldn't be like us. Yet why not? It was natural. She was a loving girl. Damn her!

"You want him to escape with you?" I asked.

"Yes."

I remembered my cigarette and lit it. I got up and walked around the room. I came back to the chair where Celia perched. Her dark eyes were wet, but she held up her head proudly.

"All right," I said.

She ran into my arms, sobbing. It didn't make sense.

"I hate you! I *hate* you!" she said and pounded my chest with her small fists. Tears spurted from her eyes. Her voice squeaked to silence. I tried to comfort her. My big hands were clumsy. I managed to stroke her hair and hold her softly in my arms, to pat her back and kiss her tenderly on the forehead.

Then she squeezed my back very hard with her fingers, her nails digging through my shirt, and she kissed me. She was all over me. Her lips were demanding. Mine were too. My hands dropped to her small waist and then to her hips as I felt her legs move apart and the soft inside of a thigh pressed to one of my legs.

I put my hands on her shoulders and pushed her into a chair. Her hands were limp in her lap. She had a gone expression on her face. I must have looked twice as stupefied.

"I *do* hate you," she said slowly.

"Sure you do," I told her. I felt wonderful. I would fly through hell to save her.

"Luke?"

"What, darling?"

"We shouldn't do that. It is wrong, honey, but I can't help it. What is the matter with me? I love to be loved by you, but it is not what I am meant for. I am meant for Carlos."

"That's right," I said, laughing.

"It is not funny, Luke."

"Yes it is, and we'll all die laughing if we don't make some plans to get away."

"My aunt and uncle will be right back. What did you want to say to me alone?"

"That I love you. And will you marry me?"

"I can't."

"Believe it or not," I said, "I have Coronel Romirez' permission to marry you, but he said it must be tonight. The bastard even threatened to harm you if you stayed with your family."

She looked at me coldly. "Would *you* do that to me, Luke?"

"What?"

"Would you threaten me?"

I hadn't meant for her to take it that way. Before I could say no, she said, "I won't marry you just to save myself!"

I wasn't surprised. And I *had* come to save them all, even Lacayo. Their danger was my danger now.

Tears were filling Celia's eyes again as the doors opened and the threesome filed in, Caldéras in the lead. They stood in a half-circle and looked worried. Carlos had worked up a scowl for me. I laughed in his face and looked around for my cigarette. It had burned out in an ashtray.

I lit another and spoke to Carlos. "Do you still pack that Luger?"

He reached for his belt and patted a bulge there. Wow! He had controlled his temper pretty well up to now!

"You'll need it, Charlie," I said, "because you're going out in the streets. You're going over to the United States Embassy and ask for Harry Donahue. If he's not there, go to his apartment, the Casa Real, on Avenida Santa María. Don't speak of this to anyone else, but ask Mr. Donahue where to find Ycaza Lacayo."

"That rabble-rouser? Why?" Carlos asked disdainfully.

"Because you need him for the plan I have, and he wants to get out of the capital just as much as you and the Vidals do."

"What should I tell Lacayo?"

"Just tell him we're flying somewhere tomorrow and to come here with you tonight. Do you think you can do it? Don't bring the enemy here after you. This is not like it was at the cockfights."

"I can do it," he said, mean-eyed, hating my guts.

"Then get going!"

He didn't move. "I think you are trying to get rid of me," he said, looking at Celia.

Celia said to him, *"Vaya!* Go quickly! We will wait."

Carlos went over to Celia and kissed her on the lips. It took something to do that in front of me. I hoped he had enough for the rest of the trip.

"What is this of the cockfights?" Dr. Vidal asked.

"It is nothing. A joke between us," I said.

"I think not," Doña Felisa said and looked at me in a certain way. She hadn't looked at me that way very often. It made me proud. Celia was looking out the window, watching Carlos leave.

"What is your plan?" the doctor asked.

I sat on the down-filled red velvet cushion of a French Bergère chair. I was tired. I had a half-drunk, dizzy hangover. My eye hurt again. I put my hand over it. "We can talk about the plan when Lacayo gets here," I said. "I'm bushed. I don't want to go through it twice."

Outside, the sound of sirens came closer and closer until they were right out front and then faded in the distance.

"Ycaza Lacayo is a radical, but he has stature," Dr. Vidal said.

Doña Felisa asked, "Can we take Celia's mother when we go, and perhaps our two old servants?"

"I don't want to discuss it now, I told you."

"As he wishes, *por favor,*" Celia said, God bless her.

"You need not talk," Dr. Vidal said. "Since you did not hear Ortega on the radio, I will tell you what has happened. I will tell it from the beginning."

The doctor's face was pinched as he held himself in, and his voice was tense. "I was summoned to a six p.m. meeting at the Maya Club, escorted by my own traitorous *federales*," he said. "All seven ministers were brought into the board room—but not Ortiz, of course.

"Romirez stood at the end of the long table. He proposed a junta of three men to take control of the government. I think we were all genuinely surprised. The Coronel had control all by himself. Why should he make concessions?

"I was to be one of the three men to take over, I suppose for appearances; also Fernandez, Minister of Agriculture; Romirez, of course, the third. Then Romirez relinquished his position at the head of the table to Ortega, as though the poor man were still President.

"Ortega then asked for a vote. Three ministers voted in favor of the junta, and Romirez' vote made four. I, the Minister of Mines, and Moncado Flores, the Minister of Justice, voted against it. When President Ortega cast his vote, it was a deadlock.

"The Coronel was furious. He swore at us. He raved like a lunatic. Then he proposed calling on Sagasta to return from exile to join the junta as a fourth man. It was a threat. I rose and tried to make a speech against that proposal, but Romirez made my objection unnecessary by demanding a vote on a different junta, this time with Ortega replacing me. This was very strange in view of what you say, Capitán—that Romirez takes his orders from Sagasta. The deadlock should have pleased him."

I nodded, fascinated.

"The second vote was six to two in favor of the junta. Only the President and I held out against it. But Ortega said he would accept the majority vote, for that is how he feels about democracy.

"I left the club in a government limousine, and no one tried to stop me. On the radio in the car I heard Ortega make his statement to the people—that he recognized his duty in the new government, the junta, that he would continue to serve the welfare of all Ruedo to the best of his abilities. He is our hope for sanity in the new government. He made a plea for law and order, and that was all. The *coup d'état* was complete."

"You think Romirez has double-crossed Sagasta?" I asked.

"Possibly, but I doubt it. Somehow I still fear *El Sagáz*. And Fermín Sagasta has no love for the Vidals. He put my brother to death," the doctor said. "I must have had a premonition when I moved my wife, my sister-in-law, and my niece here to the Chilean embassy, taking every precaution. Chile has had time with democracy. I knew my friend their Ambassador would understand and give us asylum. Have you proof of Sagasta's authorship of the Romirez coup?"

"I never knew the details," I said. "I just know Romirez took Sagasta's orders—to the letter—but that was two weeks ago."

"So much has happened in two weeks," Celia said. "You would not believe so much could happen!"

"This junta has the intricacy of something planned by *El Sagáz*," Doña Felisa said. She looked from me to Celia and back, as if our relationship too was part of some insidious plot.

I felt awful. We were quiet a long time. I closed my eyes and thought how that morning Romirez had said he would arrest the doctor, probably the women too. When I opened my eyes, I saw Celia was watching the street again from the front window. "Here they come!" she cried.

I heard Ycaza Lacayo's voice at the opening doors. He strode into the room with Carlos behind him.

"*Señoras y señores*," Lacayo said politely, kind of mournfully, "I am sorry to bring you more bad news. Felipe Esteban Ortega is dead. Assassinated."

Doña Felisa's hand flew to her mouth. There was fear in her eyes as she looked at her husband.

"Please sit down," Dr. Vidal said. "Tell us!"

"Of course, I did not see it myself," Lacayo said, "but I have an organization. I had men at the Maya Club—waiters. Word came to me of how Ortega died. He made a fatal mistake. He trusted Romirez. Nobody will do that again in this country and be fit to govern. Ortega was a weak fool. He actually believed he was to be part of that junta!"

"*Por favor*," Dr. Vidal said, "do not make a political speech, Señor Congressman. Just tell us what happened."

"I will tell it in my own way," Lacayo said, his hot eyes flashing. His words were a sharp staccato: "Romirez held a banquet. Imagine! After you left, a banquet to celebrate. Pigs at the trough. All the other ministers. They drank a lot of wine, a lot of brandy. Ortega went on the radio. Then there were toasts to the new government. They sang *Salve a ti, Ruedo!* They went outside to be photographed together. It was Romirez' idea. They posed beside the swimming pool. Then Romirez left his position in the middle of the group. He went to the photographer to look at the viewing plate under the black cloth and check the composition. A moment later Fernandez, the Agriculture Minister, who is, of course, for cheap beans and rice, stepped to one side. There was a machine gun under the camera's black hood. It is believed that Romirez used it himself. Ortega and the others were blown like cane back into the swimming pool. I am told that the water turned pink with their blood!"

Lacayo stood there holding an imaginary machine gun and imitated the sounds it would make as he sprayed it back and forth.

Celia and her aunt shuddered, but the doctor held himself erect and firm. "Why did he kill them? Why?"

"*Quién sabe?*" Lacayo said. "Romirez is a treacherous animal. Who knows what he will do or why? But if he planned to kill the opposition ministers, why the pretense of a junta? Why permit Ortega to speak on the radio? Perhaps he is getting drunk with power and the assassinations were an impulse. Perhaps he is insane. *Quizás.* Perhaps he follows orders from *El Sagáz,* who also has reasons beyond understanding."

"Mother of God!" Doña Felisa said. "They will come for you!" She held her husband's arm.

"Not here," Carlos said. "They would not dare."

"They will come back," Lacayo said.

"Back? They have been here once already?" Celia asked.

Lacayo looked from side to side as if for a place to spit, thought better of it, and continued. "One of the guards told me as he escorted us up the drive," he said with a superior smile. "I have men loyal to me even in the *federales*. I was told that Romirez himself and the German pilot passed slowly by in a car with eight motorcycle escorts and sirens. They pointed to the Italian car in the driveway and drove on. They were shouting and laughing, my man said."

"It is my Italian car," I said, "a present from Romirez. I have not used it until tonight."

Their looks told me they despised me. Well, let them, I thought. Romirez had at least remembered the car and fortunately, too, he had remembered his promise to me about visiting Celia—about marrying her.

I had nothing to lose now, except maybe my life. I felt as though I'd lost everything else that mattered, except one thing—a commitment. I had found out in the last couple of hours that I could do what's right—not that I would, but that I *could,* and it was important to me.

I was going to make them understand my plan. It would require saying some things that would hurt Celia, maybe hurt Carlos too, and even that didn't make it any easier.

"Celia," I said, "you know I love you. If you believe that, you can believe the rest I have to say. You can trust me."

"I trust you," she said.

"I never really accepted the Lancia," I said. "Now I have broken with Romirez, but he doesn't know it yet. Meanwhile, my uniform and that damn car can be useful. A promise the Coronel made can also help us all to escape."

Doña Felisa spoke as if I were not there. "If Celia can trust him, so can we. Anyway, let us be practical. The Capitán has the plan he mentioned. What other choice have we?"

"Indeed, what other choice?" Lacayo snorted. "El Señor Donahue of the State Department of the United States trusts Hadley too. So *I* trust him. But I do not trust a Romirez promise!"

I spoke only to Celia. "You know I hoped to marry you. Coronel Romirez found out that I—had courted you in Puerto del Sol and that I have tried to see you here in Santa María. For this contact with a Vidal I have been tortured and a friend has been killed. Romirez has scared me. I don't deny it. But I have worried him a little too. He thinks I possess some evidence of his grafting, so he made a deal. It adds up to the fact that he has forbidden me to see you again unless you become my wife—*tonight!*"

Lacayo snorted, "And if she refused?"

"Then that was the end of it, and God help the Vidals—all of them!"

"You have retained your position in the airline?" Lacayo asked mockingly.

"Well, yes. That's the whole point. I report for duty tomorrow morning. Perhaps I will have a new superior—the German, Major Heinen, but I'll be flying."

"Romirez may still have you shot," Lacayo said.

"He is short of pilots," I said.

"As your wife, this girl will achieve protection from the new dictator, I suppose," Lacayo mused. "She will no longer be a Vidal, so to speak. It will appear she has deserted her family. Then what?"

"If you will please ask the servants to leave the room for a moment, we can talk it over."

"They can be trusted." Dr. Vidal bridled.

"Why give them the responsibility of knowing too much?" Lacayo asked.

As soon as they left the room I said, "I will be given a cargo flight going somewhere in Ruedo tomorrow, and I'll be expected to take my bride with me. Somehow I will manage to get the rest of you on the plane."

"*Perfecto!*" Lacayo said to the others. "All Hadley and the Señorita Vidal have to do now is get married!"

"No!" said Carlos.

"I have already refused," Celia said to Carlos.

"Don't be foolish," Lacayo said. "The wedding will stall Romirez long enough for everybody to escape this embassy. I say send for a priest. In this romantic nonsense I still trust a Romirez promise."

"But Celia is not going to marry him!" Carlos yelled. "She is going to marry me. We are betrothed."

"Oh, so that is how it is?" Lacayo looked from me to Carlos and then at Celia. She lowered her eyes.

"I have forbidden Celia to even think of marriage to the *Norteamericano!*" Dr. Vidal said. "He is already married!"

"I am divorced," I said.

"In the eyes of God you are still married. No priest will perform the ceremony." The doctor was adamant.

"Were you married in a church?" Doña Felisa asked me.

"No," I lied, to see what she would say next.

"We can call the Bishop. He is a distant relative," Doña Felisa said to her husband. "Things can be arranged."

Lacayo made a vulgar sound. "It is a great plan!" he said to me.

"It's a lousy plan," I said, "but it is the only one we have."

Now everybody looked at Celia. No one urged her. The choice was hers. She looked at me. "I will marry you, Luke, to save the others." It was said without enthusiasm.

"All right, Doctor," I said, "you get on the telephone. Call the priest or Bishop. Assume the wire is tapped. Tell him to come here at once to perform the ceremony. Tell him to try to reach Romirez by phone to request safe transportation here. I think the Coronel will provide it. Do it now."

The doctor looked unhappy, but he did as I told him. Then the Bishop was on the wire, and the doctor had trouble convincing him of the urgency, of the justification for not marrying in the chapel. "Yes, we must have a priest tonight!" the doctor insisted. He was having a hard time making his point.

"Tell him Celia is pregnant," I said irritably and wished she were.

He spoke into the phone again and hung up.

"A priest is coming?" Lacayo asked.

"Yes, but there will be delays. His vestments, such accouterments as are necessary to perform the ceremony—everything takes time. But he will hurry. I reminded him of the school I helped to finance for his parish." Dr. Vidal looked at me with distaste.

Celia had gone to the far side of the big room. I followed her.

"I didn't think you would do this to me," she said.

"I have slept with you," I said. "Now all I am going to do is marry you!"

"I didn't ask you to make an honest woman of me!" She was cold and proud, and I thought—I don't know what I thought.

"And after the wedding," I said, "I will not sleep with you. There's a switch. You can get the marriage annulled."

I went back to where Caldéras was sitting with his head in his hands. I stood over him. I wasn't getting any kick out of this. "Charlie," I said, "when the wedding is over, Celia and I are leaving here and we're going to my hotel. Only for appearances. I have a hunch Romirez will be waiting there to toast the bride and groom. If you have any objections, I'm going to kill you right now."

He stood up, tugging at the Luger in his belt. I was almost glad. I reached in my side pants pocket for the little .32, but it wasn't there. I had changed pants and forgotten it.

Carlos got his gun loose. I heard Celia scream a protest. Lacayo was standing very near. His hand came down in a judo cut on Charlie's wrist. The Luger went down on the rug with a thud. Lacayo picked it up and kept it.

"We either take Caldéras with us," Lacayo said calmly, "or we kill him. If we leave him behind, he will talk. Everybody talks to *Sargento* Molina."

"For God's sake, take him with us," Celia cried. "Luke, you told me you would take him!"

"Then make him understand what we have to do. Tell him you don't like it any more than he does. Tell him I don't like it either. Tell him it is a marriage in name only."

A little later Father Tomás was ushered in by the two Vidal servants.

The priest was fussed, his face purpling over his round collar. He pontificated, "The Bishop says no bans are posted for this marriage. It will not be legal."

"It doesn't have to be!" I said. "We will have a mock wedding, but nobody outside this room will know it until we get out of town."

"You are crazy about this girl," Lacayo said to me under his breath.

"Yes, damn it, yes!" I said loudly.

Vidal heard my outburst, and the pain lines in his face deepened.

Celia had gone back to the window. She said, "There is a jeep outside and men in blue uniforms."

"They brought me here," the padre said. "I asked them to wait to take me back. The officers said they would like to be invited in for a glass of wedding champagne."

"Why not!" Lacayo chuckled. "I will get out of the way so the masquerade can proceed with a small family reception. All the more convincing. The wedding couple should leave with the padre and Romirez' men as escorts. Then when they are gone, we must leave also, by a back way. I know how we can get to the *aeropuerto* undetected, but how we will board the plane tomorrow I do not know."

"I have some ideas about the airport fence," I said.

"What is this of the fence?" Dr. Vidal asked.

"You don't think you are going to buy a ticket for this flight, do you?" I said, not knowing why the old man got on my nerves. "The southwest runway is the longest and it comes closest to the fence. The cover is good there, too—lots of banana palms outside and the grass is pretty high inside the fence. But it's a ten-foot cyclone fence with barbed wire on top. Three strands. You'll need wire-cutters and a ladder to go over the top. Darkness, too. Otherwise, if you get there early enough, it would be better to dig a tunnel underneath."

"I am for the tunnel," Lacayo said. "Are there soldiers patrolling the fence?"

"There weren't any before," Dr. Vidal said, "but it is a logical order now."

"We dig tonight," Lacayo directed. If there are guards in the way when we come out of the tunnel for the airplane, we will shoot them. How will we get into the plane, Señor Hadley?"

"How many people?" I asked the doctor.

"Celia's mother—poor woman—my wife, the two servants, Caldéras, Lacayo, and I—seven."

"I don't think so," I said, shaking my head. "The cargo will probably be weapons or gasoline, a heavy load. Eight passengers with Celia, and, perhaps, a co-pilot—that is too many."

"You still wish to go without me!" Carlos grumbled.

"I have men everywhere; also at the *aeropuerto*," Lacayo said to me. "Something might be done to lighten the cargo. I will give you the password so you will know which mechanic to trust."

"What is it?" I asked.

"Later," he said, eying the others suspiciously. To them he said, "The best service the *viejo* and his woman can give the Vidals now is to stay behind and take care of the mother of the *señorita*."

"We may be separated for many months," Doña Felisa lamented.

"It is a pity," Lacayo said sarcastically. "No servants. You may not bring any luggage either!" To me he said, "Let us get on with the boarding plan. The door of the airplane will be open?"

"At the proper time. You will stay hidden and watch for the plane, a DC-3. Do you know the type?"

"*Sí.*"

"There are three more of them on order—they could have arrived, for all I know—plus the two LARC had. So you can be sure which one we are in, I will signal with three short blips of each of the engines, like this." I imitated the sound. "While I am doing this at the very end of the runway, I will turn the ship so the door on the left side faces away from the terminal, and Celia will open it for you. Clear?"

"*Claro!*" said Lacayo. "We will dig the tunnel under the fence at a place where the airplane will cover our coming out. The *señora* will come out first, but we three men will be able to run faster and reach the door first to help her up, as I do not expect any steps."

"That's right, the floor will be about chest high."

"I will board last in order to cover us against attack. If possible I will obtain a carbine," Lacayo said, gripping an imaginary gun again. He loved guns.

"Shooting could ruin it. Try to get away clean," I said to Lacayo. "I hope you have some organization outside the capital."

"Do not worry, Señor Hadley. In the provinces Ycaza Lacayo is a very big man."

"I suppose we will all be fugitives," Carlos said, "and the Capitán will be a deserter, hunted down like a dog."

"Are you thinking of informing, Charlie?" I muttered coldly. "Maybe you can't wait for a fake annullment for the fake marriage."

"Stop it! Stop it!" Celia cried. "Let's get on with it."

"Take a few minutes to dress properly and pack a suitcase for your wedding trip," Lacayo said. "Make everything look correct."

To me he said, "I may not see you again until tomorrow at the airplane." He lowered his voice. "Remember this: the password for Lacayo is *El diente de tigre*—the tiger's tooth. My friends will make themselves known by talk of such a tooth. *Claro?*"

Then he frowned fiercely and left the room.

"Hasta mañana," I said under my breath.

The Chilean Ambassador, his wife, and three little daughters had been invited to the mock wedding, thinking it was the real thing, of course, and the foreign dignitary was prevailed upon to permit the jeepload of Air Corps officers to enter. Among them I recognized young García.

The priest was ready with white surplice and stole over his black cassock. A sofa cushion was placed on the rug so we could kneel comfortably. Flowers were no problem. Outside the door of any house in Ruedo it was possible to cut armfuls of blossoms that would make New York florists envious.

Celia's melancholy mother could not be persuaded to come down, and Doña Felisa was already weeping just as though it were all real. The good doctor had a suitably grave expression and Celia on his arm in a virginal white tulle dress that had probably once been to a spring dance at the country club but served the purpose as a wedding gown with a white Spanish lace veil. Carlos, to make a perfect mockery of things, was my best man and held a ring he had purchased for his own use.

I had a purple shiner, a hangover, and I needed a shave.

The ceremony in Latin confused me, and Celia had to tug at me to kneel and to rise at the right times. We got through the responses somehow, and our kiss at the end was perfunctory.

The iced champagne, furnished by the Chilean cellars, came from the Ambassador's own vineyards on the slopes of the Andes. Celia and I linked arms to drink some, and I had a moment when I wished it were real. The guests said Celia was a beautiful bride, though they always say that, and I loved her. She cut the small cake the kitchen had somehow provided. Carlos kissed the bride, while I winced.

Her uncle lectured me. "It should not be necessary for my niece to be alone with you," he said sternly. "She is a properly brought-up Spanish girl. I must ask you, on your honor, not to—"

"Don't worry, sir," I said, "Celia will be safe as in church. We'll only make it look the way it should."

The Little Boy Blues of the Air Corps had begun to pop champagne corks at one another like artillery. Father Tomás looked at his great gold watch that was fastened to a long loop of chain under his habit with his rosary, his gold cross, and his keys to whatever treasure or sacramental wine he locked up in the cathedral. It was time to go.

Lieutenant García gave me an *abrazo fuerte,* as did the doctor, and even Carlos. Celia was kissed good-by, and we were helped into the Lancia along with Celia's suitcase. There were ribbons tied to the rear bumper. We took off with the officers' jeep behind us, its horn blowing.

Chapter 28

THE Hotel Mirado was lit up like New Year's Eve. Romirez was throwing a victory party. When Celia and I arrived, with García ahead of us trying to pry open a path through the lobby, the celebration had reached a stage where the people were spilling more than they drank. García shouted a command that got the drunken officers to cross swords for us to pass under, except that a few crossed pistols and leather riding whips and others crossed bottles. We ducked through that arch. It led us into the seldom-opened grand ballroom and toward a table dais where sat the great Juan Miguel Romirez with a mountain of food in front of him. He had six rows of ribboned medals on his chest. Some were gravy-spotted. A half-dozen pretty girls crowded around him admiringly, reading aloud cables of congratulations from Ruedan ambassadors who wanted to keep their cushy jobs outside the country. The Coronel ignored us, and we had to stand humbly in front of him while a gushing telegram from the Alcalde of Puerto del Sol was read to him. That was the Mayor I had met. He was quick to get on the bandwagon. But Romirez didn't look happy. He complained that there was no message from Mexico—from Sagasta. He pawed through the stack of wires with his fat fingers and couldn't find any from Matanzas or Las Piraguas either.

Finally Romirez took notice of us and grudgingly gave us his congratulations. Celia, who hadn't said a word till then, whispered in my ear, "If that pig tries to kiss me, I'll spit in his face!"

There was enough noise in the place to smother my reply. "Not if you want to save your aunt, your uncle, and your precious Charlie, you won't," I said.

Then damned if she didn't turn out to be quite the little actress. When Romirez got loud about kissing the bride, she took his bushy mustache right on the mouth and even congratulated *him*. Celia charmed all of them at the head table, where they made room for us between Padilla, who now headed the *federales*, and the Minister of Agriculture, who had passed out with his head in a salad.

We tried to eat something from the sumptuous spread before us, but the musicians struck up "Here Comes the Bride" with a sexy rumba beat and the bridal couple was commanded to dance.

When it looked as if everybody, starting with the Coronel, wanted to dance with the bride, Celia whispered, "Enough is enough! Do I have to go through with this too?"

"No, just act as though you can't wait to be alone with me," I said bitterly.

She managed that bit of histrionics too. The fat man laughed and shouted, *"Olé, olé, olé!"*—punctuating with hard slaps on my back. Amid vulgar wisecracks we were hustled off. Hotel porters carried Celia's luggage, a bucket of iced champagne, and bunches of flowers to the bridal suite, no less. They moved my B-4 bag from my room.

I fussed around the edges of the suite, keeping out of Celia's way because her eyes were like black flint. I began wondering if I could steer the airplane across the border in the morning instead of to some still free Ruedan town. That would get me the hell out of it. No, I thought, I had bought in; I'd have to play the hand.

Raucous laughter and shouting in the streets eight floors below were mixed with some distant small-arms fire. Were the shots catching the Vidals and Caldéras and Lacayo in the open? Celia heard the shots too and stood in the middle of the sitting room, looking forlorn in her wilted party dress. My heart went out to her, but I didn't know what to say except, "You take the bedroom. I'll sleep in here on the couch."

"I have made you very unhappy, haven't I, Luke?" Celia said, her eyes warm again.

"I'm used to it," I said.

"I wanted always to be able to make you smile, make you laugh. It was very important to make you happy," she said without looking at me.

I went over to the champagne bucket on a sideboard and decided to put out the fire in my throat. Thumbing the cork loose, I thought I would have liked to smile for her, but it just wasn't in me.

I poured two glasses of the fizzing wine and didn't bring hers over. I just picked mine up, and she came over to me.

We raised our glasses in a silent toast and drank, and I could feel her nearness. I ached to hold her.

After pouring more champagne, I had to corn it up. I said, "According to Cole Porter, it was just one of those things."

"I'm sorry, Luke," she said.

I felt sorry enough for myself and turned away.

"Look at me, please, Luke."

"Then don't be sorry," I said and looked at her pale, sweet face over the rim of my champagne glass.

"Oh, I'm not," she said, "not that way. Just sorry I acted bitchy."

"You were fine," I said. "Under the circumstances, you did it all very well—the wedding, the reception, downstairs, everything. You're an accomplished little faker!"

"That's unfair!" she said, and the hurt showing on her face wasn't faked. "Do you feel betrayed?"

I didn't answer right away, because the answer was yes. I poured the last of the wine, her question still bothering me. Then I told her. "Yes," I said.

"You shouldn't," Celia said. "I knew *him* first. It is still *his* ring I wear now. And I never was your whole life."

I thought there was some logic in what she said. "Okay, forget it," I said, which made no sense at all, and she knew it.

"Now you are acting like a spoiled little boy who isn't getting his own way!" she said, showing exasperation. "You know, most girls my age in Ruedo are married, so maybe I just decided I didn't want to be a virgin any longer. You helped me come to that conclusion just by being you. Big, kind, understanding you! I felt it irresistibly about you. You had to be my lover, because I thought with my insides about you. But something went wrong! It got so complicated!"

As she talked I remembered our very first days together, how we worked at the office with a studied avoidance of touching hands when tracing routes on the map. Unconsciously we were learning what was there for each of us, long before we made up our minds about it and sort of arranged in the least possible deliberate way to meet in Puerto del Sol.

"It went wrong," she said again, "because I felt the need to make you happy. First I was selfish about you, so selfish that maybe I only meant to use you for the end of my girlhood and then eventually go on about the good little Ruedana's business of becoming a wife and mother the way I was supposed to. But—*damn* you, Luke, honey—I found myself caring about you, how you were, if you were happy. I loved you so *hard!*"

"I love you now!" I said.

"I think you do, poor honey, though you didn't at first—not so soon as I fell in love with you, and that didn't matter. It was wonderful when you did, your surprise! Oh, Luke, it was like a dream—but only a dream."

"No"—stubbornly.

"Oh, yes!"

She seemed much wiser than I. Here she was telling me it was over, letting me down easy, and I was behaving very badly.

"You will be fine with Carlos," I said.

"Never like with you."

"It isn't necessary to say that." With an effort I smiled. "I think— yes, I can predict you will find it with him. I can say that because I am older than you."

"Don't start acting like a big brother!"

We were smiling at each other. It was incredible.

"It will never be the same with him," she said.

"But it will be fine. Maybe it will take some time, but you can help him, if you aren't too much woman for him."

"Shut up!"

"I still love you," I said and never meant it more. "I can't think of a time when I won't love you. And I still want *you* to be happy—even with him. That will never be enough for me, but it will do me some good to remember you and to know you are alive somewhere in the same world, sometimes seeing the same sky."

"I'll hear a plane and look up, wondering if you are flying it."

We still stood beside the empty bottle in the ice-bucket, as if sitting down would be a too easy acceptance of the set-up. It was as if we had to be uneasy.

"I'll go away," I said. "I'll give us both a chance to forget." Then I stopped talking, because she had come closer to me, and my vision was getting kind of misty. I knew, somehow, that if I didn't stop talking to her the way my voice sounded, with the caring in it, she would come still closer, and then I knew I would touch her, and if I touched her a chemical process would start in her and in me and it would be easy not to be fair or honest. The right thing to do was to back off, and, so help me, I did. And the minute I did, I knew it was right. I didn't have to lie down with her again to know we had that for each other, only to have to say good-by all over again. It wouldn't make anything better for us than a dream would, or a memory.

I said, "Go to bed in there," and I pointed to the bedroom. "Get out of here!" I said it rough.

Her dark eyes held mine and went wide and soft, but she did as I told her. She went by me within easy reach. I swear she expected me to grab her or follow her, but I didn't and the moment passed.

She shut the door behind her, and I waited for the lock to click. When it did not, I closed the bolt on my side, feeling priggish. Then I took a cold shower, glad there were separate bathrooms. I found some aspirin in my B-4 bag and, while digging into it, discovered that my little gun had been swiped. The hell with it, I thought, and lay on a big bath towel on the couch and felt spent, old. My head ached, and my sore eye was full of sand. For the worst ache of all they haven't invented a pill.

I was still awake when the telephone rang in the morning. It was Rudy, trying to be friendly. "How are the bride and groom this morning?" he asked.

I kidded with him just a little and said something insulting too, to make our relationship seem as usual, and I asked him how things were.

"Quiet. Calm here, except around the university. Puerto is with us, but there is still trouble in the other cities. We have to work them over one at a time, Matanzas first. They are calling for an election there, offering Ycaza Lacayo as their candidate for president. Imagine! In Las Piraguas the *federales* are reported to be still loyal to Vidal—the fools! The new DC-3s arrived this morning, just in time to move troops to Matanzas and then to the south. You are to fly a load of gasoline to Matanzas so we will have fuel there for the P-51s. Hurry up, will you?" The last was said in a way to remind me who was boss.

"Yes, sir, Major Heinen," I said to make him feel good. I didn't want any trouble with him now. My mind was racing ahead to the end of the

.

southwest runway, where my passengers should be hiding. I had a crawling feeling in my stomach.

Celia must have heard me on the phone. She rattled the door. I opened it and she came into the sitting room wearing the cutest pajamas. Without any lipstick she looked fifteen years old. I wanted . . . The hell with what I wanted!

I scowled and told her our flight plan for the morning was a quick breakfast and out to the *aeropuerto,* but she countermanded me just like a wife.

"It's Ash Wednesday," she said. "We will have to stop at the cathedral first."

"All right," I said. "Let's get going."

I left the Lancia in the hotel garage, and the doorman got us a taxi. The cathedral was our first stop, and the driver and I waited until Celia returned from mass with a small charcoal smudge on her forehead. Then I remembered my Saint Christopher medal, got it out of my wallet, and put it on.

When we got to the airport I left Celia with our bags at the terminal *cantina* and walked over to the hangar alone. I admired the LARC fleet of five DC-3s parked there.

The twenty-two seats in my ship had been folded up along the inside of the windows, and I counted thirty drums of gasoline lashed in place down the length of the fuselage. The front hatch and side door were open for ventilation, but I could smell the high-test stuff. It was a hot load.

Pepe Lopez hailed me and came over with the manifest on a clipboard. We said, *"Buenos días,"* and I whistled at the weight figures he showed me. I borrowed his pencil and did some calculating while I idly asked him what he was doing here.

"I have been assigned this flight as co-pilot," he said unhappily.

"I don't need any goddamned co-pilot on an hour-and-a-half trip to Matanzas, especially not you," I growled.

"The major's orders," he said. "I prefer to fly the bomber again."

I didn't want to have to kill the guy, but that was going to be the alternative if Rudy insisted Pepe fly with me, and I had to think about getting some kind of weapon. He wore a pistol in a holster.

I went on with my figuring. An empty gas drum weighs 50 pounds. The fuel, averaging 54 gallons each drum, figured to weight 368½ pounds, for a total payload of over 5½ tons. I re-counted the drums to be sure, and whistled again. With six people aboard, our overload would be about 1500 pounds, plus or minus, depending on the fuel in the DC-3s tanks.

"I'll talk the major out of your assignment," I said to Pepe. "We're too heavy anyway."

I tossed the clipboard onto the cabin floor and walked around the ship, giving it a pre-flight inspection. The tires were flattening with the weight. I didn't see any mechanics anywhere to try Lacayo's password on. Then I walked Pepe back to the administration section of the terminal, watching the windsock above the tower. It sagged limply. It was a hot day, too. I was going to need some wind right on the nose to get off with that load, even on the longest runway.

I wondered how my passengers were making out, if they had their tunnel dug. I bet they had missed mass.

"Pepe," I said, "you speak to the major first. I'll talk to him later. I want to see how my bride is for a minute." I was the dutiful husband.

Celia was sitting in the *cantina* sipping a *café puro* just like any tourist waiting for her flight. I bent down and kissed her on the cheek the way a guy who had just been married a day would. With my head beside hers I whispered, "I've got a co-pilot to get rid of and no gun or anything."

"I have a pistol," she whispered back. "Uncle Luis gave it to me last night to protect myself from you." She turned on one of her big, wonderful smiles.

"Give it to me now," I said softly and nuzzled her cheek with mine. She opened the large purse in her lap, and inside it was a nickel-plated .38 Webbley revolver. She wrapped it as well as she could in a handkerchief. Pushing her body close to mine, she slipped the gun in my nearest side pants pocket. Nobody could have noticed anything but two affectionate newlyweds. Her lips were so close to mine, I kissed them. I sort of told myself it was part of the act. The kiss I got in return was no act.

Then I left her and went looking for Rudy, and I was confused as hell. Celia loved Charlie, she said, but the way she kissed *me!* What the hell was going on? Maybe it was me after all, and not Charlie, or maybe I was a mixed-up product of my country's middle-class morality. Suppose it was only a kiss, just for the fun of it—what then? Then she was a sensualist. What else? She could be a cool one too. I talked of murdering a guy in cold blood, and she never batted an eye. Some things I was never going to understand.

I went into the pilot's ready room. Rudy was there, studying a chart, and Pepe was arguing with him. Other pilots crowded in for their briefing.

"I want to fly the B-25," Pepe kept insisting.

"You have your orders!" Rudy snapped. "You make the Matanzas trip with Capitán Hadley!"

"I will speak to my uncle," Pepe whined. "It is ridiculous to put a co-pilot on such a short hop!"

"That's right," I chimed in. "Besides, the plane is overloaded."

"Who asked you?" Rudy exploded. "I remind you that I am running things here. If the load is too much, leave your wife home!" The German's face was red; his eyes were narrow slits of blue ice.

Then Coronel Romirez was in the doorway with two bodyguards carrying sub-machine guns.

"Let *him* settle it," I said to Rudy with a shrug.

"Settle what?" the Coronel asked, laughing and blowing great clouds of cigar smoke. He was in a top-of-the-world mood but with a threatening edge of impatience. "Can't I appoint officers good enough to take charge of things without bothering me with petty details all the time?" he asked.

The Coronel was obviously busy with the whole damn country now. The problems here were too small for his attention. But he did inquire about the DC-4 turnaround. Having checked communications when I came in, I told him Fuentes and Carter had landed in Mexico on the way back, adding that they should arrive in Santa María inside an hour.

Rudy resented the attention Romirez paid me. He sputtered. "My Coronel, Capitán Hadley refuses to fly with an assigned co-pilot."

"The Capitán is right, I think," Pepe said, which probably saved his life.

"Capitán Hadley still runs the commercial end of this, doesn't he?" Romirez asked, trying to be patient.

"He is going to resign as general manager," Rudy said.

I smiled at Rudy with my teeth. "But as operations manager and chief pilot I would still name the crews," I said.

"*Por Dios!*" Romirez roared at the German. "Haven't you enough to do with command of the Air Corps? Don't we need every available pilot for the three new transports to carry troops?"

"I do not trust Hadley alone with the aircraft," Rudy said. "Suppose he flies out of Ruedo!" The other officers watched this show of strength with mild interest. To them, one superior was like another, particularly foreigners. They'd be happier if we both got shafted. Some of them started treating themselves to sniffs from oxygen bottles, a great hangover cure. The 51s could be mercilessly unforgiving to slow reflexes after an all-night party.

"In times of military operations, the Air Corps should control the airline absolutely," Rudy declared, as if quoting a dictum from the German war college.

"Then control it in a sensible manner," the Coronel said, laughing again to show what a really big man he was, so far above this petty wrangling. "Do not waste a second pilot on a cargo run. Send a P-51 out as escort to Matanzas if you are afraid Hadley will fly somewhere else."

Rudy should have known when to quit, but he didn't. He said, "I think—"

"Don't think; give orders!" Romirez exploded.

I tried hard not to laugh. Major Heinen saluted and led his fighter pilots outside to inspect their planes.

Then Coronel Romirez gave me his full attention. "What is this again about resigning as general manager? I am sorry to hear it, if it is true. You married your girl, so you must need the job. I am sure that now Doctor Vidal must hate you almost as much as he hates me. He will cut his niece off without a penny. Ah, but when I get around to executing him, she will inherit a fortune. Then you will be rich, *señor!* Is that why you want to resign?"

"No," I said. "It's just that your Air Corps is too small for the German. He wants my job too."

The Coronel exhaled cigar smoke with a laugh. "It is a competition! *Bueno!* Is that not what you *Yanquis* approve of?"

I nodded enthusiastically, and Romirez propelled his fat body into the communications room while I looked out the window at the Ruedan flag. No breeze stirred it.

I heard Romirez shout at the radio operator, who had earphones on, "Did the DC-4 pick up a courier when it stopped in Mexico?"

"Courier, my Coronel? No, only a woman, a Señorita Shelton," the man said, looking at his message log.

"That is the courier, you fool." The Coronel laughed wheezingly.

So Lita Shelton was coming to Ruedo with a message from Sagasta, and the Coronel was feeling expansive again and he turned to me, saying, "My fighters will open the southern airports with strafing attacks; then, with six transports, I can command more than two hundred airborne troops with heavy weapons, a military operation just like in the war, is that not so, Capitán?"

I nodded. There goes the rest of Ruedo, I thought, and wondered where the hell I'd land my refugee passengers.

"When the fighting is over," the Coronel said, "you will be in charge of the biggest airline in Central America. I can trade you that for some pieces of paper!"

"All right." I smiled. "When I get back." Resistance elsewhere in Ruedo gave my supposed graft evidence a somewhat longer life, but for a second I almost wished there were an existing first draft of the report. Without it I would be a fugitive instead of a big *Jefe*.

"Perhaps with the Vidal wealth you can purchase LARC from the government and run it as a private business," Romirez suggested archly.

I laughed and pushed the palms of my hands at the Coronel, shaking my head negatively. "Then maybe you'd confiscate it right back!" I said, kidding.

"You are learning Ruedan politics!" he said laughing.

Through the window I saw Celia standing outside at the lattice brick railing that keeps passengers off the runway. I started out to join her. "She must be pretty good, eh, if you cannot stay away from her for a minute," Romirez said, leering. He made a vulgar gesture with his fat fingers.

"I'm a lucky man and I owe it all to you," I said and went out.

Outside I noticed the windsock was beginning to flutter. The troops and their equipment were assembling in the area where the transports were parked. Six of the P-51s were gassed up and ready. As soon as the DC-4 landed and loaded up with troops and mortars and small cannon, the movement would start. My official flight plan was to bring up the rear and land the gasoline after the airport in Matanzas had been made secure, but I had to plan a detour, try to land someplace else, unless Vidal and Lacayo thought they could escape in Matanzas. I went over to Celia, and she must have noticed how grave I looked.

"I pray my *tía* and *tío* are all right," she said.

"And Charlie too, and Lacayo," I said.

"Yes, Carlos and that Lacayo too," she said.

"He's not *that* Lacayo," I said. "He's got a lot of Indian blood, but he's a better man than Charlie."

"Don't call him Charlie!"

"You know what?" I said. "Maybe you did marry me last night after all. A license, a piece of paper, would make it so; besides, half of Santa María thinks you did. It will be embarrassing for the Bishop or the padre to deny it?"

"How can you say such things?" Celia said, truly shocked. "We are not married; that is that!"

"It will look odd if you marry Charlie now," I said, needling her. "It would be better if you were a widow first."

I had succeeded in making her angry. Her dark eyes flashed hotly. "Perhaps Carlos will oblige me by killing you!"

"Not if that gun you gave me is loaded," I said. "He hasn't got the guts to go up against me unless—" I stopped.

"There it is *again!*" she said, very disturbed. "You allude to something between you and Carlos, but you won't say what it is!"

"No," I said, looking away. "It's nothing. Forget it."

"You don't know Carlos. He is a fine, decent man, and he loves me very much."

"And do you really love him? A great man named Frank Lloyd Wright said, 'Marriage without love, not love without marriage, is a sin.' "

"You are one to speak of sin!" she said sharply. "What *do* you believe in?"

The DC-4 came into view from over Santa María at about three thousand feet. I believe in that, I thought, and in the science that made it, which is nature given some help by man.

"I believe in myself," I said.

"Such ego! Not in God?"

"Perhaps in many gods—and a certain Mayan goddess." I chuckled.

"Pagan!"

"Maybe," I said, "You should listen to your Indians sometime, and not the ones you have forced to their knees. The Indian I know believes in God as the good in himself and in all people. There is a lot of such natural good in everybody, but so-called civilization has made it difficult to get it out."

"You are good, Luke," she said softly. "Forgive me?"

"Sure," I said, watching the DC-4 touch down on the runway. It bounced a little, but it wasn't a bad landing for an empty plane that would have a tendency to float.

It taxied up to the gate in front of us. As soon as the propellers stopped turning, Carter opened the door and called for a ladder. LARC had no ramp steps high enough. Then he helped Lita down. She gave him a big smile and got close enough in his arms to make his courtesy worthwhile.

Fuentes climbed down, and then an attendant brought out a small trunk and three pieces of matched luggage, all the redhead's. It looked like she was staying awhile.

Lita had on another of her too tight suits and carried a small cosmetics case. She saw me at the railing and waved a big hello.

Celia said, "Why do you want me? You could have a girl like that— lots of girls. I am not good for you."

"I don't want lots of girls. Not any more. That's how good you are for me."

Johnny Michaels came out to greet Lita, and he called to me, "Hey, Luke, come inside a minute!"

I gave Celia's hand a squeeze and smooched her for our public. "It won't be long now," I said as reassuringly as I could. "Wait here."

I was close to her. She said softly, "Damn you! Damn you!"

There was no figuring her.

It was getting hot and stuffy in the ready room. In addition to Ruedan flying officers who had returned, there were now nine Yank pilots, including me. Romirez was having his picture taken by a battery of photographers. He stood in the doorway of the connecting communications room and had the radio head set on. He held a mike to his mustache as if broadcasting. I could see the picture caption in my mind: "Coronel Romirez directs operations as Ruedo's national airline expands to meet growing needs for transport." It would be true, too. I had written the plan for it.

"Hello, Luke darling." I heard Lita's voice in the din of chatter.

I turned to her and said, "How are you, Lita?"

"Just great, sweetie," she said emphatically. "Who gave you that eye, an irate husband?"

"It's a political eye," I said. "You staying long?"

"Long enough to get me a new boy friend," she said. "I ought to be able to beat the time of those broads on the sixth floor, don't you think?" Lita had her pride back, that cocky, hysterical kind of pride that might have come out of a Benzedrine pill.

Johnny came over and asked, "You want to proposition these new guys from the States? They could start today hauling troops."

"I have a flight to Matanzas. You pick 'em over, will you? If you don't, Rudy will get in the act and scare them off for sure." I said that as though it really mattered to me, but I didn't want any part of selling those Yanks on LARC as a career if I was going to wind up on the other side, maybe fighting them.

"Okay, Luke," Johnny said, and then Romirez joined us.

"Congratulations, Coronel!" Lita said and actually managed a sort of bowing curtsy that wasn't corny.

"Congratulate the *capitán* also. He was married last night to the niece of Doctor Vidal," Romirez said as if to cut me out with her.

"I must kiss the happy bridegroom!" Lita said and did. Close to me, in rapid English, she added, "Poor boy, did you *have* to?"

"Any messages for me?" the Coronel asked pettishly as I rubbed the smear of lipstick off my mouth.

Lita gave him both barrels of her uplift personality and batted her long false eyelashes, getting her timing right. "Yes, my Coronel, I have a message," she said and waited.

"In my office, then," Romirez said stiffly and took the redheaded prize that all the Latinos were having mentally.

The door to the Coronel's office closed, and I wondered what Lita's pitch was. With Sagasta returning to Ruedo, her messenger-service job was over, and I guessed her rent wasn't going to be paid any longer.

Two minutes passed. I looked out the window at Celia and thought about the people waiting in a dirt tunnel under the southwest fence. Then the door opened. There was a trace of lipstick on the Coronel's kisser, and he was beaming. He shouted for attention and got it.

"Tell them," Romirez commanded, "the message from *El Sagáz*."

It was a big scene for Lita. Her audience waited in silence. I saw Rudy with his mouth partly open, a kind of stupid expression on his pink Teutonic face.

"You all know how Fermín Sagasta likes to play with words," Lita began, and there was a murmur of *"Sí, sí."* "Well, he asked me to tell it like this: 'Ruedo is governed by a simple plan: he takes who has the power and he should keep who can.' " In Spanish it had quite a ring to it, and there were cheers, but I guess only I knew Sagasta had stolen the lines from Wordsworth.

Lita turned to Romirez and held out both her arms in a dramatic gesture, padding her part. "Sagasta concedes that Ruedo is rightfully the Coronel's, that he has earned its leadership!"

There were more cheers and everybody giving everybody else *abrazos*.

So the sagacious one decided he liked retirement, I thought. That was a surprise. Romirez' little pig eyes were popping with delight.

Rudy moved to Romirez' side and said, "Excuse me, Coronel—"

"*Excellency!*" Romirez exploded, "Call me Excellency. I am Prime Minister now!"

"Your Excellency," Rudy corrected himself, giving Romirez a heel-clicking salute, "may I remind you that only the capital and Puerto del Sol are yours, that we must move to make your victory complete? With your permission, the troop transports will now take off, and I will lead the fighters ahead of them to strafe the Matanzas airport if there is any resistance to your taking the town."

"The wind is freshening; what are you waiting for?" Romirez replied.

Rudy Heinen saluted again and backed away.

"What are my orders?" I called to the German.

"Don't land until after the fighters are on the field," Rudy barked from the doorway.

"Okay," I said wearily. Damned if I was going to "sir" him again.

Johnny had got four of the Yank pilots to fly to Matanzas. A month ago I'd have grabbed a job like that. I collected Celia and her luggage, and we walked the fifty yards to the plane in silence. I polished my sunglasses. A mechanic was waiting for me.

"All set?" I asked him.

"*Sí, todo,*" he mumbled, bored with it. I got no password out of him.

I lifted Celia onto the cabin floor. In English, because the mechanic hung around, I told her how to latch the doors from the inside and how to unlatch them too. I told her to sit on my soft B-4 bag and to hold on tight as there was no safety belt.

The mechanic wandered off to the front of the plane, and I quickly told Celia what had happened—how Romirez was Prime Minister.

"Poor Ruedo," she said. And then I pulled the double doors around, and she latched them on the inside.

The mechanic had a ladder for me to reach the higher front hatch to the cockpit. It was easier than climbing over all those drums of gasoline.

While I fired up my engines I watched six P-51s line up to take off, one after the other. The leader—it must have been Rudy—did a chandelle at the end of his takeoff run. The crazy Ruedanos tried it too, right off the ground, with wingtips nearly scraping the runway. The last one, in a hurry to join up in formation, wasn't quite airborne when he retracted his wheels. He skidded into the fence, throwing a lot of sparks, but he didn't burn. Good thing, too; the airport fire truck wouldn't start.

Crews and soldiers climbed aboard the DC-3s and the DC-4. The ships cranked up, and Johnny waved them off. They all taxied toward Runway 23, where I was supposed to go. I hoped Lacayo remembered the signal I said I would give with my throttles, and would not be confused by the other planes.

I started rolling and got on the horn to ask the tower for wind velocity. Some of the kids who worked the tower didn't know how to read the anemometer accurately, but I hoped for the best.

"Five to ten miles per hour," the tower reported, "variable easterly to northeast."

That checked with the little breezes that occasionally made the windsock twitch, but what bothered me was that the wind was shifting.

I waited on the apron for the other five aircraft to take off. By the time they were gone, the wind just wasn't quite right for the southwest runway, but that was where four people should be waiting for me. I taxied down there and turned my ship as close to the grass as possible, keeping the doors toward the fence. I revved up the port engine three times, as I had told Lacayo I would. We were four hundred yards from the tower, but I also lowered my flaps all the way to provide that much more aluminum to shield four people from view. Then I blipped the throttle of the starboard engine three times, completing the signal.

Nothing moved in the high grass beyond the blacktop of the runway. I looked into the banana-palm fronds beyond the fence. Nothing. I didn't see any patrolling guards, either, which was luck.

I felt rather than heard a door bang open against the side of the ship. I stuck my head out of the cockpit window and watched the fence where Lacayo should be with the Vidals and Carlos. I still couldn't see them. I had to run up the engines and began with the one on my right to minimize the slipstream blowing back when they boarded—*if* they boarded.

I looked at my instruments, and when I turned to the window again I saw the high grass opening like a furrow. Where the furrow ended I saw Lacayo rise up from his hands and knees and sprint toward the plane. Then came the stout Doña Felisa, panting hard, with Carlos and her husband on either side of her, half dragging her in their hurry to cross the open space. Their clothes were covered with dirt.

Through the open cockpit door behind me I looked across the stack of gas drums and saw Carlos and Celia reaching down to pull her aunt up while the others boosted from outside.

I had to run up the port engine, and I did as soon as the woman was aboard. The doctor and Lacayo took quite a buffeting, but as soon as I throttled down I heard the door close. Then I raised my flaps, poured on the coal, and released the brakes.

Chapter 29

I CROSSED my fingers on the wheel as we lurched forward. The DC-3 would fly with what we carried in excess of its gross weight limit, but it figured to drag its feet getting off the ground. The old ship vibrated and rolled. But it only rolled. It wallowed across the east-west runway intersection where normally I'd be airborne, but I didn't even have my tail up.

I pushed the yoke, but the elevator control was mushy. I shoved the throttles that were already against the firewall, popped one-quarter flaps, and began to exert body English on her. So help me, I began to talk to that airplane. *"Arriba,* baby," I said. *"Arriba!"*

Another shove got the tailwheel lifted and cut down some of the drag. The goddamned wind was quartering from the east, and the end of the runway was rushing toward me. I knew she wasn't going to fly herself off at the speed we were making, so I kicked the right rudder pedal and we staggered off the blacktop onto the rough dirt surface of the field. We bounced a couple of feet into the air but settled right back down again and bounced a little harder. This time, with the wind on her nose, I horsed her up, and we stayed up—just barely. I yanked up the gear to cut more drag and kept her flat over the fence at the end of the field. I think my wheels would have snagged on the fence if I hadn't retracted them. It was that close.

The engines screamed in pain, but I didn't cut them back from max power. We inched upward. I loved every rivet and connecting rod that stood the strain. It seemed like a year later when we had a couple of hundred feet and I took some of the agony out of the engines.

Still heading east into the wind and climbing slowly, I rolled the elevator trim tabs up and I could see the Atlantic ahead. If I had any ideas of flying to some Caribbean island, a P-51 cut in front of me and changed my mind. The fighter bored in from the north and fired a burst of his six .50s across my nose—no doubt Rudy's orders. I turned south obediently, and he crowded me until I was on course for Matanzas. Since he didn't shoot me down or force me to land, I could assume my refugee passengers hadn't been spotted.

I looked back at them, huddled on the floor behind the gas drums. Lacayo waved, his white teeth grinning in his mahogany face. Dr. Vidal gave me a small salute. Carlos was talking earnestly to Celia and her aunt.

My fighter escort stayed with me, playing with my wingtips. "Matanzas, or else!" I thought aloud.

Then the game the P-51 pilot was playing with me finally bored him, or he had a call for another duty. Anyway he peeled off and dove out of sight.

I looked for the other five transports but didn't see them. Good. Their head start had separated us, also my slower turn and my weight held me back. I had enough gas in my tanks for five and a half hours of flying— enough to get clear out of the country—enough more in the drums to fly for a month. But our destination had to be chosen by Vidal and Lacayo. I signaled for them to come up forward over the tops of the gas drums.

Only Lacayo came. I pointed to the empty co-pilot seat. He wriggled into it.

"Do they know better than to smoke back there?" I asked him first. I had the No Fumar sign lit, but I was a worrier.

"*Sí,* they can smell the *gasolina.*"

"How did it go last night?"

"It was dark enough. We are here. What is the news?"

"Romirez has made himself Prime Minister. Sagasta has pulled out. I don't know what choice the other cities have."

"They have *me!*" Lacayo punched himself on his dirty shirt.

I was thoughtful a moment. A hell of a lot depended on this one man sitting beside me—but why was it always *one* man down in these latitudes?

I told him the people of Matanzas were for him, but that fighters were going to strafe the airport if there was any resistance; that five planeloads of troops would be landed to take the town. The gasoline we were carrying, I supposed, was for a similar operation against Las Piraguas.

"Where do you and the doctor want me to take you?" I asked.

"Matanzas! I would like to blow up this load of *gasolina* in the army's face!" He showed me a coil of powder fuse he had brought with him. "Are you for it?"

"What does Doctor Vidal say?"

"He is for it."

"The plane too?"

"*Sí, cómo no?*"

"I don't like to destroy the plane."

"It is not a time to be sentimental about an aircraft. We will blow it with the drums inside, and before the smoke clears we will escape. There are those who will hide us."

It made sense to blow up the gasoline and delay Romirez' action against Las Piraguas, but I argued with Lacayo. "It is a waste to destroy this airplane. One plane less weakens Ruedo more than you know. The rains will come soon, and the things that one plane can move in six months would amaze you."

"Destroying the plane weakens Romirez," he insisted.

He had me there. I nodded. He squeezed my arm. I looked back at my passengers again. What I wanted was a glimpse of Celia. She was weeping on her aunt's shoulder.

Lacayo saw her tears too and said, "It is for her mother she cries."

"What happened?"

"Dead. Before we left the Chileans."

"How?"

"In a moment of sanity she killed herself—cut her wrists."

"*Jesus!*" I said.

"Somehow the mother heard the talk of Sagasta returning to Ruedo— from the servants, perhaps. The dream world she had escaped to collapsed."

"And now Sagasta is not coming back," I said.

"I do not believe it," Lacayo growled.

"Romirez believes it."

"He is a fat, self-inflated fool!" the dark-skinned man said angrily. "I am preparing for a long fight—and against Sagasta, too."

I let more air in through the front ventilating scoop. It was the clean, cool air of altitude. It made me feel better. I looked down at the eroded dusty mesas, the barren mountains beneath my wings. *My* wings. I often felt above the trouble down there when I was flying, almost godlike, but

I never spoke of it that way any more, because some people had a way of looking at me funny when I did. I felt it just the same. I think most pilots do. But what goes up must come down, if only to refuel, and down there I was a member of the human race.

I watched Lacayo peering out the windshield at the mountains. He could see a lot of geography from nine thousand feet, and we were still climbing.

"You have a map?" he asked.

I handed him the chart I had in the side pocket, pointed to a mountain peak on the chart, and showed him where it was ahead of us.

He nodded, and I watched his brown finger trace other mountains around the Copa Verde. He was smiling.

"Bombers will not find me in such places, and *federales* will not come into the bad country after me. One day I will be strong enough to come down into the valley and liberate Matanzas—then the capital!"

He stopped speaking, deep in thought. He looked very tired. It couldn't have been an easy night for him with the three aristocrats. I hoped he had made Charlie do a lot of the digging.

"Try to sleep," I said. "We have another hour."

He nodded gratefully and dropped right off. I looked back into the cabin. Celia slept with her head on her aunt's ample breast.

The engines droned. The plane flew steady and true, and then I was the only one awake. I was responsible. For what was to come after, Lacayo would be in charge. He must have seen the gasoline being loaded during the night and then gone after a fuse.

I wasn't relaxed about taking his orders. I had been in a position of command too long to give it up easily. No, that wasn't it. I hated to admit it even to myself, but I was worried about Matanzas. There was no use saying the reason for my fears was doubt about the others' leadership. Lacayo and the doctor had the guts to choose a hot spot like Matanzas to sit down in when I could have flown them to a quieter town. They weren't running away from trouble and they had enough confidence to take two women into this. And there was Carlos, who would have to take orders just like me.

The feeling I had was different from the sudden fright that comes from unexpected danger that could be met defensively with a fighter's re-flexes, or endured somehow more easily because it could go as fast as it came. This hand sweat was worse because it derived from deliberate, cold-blooded planning to put myself and others in a hell of a tight spot. This was knowing the lousy odds in advance. And this was playing for keeps, even if Celia wasn't the prize, as I first thought when I went so gallantly to the Chilean embassy to rescue her. Then what in Christ's name was I doing with a maniac like Ycaza Lacayo and his goddamned coil of fuse? I was staying on course for Matanzas, that's what, and with all of them asleep and trusting me. With the bitter penny taste on my tongue, I was heading into it. A half-hour more. All I had to do was hang in there and help blow up sixteen hundred gallons of high-test aviation gasoline. It was to be done in such a way that it would hurt Romirez militarily. And the importance of it to me personally and to a few who might learn a lesson from it was not to be ignored.

I looked at the white indicators on the black dials in front of me. Everything read nice and safe. I looked at the sleeping Lacayo. No dials or gauges on him to tell me if his manifold pressure was too low or too high. But he was a good man. Harry was a good one too. Maybe I could be pretty good in there today myself, because I was learning almost every day that there were worse things than getting clobbered. There was being too careful, too calculating, for instance, and losing anyway. I hoped I wasn't kidding myself, but the feeling of commitment was a fine, satisfying feeling when I concentrated on it. I was still scared, but I didn't give a damn any more about being scared. I even felt my love for Celia becoming a bigger love—win or lose her—because I loved her now aside from what else I had to do. I was my own man.

I tooled the plane down into the Copa Verde, lining up my approach with Mount Diablo. In the next minute I saw that *Aeropuerto Matanzas* had been occupied. Five P-51s had gone in ahead of us, and also the DC-4 and the four DC-3s, their missions accomplished. I didn't wake Lacayo. He'd know soon enough how things stood.

When I called Matanzas tower, a voice responded with *"Viva Romirez!"* and cleared me to land. My glide path was straight in. I put our heavy, explosive load down very gently.

The squeaking rub of my tires on the runway awakened Lacayo. Out of the corner of one eye I watched him take in the situation on the field. His expression didn't change. Indians! What a people!

I taxied past the Spanish-style terminal to the far end of the farthest right-hand hangar and wheeled the ship around so our doors would not face the terminal guards.

Before our props stopped turning, a Clark lift truck drove out toward us. There were two mechanics on it. It looked like they wanted our cargo of gasoline in a hurry.

"Hope they are friends of yours," I said to Lacayo, who was ducking down in his seat, out of sight.

"Open your window and say to them: 'Who is the customer for the tiger's tooth?' " Lacayo instructed.

I opened the front hatch, leaned out, and asked the silly question as soon as the Clark stopped at the unopened doors.

"*Un diente de tigre?*" one of the men repeated, mystified.

The other winked at me. "*Sí,* a curio for a *turista.* I am one who can take the tooth to whom it belongs."

"Before the unloading?" I asked hopefully.

"I don't think so," he said in English, shaking his head and pointing his thumb at the other mechanic. "This one knows nothing of the tooth, but he is in charge of unloading the gasoline. However, he speaks no English."

He had clearly stated the problem. I said slowly in English, "If the other one were to become ill, would you be in charge?"

"Yes. You advise it?" He showed me a folded jackknife in his front overall pocket as he took out a cigarette to hide the motion.

"Don't smoke near the plane, *hombre!*" I shouted in Spanish, then, switching back to English, said, "I do not advise such a sickness. Is there no other way? Make him ill with something on the head."

Lacayo snarled behind me. "Where were such fine sensibilities that night in the Linterna Azul?"

I knew what Lacayo meant. We couldn't take prisoners and couldn't afford to leave talkers behind. But I didn't want to watch it. I'd been a popular target for cuts lately myself, but seeing somebody else get it bothered me.

"I will open the doors," I said out the window. "Do what must be done."

From inside the plane, as I scrambled back over the gas drums to the rear, I could hear the truck's gears raising the fork lift to the level of the cabin floor, and then I heard a muffled cry. When I looked out the little round window in the door, our man waved at me. The other one was doubled over as if with a stomach ache. I opened the doors. Lacayo was right behind me. The Vidals and Carlos were back against the rear bulkhead, trying to look invisible.

Our man called out, "The German major is very insistent about getting all the *gasolina* unloaded immediately."

"Carajo!" Lacayo swore, "If the German comes nosing around here, we won't have time to set the fuse and get out of the plane!"

"Begin unloading and stack the drums near the hangar," I said to the mechanic, and softly to Lacayo I added, "We can blow it up there just as well and maybe catch the P-51s in the blast when they refuel."

Lacayo looked at me with amused respect, and then I realized I had given orders which were his prerogative.

"How is that one?" Lacayo asked, indicating the man slumped over in the truck.

"Muerto!" our man said.

I wished it hadn't been necessary, but there were seven lives in the balance, including the mechanic's. Lacayo told our man about this.

"Two women and two men, as well as the Capitán and you and myself, must get away from this *aeropuerto* as soon as the *gasolina* is exploded."

"It will not be easy," our man said. "Now all the *federales* here have gone over to Romirez."

"It is a shame to destroy this beautiful *aeropuerto*," Dr. Vidal complained.

Lacayo looked at the doctor briefly as if to say, We must destroy in order to rebuild better. Then he proceeded with the grisly business of dragging the dead man inside the cabin, removing the overalls from the corpse, putting them on himself, and disposing of the body in the tail cone of the plane. Swarms of hornets something like yellowjackets flew in, attracted by the blood.

Meanwhile Dr. Vidal philosophized. "Perhaps our Ruedan cities are to be like Rome, which stands on many layers of the rubble of former cities—but which Rome was best? Which should have been saved?"

In his disguise Lacayo was ready to help unloading the gas. He said to me, "You'd better report to the German. That would seem proper now. Take your—your bride with you so it will look natural."

Doña Felisa and Carlos clung to Celia stubbornly. "She must not be separated from us until we know how to plan our escape," Carlos said.

"There is no other plan than the explosion and fire. Everybody will be running out the gates then," Lacayo answered.

"The Caldéras family has a *finca* in the valley," Carlos said. "We can all meet there. My farm people will remain loyal to me."

Lacayo's comment was to spit on the floor of the plane.

Celia and I rode to the ground on the fork lift and started walking toward the terminal while the men began wrestling the gas drums out the door.

I lit two cigarettes and handed her one.

I tried to find the right words of condolence about her loss. "I'm sorry —about your mother," was the best I could manage.

There was grief in Celia's dark eyes, misting them, but she shook her head as if to clear it of memories and said, "It is a sin to— But I can't help thinking she is better off now, somehow. She had no life the way she was."

The airport was quiet. None of the usual crowds were around, just the troops standing guard. All the blue uniforms were in the *cantina,* and the pilots were drinking coffee, which meant they planned to fly again soon. I spotted Rudy and left Celia, who was ordering sandwiches and coffee in a large container. Apparently she planned to take the food back to the plane for the others, who hadn't eaten since last night.

As senior officer, Rudy Heinen sat alone at a small table. No fraternizing with the troops for him. I gave him a half-salute for his ego to feed on. It made him friendly.

"Luke," he said amiably, "when will you have the gasoline unloaded?"

"It is started," I said and sat down without an invitation. I ordered a *café puro* and, trying to sound only casually interested, asked, "Where are you headed?"

"Las Piraguas. To corner another supply of fuel. We are short in Santa María with the railroad out," Rudy said.

"You didn't have to bomb the railroad to take the city," I said, feeling that I would be out of character if I agreed with everything he said.

"It seemed like a good idea at the time." Rudy laughed.

"How about Pacific tankers off Puerto del Sol? Lighters can bring in a load of gas." I wanted him to know how helpful I could be.

"His Excellency the Prime Minister had wireless messages sent, and only one ship was contacted in the Pacific that was near enough and could do business. But it is still three days out of Puerto." Rudy shrugged.

I almost laughed in spite of myself. They were in a spot. My load of gasoline here in Matanzas was what they needed to move against Las Piraguas and secure additional fuel there right away.

Over the edge of my coffee cup I asked, "Is Romirez expecting any resistance in Las Piraguas?"

"Only from a misguided minority," Rudy said disgustedly, "but they can cause trouble. Lieutenant Lopez radioed that the B-25 was shot at."

"It might get rough in the south," I said, "especially if they hold the airports in Las Piraguas and Boca Culebra. You may not knock them out from the air, at least not with just a few passes, and your gas supply won't permit much more. Then you won't be able to land troops or refuel."

"We will make every flight count!" Rudy smacked the table with his fist. "We will throw a scare into the city; a few bombs from the B-25 and the fighters strafing the streets should result in the airport's being deserted by the local garrison. They will be called to keep order in the city."

"But bombing civilians!"

"Of course. You did it yourself in the war."

"Your people invented it!"

I had got his goat again. The twinkle was gone from his blue eyes. "Listen," he jeered, "these natives are not like the British; they won't stand up under bombings. And, don't forget, LARC radio can transmit messages, the kind of propaganda that will break their will to resist. You will see!"

"You may be right," I conceded, "but it's a hell of a way for Romirez to win the affection of his people."

"We have no time for a popularity contest!" Rudy said snappishly and, rising to his feet, added, "Surrender and obedience are sufficient today. Also, the longer Las Piraguas holds out, the more unrest we face elsewhere. Come. Let us see if the gasoline is unloaded."

I walked with him out of the *cantina,* and then he saw Celia leaving the terminal ahead of us. "Tell your wife His Excellency has offered her father safe conduct out of the country."

"You can tell her yourself, if you're coming over to supervise the unloading," I risked saying because I could see, even from that distance, fifteen drums on the ground. The job was fortunately half finished.

Rudy said, "No, I will wait here. I must radio the capital to ration gasoline to civilians. Maybe we should stop all auto and bus travel until we take Las Piraguas."

"Where do I fly next?"

"You will rendezvous with the other transports back in Santa María to pick up more troops and heavy weapons, but wait there for orders."

I must have looked unhappy.

"I forgot! You are on your honeymoon!" Rudy said. "But we need every available pilot. After this mission today or tomorrow, you can enjoy your honeymoon more—counting the Vidal estate you will inherit. Unless, of course, the doctor chooses exile." The last was said slyly, as if I might turn my father-in-law in for the inheritance.

I tried to look thoughtful and gave Rudy Heinen a non-committal half-salute before walking back toward my ship. I had to believe that any Romirez promise of amnesty or exile for Dr. Vidal was as worthless as the deal given Ortega and the other ministers who posed for a picture with him. And I knew now, more than ever, that our plan to explode the fuel dump must not fail.

The row of shiny black drums near the hangar was growing fast. I rounded the tail of the plane and saw Lacayo swatting at hornets in the doorway.

"*Qué pasa?*" he called.

"The German talks of bombing Las Piraguas and flying in troops to take the airport there."

"*Coño!*" He cursed and spat out the door.

Dr. Vidal appeared behind him. "Please, such language!" he said, "There are ladies present."

"While you are minding my manners, Señor Doctor"—Lacayo spat again—"I am thinking." He paused, and the lift truck came up to the door. He held up his hand as if for quiet, and no move was made to dance another drum onto the lift platform. Lacayo's dark face was seamed with a fierce scowl as he said, "I can only conclude that there is a strong resistance in Las Piraguas. As there is none here to speak of, I should go there."

"And I shall go also," Dr. Vidal said.

"What for?" Lacayo asked, surprised. "When we blow up the gasoline here, you and your family can escape to the Caldéras *finca,* where you can get lost on at least two hundred thousand acres. Lucas Hadley and I will fly south."

"May I remind you, sir," the doctor asserted, drawing himself up tall, "that I am the ranking government official in opposition to Romirez' revolution, and that it is doubtless my own disciplined police troops who are holding out in Las Piraguas!"

"May *I* remind *you,* Señor Doctor," Lacayo said, pounding his chest, "that I am the new revolution!"

Dr. Vidal began shaking his finger like a school teacher. He scolded.

"What I think you want most, Señor Lacayo, is to make your bid for personal power in the jungles of the south. Your followers will be no better than *bandidos!*"

Ycaza Lacayo's face was darkly terrible, but he was silent. The only sound was the buzzing hornets. Then Lacayo shrugged and, with a half-secret smile, he began wrestling another gasoline drum out the door. Carlos helped him. The doctor went forward in the mostly cleared cabin space to join his women.

I hoisted myself aboard and saw only two more drums remained to be unloaded. One more trip for the Clark truck. Lacayo was fingering his coil of fuse, measuring loops of it while deep in thought.

"After the fighter planes start to move toward me," Lacayo said, "I must judge the time it will take for them to assemble near the *gasolina*. I will cut my fuse accordingly and hope to light it at the correct time. Don't wait for me and the mechanic. When the fighters move, you move this airplane away from here pronto. We will follow in the lift truck."

"If you don't get them all in the blast—if just one escapes, it can intercept us on our way to Las Piraguas," I said.

Lacayo nodded and he patted his pockets. "Of all things!" he muttered. "No matches!"

Everybody searched his pockets. Nobody had any. It was ridiculous. Then Celia handed him her gold lighter.

"I hope it works!" Lacayo said doubtfully.

The Clark truck pulled up to the door again. This time I helped Lacayo move one of the last two drums out.

"This is enough," he directed. "We will save one of them. It may be useful. I do not like waste, and we have enough to destroy the entire *aeropuerto* if I do it correctly. Now I will go with my man to open the drums and place them for a better chain reaction. Look well at the movement of fighter planes and remember when to move."

"*Sí*," I said and gripped his hand.

I went up forward to the cockpit. The doctor, Carlos, and the women were crouched down away from the plane's windows and behaving very well, which I had to admire, because it is difficult to be brave when you are not a part of the action but just waiting. I smiled at them, because I knew I too was taking orders well and not getting clutched up. Hell, I was having a fine time.

Out the side window of my cockpit I could see Lacayo and the mechanic redistributing the drums so that several P-51s could plan to gas up simultaneously. I guessed they were also unscrewing the threaded plugs in the tops of the drums, letting the volatile fumes escape.

The P-51s didn't move, but four of the five transports started out on the field, including the DC-4. Their departure for Santa María would make our moving less conspicuous.

Then the first of the P-51s cranked up with a cloud of blue smoke and started taxiing slowly away from the terminal toward the gas dump. One by one the other fighters followed. Their pilots were probably not anticipating with any pleasure the slow process of wabble-pumping fuel from the drums. I did not react to the fact that they would soon be dead with the impersonal, so-what? attitude of the war. I *knew* some of those pilots. I kind of hoped Ramón Fuentes and the García kid were in the transports.

I got busy with my panel switches, thinking that revolution is a strange kind of war. My engines hadn't cooled so much, so they started quickly. If Lacayo's fuse was already lit, it was time to put some distance between me and those twenty-nine drums, but then I realized I had no mechanic outside the plane and I had forgotten to remove the wheel chocks, so I left the engines idling and ran back down the cabin and out under the wings to pull them free, then back aboard and up front again with lots of hustle and breathing hard. I gunned my ship out of there fast, hoping for a slow fuse. I speeded up so much that our tail left the ground.

I wished I could see how Lacayo was making out, but my cockpit was blind to the rear. There was no sign of him coming in the Clark truck. Then I saw a jeep racing alongside, about even with my wing. The blue-uniformed driver was waving hand signals for me to stop. "What now?" I wondered aloud.

Celia stood close behind my seat, holding onto the back of it. We were going as fast as I dared without becoming airborne. She must have heard me swearing fervently, but she thought I was praying.

"The good Lord protects us," she said, reaching one hand around my neck and touching the medal she had given me.

"Nuts!" I said, keeping one eye on the speeding jeep.

"Now you sound just like my father when I was a child," Celia said. "I used to ask him to come to mass with me and he would say, 'No, it is for the women. Go with the maid.' "

The jeep was gaining on us. I wondered what had gone wrong. What made one of the pilots chase me down? But in this tight spot I still felt pretty good, oddly free of the misery of loving Celia without her love in return. I let her hear my goddamns and Jesus Christs."

"You will go to hell!" she said bitterly.

"Maybe in the next two minutes," I said and laughed.

The jeep driver's hat was off, and as he pulled closer alongside I could see his blond hair. It had to be Rudy Heinen. Again he signaled me to stop with a down motion of his hand.

Some distance behind the jeep I saw the Clark truck trying to catch up. I also saw the first of the other DC-3s take off.

Then, fresh out of airport, I had to stop. I cut the throttles, but not the switches, and hit the brakes.

Rudy braked the jeep to a stop and backed and turned until he drove his radiator up to the open cabin door. The second DC-3 roared overhead at full throttle, drowning out Rudy's shouts, then the third and fourth ones took off, followed by the DC-4, which made even more noise. Rudy kept on shouting, but I'm no lip-reader, so he sat down in disgust from his futile efforts to communicate to me. Meanwhile the Clark pulled up right behind him. Lacayo jumped down and then climbed into the cabin, using the jeep's hood as a step. He saluted Major Heinen belatedly from the doorway, and, looking like just another dark-skinned mechanic to Rudy, got a chewing out. The German stood up in the jeep and made a motion like cutting his own throat, which was a signal to shut off my engines.

I got out the Webley revolver Celia had given me and reached for the switches.

In the sudden quiet I could hear Rudy yelling, "What the hell are you doing? Didn't you see me wave you to stop?"

I stuck my head out the cockpit window and shouted, "I thought you said I was supposed to join the other transports back in Santa María."

"Come down here!" Rudy yelled impatiently. "I wanted to tell you something first!"

As I started back down the cabin, I wondered. Had somebody pumping the gas discovered the fuse?

The cabin was swarming with hornets again, and Rudy must have smelled trouble then. Through the cabin windows I saw him do a Western-style quick draw, and he had his Luger out and aimed at Lacayo, who stood in the doorway.

A lot of things happened fast. The mechanic, still seated in the Clark, had hooked his fork lift under the tailgate of the jeep, so he shoved the lever to make it rise. The jeep's rear end tipped up, and Rudy lost his balance, falling across the windshield. At the same instant there was a blinding flash, followed by a boom like thunder and a shock wave we could feel clear across the airport.

Ycaza Lacayo had Carlos' Luger out, and the trigger-happy guy was banging away at Rudy, but the angle was bad for him. He hadn't found the range by the time I reached him. He had missed three or four times and made holes in the jeep.

Rudy had thrown his gun down and was whining, "Don't shoot! Don't shoot!"

"Cut it out!" I shouted at Lacayo, and then the mechanic jumped off the Clark and retrieved Rudy's gun. The doctor had another Webley like the one Celia had given me. Even Doña Felisa had a little pearl-handled .25 in her hand. We were lousy with guns and didn't need them now.

At the other end of the field, gasoline continued to explode. Through the cabin windows we could see pieces of the P-51s and crumpled gas drums in the air, turning slowly end over end, higher than the huge plume of black smoke.

"Back up that Clark and pull the jeep out of the way," I shouted to the mechanic above the fire's roar. I had to have my tail clear to move again.

Lacayo went out and forced Rudy into the cabin at gun point. He held his Luger to the German's head, saying, "I like to shoot this *pistola,* but why couldn't I hit him before? How could I miss? I want him to make a funny move now. I want him to say something I don't like so I can shoot at him again and see the holes I make in him!"

"He will make a fine hostage," Dr. Vidal said. "Don't shoot him, please."

Rudy was completely cowed. He had absolutely nothing to say.

The mechanic moved the vehicles out of the way and climbed aboard. I should have cranked up the engines and started us out of there, but, like the others, I watched the fire, fascinated. I could see tongues of flame leap into the air, detach themselves from the main fire as if carrying their own fuel with them, and sweep to other airport buildings and hangars, where they instantly touched off new fires. Everything was tinder. The DC-3 still on the ground in front of the terminal started to move, but not fast enough to get out of range of arching firebrands. One landed on its wing. There was a flash as the plane blew up. What was left of it seemed to melt.

A baking heat wave reached us. The booming, crackling roar of the fire made it necessary for Lacayo to shout. *"Vámonos!"* Everybody echoed it.

"Okay, let's go!" I agreed. "Shut the doors!"

"No, not the doors." Lacayo shook his head stubbornly.

I didn't waste time arguing. I went up front and got us rolling. The awesome noise of the fire nearly blanked out the sound of my engines. Where hangars had been, sparks as big as pumpkins shot up and fell back to rekindle smoldering ruins. All five fighters were destroyed. The once beautiful terminal was gutted and black.

My ship was light enough to chance a downwind takeoff and that let me use the runway farthest from the fire. When I got us out there, I looked back into the cabin and saw that somebody had rolled the last gas drum down the sloping cabin floor. Lacayo was sloshing gasoline out of the drum onto a groveling Rudy, while the mechanic held him at the open door. Then the men upended the drum and spilled gasoline out on the runway. If a spark from the exhaust . . . !

Carlos or somebody went through the hinged bulkhead into the tail cone and brought out the body of the dead mechanic. It was dumped out the door, then Rudy, then the empty drum.

Lacayo was leaning far out the door for some damn reason, so I gunned the engines to warn him we were going up. He got helped back by the other men, who pulled him in by his belt, and he had hold of the door, which he closed.

We shot down the runway as I leaned on the throttles, and we bounced into the air on the heat thermals. I turned us away from the big blaze and saw another fire behind me on the runway. Crawling on all fours away from the flames was a man. His legs burned like torches.

Lacayo was behind my seat, watching too. In one hand he held the plane's flare pistol.

"Why couldn't you just shoot the German?" I asked.

The spreading incandescent pond of fire caught up to Rudy Heinen for a brief and literal hell on earth. Then he was a clinker.

"Do you remember Paco Gonzales?" Lacayo asked softly.

I nodded.

"He was one of my men. The German turned him in to Molina." Lacayo's voice was both judgment and doom.

Dr. Vidal joined Lacayo behind me. He had helped burn Rudy, this conquistador-descended aristocrat who still had in him the kind of ruthlessness I thought would have been bred out by now, but I remembered Armando and Elena Ortiz, his friends, on that pile of corpses. Vidal and Lacayo believed that two wrongs make a right.

Carlos crowded up front too. He asked, "Can a fighter plane intercept us from Santa María?"

"Yes," I said and grinned at him, not enlarging on the possibility. The other transports would have seen the fire and radioed ahead to Santa María. There were still three P-51s there. My passengers went to the cabin windows to keep watch. If just one had been sent to look for us, it was permissible to say, "We've had it!"

Chapter 30

OUR luck held, and we had Las Piraguas in sight without any pursuit. I talked to Alvarez on the radio while making my approach. He said my blue uniform would not be popular, that the *federales* were loyal to the old regime. He cheered up when I told him I had Dr. Vidal and Lacayo aboard.

It was a friendly reception committee that poured out on the field, despite their rifles. The police troops seemed to grow nine feet tall at the sight of their leader. The doctor was very proud. Lacayo looked almost disappointed.

Doña Felisa came over to me, put her hand on my shoulder, and looked for something in my eyes. There was a sadness in her face. "We will never forget you, Lucas," she said, and I looked over at Celia, who was several steps away. Carlos had his arm around her waist. "She must do what she is meant to do," her aunt said. "It was planned long ago."

Dr. Vidal came over to me and held out his hand. I took it and he said, *"Mil gracias,* Capitán. We are very grateful. My whole family appreciates your sacrifice." A wave of his arm took in Carlos as well as the two women. "You have given up much," he went on. "You are a great gentleman." The word he used was *caballero,* which sounds more dashing—only I didn't feel dashing.

"Por nada," I said, "and please drop the Capitán stuff. I'm a civilian now."

Celia didn't come near me, which was probably the way it had to be. She looked off somewhere—not at me and not at Carlos, but with a smile that for me had hope in it, a kind of dreamily meditative smile. Aside from her smile, what I took in to remember when alone was not the usual female shape, but her thinnish arms because I liked the way they felt around my neck.

Dr. Vidal and Lacayo gave each other the *abrazo* hug and back-pounding. I could almost see the knives. The doctor said to Lacayo, "You and Señor Hadley are welcome to the hospitality of the police officers' quarters."

Lacayo answered for both of us, *"Muchas gracias,* Doctor, but we can take care of ourselves."

Then the family got into a big black Buick and rode off with a motor-cycle escort. Nobody waved from the windows. To myself, I said, Be seeing you, Celia. I asked Lacayo, "Do you know where they are staying?"

"At one of the big plantations!" he said and spat. "I will take you to a better place. But first let us talk to the man in charge of the *aeropuerto."*

It was humid and hot in Las Piraguas. The short walk over to the terminal shack made us sweat. We found Alvarez there and heard a clatter of dots and dashes coming through the radio.

"You are in much trouble, Capitán," Alvarez said, winking at me. "Romirez wants you dead or alive!"

"What have you told them in the capital about *me?"* Lacayo asked sternly.

"Nada, Señor Congressman. Let them think the worst, which is always the case when there is no news."

"What else do they say on the radio?" Lacayo asked.

"They say they are sending the bomber again to punish Las Piraguas for not cooperating in the matter of *gasolina.* The first flight this morning was to warn us. They say they will fly troops in here tomorrow to take the *aeropuerto."*

"They are bluffing," Lacayo said.

A lieutenant of federal police came into the shack. "There will be no communications with the outside without my permission and clearance," he said brusquely.

Alvarez looked sheepish a moment and said, "I tried to raise Matanzas on the radio to ask them what goes, but they do not answer my call."

"Their radio is out of order," I said.

"Excuse me," Alvarez said, and he began to transcribe incoming dots and dashes that beeped excitedly.

"Give me the message," the officer said.

Alvarez handed over the page from his pad, and after a glance the lieutenant read: "The bomber will come in the night to give Las Piraguas a taste of what traitors deserve. Signed, Romirez."

"Any reply?" Alvarez asked, alarmed now.

The lieutenant hesitated.

Lacayo said, "Tell Romirez we will blow up the *gasolina* before we surrender it to him, no matter how many times he bombs us. Sign it Lacayo and Vidal."

The lieutenant grinned. He liked the reply. Then he realized he was talking to Lacayo himself, and he saluted.

"Come on," Lacayo said to me, taking my arm. We actually found a taxi waiting and started into town.

"My radio message is a great strategy," Lacayo said, spitting on the floor of the cab. "I think I can count on its leaking out in the capital. My people will know what to do about a shortage of *gasolina*. Then I will have a meeting with Doctor Vidal. But now I am going to sleep for two, three hours. How about you, *amigo?*"

I began to realize how tired I was. Though it was not yet dark, the idea of a bed sounded grand. When the taxi stopped at the street address Lacayo had given the driver, his choice of a place to bed down surprised me. We were in front of the Club Zerape.

All night clubs have that dirty, beat-up look by daylight, but the Club Zerape needed a good hosing down. Stains and finger marks showed on the walls. The palm-thatch roof and ceiling and the bamboo supports looked ratty and dusty. In a corner there was a hideously garish juke box that I hadn't noticed on previous visits. It was unplugged and dark. The couple of painted whores you had to expect sat at the bar with two straws in one bottle of Coke. One was stroking the other's wrist. They looked at us and smiled mechanically.

"Where is Fidel?" Lacayo asked and spat on the floor at the girls' feet.

On cue Fidel Salas, the proprietor, came out from the back. *"Hola, amigos,"* he said listlessly. "You want some girls?"

"No," Lacayo said sharply, "just empty beds for a nap."

"You must be very tired," Salas said.

"And hungry," Lacayo said. "Get us some tortillas and beans."

"I will get them," Salas said, "and coffee for you, Ycaza Lacayo, and a beer for the Capitán." He went back into the short-order kitchen.

All the tables had chairs stacked on them, so we sat at the bar, leaning on our elbows, until Salas came back with the plates of hearty peasant food.

"I suppose you will make the counterrevolution here?" Salas asked Lacayo.

"*Sí!*" Lacayo said through a mouthful of beans.

"Too bad," Salas said sadly. "Is bad for my business. Why do you come here to my place?"

"The best revolutions are made with a lower class of people." Lacayo laughed.

When we finished eating, Fidel Salas led us to the back rooms. "I recommend you use the bathroom now," he said. "It will be very busy later, I hope."

Lacayo and I were given rooms on opposite sides of a narrow hallway. Mine looked vaguely familiar—the small bed, the icon over it, the rattan chair, the cracked mirror facing the bed, the night stand with a rose-colored lamp, the one little window with a reed shade drawn. It was a dump, but I had never noticed that before.

I just about got out of my pants and shirt before surrendering to the bed. I lay on my stomach and kicked off my shoes. It was the last thing I remembered until the music woke me up. It wasn't like any music I had heard at the Club Zerape before. It was slower, and sad-sounding.

My first thoughts were of Celia; then I switched on the sexy red whoring lamp and looked at my wristwatch. It was nearly eleven p.m. I had slept much too long! I wondered why Lacayo hadn't waked me.

I rubbed the stubble of my beard and looked into the watch-yourself-do-it mirror as I swung my feet to the floor. My shiner was a beaut. There was a thin scar on my cheek.

Tossing my uniform aside, I got dressed in slacks and a rumpled *guayabera*. Then I went out front where the music was. Only a few customers sat glumly at the tables. Two grouchy-looking hostesses danced together.

Carmen saw me before I saw her and came over. "Loo-kay," she said and stood very close.

"Hello, Carmen," I said.

"Dance with me," she said and began a subtle suggestive movement.

"Not now," I said and turned away from her to give Salas an order for a dark rum and soda.

"One for me?" Carmen begged.

"Sure," I said, "but please drink it over there." I pointed to a faraway table.

Salas splashed the drinks quickly, and Carmen went, pouting.

"Slow night," I said as Salas held a match to my cigarette.

"*Sí,* nearly midnight and not a towel wet!"

"T.S.," I said.

"I am going broke with this revolution," he complained. "With both Vidal and Lacayo here and Romirez sending a bomber, is going to get worse before it gets better."

"Is Ycaza Lacayo still sleeping?"

"No. He went to see Doctor Vidal."

"No message for me?"

"None."

If Lacayo was with the Vidals, Celia knew where I was. She could have sent a message—but then, why should she? Salas pushed the black leather dice cup toward me, and I pushed it back.

"You act like a man in love," Salas said.

"It shows?"

"Always it shows."

"You believe in love? A whoremaster like you?"

"Why not? I was not always running a cheap little club such as this. Once I was the *gran empresario* of theater arts and circuses in Argentina. In BA. Until that *cabrón,* Perón, kicked me out, but there I learned that love is a theater."

"What the hell does that mean?" I asked and sipped my drink and thought that it helped a little to talk about love. I wondered whom Celia confided in. A girl always had to talk about it with someone.

"Love is like a theater you build for a girl," Salas continued, "and every girl is a born actress. Is impossible for girls to resist a stage in the form of a true love."

"That sounds loco," I said. "I am in love all right, but this of theaters —I don't know."

"I will explain," Salas went on and mixed another drink for each of us. "I imagine that your love has been *muy romántico* and so has built a big stage in a big theater that has wonderful acoustics. The girl must perform in spite of herself."

"What you're saying is that her love in return is just an act." I didn't like that idea. "You are a cynical bastard," I said.

"Do not suppose the girl you love is any different from the others. All women are the same. Every one of them is a frustrated actress, an exhibitionist. I have been through this experience many times in the days when I could care enough about a girl to put her on my real stage."

"Fidal Salas," I said, "if you're so smart, tell me how does it end, this play of love?"

"Well, one day you will get tired of her act and kick her out of the show for her understudy. Or maybe another producer will offer her a better part, perhaps with a piece of the property, a contract." He shrugged eloquently.

"All this talk of the theater makes me thirsty," I said, showing him my empty glass.

He poured and said, "Is not possible, real love. Lovers are actors. Very excitin', but just a big act!"

And then I heard it. I heard it before anybody else in the place. I should have, because my ears were trained for it. It was the faraway drone of the B-25!

I didn't say anything about it. The few people were still listening to the little combo playing sad music. The Spanish word for sad is *triste* and sounds sadder somehow, and the people's gloom for their country in this *triste hora* didn't permit the emotional musicians to pound out their usual rhythms. They sang laments. It was easy for me to feel sad with them.

There were no air-raid sirens. I caught Salas's eye and pointed upward. He heard it then and shouted, "I am turning off all the lights! We must have a blackout as we were ordered on the radio!"

He darkened the place with a master switch behind the bar. The neon sign outside went out too. The noise in the night sky was closer now. It was the throttled-down sound of the B-25 making a shallow run. The girls shrieked, but in a way that was expected of them, not really frightened screams, more in anticipation of slightly scary fun in the dark. The guitarplayer continued to pluck out thin melody of heartbreak.

Somebody bumped into a table in the dark, and there was a hoarse curse and the sound of a glass breaking on the tile floor. Then I felt a girl pressing close to me. She found my mouth with hers, and her hands were rubbing me. I was disentangling myself as the first bomb whistled and exploded.

Screams had terror in them now. Dust settled on our hair from the thatch overhead. The next bomb howled down, and the explosion made the floor rise and crack underfoot. It was close enough to smell, but I

could tell it was on the other side of us, which meant we had been strad-
dled and missed.

Someone lit a match for a cigarette and got yelled at, but the smoke
was passed around until a half-dozen cigarettes glowed in the dark. It got
passed to me, and when I lighted up I knew the girl hanging onto me, now
in fear, was Carmen. She stopped whimpering when the next bomb went
off a mile away. She put the tip of her tongue in my ear, her hand inside
my shirt, and worked on the side of my leg with her pelvic bone. I reached
for her buttocks, which were small and round, and I felt them tighten under my hand. She had nothing on under her dress. I was a guy who had
lost his girl, been rejected and hurt. After a crash you're supposed to go
right up again—wasn't this the same? And then I thought of Celia somewhere in the bombing that went on farther across the city, and I put my
hand gently on Carmen's throat and held her away from me. What she
aroused in me was passing, and she knew it. I felt her teeth at my wrist and
her fingernails tearing at my shirt. I slammed her back against the bar.

Salas said, *"Hija de la gran puta!"*

The goddamned B-25 was making another run our way. I wondered
how Johnny could do it. Pepe, yes. But why Johnny? I cursed him. Carmen thought the curses were meant for her and went somewhere else in
the dark.

None of the bombs from the second run was as close to us as the first,
but firelight came in the windows. I went outside and stood in the middle
of the narrow dirt street. The sky was alight with fires. I heard a fire-
truck siren far away. The bomber made a low strafing run with its tail
gunner and belly turret firing into houses, bringing tragedy to innocent
people who had enough troubles already. Then the plane winged north
out of hearing.

I heard a mob coming down the street, and they were singing. They
came closer, and I could see men marching raggedly, carrying either pitch
torches or machetes in the air. It was a barefooted, ragtail army of Indians and breeds. Those with guns had an assortment of ancient pistols,
World War I Springfields, sporting rifles, and mail-order shotguns. Several wore their ammunition in crossed bandoleers and carried their rifles
on rope slings, barrel down, off the shoulder. Lacayo marched at the
head of them with a half-dozen hand grenades on his belt. He was singing
his head off. The chorus was: *No le tema la vida, porque la vida no vale
nada!* It meant, don't be afraid of life, because life is worth nothing! It
was a thought.

Lacayo held up his parade to embrace me and hammer my back. The murdering mechanic from Matanzas was with him; also my fishing guide, and he hugged me too. We had all survived an air raid and now we were feeling expansive.

"I am recruiting an army!" Lacayo said. "We march through the streets singing, and many join me. The bombing has made the people angry."

I was glad that Rudy had been proved wrong about that, dead wrong. I grinned at Lacayo as he tried to get his Indians to form something like ranks. I heard their falsetto laughs that always sounded like roosters crowing. Well, Lacayo could drill them, but could he get them to fight— and fight whom? Would they take on Romirez' airborne troops in the morning? Or would the enemy be Dr. Vidal's *federales?*

Before Lacayo could get them all started down the street again I asked him, "How are the Vidals? Are they safe?"

"You worry about the girl, *verdad?"* He winked at me.

"It is the truth, I do," I said, watching the sky full of the flickering light of many fires.

"Romirez' bomber didn't hit any of the rich haciendas!" he said. "Wait for her here at the Club Zerape. When I talked to your father-in-law, she asked me where you were."

"You think she would come here?" I asked hopefully.

"Cómo no? If she loves you, what is a place? *Adiós, amigo."* He marched off, singing.

I thought about the two leaders who were uneasy allies. The doctor might have the police, but plainly Lacayo had the people out of the huts that crowded the slum side streets and alleys of Las Piraguas, ten to a room. The mud, packing-crate, and palm-thatch, tumble-down huts I could see from where I stood now held only women and children huddling in the dark. Their men, to whom life was worth nothing, marched with the brown-skinned hater of the ruling class.

The Club Zerape combo had picked up the melody of *"No le tema la vida"* and given it a mambo beat. There was a bigger crowd inside. I had the feeling that Lacayo had lost whatever marchers had the price of a drink.

At the bar Salas joined me in another rum and soda and pointed to Carmen sitting at a far table and glaring darkly at me. "She wants you *sin dinero,"* he said, shrugging. *"Muy* loco, that *mulata!"*

So I could have her now without paying, if I wanted to; but I didn't want to.

Salas kept the rum flowing and kept on trying to pimp Carmen to me. "Me, she would kill, one way or another." He shrugged and laughed. "I have too many years now. What is your excuse?"

"I am in love, as you know," I said.

He laughed so hard he choked, and he refused the duros I pushed across the bar to him for the drinks. "You *Norteamericanos* are not practical about love," he said.

Maybe he was right, but I wasn't just a bunch of glands and nerve endings. To myself, I said, *"Nadie más que tú,* Celia, my darling. *Solo tú!* Only you!" But I also knew it was more than that. It was also the good feeling of being my own man. I hung onto the feeling.

After a while we heard shots all over town.

"Looting!" Salas said. "It is the opportunity of a lifetime for some of them. Besides, many Indians say, 'This man has more than me. Is right to take from him, no?' "

I shook my head unhappily, thinking of how it had happened in Palmas too. It was very late, and I started back to my room. *"Buenas noches,"* I mumbled.

"Shall I send Carmen to you?" Salas called after me.

"You keep her the hell away," I said.

Sometime later that night, Fidel Salas failed me and let Carmen get into my room. I was sleeping the restless, sighing, intermittent sleep of the very troubled when the turning of the lock in my door awakened me.

By the little light from the hall I saw her come in, cat quiet. I closed my eyes, faking deep sleep, and she didn't come near me, but left the door open and went rummaging around in my B-4 bag. With one eye narrowly open I watched what I thought was plain robbery and I was about to catch her in the act when I realized she was gathering my soiled and rumpled laundry.

My wallet and gun lay beside my pillow. She never went near them, and I closed my spying eye again when she turned and I felt her look at me for a long and uncomfortable minute. I thought how I had treated her simple, savage affection rather badly, and it crossed my mind to quit pretending sleep, but the monogamous feeling I had about Celia was a stubborn thing. I had never felt like that before, and damned if I didn't kind of admire it in me.

I must have tricked myself into really sleeping again, because the next thing it was morning. I got out of bed and saw freshly starched and pressed shirts on hangers hooked over the mirror. That damn fool Carmen girl had been up all night with my laundry.

I put on my old uniform pants to get to the bathroom for a tepid shower and much-needed shave and then, in clean slacks and *guayabera,* I headed for a cup of black coffee.

I found Fidel Salas bawling out a girl who couldn't have been more than twelve or thirteen who was about to put another coin in the juke box. The kid took a deep breath inside her off-the-shoulder peasant blouse and arched her back at Fidel, showing him how well developed she already was, and she played another record despite his hollering.

"I will put you to work here, *muchacha,* if you are so proud of what you have, and then, *por Dios,* you will sleep late in the morning and not bother my poor head with mambos when I want peace and quiet!"

"Café, por favor," I said, but Salas didn't pay any attention. He was watching the dark little girl as she sensuously stroked the inside of one of her thighs with the flat of her hand, daring him, mocking him with her body to the music's beat.

"For Christ's sweet sake, may I have some coffee!" I shouted. "And a bottle of rum to lace it with!"

Salas shrugged and sighed and came back from wherever his mind was and said, *"Un momentito,* Don Lucas."

When he brought the coffee and the bottle he pointed at the girl doing a solo. "They start young here," he said happily. "I think I could build a small theater for *her!"*

"She's just a kid, thirteen or so!" I said righteously.

"Ha!" Salas grunted. "How old do you think that Carmen is who sucks around you like a cat in heat?"

"In her early twenties anyway," I said.

"A lot you know!" he said. "She isn't a day over sixteen!"

I was speechless and, I've got to admit, shocked.

"They are all little jungle cats, these girls," Salas said. "We call them *naturales.* No fathers they can name. Every one of them is born nine months from fiesta time, like clockwork."

With the hot coffee and rum to equalize the outside heat, a tolerant lassitude spread over me, and nothing seemed bad or wrong in this languid tropical morning. I puffed my first cigarette of the day and turned on the bar stool to join Salas in watching the youngster dance. How the hell could you really fault what she had for her world?

Fidel's way of countering his temptation was to pull the plug on the juke box, and damned if the little gal didn't retrieve a hoop and stick from under a table and go outside to play with them.

"I want to get the nine-o'clock news broadcast on the radio," the proprietor said sheepishly.

The radio had mambo music on it too. The new rhythm was becoming a national disease. Then after a long commercial about Espíritu de la Caña, the government rum, the news announcer came on sounding very excited.

"A special bulletin has just been handed to me," the newscaster said. "It is reported on good authority that in the early hours today the former President of Ruedo, Fermín Sagasta, landed at Puerto del Sol from a private yacht and was greeted there as *El Libertador!* Sagasta's triumphant return to the Pacific coast city is said to be the prelude to his plans for ousting the hated Romirez faction which recently assassinated our beloved President Ortega and Vice President Ortiz. There has been no report from the capital. Radio Santa María has been off the air. Please stand by for further bulletins on this new development in the sadly chaotic politics of our nation."

The rest of the newscast was about the ruthless bombing of civilian population in Las Piraguas, the extent of damage and loss of forty-two lives, the fires which were now under control thanks to a heavy rain during the night. He restated old news of the arrival of Dr. Luis Vidal and Congressman Ycaza Lacayo in the city and droned on about ultimatums received last night from Romirez for the delivery of aviation gasoline to the Air Corps.

"Well, what do you know," I said. "The old son-of-a-bitch came back after all."

"What do you mean?" Salas asked.

"Sagasta!" I said. "I had the distinct impression he was Romirez' sponsor and wished him well."

Salas shrugged expressively and let the radio's mambo music stay on. "Politics in Ruedo are very *complicado*," he said wearily, watching the open door to the street, no doubt hoping his little doll would return.

Then the music was interrupted and the announcer was saying, "The news of Fermín Sagasta's return to Ruedo reached Doctor Vidal, the honorable Minister of Peace, this morning, but he has refused to make any comment at this time."

The announcer paused lengthily and then added, "In a telephone interview with Congressman Ycaza Lacayo, he said, and I quote, 'The only true counterrevolutionary movement in Ruedo is headed by me.' Señor Lacayo has also claimed responsibility for the destruction by fire of six planes and gasoline supplies at the Matanzas airport before making his escape to this city."

Mambo music blared out of the radio again.

"Do you think Lacayo can win it?" I asked him.

"He has not many guns and no money. A Garand rifle costs a thousand dollars American! How can he win?"

"What about Doctor Vidal?"

"A good man, but an intellectual!" The last word was invective in Salas' mouth.

"Then Sagasta?"

"Very strong. Ruedo needs a strong man."

"A dictator, you mean?"

Salas shrugged. "Dictator is just a name. Either Romirez or Sagasta will be good for business."

As he spoke the room suddenly darkened and a sound like ten thousand wide-open garden hoses on the roof all but drowned out the radio. Salas frowned as he saw some leaks in the thatch make puddles on the floor. The sudden tropical rain turned the road outside into a splashing sea of gumbo. It chased a couple of half-drowned, half-uniformed young men into the Club Zerape. The word for them, hissed by Salas from behind the bar, was *Lacayistas,* which I was sure Lacayo's followers would soon be called by everyone in Ruedo. The downpour also returned the *muchacha,* who cadged a coin from one of the young men and fed it into the juke box.

Salas was jealous. "You men of Lacayo's camp will lose all your bravery in that one," he said.

"How goes it with Lacayo?" I asked them and stood a round of drinks. Free rum changed their scowls at Salas into contented smiles.

"We were on our way to the *aeropuerto* to find out," one answered me. "Our leader contests the protection of the *gasolina* with that old woman, Vidal."

Oh? So that's how it was, I thought. Another strong man. And I had believed Lacayo wanted a strong people.

It stopped raining as abruptly as it had begun. The juke stopped too, and the quiet was awesome until a fresh, clean breeze stirred the muggy air. It got a little windy as the sun rose higher. The young men didn't hurry their drinking and leave. Everything moved slow and easy in their lives, even a revolution.

Salas turned on the radio. The announcer was talking again: "... Verde province has declared itself for Sagasta. Radio Santa María is still off the air. There are rumors of street fighting in the capital and of many fires. Stand by for a repeat broadcast of a transcribed statement from Fermín Sagasta, who has declared himself Premier of Ruedo. The next voice you hear will be that of Fermín Sagasta, speaking from Puerto del Sol."

There was a pause and then I heard that remembered, resonant voice: "Good people of Ruedo—greetings! You know me. I am a proven man. I am a man with a long record of my willingness and ability to serve my country well. I am your humble servant. The work I have been called back to do again for Ruedo is inspired by your needs. Always I am at your orders. I have heeded your desperate call. I am here. Romirez is the betrayer of the revolution. His attempt at governing you is a disgrace. The destructive rebellion of Ycaza Lacayo is also a disgrace. I will rid you of these disgraces and make you proud. History will record my past and future tenure of office as head of the Ruedan state as the embodiment of the most revolutionary movement the nation has ever known, and within a regime of peace. I reaffirm my faith in Ruedo as you reaffirm your faith in me. Onward to peace and security, we will march together. *Salve a tí, Ruedo!*"

Then a military march record was played. The two young men slipped off their bar stools and started in the direction of the airport. The little girl followed them.

Martial music continued pounding out of the radio in back of the bar. It came to me that Sagasta had not mentioned Dr. Vidal in his speech.

Chapter 31

THE last announcement I had heard over the radio before starting for the airport was an appeal from Dr. Vidal to the people of Las Piraguas to stay away from there. On the road to it, it looked as if everybody in town had disregarded him. The people had brought their lunches and musical instruments and were in a fiesta mood. There was no transportation, and I found it hot walking. The sun had already dried up every evidence of the rain, but the wind had not died down. The wind kicked up dust from the road into my face, where it caked on my sweat and darkened my spit.

Several green Army trucks with horns blowing plowed through the foot-slogging crowd and I heard a shout from the lead truck's cab: "Señor Hadley!" It was Dr. Vidal with Carlos and a driver. The back of the truck was full of grim-looking *federales* with rifles and their steel helmets still bore the US stencil markings.

"*Buenos días, señor*," Dr. Vidal said as I climbed up on the running board. "Why do you go to the *aeropuerto?*"

"Why does everybody?" I laughed, looking around at the kids trying to hitch a ride and being shoved off the truck's sides by the soldiers' rifle butts.

"Come with us," the doctor said. "You have heard the news?"

"Yes. Sagasta has double-crossed Romirez and come back to take over." I summed it up.

"It was a sagacious plan," the doctor said, shaking his mane of white hair. "I should have considered the possibility. *El Sagáz* used Romirez as a pawn, set him up with deliberately bad advice for bombings to turn the people against such leadership and make them welcome a liberator."

"I guess so," I said and asked, "How is Celia? And Doña Felisa?"

"They are well," Carlos answered.

The trucks speeded up, throwing back clouds of dust like rooster tails, which the wind blew over the walking families. If Romirez made good his threat to fly troops in to capture gasoline, these *federales* were supposed to stop them. It was bound to be dangerous at the airport for the crowds of people, but they didn't seem to care. The revolution provided a break in the monotony of their lives. It was their baseball game, and they didn't need a program to know the teams and players.

Near the airport we came to a little suburban cluster of stilt-raised houses crowded close to the road. A clumsy barricade had been thrown up there—odds and ends of lumber, a broken iron bed, a few bags of sand, some piles of bricks and stones. Behind it were posted a dozen of Lacayo's Indian irregulars, soldiers in gaudy sport shirts. Our truck drove right up to the roadblock, into the barrels of rifles and shotguns that rested on the debris.

Dr. Vidal had the driver crank the windshield open and then, calmly, he said, "Clear this road at once! I am Doctor Luis Vidal and I have four platoons of trained *federales* in these trucks."

It seemed senseless to me for the doctor to confer with Lacayo's men while they had a bead on us. It must have seemed so to the driver too, because he got down out of the cab and went over to the other side. In another minute the troops climbed down from the trucks with their rifles slung, barrel down, from their shoulders and walked quietly over to the enemy, who greeted them like brothers.

"What do we do now?" I asked the dumfounded doctor.

"We walk," he said, and led the way, carrying his white head high. I admired his guts if not his military judgment. Nobody stopped him. Carlos and I followed.

The crowds of civilians were well contained outside the airport fence by renegade *federales* and barefooted *Lacayista* rebels in parts of uniforms, some armed only with machetes.

Carlos and I were allowed through the gate with Dr. Vidal. A guard said the doctor was expected by Lacayo, and we were politely escorted to the terminal shack, which had become the command post for the expected airport battle.

Lacayo greeted us like a general, from behind a desk flanked by two guards, an airport map in front of him.

"I am sorry, doctor," Lacayo said, "but your *federales* would not want to shoot their neighbors or risk dying themselves in a stupid, meaningless fight. Besides, who will pay them their sixty duros this month?"

"I am not completely ignorant of the situation, my good man," Dr. Vidal said, smarting under his political and military failures, "but I can still give you advice."

"I may not take it," Lacayo said, spitting on the floor.

"Let me tell you that I know it is too late for me, but that I also know it is too soon for you. Sagasta will win all Ruedo," Dr. Vidal said, his face pinched as if close to tears.

"I am fighting only one revolution at a time," Lacayo said. "I have not yet finished with Romirez. But almost. Almost. My followers in the capital have sabotaged the remaining fuel supplies there. They burned all the gas stations in Santa María."

"How did you hear of it?" Dr. Vidal asked.

"My men managed for a time to hold the Army communications center. A wireless message was received here at the *aeropuerto* of their deeds in my name."

Alvarez, my LARC man, joined us. He gave another message to Lacayo.

"*Coño!*" Lacayo swore, reading it. Then he told us it was from Romirez—a threat and a demand. The Coronel had sent the bomber and was coming himself in the DC-4. Lacayo was to permit the DC-4 to take on full tanks of gas, or Las Piraguas would be bombed again. "He must have found enough gasoline left in the other planes to make this trip. Perhaps they siphoned some from every automobile in Santa María, but they don't have enough to fly four planeloads of troops here. My guess is they don't have even enough to escape from the country either!" Lacayo was gleeful. He was the victorious general. "My men in the north harassed him. Sagasta returned as his enemy. Now Romirez is on his way here, begging me for gasoline!"

"If you let him gas up, he can make the LARC Miami run quite legally," I said.

"Never!" Lacayo shouted. "We have a pilot who can shoot the bomber down!" He pointed at me.

"In what?" I asked, surprised.

"We have two AT-6s here with machine guns. Take your pick!"

"It can't be done," I said. "A trainer would have no chance against the fourteen fifty-caliber guns of a B-25. The bomber has turrets to fire in every direction!"

"I thought you were my *compadre!*" Lacayo said scornfully.

"I wish you well, but you always want me to die to prove it," I said.

"I will not give the *cabrón* the fuel he wants!" Lacayo swore.

"But the bomber pilot will see these crowds of people," Dr. Vidal said anxiously. "He may drop his bombs on them, and use the many guns Señor Hadley speaks of."

"That makes no difference!" Lacayo pounded the desk. "Don't you realize that Romirez was sure to go to the Ruedan treasury first with a truck and a shovel? I want that DC-4 full of money to fall into my hands!"

"So you can finance your revolution?" Dr. Vidal asked sarcastically.

"*Sí!* Should I let the money get away? Should I give it to you or Sagasta?"

"The bomber can kill many in this crowd of people," Carlos said. "Would you sacrifice them for the money?"

"It will be Romirez' bombing, not mine," Lacayo argued. "And there will be many sacrifices before my battle is won."

I began to feel like a heel for not considering a try at the B-25 with the trainer, but it would be suicide. Hitting the faster DC-4 would be no cinch either.

"When are the planes expected?" Dr. Vidal asked. "If there is time, let us together try to disperse the people."

"*I* will tell *my* soldiers what to do!" Lacayo said and left the shack.

"The radio reception was very good," Alvarez said. "They must be close."

Dr. Vidal and Carlos sat down on camp chairs and waited near Alvarez and the radio equipment. Some kind of reply would have to be sent to the desperate Romirez. I went over to a window to see the huge crowds outside the fence. They weren't leaving. The wind was blowing stronger, making the palms rattle and bend. I remarked about the wind to Alvarez.

"If it is going to blow, it is going to blow," he replied. "You are not in charge of that now."

I wondered what I was in charge of. I worried about misplacing the sense of mission I had felt yesterday, flying into Matanzas and helping to blow up the gasoline. I sure as hell didn't feel it for attacking a B-25 in an AT-6. "Life is worth nothing!" they sang. Some battle cry! I said to nobody in particular, "Sometimes their indifference to death is more terrible than their violence."

"It is stupid!" Dr. Vidal said bitterly. "Even with schools we have failed with these people. We cannot erase that stupid expression from their faces in less than three generations. Perhaps in this climate we will never remove that underlying aggressive stupidity. I tried to educate and enlighten my police, but today two thousand men follow either Romirez, Sagasta, or that Lacayo!"

The building shook from a gust of wind that howled through the jungle trees. I went outside and had to lean into the wind to take a look at the windsock that stuck straight out from a pole on the hangar roof. Clouds of sand and even pieces of gravel blew across the runway.

"*Un huracán!*" Carlos said behind me.

"No, just a *papagayo,*" Alvarez corrected him, "but it could blow the skin off a mango!"

"Straight across the runway," I said. "A hell of a day to try to land here!" We heard the sounds of a plane approaching. I knew it was the B-25.

Lacayo returned. "The people won't go away!" he shouted above the noise of the wind. The gun-crazy man had two .45s in his belt now, and he carried a beautiful new carbine, but I felt Lacayo had the right posture for his people. He was a straight-backed, bold man, as dark-skinned as most of them. I could buy half of his battle cry—"Don't be afraid of life."

Inside the shack the radio receiver squawked into life. It was Pepe's tense voice in the B-25, doing his uncle's dirty work.

"B-25 calling Las Piraguas . . . calling Las Piraguas . . ."

"Answer the *chulo!*" Lacayo told Alvarez.

"Las Piraguas to B-25, over . . ."

"Hear this!" Pepe said hysterically. "The DC-4 is coming in two minutes. I will stay over the airport. If Coronel Romirez is not given the gasoline I will drop my bombs on the people. Over."

"What are you going to tell him?" Dr. Vidal asked.

"Tell him to go to hell!" Lacayo shouted at Alvarez.

I went outside and got the full force of the crosswind. It was mean. I wondered who was flying Romirez in the DC-4. Johnny maybe, or Fuentes, who was good. Maybe fat stuff was doing his own flying. He could, but this was going to be a tough landing to make. I called to Lacayo. He came out, and I pointed to the DC-4 letting down in the distance. It looked as if it was going to fly a 180-degree pattern and wait for radio clearance instead of coming straight in. That would give the bomb scare plenty of time to work.

"Look," I said, pointing at the windsock. "Let Romirez try this landing. It won't be easy. They may crack up, so why not tell the bomber to lay off? But if the DC-4 makes it, pretend to let Romirez gas up his plane. Then block him with the gas truck and take him. That way you get the loot, and if I know Pepe Lopez, he'll hightail it for someplace else fast. If he doesn't I'll keep him busy with the AT-6. Okay?"

Lacayo nodded. "Call the bomber," he shouted into the door. "Tell him I agree to let Romirez refuel."

Dr. Vidal came out and shook my hand. "I don't know what you told him, but it was a fortunate day that brought you to our country, *señor.*"

I looked at Carlos, who wouldn't quite agree with that. I shook my head, saying, "I just stuck my neck out. I may have to chase Lopez in one of those little planes. Say good-by to Celia for me."

That got a smile out of Charlie.

Gusts of wind slammed at us. I headed toward the end of the field with Alvarez to help me get an AT-6 untracked where two of them were tied down. Dust devils like little tornadoes swirled over the strip. I kept looking back over my shoulder at the DC-4. It was turning on its base

leg at the other end of the jungle clearing. The bomber was circling at
three thousand feet directly overhead. I thought: I ought to be able to
outfly Pepe, even in a slower ship. If I couldn't shoot him down, I could
at least spoil any bombing run he might try when he realized the DC-4
was captured.

I looked back again and saw some *Lacayistas* climbing up on the
hangar roof. They knocked down the pole that held the windsock. Ycaza
Lacayo was stacking the deck in his favor.

The DC-4 turned on final off its left-hand pattern. The pilot should
have felt the drift, even without the windsock to guide him, but he goofed.
He took the ninety-degree crosswind broadside with insufficient correction. Whoever was at the controls finally dropped his upwind wing, but
he wasn't lined up with the runway any more. The tricycle gear and
flaps were down, and the nose was down steeply, but the big ship was
light and it floated.

The pilot tried to S-turn back on his approach, but the maneuver was
a case of too little and too late. The gusts across the runway must have
been hitting them at over seventy-five miles an hour.

"Je-*sus!*" I shouted aloud as the big plane banked and turned against
the wind so close to the ground that a wingtip nearly dragged. "Go
around! *Go around!*" I heard myself shouting, putting body English into
it, hating to see a crash, even if Romirez was aboard. Who the hell was
doing that sloppy flying? Not Ramón Fuentes. Certainly not one of the
Yankee crews. The Coronel hadn't been checked out in the big ship.
Neither had Johnny. Must be them!

The four engines were throttled back, and the plane crabbed forward,
bearing down on where we stood beside the parked AT-6. It was still
drifting too far off to the right of the strip and couldn't be landed in
that attitude without damage. Then there just wasn't enough room left
to land, so the engines roared a few feet over our heads and the plane
lifted. They had finally decided to make another pass, but I could tell
they had waited too long for that decision.

I found myself running toward the end of the field. It was as if I had a
certain instinct about what was happening, not shared by other watchers.
What I knew was that the DC-4 was too damn low in relation to two
hills that rose sharply at the end of the Las Piraguas airport. Those hills
could fool you. They got steeper and higher as you approached them,
and they were covered with big jungle trees. I ran on. The plane couldn't
possibly climb over them now. And it was too late to turn downwind to

the right because trees blocked that way out too. Besides, the pilot needed the wind on his nose for lift. His only chance was the one he took, a climb to his left.

"They're going in!" I said to myself. . . . "No, they're going to make it!" I stopped running; I was glad. *"Oh, Jesus, no!"* I was running again.

The thing a pilot gets to know about accidents is that it isn't the last mistake that kills you but the series of errors going back to the first one. The DC-4 pilot had accumulated his fatal share. He had been late for a left turn, too. He had run out of ideas and altitude at the same time. The last desperate maneuver the pilot made was to pick up his steeply dipped left wing to avoid hooking it on the fence at the end of the runway. Then the crosswind drifted him smack against the nearest hill.

The thick green tops of the jungle trees squashed like broccoli under the big silver plane and swallowed it up with a sound that wasn't really a sound but rather the abrupt end of sound. Even the screaming mob at my heels was silent for a few seconds.

At the fence I paused to look up at the bomber and back toward the AT-6, just in case. I had been right about Pepe Lopez too. He dropped no bombs. The B-25's engines faded in the distance as I climbed over the fence. I wondered, without giving a damn, where the bastard could sit the bomber down without facing a Sagasta firing squad.

I had a head start on everybody running toward the wreck and managed to clear three strands of barbed wire on top of the fence with only a scratch on my wrist. There was no fire to guide me to where the plane hit, but I had a bearing on its location in my head, and I needed it, because at the end of the field I was in thick tangled jungle.

I would have made better time with a machete to cut through the creepers and vines and the green walls of enormous leaves that limited my vision to three feet ahead. I didn't feel the wind any more, but I could hear it howl above in the treetops. A fine spray of rain forest humidity bathed my face. Bugs buzzed around my head and flew into my sweating eyes, ears, and nose. I swatted at them, but I kept going.

Then I was panting uphill through the rotting vegetation that spread its sickening mulch-like stink in the mist. Insects stung my ankles and crawled up my pants legs, biting as they went. A colony of them settled under my belt and fed on me there. I scratched and cursed—and scratched some more. Steamroom heat melted down the tallow in me as I pushed on. Birds and monkeys made weird complaining cries. I came upon an area where the sky showed through clearly and where tops of trees had been sheared by the falling plane. I made a slight correction in my heading, following the debris left behind the hurtling hundred-mile-an-hour smash-up. Jagged pieces of aluminum were caught in some mahogany branches that didn't break. The tail section, in one broken-off piece, reared straight up out of the jungle floor like a cross. When I stopped to rest a minute, I heard machetes chopping behind me. A cigarette served to keep some of the bugs at bay. Then I went on up the hill.

The main body of the wreck lay upright on soft, level ground. There was a gash in the side of the fuselage where a wing had been torn off. There wasn't a sound, but somebody could be alive.

I went inside the cabin through the tear in its side. The first thing I saw was Lita. She obviously hadn't been belted to her seat and had been thrown against the forward bulkhead by the sudden stop, in a grotesque disarray of arms and legs that bent in wrong directions. Her gold anklet gleamed under her twisted nylon stocking. I felt such pity for her, I touched her once, but quickly took my hand away. She was mushy.

There was nobody else in the askew cabin, only several tumbled trunks and suitcases. One piece of leather luggage had burst open and spilled American greenbacks under the seats. I picked up a taped bundle of bills. They were all hundreds. I put the money gently down on a seat. There are some things you don't do or can't do.

I forced open the jammed door to the cockpit. There was Johnny, sure enough, in the left-hand seat. He had been killed instantly when his head snapped forward into the knobs on the panel. And he stank of rum even in death, but one of his hands was on the gas shut-off switch. His last act had been by the book. They didn't burn.

Romirez was still belted into the co-pilot seat. His fat flesh had burst out of his sky-blue uniform, but he was breathing. Frothy pink bubbles formed on his mustache.

"Coronel!" I said to him sharply, but his beady eyes stared sightlessly. He made no response.

I heard shouts outside the wreck. I said, "Here comes Lacayo for the jackpot!" If Romirez heard me, it was the last bit of information he took with him to wherever he was going. The bubbles popped on his mustache and didn't form again. I stared at him. A dead dictator had a certain fascination. Who would mourn him? His wife and kids might, but maybe not as much as the girls on the Mirado's sixth floor, who had lost their meal ticket.

Then I worked Johnny's seat belt loose and dragged him out of the plane. Lacayo was out there with half a dozen men holding green-stained machetes.

"*Qué pasa?*" he asked.

"All dead. I'm going to bury my countryman, if you don't mind."

"The money?"

"A ton of it!"

I carried poor old Johnny to a clearing not far from the wreck and put him down. Lacayo and his men went inside the cabin, and I heard them shout for joy.

Lacayo ordered his men to form a sort of bucket brigade to pass the treasure out of the wreck hand over hand. There were canvas money bags in the trunks, more suitcases full of United States currency.

I went back inside the wreck and could hear Lacayo talking to Romirez. It didn't matter to him that the fat man couldn't hear any more. "This will buy many guns, Coronel," Lacayo said. "You have financed the true revolution."

I saw that Lita's body had been unceremoniously dumped to one side to make room for the unloading. Her gold anklet was gone.

Up forward I found the GI folding shovel that was standard survival equipment aboard. I took it and went back out to where Johnny lay. I began to dig.

Lacayo came out, carrying Lita. He put her body down with a tenderness that conflicted with the mockery in his eyes as he watched me hack away at stubborn roots in the loamy black soil.

"To bury them is not necessary," he said and pointed to the black vultures roosting in the branches overhead. "Those *gallinazos* are the jungle's sanitation squad."

"I will bury my own people," I said.

"That woman is rotten enough to make good compost," he said.

"Why don't you shut up!" I said, stopping my digging to scratch the bites under my belt.

Lacayo pointed to the way his pants were tied at the ankles with handkerchiefs and said, "To keep out the *niguas*. I think you call them chiggers. Little red ones. Devils! They dig under the skin where clothing is tight."

Scratching only made the bites worse. I went on shoveling and sweating. It would not be a deep grave, but it would hold both of them. When I finished digging, I dragged Johnny Michaels' body into the hole by its feet. Then I folded his arms over his chest. Lacayo squatted there and closed the staring gray eyes.

"He got what he was looking for," Lacayo said. "We always say that down here when a man dies violently, but it is true. A man's death explains his life."

I eased Lita's body into the grave. It felt like she was coming apart. There was an obscene nakedness to her dead flesh where her skirt had slipped up, so I pulled it down and tried to arrange her limbs more naturally. She felt cold as a fish. I shut my eyes. Lita had thought I liked her, liked her as a person, but I never did. Not really. I thought she was nuts. I was just halfway polite to her and not deliberately unkind to her and didn't ignore her as a person, that's all. I felt sorry now to be burying her and trying to fan away the big bluebottle flies that settled on her still pretty face and the hornets that always came. A buzzing requiem for a bitch and a lush. They might have had it better, both of them.

I shoveled back the pile of dirt onto the bodies, and when they were covered I packed it down with pats from the back of my little spade.

"Wild pigs will come in the night and root them up," Lacayo said matter-of-factly.

"It figures," I said, and in English I added, "the poor slobs." That would have lost something in translation, but it was all the prayer I had in me. I picked a wild orchid from a rotted tree trunk and put it on the grave mound. As for Romirez' body, he was buzzard bait.

"*Viva Lacayo! Viva Lacayo!*" the men shouted when the last of the loot was out of the plane.

The dark man went over to them and began making arrangements for moving his treasury to some safe hiding place. He sent a runner to get more men from the cordon below the hill that was holding the curious crowd back from the wreck.

Lacayo saw me start down the hill and called, "Lucas, *amigo,* I could use a pilot!" He trotted after me. "You could hide those AT-6s at Lajas or some other mountain strip. Some flying operations would be a help in my fight against Sagasta. It is a job with little to offer you now, but it has a fine future. I will make you my minister of aviation."

"You must be planning on a long-drawn-out fight," I said. "I thought you might take the DC-3 back to the capital right now with a few hand-picked troops and sign up what's left of Romirez' flyers on your side. After all, you have the money and you control all the gasoline for another day or so. Sagasta hasn't flown to Santa María from Puerto yet, as far as we know."

"That is a plan I thought of myself, but discarded," Lacayo said. "It would be a compromise. I do not want to do business with any of the old cliques. They would want certain guarantees. I would be starting a kind of negotiation that would never end—first with the pilots, then the Army people, then the landowners, then the *Norteamericano* shippers and importers. Finally I would be *their* man. *No!* I will make no deals!"

"I can afford to be patient," Lacayo said. "Do not forget I am rich now. Soon I will withdraw from Las Piraguas and go deep into the jungle. Sagasta will take over, but he will be sitting on a keg of dynamite when I begin importing it. I will booby trap the whole country for him! What do you say to joining me?"

"No. I must go back. I may regret it, but I must."

"It is the girl, then?"

"I think it is hopeless, but I love her."

"I can understand that. It is too bad. Love makes men do foolish things."

"Yes."

"And she is a Vidal. It might be different for you if she were not a Vidal."

"Thank you."

"No. *I* thank *you.* I owe you much. I will not forget that and I will understand that you have to compromise to live. Not I, but you. Will you fly for Sagasta?"

"He may not want me, but I need a job. The airline needs me, too."

"I think Doctor Vidal will compromise also, and Sagasta will use him someplace in the government. He is a very useful man. Someday I may find a place for him in *my* government."

"Good luck with all of it and *hasta la vista,*" I said.

"My men are saying '*Hasta la muerte*'—until death—but *buena suerte, compadre!*"

With his wish for good luck I started back down the hill through the trail the others had cut with their machetes. When I came out of the steaming jungle, scratching a new set of *nigua* bites, I found the wind still blowing hard. The afternoon sky was slate-gray.

I hitched a ride into the town on a two-wheel ox cart with a half-dozen other sweaty, dirty peasants. I looked like one of them. I went back to the Club Zerape. Where else could I go?

Chapter 32

I WAS soaking in the tub with a double rum and lime when Fidel Salas knocked and told me I had a visitor. It was Carlos Caldéras.

"Send him in with another drink," I called through the bathroom door.

"I will, but do not be too long in there. My girls want to use the shower."

"Build another bathroom!" I muttered crossly.

Carlos came in presently with my drink and one like it for himself.

"Hello, Charlie," I said, lolling in the tub, beginning to feel human again.

"*Qué tal?*" he asked.

"Not bad. Not too bad," I said and raised my glass to him.

He sat on the lid of the toilet and we drank slowly. The juke box was getting a play and the music of a romantic bolero came down the hall to us. I held one leg out of the water and looked at the *nigua* bites. I had six of them on one ankle bone, others under my knee, and several in my crotch and around my waist. They were red and swollen and itched ten times worse than mosquito bites.

"Not much can be done," Carlos said sadly. "The insects have burrowed under the skin to die. They will come out with the infection, something like the head of a boil. Alcohol helps."

"Inside or outside?"

"Both." He laughed a little. He wasn't such a bad guy—maybe.

"Go tell Salas to send in another kettle of hot water," I said as I soaped myself. Something nasty in me impelled me to push him around.

Carmen came back with him, carrying the steaming kettle. Without a smile or a by-your-leave she poured the hot water out of the kettle spout right over my head. I yowled. Carlos laughed, and Carmen ran out. As soon as I got my breath and ascertained that I had not been scalded, I laughed too.

"What's on your mind, Charlie?" I asked.

"Dr. Vidal had a telephone message from Fermín Sagasta," he said gloomily.

"Well?"

"We have capitulated. *El Sagáz* has all Ruedo now unless that loco *Indio* Lacayo tries to make a stand in Las Piraguas."

"Oh?" I said.

"Sagasta will offer amnesty to Ycaza Lacayo in exchange for return of the looted treasury funds," Carlos said, and I could see he thought that eminently fair.

"Lacayo will get a laugh out of that," I said.

"Where will you go?" he asked me. "I mean, what are your plans?"

"I'm a pilot—for hire," I said.

He shifted around uncomfortably on the toilet seat, looking into his drink. "Will you work for us? For Sagasta?"

"I need a job."

"Sagasta would like to enter the capital tonight for a torchlight parade. He would like to have Doctor Vidal by his side. Will you fly us to Puerto to pick up Sagasta and then to Santa María in the DC-3?"

"Why not? Sure. Tell them your mission is accomplished. You persuaded me. You hired the only available pilot."

I spilled the rest of my drink into the tub, climbed out, and began rubbing myself down with a towel.

"I am sorry about that time . . ." Carlos said.

"Forget it," I said.

"No. It was a shameful thing, Lucas Hadley. I was very jealous. To have killed you or tried to was one thing; to leave you like that—*no!*"

"Let's forget it," I said. "We all do things we regret. How is Celia?"

"She is well, *gracias.*"

"Don't thank me for asking, goddamn it, Charlie!" I said, losing patience with him again.

"Celia and I are to be married," he said. "I was born here," he added by way of explanation.

That was one way of putting it, I thought. I had to suppose he was important to Celia in a way I could never be. And it was tough for him to know about me, too.

"See you at the airport as soon as I can," I said.

He was gone. Carmen came back with alcohol and cotton for my bites. She wanted to apply it, but that intimate I didn't want to get. She followed me to my room, and there I discovered she had shined my shoes. I thanked her. She shrugged.

"Take me with you, Don Lucas," she said in a small voice. Take me to Santa María. I will be your servant. I will be very useful."

I believed she would. I didn't need a diagram. For a second I thought, Why not? As I packed the laundry she had done into my B-4 bag I could almost believe she was a whore with a heart of pure Mayan gold. And she would be something to show Celia. The coffee-and-cream girl was beautiful, the way some calendar art hanging in a garage is beautiful. But hell! I had changed more than I realized.

"It is impossible," I said, opening my wallet, then handing several big duro bills out to her. "I'll be back," I said. "Take something to tide you over."

She slapped the money to the floor as she said, "You want me to wait for you?" Her look was one of disbelief. "I do not understand! You do not want me, but you do not want others to have me, is that so? Do you expect me to become a nun?"

I shook my head. I hadn't even thought about what I expected her to do. I turned away from her and finished packing. My blue uniforms went in the bag, but I didn't wear one.

"Loo-kay?" Carmen called from way across the room. "Look well at this!"

I looked. She did a flirty bump and grind with her abdomen and smiled evilly. Then she picked up the money.

The wind was still blowing hard when I got out to the airport in a taxi. The three Vidals and Carlos were already there in the black Buick. Alvarez had serviced the plane and informed me that everything was okay. A lot he knew!

Celia looked so alive, so good to me. But all that passed between us was a look, merely an acknowledgment that we existed for each other in a special way. I swallowed a couple of times and went up front to chauffeur her out of my life.

The takeoff in the crosswind went all right, but I could tell what Johnny had been up against. We flew over the wreck on the hill, a scar in the jungle where the buzzards circled. My passengers crossed themselves.

We had headwinds from the north. It was going to be a long flight. I kept looking back through the open door to the cabin and felt a reckless urge to talk to Celia once more—to try again. I waved to her to come up to the cockpit. The others saw it and had a fit. Maybe that's why she came.

I helped her into the co-pilot seat, and, I guess without thinking, she said, "Hi!" Then she was all excited about the cockpit, the dozens of dials and switches, and I got impatient explaining them.

I shut and locked the door behind us. "I love you!" I blurted.

"Please open the door," she said.

"They know I can't seduce you up here," I said.

"You? I wouldn't be surprised!"

I laughed, but she seemed suddenly withdrawn.

"Luke," Celia said, "it is over. Let me be what I *can* be. It is enough. I am really very happy with Carlos—happier than I deserve to be!"

That hurt, the happy-with-Carlos part. The trouble was, I began to think, I never really knew much about her. I only knew what lovers know, which was very good, but not strong on realities. Okay, she had hurt me, and I tried to understand that she had to. I wasn't wise enough to know all her reasons, but I would have a lot of time to think about them. As I reached back and unsnapped the door lock, my arm brushed against her. Did she feel what I felt from the touch? I tried not to look at her, yet I did. I had never seen her look so unhappy before. I didn't push the door open. I put my hand on her face, cupping her chin, and looked into her dark, sad eyes.

"Don't, Luke—honey," she said with a hazy fog of endearment in her voice.

I leaned toward her, keeping just a finger on the wheel.

"No!" she said and didn't mean it. She leaned toward me too. We kissed quickly, silently, knowingly. It had been a long time. We came up for air and kissed some more. Her arms were around me. I reached back and snapped the lock on the door again.

I should have accepted the kisses on any terms, but I was too stubborn. With my lips on hers, I said, "Stay with me." I punctuated with little kisses. "Stay with me *always!*"

"It would be so easy," she said, lowering her head to my shoulder so my mouth and nose were in her sweet black hair.

"Then it's right!" I said and put both arms around her protectively. I could fly with my feet.

"You are all I ever wanted," she said softly. "But it can't be. Oh, I wish I were just a girl, a nobody, a—a stewardess on this plane. . . ."

I don't think she meant to sound snobbish, but it rubbed me wrong and made me conscious of that ever-loving family thing again.

"You will be all right without me," she said. "Because you are so strong, you will be all right. Keep some of our dream. Don't *you* change. You will find happiness with some other girl. You deserve it. And don't think so much!"

I took my arms away a little. I didn't cling to her. I played it strong, as she said I was. And I *would* think. I would think hard and maybe become a wise old man. I began by thinking that if her sympathy for Carlos or her family was going to determine her life and mine, that was too damn bad. I wouldn't beg. I tried as sophisticated a smile as I could manage. I wouldn't sulk either. I'd show her I could take it, but I already knew I couldn't. When you're a loser in one of these things, you feel like bawling.

"In a way," I said, still trying to hide what I felt, "we have been lucky. *I* have been, I mean. I'm very grateful, and look"—I kissed her lightly— "we don't end by hating each other."

The kiss she gave me in return was a biting, open kiss that was never going to end unless I ended it, so I did. I said what was on my mind. "Now *you* stop it! I don't want any more farewell scenes!" I guess she finally understood that.

"I can't say it, but it *is* good-by, then," she breathed.

I didn't say anything. I wouldn't have made sense anyway. I unlocked and opened the door to the cabin, nodding my head toward the aisle.

She kissed me once more—lovingly, sweetly, not caring if the others saw us. "Go with God, Luke. Be good, angel," she said and left me.

I began to miss her almost at once. I felt terribly alone. Celia, I supposed, would not have that feeling, because family is practically a way of life here to the old landowners, and there is authority in it, all kinds, and Celia's uncle and aunt and the Caldéras family meant a home and children with historic purpose. Maybe I wanted to be a part of that too, but it just didn't work out.

When I took us down toward the strip at Puerto del Sol, I had to look away from the laguna beach. I knew there were going to be a lot of things like that for a while.

The family deplaned to be greeted by Fermín Sagasta and his retinue. I stayed aboard. Out the window I watched Dr. Vidal and Carlos damn near bend at the waist when Sagasta acknowledged their presence. Standing there in his high-heeled cowboy boots, the dictator was a head taller than everybody around him. I also saw a P-51 parked on the edge of the airstrip. One of the pilots must have siphoned up enough gas to jump on the bandwagon ahead of the others. Then I found out who.

Ramón Fuentes came up front and, jerking his thumb, motioned me out of the left-hand seat. "Capitán Hadley," he said, "I will take over from here."

I got no polite how-are-you from him, so I just grunted my way out of the seat and went down the aisle to welcome Sagasta aboard at the cabin door.

Sagasta had better manners. He politely requested two seats in the rear of the plane—as if I could have refused them. Then he said, "You are out of uniform," and wrinkled his nose distastefully at my *guayabera*.

Ten more people, including the Vidals and Carlos, got on board. The two bodyguards from Mexico, now carrying sub-machine guns, were among the passengers.

It was dark when we were airborne. Then one of the gunmen tapped me on the shoulder. He told me Sagasta wanted to see me and he frisked me before I went into the cabin. Sagasta didn't offer me the empty seat next to him. I had to squat in the aisle beside him.

"I am sorry," Sagasta said, "but this is your last flight for me. I must discharge you." His resonant voice carried five seats away.

People looked around with more curiosity than pity. I felt no shame at getting fired, but I was broke and needed the job.

"Why kick me out?" I finally asked. "I don't think you have anybody around who can run LARC as well."

Sagasta looked out the window at the few lights of his homeland with God knew what expression behind his dark glasses. Then he said, "I cannot trust you. I could once. You were a cynic. Formerly I could buy your loyalty. Not now."

"That's a compliment," I said.

"I can deport you as well as compliment you," he said sharply.

"I want to stay in Ruedo," I said.

"Then your visa will be stamped," he said, "because it amuses me to keep you around, but be amusing, señor!"

I went up forward to help with the night landing at Santa María. Fuentes didn't need any help. I had taught him all I knew.

"Congratulations," I said to Fuentes. I meant more than the landing. Could be he was slated to be minister of aviation.

"I owe it all to you," he said.

"You sure do!" I said.

"I am Ramón, your friend. Remember that," he said. "I told the Premier you are a good man."

"Yeah? What else did you tell him?"

"You really want to know?"

"Damn right!"

"I said to him that he should either have you shot or leave you alone, that you were not like some others he could play with, that he couldn't pull your wings off like a fly's, that you were more like a bee with a stinger."

"That's pretty good," I said and felt much better. Then we cut the switches and there was a big crowd waiting to greet *El Libertador*.

Sagasta arranged it so he'd be last out the door, except for the pilots, of course. I came down the aisle, and he waved me over to him.

"We have some tastes in common," he said. "I understand you took a fancy to a piece of land I own up the coast from Puerto del Sol."

The son-of-a-bitch knew everything!

"I would like to buy it," I said, like making a raise in poker, without eagerness—and what the hell, I didn't have any money.

"I am glad the property tempts you," he said with satisfaction. "I may need your services again, and it reassures me to know that you still have a price."

Compulsively, I scratched an itching *nigua* bite on my hip bone. Then Sagasta went out the cabin door, smiling into the floodlights, accepting the cheers of at least fifty thousand people jammed around the airport.

I followed him out and was highly visible at the airport—a tall man, taller than Sagasta even, among a short-statured people. Andy Cluette and Ben Green saw me and called my name. It was one of those times when I was glad to see other Americans. We were long-lost friends and loud about it.

I gave them an eyewitness story of the DC-4 crash, of Romirez' death, and of the *Lacayista* movement's sudden wealth.

"Lacayo could go bad," Andy said. "I've seen it happen before to men like him. They just go bad. He will be all right if he doesn't go bad."

Then Ben slapped my back and told me they'd learned of what we had done at Matanzas. "What now, hero?" Ben asked. "Going home?"

"No more heroics," I said, "but I'm staying."

We watched the Sagasta party leave in a motorcade of Cadillacs.

The Vidals got their share of cheers. Torch-bearing motorcycles and jeeps flanked the cars.

"Donahue is gone. Schlomer too," Ben said as Andy Cluette drove us to town.

"They were recalled," Andy added, "but Harry was glad to leave. He's gonna be a cat's-paw candidate for Congress in his home district, where the Democrats figure they ain't got a Chinaman's chance next year. It's a service he's doing for the party and it will get him better known. What the machine doesn't know, though, is that Harry will make a million speeches, sho'nuff. He'll be a big deal if he pulls an upset. We all may be proud to know him some day."

"I know a lot of big shots," Ben said, "and I'm not proud."

The reporters dropped me at the Mirado. I thanked them for the ride and said, "Keep in touch, will you? Not here, though. I'm moving to the Hotel Colón."

"Broke?" Ben asked.

"Busted," I said, "and unemployed."

"Good for you!" Ben said, treating this aspect of my life as if it were necessary for my character.

"I'm going into business for myself," I said and, frankly, had just got the idea.

"Capitalist!" Ben said, but laughing. "Good luck!"

I went around to the Mirado garage for the Lancia. For the first time I regarded the car as mine. It was a possession out of the past. It didn't commit me to anything now or in the future.

I checked into the cheap Hotel Colón, and when I showed the cashier my $350 LARC paycheck signed by Romirez he laughed in my face. Then I gave him ten duros in advance from my thin wallet and went up to see my small room just two stories over the noisy Plaza Libertad. The bath and toilet were down the hall, but there was a cold-water sink on the wall and the rate was just seventy-five cents a day.

The town was jumping when I went out again. Nobody wanted to miss Sagasta's balcony appearance at the palace. They all wanted to be sure they were cheering loudly enough. I bought a couple of *tacos* from a street vender and kept my personal austerity program going by taking a bus back to the Mirado.

The Mirado room clerk handed me two envelopes. One was my bill; the other contained a note from Harry Donahue. I read:

Dear Luke: I'm giving up this errand-boy stuff with the international intrigue set. Heard what you did in Matanzas. Olé! Glad you survived, but don't push your luck. Take care, you big lug. If you come back to the States, look me up. Maybe I can be of some help.

Sincerely,
Harry

It seemed everybody considered the possibility of my going home but me. I wished I had the good sense not to hang around in this country like a rejected lover who ought to go away but shamelessly doesn't.

Chapter 33

ALL kinds of cars were still scarce since the war, so I got nearly five thousand bucks for the Lancia. That was my capital for starting an air-service business. The only plane for sale was a quite new Aeronca, a cream-yellow side-by-side two-seater with low hours on its 85-horse-power Continental. I bought it for a price that left some change from my five grand. Then I had a crop-dusting gismo installed and modified the luggage compartment for bulkier loads. She'd cruise at an even hundred and give me fine small-field performance. I bought some red paint and did a fair hand-lettering job on both sides: *Hadley Air Service.*

All I needed was customers, so I wrote an ad and placed it in *La Hora* for weekly insertions until further notice. Copy said my services were available seven days a week and urged that reservations be made early. I put in the Hotel Colón phone number and made a deal with the switchboard to take messages.

Although a couple of calls came in, I wasn't really in business until I had completed a lot of bureaucratic paperwork for licenses and permits. The gasoline shortage was the toughest problem to solve, but until fuel started to come in over a repaired track to the coast, bribery still worked in Ruedo for gas or whatever was needed. I also paid commissions to the hotel managers for every customer they turned in.

I was very busy at charter flights, light cargo hauls, aerial property surveys, and crop-dusting. I liked being my own boss and I gave value for what I was paid. That was satisfying, and working hard helped keep me from thinking about Celia.

The rainy season came, and one morning when I was socked in, I sat in a barber chair getting shorn and checking the position of my ad in *La Hora.* I found the barber-shop gossip a lot more enlightening than the newspaper. For example: The paper contained a hint Sagasta must have planted that Dr. Vidal was slated to represent Ruedo at the OAS and as a delegate in the United Nations. The barber whispered that this was how *El Sagáz* planned to keep the liberal politician out from under foot. Another example: Buried on a back page was a small item about deplorable counterrevolutionary activity near Las Piraguas; *federales* under Sagasta's new officers, the paper said, were preparing to put down the small civil disturbance. Lacayo's name wasn't mentioned, but there was a slightly hysterical editorial tone about the dangerous Communistic tendencies of the rebels in southern provinces. When I asked the barber what he thought about that, he lowered his voice and told me he wouldn't dare say anything about it except to a *Yanqui,* but the fact was that Ycaza Lacayo's recruiting was so successful that now you didn't have to do anything obviously counterrevolutionary to be arrested. *El Sagáz* had proclaimed a new law for a crime called Imminent Breach of the Peace. It meant you could be jailed or shot on mere suspicion.

When I returned to the Hotel Colón, the switchboard had three messages for me:

Sr. Gómez called twice. Has several cargo shipments for the south. He is at the Mirado.

Estrada Mining Company called. Want you to pick up a passenger at Puerto for Minas tomorrow.

A Señorita Vidal called. Left no number.

I looked at the third message slip and thought: Damn it! Just when I could go two whole hours without thinking about her!

I called Estrada's Santa María office to check details on the Puerto passenger pick-up. They told me how glad they were to hear of my charter service, as LARC hadn't got back to normal yet.

I didn't have to call my other customer. He came to see me in the lobby. His card read: *Gómez Importing Company, S.A.* The oily little man wore cologne and was evasive about the nature of the cargo and its destination.

"Look," I said, "I've got paper work to do for every flight. The law requires it."

"Suppose we call it a shipment of toothpaste for Las Piraguas," Gómez said.

I caught on fast. It was for the tiger's tooth.

"Who pays?" I asked.

"I do."

"Cash in advance."

"How much?"

"A dollar a pound. I can carry about three hundred pounds per trip."

"It is robbery!"

"I'll pay my own bribes to clear the cargo if I have to. Are you giving the guns away?"

Gómez smiled for the first time. "All right, perhaps your price, like mine, is equal to the risk. I won't quibble. We can do a steady business?"

"Maybe I'd better expand. I'll buy a couple more planes," I said, kidding.

"A good idea. I will keep them busy." Gómez didn't kid. He looked over his shoulder and added, "The packages will look like wrapped-up outboard motors. When can you be ready?"

"Day after tomorrow," I said.

"Está bien," Gómez said. The little man walked away abruptly.

"Hasta la vista," I said to his back.

Gómez didn't say good-by, and he wouldn't know me if I got in trouble. Nobody would.

A bellboy paged my name for the telephone. Business was getting brisk. I picked up the house phone and said, "Hadley here. *Dígame.*"

"Hello, Luke." Celia's voice. Oh, my God!

I spoke: "Hello, Celia."

She spoke: "How are you?"

I spoke: "How the hell do you think?"

Pause.

She spoke: "Aren't you going to ask how I am?"

I spoke: "How are you?"

She spoke: "Fine. Everything is fine."

I spoke: "Good!"

Long pause.

"How is your new business? I have seen your advertisement."

I thought of the old gag about a flying-service business having its ups and downs. It didn't seem funny.

I heard her: "Oh, Luke!"

Another long pause while I thought: Oh, Celia! Then I said, "Give my best to your family—and to Carlos."

"I—"

"I know you won't even say you talked to me," I said as rough as I could. "So don't talk to me! Don't call me. Get married and be happy, but don't keep me up-to-date on it. I can accept the idea now, but I don't want to watch it or hear about it. Leave me alone."

"I'm sorry—"

"And don't be sorry! Good-by."

"Luke! Luke! Luke!" Celia cried across the wires.

Then the black instrument was back on the hook and damp from the sweat of my hand. It was a final silence in which I knew I had cut it clean off. I was hurt more than I'd expected I could be hurt.

I went up to my room, got my B-4 bag open, and pulled out the sailfish picture of the two of us and knew that I would always love her and that always was a hell of a long time. I would always care, really care how she was, and they would have to kill me to make me stop that. I put the picture away, at the bottom of the stuff I kept packed for quick trips.

Then I went to the Mirado for dinner and a waiter made things worse by asking for my order in English. It was a goddamned conspiracy not to let me belong.

Back at the Hotel Colón, there was another message from Celia, this time with a phone number.

For a minute or two I thought there was no use fighting it. I found myself daydreaming about calling her back, even of seeing her again secretly and how she would love me, but I didn't call her back. I did keep the little piece of paper with her phone number on it. I carried it around in my pocket to three or four different bars. The rum didn't drown my sorrows, but by taking them swimming in the stuff, I wore them out a little.

I was just walking in the night when it rained hard without warning and soaked me good. Then the rain stopped and the plaza glistened in the street lamps. The washed sweet air went deep into my lungs. A rooster crowed because it was coming up morning. And I knew it would be a beautiful day—another monotonous beautiful day. I would fly over a beautiful green world to a beautiful blue sea and a place where maybe I still had one friend who felt I belonged here. I decided to help Curro Aboroa plant some trees and try to get my roots down with theirs on that hill by the laguna. After that I would fly my passenger to Minas. And then tomorrow I would pick up some guns and deliver them to Lacayo.

A crippled lottery salesman braced me in the hotel doorway. "I have lucky numbers . . . lucky numbers . . ." he said over and over, probably in his sleep. I gave him a duro but didn't take a ticket. Well, I'd been cured of something.

I had my coffee, lots of it, at the airport *cantina* and was trying to drain some wakefulness out of the demitasse cup when I heard my name called. It was Ramón Fuentes. He, García, and Teddy were sitting at a table in the corner. They were in uniform. I joined them. We said all the polite things to each other in Spanish.

"I am getting Flight oh-nine-hundred out on time today," Ramón said proudly.

"Glad to hear it," I said. "Hadley Air Service can use some competition."

"He always makes jokes," Ramón said to the others.

"Not always," I said. "How is the other LARC equipment?"

"We will have all four aircraft in operation by next week," Ramón said. He liked running things. So had I.

"The new pilot, Capitán Carter, does very well," Teddy said—and I could believe that, in more ways than one, because Ramón gave her a black look. Things hadn't changed much.

"Business should be good," I said.

"*Sí*, there is much cargo that has been held up in all directions," Ramón said. "And Señor Reynolds is coming back, I think."

"Good," I said. "Well, I've got to get going."

"What is your flight plan?" Ramón asked.

"Puerto. Be seeing you." I got up, and Ramón got up, because he was really very well mannered, and we stood there as if there was more to say.

"What happened to Pepe?" I asked Ramón to fill the void.

"He cracked up the B-25 trying to land it at Palmas. He is in the hospital there. Broken leg."

"They taking good care of him?"

"Why not?"

I didn't say why not. "Well, so long," I said.

"*Suerte!*" he said. Luck? I didn't believe in it any more.

My little plane and I chugged into the air and headed west. I had lots of time to think. Too much time. So Ken Reynolds was coming back— there! That was a different thought. Who else would I see again? I'd heard Sam Warren was returning. Maybe J.K. Bullard would be back in business with his resort-development plans for Puerto del Sol. Good. Perhaps he would pick up the land above the laguna along with the rest of it, assuming Sagasta still wanted to deal with him. That way, if I continued to make money with my air service, I could get an option on it; unless, of course, *El Sagáz* intended to keep that lot to tease me to death with it. But what the hell did I want with the piece of land now—without Celia?

The DC-3 passed me on my left at a higher altitude. The LARC flight was on time and it would be long gone out of Puerto when I got there. I slouched down in my bucket seat and watched the silver plane pull away in front and fade from sight.

It was nearly noon when I sat down on the Puerto strip. I had to jockey around to find a place to park my Aeronca because some road-building equipment was scattered there preparing to surface the runway. LARC was moving fast on my recommendations. It put people to work too, and that made Sagasta look good.

The field agent came out of the terminal shack, waving two pieces of paper at me. One was a message from my passenger asking to postpone the trip to Minas until tomorrow. The other was from the El Cortés. They were holding a mounted sailfish for me, and the invoice. I'd forgotten about that order. Well, now I had time to deliver the trophy to the Aboroas, and Lacayo's guns wouldn't be delayed too long.

I checked into the El Cortés, taking a cheap back room. Then I loaded the mounted sailfish in a taxi and went to the market place. There I picked up some rum for Curro and Marguerita and a couple of children's books for Niño and Chico. The taxi took me out as far as the road went, and I told the driver to come back for me and toot his horn before dark.

Curro must have spotted the taxi and came barreling down his hill like a mountain goat to give me a big *abrazo*.

"Patrón!" he cried. "You came back!"

"Didn't you expect me to?"

"*Ciertamente!*" he shouted, pounding my back. "Sometimes good news travels as fast as the bad, Don Lucas."

I grinned at him and gave him my small gifts. He was stunned by the sight of the eight-foot stuffed fish. We carried it up the hill to his hut. His wife greeted me fondly too, and Curro showed her the books for the boys' reading lessons but hid the rum from her.

"Where are Chico and Niño?" I asked Marguerita. "There is no time like the present to begin their lessons."

"There is plenty of time, *El Profesor*," she chided me. "The boys have waited ten and twelve years, each of them. They can wait a little longer. Why do you not take a swim in the sea while I cook some tamales for you?"

I had the distinct feeling she was trying to get rid of me, so I went down the hill toward the laguna. I came out from behind a clump of cactus at the edge of the cliff, and there I looked at the beautiful curve of beach and the dazzling turquoise water and at somebody else there ahead of me, standing at the water's edge.

I do not remember getting down that cliffside and over the rocks to where she stood waiting for me. The next couple of minutes, as we stood wrapped in each other's arms, are pretty blurred too.

"You didn't answer my telephone call," Celia said breathlessly, "so I followed you here. The LARC flight. I saw your brave little plane, so alone in the sky, when we passed you."

"But why . . .?"

"Carlos told me . . ." she said, her voice so low I had to listen very hard. "He was very ashamed. . . . He told me what it was between you —about that time at the cockfights when . . ."

"Well, I'll be—"

"Carlos could see you were everything to me, so he told me. He knew I could never marry him, knowing . . ."

I was dizzy with my happiness and staggered hugging her and we kissed and kissed and I said, "I love you! Will you marry me?"

"We *are* married! Remember?"

"Is that good? I mean . . ."

She smothered my question with her mouth and then she said, "It is more than we had before. The piece of paper—we will get it sometime."

I didn't argue.

"The Aboroas are letting us have their house tonight to begin our new life here," she whispered. "Then we will build our own house."

I didn't argue about that either. I just held her tight. Maybe there were a couple of things we had to get settled between us—but later. Now wasn't the time to say I wouldn't work for Sagasta, house or no house. I would try to explain to Celia what I knew now about a man's work, the need to have a good feeling about it—but later. Ahhh . . . a little later.